❧

An American from the Deep South, Kenneth Ray Taylor currently lives on the island of Phuket in Thailand. He is a writer, public speaker, and humorist. He has researched psychic phenomena and spiritualism for thirty years. He is currently finishing up the sequel to *Beyond the Shadow of Death*, and has started a third book which puts his lead characters on the beaches of Phuket, Thailand, on December 26, 2004.

To Mom,
If I searched I might could never find a better wife but a better mother-in-law.
Love you,
Ken

BEYOND THE SHADOW OF DEATH

A Novel

BEYOND THE SHADOW OF DEATH

A Novel

Kenneth Ray Taylor

ATHENA PRESS
LONDON

BEYOND THE SHADOW OF DEATH
A Novel
Copyright © Kenneth Ray Taylor 2005

All Rights Reserved

No part of this book may be reproduced in any form
by photocopying or by any electronic or mechanical means,
including information storage or retrieval systems,
without permission in writing from both the copyright
owner and the publisher of this book.

ISBN 1 932077 89 8

First Published 2005 by
ATHENA PRESS
Queen's House, 2 Holly Road
Twickenham, TW1 4EG
United Kingdom

Printed for Athena Press

Dedication

As I consider my life, it's obvious that many people deserve recognition in this dedication for a number of reasons, but in the larger sense, no one I have known is undeserving because each individual has been my teacher. Nevertheless, there are many whom I have not met who are perhaps the most entitled.

I dedicate this effort to the children who are forced to take up arms and fight wars not of their making; to the children who have been crippled by land mines and ruthless disregard for their well-being; to the children who are or have been sexually, physically, and/or psychologically abused; and to the many children who don't have adequate food, clothing and shelter.

I also dedicate this effort to the proposition that monsters – human and situational – don't just create themselves; we all participate.

To Jerry, Joey, and Jo, who are alive and well beyond the veil.

To the late Reverend Marjorie Back, a teacher and mentor.

To V.T., just because.

Author's Foreword

The characters and events in this book are fictional. Any similarities between them and yourself or someone you might know or actual events are purely coincidental. Nevertheless, the people who live within the pages of *Beyond the Shadow of Death* are real. Someone of us somewhere each day meets aspects of these personalities or greets one of them in the mirror each morning. That is one of the ways that we can learn our most valuable lessons; by bumping into a clone or someone with a similar trait, and taking a long, appraising look. Unfortunately, we don't always recognize the opportunity.

As a matter of convenience, some of the place names are fictional, while others are real. The area of Tampa called the Oven is fictional; however, I suspect that every major metropolis has a Sodom and Gomorrah. Tampa and St. Petersburg are of course major Florida cities separated by Tampa Bay, and their respective newspapers, The *St. Petersburg Times* and the *Tampa Tribune*, are both respected publications to which I have been a subscriber.

Also real is the Latin Quarter of Tampa, Ybor City, party central for locals and visitors alike. But restaurants, bars, and live entertainment are not the only reasons to visit, even though the five-star Columbia Restaurant has anchored the area since opening in 1905. There you will find authentic Spanish and Cuban cuisine accented by lively flamenco dancers. Thinking about it now, if I were currently in Ybor my first priority would be a pressed and heated Cuban sandwich. If you have never experienced one, a trip to Florida would be worth the price in my opinion.

When you enter Ybor City, you step back into the smoky history of Tampa. Cigar making started there in 1886 and today visitors can still see hand-rolled stogies in production and sample the finished product. But not only has the area's unique craft been preserved, so has the turn of the century classical and Mediterranean architecture, complete with red brick streets and wrought iron street lamps. I haven't personally had the pleasure of meeting one, but if you'd like to try, take a walking tour and visit the ghostly hangouts where some early citizens met an untimely death.

Hyde Park can also be found when you visit Tampa on your next vacation to the Sunshine State. It is an historical area of refurbished homes and it abuts the beautiful tree-lined Bay Shore Boulevard that runs parallel to Tampa Bay. If you enjoy quaint, picturesque neighborhoods, this one is worth a drive through.

David Islands – actually it is now only one – is just a bridge away from downtown Tampa, and offers urban living in a suburban setting. The most prominent fixture is the Tampa General Hospital located on the north end of the island. You can find a great picture of this mammoth institution on their homepage at www.thg.org. If you need medical help you can get it there, and know that you are getting aide as good as it gets. I never checked, but the cafeteria or coffee shop might even list a Cuban sandwich on the menu.

On the southern tip of Davis Islands you will find a yacht basin and public beach, as well as the Davis Island Yacht Club that is unashamedly billed as "the Sailingest Club in the South". This is a "sailors" club, a private club for racers. If you love to sail and visit Tampa, check www.diyc.org: there may be a regatta scheduled.

Across the bay, St. Petersburg is no longer just a retirement home for snowbirds and a winter hangout for retired Canadians. Spiritualism has a strong presence there and can be experienced in the many metaphysical churches that dot the area. Both psychics and mediums abound. Although I chose the St. Petersburg locale to present an unscrupulous parasite who preys on the unwary, this is in no way intended as an indictment of that fair city, of Spiritualism, nor of individuals who use their insight to aid others. The reader is introduced to a fake psychic con artist as well as a genuinely gifted psychic/medium. Hopefully, the uninitiated reader will become wise enough to be wary, but open-minded enough to investigate the possibilities.

All that aside, I don't wish for the readers to think of St. Petersburg as synonymous with seedy neighborhoods and shameless characters. The city is a vibrant community balanced with mixed demographics that includes major league baseball hosted by the Devil Rays. You won't find a more beautiful and people-friendly downtown anywhere.

Several miles of waterfront have been preserved for public use by creating parks between developed areas and the shoreline. If you are into jogging, power walking, or strolling, the waterfront stretches far enough to satisfy your need. There are beaches to enjoy, boats to admire, and friendly people to keep you company. The green areas border neighborhoods listed on the National Register of Historic Places, and a downtown where one can walk to a favorite restaurant or nightclub, shop the specialty shops that line Beach Drive, or choose to visit the impressive Baywalk for shopping and a movie.

While you are at it, you may also wish to walk The Pier. The pyramidal building at the end is inverted, but don't worry, it's safe. Now that I think about it, the Columbia Restaurant has a location on the third floor of The Pier that offers the same quality food and service as its parent in Ybor. There are no flamenco dancers, but the panoramic view is unparalleled. Take a look at www.stpete-pier.com. You will also see why the city is recognized for its many trees and shrubs. Now if only I had a cold pitcher of sangria to drink with my Cuban sandwich…

Cassadaga Spiritualist Camp in Cassadaga, Florida, located between Orlando and Daytona, is also real, although you might not think so when you first arrive. It is easy to believe that you have somehow been teleported to a New England village or perhaps have slipped into the Twilight Zone. There is nothing weird or frightening about the hamlet, but it does give one the sense that here time stands still. Organized in 1894, the camp is designated a Historic District on the National Register of Historic Places, and according to association literature it is the oldest active religious community in the Southeastern United States. It is pleasant to just stroll down the narrow lanes bordered by quaint cottages, or to explore the several lakes and parks to find a quiet bench on which to sit and appreciate your blessings.

The camp itself has strict rules governing the members who practice mediumship and spiritual counseling, but the association's controlled fifty-seven acres is bordered by many practicing psychics and mediums who may or may not be members. If you are interested you may visit the camp website at www.cassadaga.org. The foregoing information, however, is in no way meant to be a recommendation nor an endorsement, as it is presented here for informational purposes only. Additionally, the ideas presented in the novel as occurring within the Cassadaga Spiritualist Camp result from my own studies, research and personal experiences. They do not intentionally mirror or present the association's teachings. The events are fictional.

Have I missed anything? Oh, yes, Plant City and its five thousand acres of berry patches. What can be more real than strawberry shortcake, and you can gobble your fill at the Strawberry Festival held each February. It's a community fair showcasing ethnic traditions and comes complete with rides and live entertainment – the heel-kicking country music kind – and of course the crowning of the Strawberry Queen. Again, interested readers may learn more about the actual event by searching the web for the Plant City Strawberry Festival.

The fishpond complete with waterfalls and an oval bridge, it's real too, or it was the last time I saw it. Only it wasn't in Tampa, it was located in St. Pete and it belonged to me. If you ever visit Tampa you can see a picture of the pond hanging at Pondscapes on South Manhattan, a full service koi pond construction and maintenance company that also carries everything the avid pond owner needs. They have a great website: www.pondscapesfl.com.

The 1957 green Chevy is also from my memories. It was owned by a boyhood friend with whom I went through school and beyond. He got stuck in the quicksand and left behind a wife and two daughters. As a functioning form the car no longer exists; however, I believe that beyond the shadow of death, my friend is alive and well.

Now, however, I've occupied enough of your time. A bunch of fictional characters eagerly await your arrival in their world. Kick back and enjoy your trip as each one creates his or her individual pathway. Who knows, the visit might even prompt you to generate a bit of change in your own.

Kenneth Ray Taylor

Prologue

With his pudgy hand, Kyle Keysor searched a dark corner of the closet and located his secret stick. The well-worn staff protected him. His mother used to, but not anymore. The boy made certain no one was watching then sneaked out of the laundry room door that opened to the garage. Patches, the neighbor's cat, was napping on a bucket seat which itself rested on a pile of other car parts that overflowed into the yard. With three older brothers and a mechanic father all contributing to the mess, the detritus of dismantled vehicles formed a part of the landscaping. "Pop art," his gruff father would challenge whenever a neighbor complained.

Since his mother's funeral, Kyle had stalked the mustard-colored feline several times, but never successfully. Although he tried, stealth was not one of the boy's talents. His whole family was big, and Kyle showed promise of becoming the biggest, and with a certainty the most clumsy. That brought ridicule from his siblings, and being only ten years of age placed him at their mercy. Sunday school, his mother's demand, had failed to help any of Kyle's brothers as far as he could see.

Kyle inched forward until his foot knocked over a useless fuel pump and the cat's head shot up. The boy froze. He held his breath. The animal lay facing away from Kyle, but somewhere in the folds of its tiny brain, Patches must have sensed danger. He bolted from his resting spot as Kyle brought his magic stick down with all the might he could manage. Dust erupted from the empty seat.

"Shit," Kyle said, then jerked his head around, expecting to see his mother before realizing she wasn't there to scold him; that, indeed, she never would be again. He almost cried, but caught himself. Only babies cry, his father had said as Kyle's mother was lowered into the ground. Anybody watching would have thought the father's hand briefly placed on the boy's shoulder was an act of condolence. The painful squeeze told Kyle otherwise. The boy stared at the intruding hand. Even at the funeral and dressed in a suit, Kyle's father still had grease under his fingernails. Kyle hated that smell.

The disturbed dust from the car seat settled on Kyle and made him sneeze. As he watched Patches scurry under the neighbor's new 1982 station wagon, Kyle used his shirt to wipe his face. He wanted to wash his hands. It wasn't that Kyle particularly disliked cats, or any other living thing for that matter, he just craved the feeling of power that possessed him when he made something suffer.

Kyle picked his way through the junk to the garage door and crawled behind the parched azaleas that hugged the side of the house. A motionless, ugly, black lizard stared at a smaller cousin that wandered too close. Kyle snatched him up, and dangled his captive over one of the numerous fire-ant beds that dotted the yard. Once the helpless creature ceased to struggle, the boy pretended the ants were Philistines and stomped them good.

The battle won, Kyle breathed deeply. He relaxed. Then he noticed the beak-nosed old man who owned the bothersome cat staring from across the street. The wrinkled old fart was always staring, his eyes burning a hole in you like he was the devil. He must not believe in God either 'cause he even glared when Kyle's mother used to load up her boys for church. Like he was trying to set the car on fire, his evil eyes stayed glued until the sedan turned the corner.

Kyle picked up his staff. God could change sticks into snakes. If need be, Kyle would smite the old man. Shit, the boy might even get one of his father's guns. Kyle had already shot a deer, a couple of wild hogs, bunches of squirrels, and a kzillion birds. Killing's easy once you get the hang of it. He sneaked his staff back into its hiding place. Humming "Onward Christian Soldiers", Kyle scrubbed his hands real good.

> *It is one of the most beautiful compensations of this life that no man can sincerely try to help another without helping himself.*
>
> Ralph Waldo Emerson
> 1803–1882

January, 1993

Unusually frigid weather gripped Florida all the way to Miami as two nights in a row the temperature remained trapped in the teens. Although it melted by midmorning, thousands of children experienced the miracle of snow for the first time. Tampa Bay area schools closed to save energy.

Adam Eden, a short but stout twenty-seven-year-old Tampa cracker, hunkered down against the fierce wind. He hated the cold. To a native Floridian, temperatures below fifty are considered life-threatening. He did, however, appreciate the solitude that the extreme weather encouraged. Adam stood transfixed as he watched the cold black water of the Hillsborough River flow slowly past. He looked around. Ten years earlier the area had been undisturbed woodland. Now, however, his favorite live oak, its twisted rambling limbs whiskered with Spanish moss, stood alone. The ancient sentinel that once guarded a small pristine section of river basin was now ignominiously demoted to a mere shade tree for yuppies. A deck overlook encircled the oak. Adam struggled to forget the sprawling apartment complex that polluted the scenery behind him.

In their youth, Adam and his friends Bulldog and Franci had climbed every inch of the bearded sentry. They fashioned rope swings on several massive limbs, and they even constructed a rickety tree house that demanded caution lest one ended up unceremoniously dumped into the river below. In that precarious perch the three of them talked about their problems, shared their happiness, cried over tragedies, and laughed at silly jokes. In that tree house Adam and Franci made love for the first time.

A savage gust of wind forced Adam to seek protection between the tree and the guardrail. He looked up, but nothing remained of the crudely built refuge. That first time he and Franci made love, she had responded willingly, but blushed when she saw Adam's manhood. She had rubbed it often, but only while it remained caged in Adam's jeans. She shyly restated her desire, but confessed her fear, and Adam had responded with patience and gentleness. He displayed maturity beyond his fifteen years. They had frequently hinted at going all the way, and almost did twice. Making out took on a will of its own. After the last time, however, and seeing how guilty Franci felt for freezing up, Adam suggested they talk about it.

Since the age of five, Adam and Franci had loved each other. Adam reasoned that real sex together should not be due to passion spiraled out of control. Sex like that could happen with anybody. It should be special. When he and Franci took off their clothes, it should be because both of them wanted to more than anything they ever desired in their short lives. That is precisely how it happened. After that first clumsy encounter in the fragile tree house, they made love eagerly, passionately, and often – that is until Franci killed herself. That's when Adam decided that God is a myth.

★

Dr. Luther Huntley, a wealthy man of letters, struggled to control his temper. The disguise required more effort than he had imagined. He fussed with the scruffy fake beard that like his chin finished in a point. A streak carelessly left on the ornate antique mirror marred his image and irritated him further. One can no longer employ decent help; people prefer welfare to work. His lips twisted with bitterness, and he made his hands into fists. Nowadays, the slightest aggravation pushed him close to screams. He gave the beard another slight adjustment. Once satisfied that his identity would be safe, he scowled at the prospect, but slipped into the faded old coat and cap. Both were made necessary by the bone-chilling conditions that waited outside.

Years ago, he had retreated to Florida with his wife, Jean, to escape New England winters. He preferred to enjoy golf and boating on his own schedule, not one dictated by the elements. Now, however, the weather was nasty, and he was bitter. He no longer enjoyed anything.

Ironically, as a wealthy man he always voted on the side of economics rather than ecology, while simultaneously vilifying insufferable liberals for mocking natural law. Survival of the fittest ensures species continuity. Now nature's just rule has been rendered ineffective. One can thank the legacy of FDR and his New Deal, and the more recent fools and their Great Society. Like maggots devouring wounded flesh, an undeserving mass of humanity chews away at the underbelly of American society. The hearty, the productive of the species, pay taxes, while bureaucrats squander the proceeds on individuals unable to survive on their own. One need only consider Dr. Huntley's personal tragedy to see the proof of his argument.

Dr. Huntley lived alone due to one of the Great Society's successes, Clarence Fardy. A welfare dependent who otherwise would have perished, the leech used the dole to keep himself in drink. Drunk, and driving with a suspended license, the disgusting little parasite rammed a piece of rusty junk into Dr. Huntley's wife's sedan. Fardy's door popped open and he flew out and rolled unharmed to the safety of the gutter. While the worthless drunk struggled to focus, Jean Huntley burned to death.

Tall and thin, vain and vengeful, Dr. Huntley examined his reflection one last time. He frowned at his appearance and slowly turned his head from side to side. Satisfied that he would pass for common and go unrecognized, he glanced at the time then darted through the cold to his car.

★

The sun set and Adam turned up his collar. His Braves baseball cap helped, but a hood would be better. He exhaled and watched his breath caress the red rose clutched in his gloved hand. Although the cold burned his nostrils, he sniffed the sweet-scented flower. He remembered the fresh scrubbed scent of Franci when they had shared their first kiss, and the taste of

Reeses' peanut butter cups. More than anything, however, he remembered the newness of Franci, her innocence, and thus her vulnerability. With a gloved finger, he dug under his wire-framed glasses and wiped away a tear.

Each anniversary of Franci's death, Adam took a rose to the river's edge and stood under the protective canopy of the oak. It did no particular good that he could see, but it did serve as a sort of penance. The only thing that would truly help would be the ability to apologize, and to have Franci hear it.

That was his Catch 22. If he could have at least said, "I'm sorry, Franci," she would not have killed herself. Once a person is dead, however, an apology, like the proverbial tree falling in isolation, may as well be soundless. After a suicide, the living can only try to accommodate their guilt. Regardless what the shrinks say, the living, innocent or otherwise, will share part of the blame. Also, there is anger to wrestle. Suicide is a selfish act committed without regard for the pain of loss and guilt that will forever torment the living. You love the lost one, mourn them, and would sacrifice everything for a second chance to help. At the same time you rail at the selfishness of their deed.

Loved ones sometimes signal their plight. Some signs are subtle, others are blatant, but if you are not suicidal you don't hear the bells. You try to lead, to pull, to push a person forward. That seems reasonable; you're secure on solid ground. The one you are struggling to aid, however, is walking on quicksand. It sucks up their resolve. You help because you care, but you don't do enough because you can't relate to utter helplessness. Indeed, you don't realize that the person is powerless until after the suicide. Then it's too late.

Sometimes you back away. From your perspective, the one you are trying to help does little or nothing for themselves. They ignore advice. You become frustrated. You take some space to regain your balance. Then you commit a weak, stupid, and an insensitive act that irretrievably shoves the suicidal person under the mire. Maybe that's a blessing. The tortured no longer have to struggle. Your guilt, however, is like a drop of black paint in a bucket of white. It may not be visible to others, but you know it's there, and it can never be purged. You learn to live with it or lose yourself as an alternative.

One by one, Adam plucked the fragile petals from the rose and watched them flutter to the river. When he dropped the last one, he watched it float out of sight. Would it wash ashore at the turn in the river where Franci's bloated body beached itself? He tossed the rose stem then hesitated. He half expected a wall of water that opened into a cavernous maw to rise like a bass after a mosquito, and swallow him whole. It did in his nightmares. He waited. No such luck.

Concerned about the bitter cold, he turned and trudged to his car. He wanted to check on his elderly neighbor, make sure that she had enough food and heat. Tragedy shapes the character of children. When it occurs to those beyond childhood, it mostly magnifies what's already there. If you were caring, you become more caring. If you were spiteful, you become more spiteful.

★

Dr. Huntley grew more irritated with each turn of the wheel. He continued to penetrate an old neighborhood of two- and three-bedroom stucco homes that had known better treatment. Finally, he located the St. Petersburg residence for which he was searching. Driving a rented clunker to go with his disguise, he aimed the rusted-out Ford station wagon next to the curb behind a string of other cars. He glanced again at the rear view mirror and fussed with his appearance. For a man of his social prominence to be recognized in such a shabby neighborhood would be mortifying. To be caught attending a séance would decimate what little remained of his dignity.

He fought the urge, the necessity to continue searching for a link to his beloved wife. He kept hearing about this Phoenix person, however, until a visit could no longer be resisted. Like masturbating when he was a boy, the more he played with himself the less he could resist. The more he gave in, the greater his guilt. Dr. Huntley hated weakness. Weakness is the plague of the lowborn.

At first, upon seeing others make contact with lost loved ones, he ached to believe. Later, after continued misinformation, doubt crept in. Frustration forced rational thought. Now, he vacillated between hope and disbelief. More than anything he had wanted his wife back. As the reality of that impossibility settled over him, more than anything Dr. Huntley wanted her murderer, Clarence Fardy, dead.

★

Adam almost had the streets to himself thanks to the cold weather, and he began to shake his somber mood. Driving did that for him, especially driving a real car like his old '57 Chevy. It felt substantial and came with a steering wheel of proper proportions. His sister, Gloria, however, said that Adam looked like a kid behind the big wheel, but the old car had been a gift from their father on Adam's sixteenth birthday and was now sacrosanct.

Besides, Franci had loved the old tank that still sported a dark green bottom and a light green top. Faded and with several paint jobs removed from the original, the colors remained unchanged. The Chevy ran as good as the day it had rolled off the assembly line, and it rolled well too considering that Adam hadn't bought tires in years. The last set he purchased came with a warranty good for as long as he owned the car. The tire dealer hated Adam.

He wheeled into the driveway of his modest turn-of-the-century Hyde Park bungalow, and saw the lights still burning in his elderly neighbor's house. The Steins had lived there for forty years until six months ago when Mr. Stein had passed away. Now Mrs. Stein managed alone. Lights shined in several rooms. He punched through the waist-high azalea hedge that marked the property line, and rushed up on his neighbor's porch. The Artic-like air stung his face. Each exhalation of his breath created a brief mist that cleared as he rushed through it. That's the same with doubts. You can't really think them away; to do any good you have to work through them. He reached out to ring the bell, but the door opened first.

"Good evening, Adam," Mrs. Stein said, "I've been expecting you." She stepped aside and motioned him in.

"Uh oh, I've become predictable. My reputation's going to suffer."

"Your reputation is already tarnished beyond redemption," she said, but her smile betrayed her rancor. "Why don't you marry one of those young ladies you keep bringing home?"

"Waiting for you to come to your senses, and drive off with me to paradise. Mature women turn me on, you know." Adam knew she loved it when he flirted with her.

She grinned. "I would today if you didn't drive like a maniac. I have to close my eyes just to ride to the store."

"What if I hire a chauffeur?" Adam said. He removed his cap. "Hmm, feels good in here. Heat seems to be working. You all right?"

"Yes, thank you for checking. I'm dressed for the cold, and the heat is working just fine."

"Need anything? Coffee, tea, or me?"

She trapped Adam's hand that was always busy when he talked. "Oh, Adam, you treat us better than the kids do, but thank you, no. We're all right for now." There were four children in all, and six grandchildren.

Adam worried that Mrs. Stein continued to talk as if Mr. Stein were still alive, but he tried to hide it. "Well, Bea, I'm just next door, it's easier for me. You need anything, call, OK? I'll be in for the evening." He stepped back to leave, but Mrs. Stein held onto his hand. She had read his thoughts.

"Please don't worry. I know Allen is no longer physically with me, but he is often near." She tightened her grip. "Oh, Adam, do you know how harsh you look when I talk about such things? You must have suffered a great loss at one time to have closed yourself off so completely from your feelings." Adam fidgeted but remained mum.

"I'm aware this upsets you, but I know Allen is frequently near because the aroma from his pipe swirls through the room. The scent of vanilla in his favorite blend is especially strong, and I often wake up embraced by the fragrance." She patted Adam's hand. "Don't worry about me, dear, try to listen more to your heart and less to your head."

"I will, Bea," said Adam, but he spoke a lie. Death is a permanent condition. His favorite T-shirt, a treasured purchase from a shop in Seattle, was printed with the affirmation that "It's not that life is so short, it's that death is so long". Adam accepted that Mrs. Stein believed her late husband hovered around like a guardian angel, but the belief obviously stemmed from her loneliness. The marriage had lasted fifty-one years. A mind would have a bundle of familiar detail to work with when creating an illusion.

An imagination can make a person happy or sad. Adam knew from experience, and when guilt grabbed him as it had earlier, he envied his neighbor's capacity for delusion. He leaned over and lightly kissed Mrs. Stein on the cheek. "Call if you need me."

★

The fake beard and mustache were uncomfortable but convincing. Dr. Huntley knew that the lights inside would be subdued. Ostensibly, lights are dimmed at a séance because bright lights are difficult for spirits to accommodate. Voodoo nonsense, of course. A cap, jeans, boots, and coat purchased at the Salvation Army store added to his disguise. He even stained his hands with the grease and grime under the Ford's hood. A disgusting sacrifice for a man accustomed to weekly manicures, but necessary.

The house, a small, two-bedroom, concrete-block dwelling painted flamingo pink, suffered with chipped and peeling paint as if diseased. Patches of hearty bahia grass browned by the lingering cold passed for a lawn. Mostly, however, a blanket of laurel oak leaves covered the sandy yard. Dr. Huntley stepped around a bent-up lawn chair and stumbled over the ubiquitous roots of the oak tree. Through clinched teeth, he said, "White trash," then cursed the cold when he saw his breath.

Once inside his mood didn't improve. As predicted, subdued light greeted him. The clutter of ceramic bric-a-brac and cheap upholstered furnishings draped with yellowed coverlets confirmed his fears. Like the rest of the house, threadbare arm rests shouted neglect, and Dr. Huntley didn't doubt that pests crawled freely about. The smell of stale air and cigarette smoke assaulted him. He struggled to appear at ease. He was relieved when Phoenix, a heavyset woman dressed in shapeless folds, strolled in and thinly greeted everyone as if she were an icon.

Only three hopefuls – Dr. Huntley, a frail little woman with gnarled hands, and a pail corpulent nobody – were in attendance. The fat man was showing the woman a picture. Dr. Huntley eased closer to take a look. In an aged black-and-white photo, a grossly overweight woman sat behind a birthday cake decorated with the words, Happy Thirty-fifth Birthday. She had a flabby arm draped around a chubby boy who looked to be ten years old. Both appeared to be laughing. An old 1948 Plymouth filled up the background of the backyard setting.

The man explained that he had visited Phoenix several times before her spirit helpers declared that he deserved the chance to visit with his mother at a séance. Rubbing her hands, the little woman expressed the same experience. Both were elated at the privilege. As the man talked about how much he missed his recently deceased mother, he began to blubber. The frail woman consoled him. Dr. Huntley marched away shaking his head.

Posing as a man named Herman, Dr. Huntley had been invited to attend only after refusing to accept the alternative. If Phoenix were legitimate, if indeed the dead can talk, then Phoenix didn't need to get to know Dr. Huntley and align their vibrations. Certainly a helper who greeted him at the door aligned herself with his fifty dollars quickly enough.

After everyone seated themselves around the table, Phoenix coughed, and in a gravelly voice said, "A little small talk to get more acquainted will help spirit align their vibrations to that of ours. It's necessary because spirit vibrates at a much higher frequency than the living. It's like a fan blade. The slower it runs, the more visible the blades. In order for contact to be successful, spirit needs to slow down their vibrations and simultaneously speed ours up. We can help by clearing our minds of any negative thoughts, bitterness and hatred. Concentrate on your loved ones; a loving person vibrates at a higher rate." She stared at Dr. Huntley. "A person must be worthy. There are no guarantees."

Dr. Huntley volunteered nothing and answered all questions directed to him in monosyllables. Finally, after coughing several times, Phoenix instructed everyone to meditate on the loved one they wished to contact. Dr. Huntley waited impatiently while she piously pressed her hands together and bowed her head. After a brief silence, followed by deep breathing, a voice came through. It expressed undying love for the frail little woman who sat weeping next to Dr. Huntley. They talked of the children, and of their memories of things done and places visited. The voice of Phoenix skillfully hinted, and the weeping woman filled in the blanks.

When the questions turned to finance, the voice advised the woman to continue to consult with Phoenix. Through the psychic instrument he would guide his wife as best he could. He explained that although he still understood the pressures of economy, problems didn't exist in spirit. It was difficult to consider negative matters. No advice of consequence was given to the lady, but Dr. Huntley noticed how the fat man perked up. When the voice explained that financial problems didn't exist in the spirit world, that indeed, no problems existed in Heaven, the crybaby bubbled over.

Phoenix breathed deeply, and the voice was silenced. Again, she examined the three participants then abruptly grunted. "Oh, I feel so heavy, my legs, my arms," she said, lifting her arms and letting them plop back to the table, palms down. Everyone gasped as the table tipped toward the psychic. She continued, saying that a jovial, loving, but very heavy woman was present and wanted to greet her son. To Dr. Huntley's amazement, the table began to wobble, steadied itself, and tilted toward the homely son who had so indiscreetly shared memories of his obese mother.

Between sobs, the corpulent man answered all the questions Phoenix, pretending to be his mother, posed. The fake psychic skillfully processed each fact surrendered. She mixed it with information gained from the man's loose tongue while talking to the old woman, and with information obviously gained during prior visits. Speaking as the deceased mother, Phoenix regurgitated only emotive responses. As with the frail old lady and her questions about finance, substantive questions from the son received equivocal answers convincing only to the gullible.

A grown man crying for his mommy. Dr. Huntley gritted his teeth. He couldn't explain the moving table, but clearly Phoenix was just another two-bit charlatan. Even her shabby surroundings shouted "fake". Obviously, communication with the dead is an elaborate hoax. Dr. Huntley prepared to disclose the ruse, but swallowed his words. The fat man looked at Phoenix and said, "Mother, I want to join you. I'm going to kill myself."

Phoenix choked and fell into a fit of coughing. She recovered quickly, however, and shouted, "No! Never! Do you understand? Suicide is the unpardonable sin. You can't ask for forgiveness if you kill yourself, then you can't join me in Heaven."

Phoenix impressed Dr. Huntley with her skill as she calmed the man, and made him promise to forget about suicide if he ever wanted to join his mother. Obviously, the last thing a psychic fraud wants is a suicide note praising her gift of gab with the dead. The man agreed to wait for God to call him home. He was a believer. Even if the deceptions were to later be explained, the homely man would not hear. He had seen the table move. He had communicated with his dead mother.

Phoenix quickly terminated the séance. "The vibrations are no longer aligned. Spirit has broken off contact. They warn that only God gives life and only God should take it away."

She continued to speak, but Dr. Huntley's mind kept replaying the scene of the pathetic fat man wanting to kill himself in order to join his mother. The irony seized Dr. Huntley like a pit bull and wouldn't let go. Here was a genetic failure. He was a time bomb of destruction who should never be allowed to procreate his worthless genes, and further weaken an already overburdened nation. He prudently wanted to kill himself. Now, however, he probably would not because to do so would be an unforgivable sin.

Like a man weakened by starvation, Dr. Huntley chewed on the irony. He experienced the first rush of energy he had felt in months. Mother Nature did not support the nonproductive, nor should society. Suicide is a natural resolution. America, in order to survive, needed to allow, indeed needed to encourage its useless members to cull themselves. Certainly no one could argue that Clarence Fardy was not a useless and destructive parasite.

Dr. Huntley possessed the money and the contacts to have the drunken little leech killed. He had contemplated that option often, but his patrician ego could never accept something so common as justice. Unable to identify exactly what was cooking in his grief-racked brain, Dr. Huntley, nevertheless, sensed that providence had just stirred the pot. He caught himself smiling and wondered how long it had been.

★

Adam always did everything at full throttle, but the nasty weather gave him an added incentive. He pushed back through the hedge, and jerked open the unlocked door. He rushed inside, but old Florida homes are not constructed for central heat and air, however, and keeping them comfortable in extreme temperatures can be a battle. The cold had seeped into the walls and floors of his home like water overtaking a leaky boat.

A clear sunny day had helped, but now darkness had fallen over the house again as it had Adam's mood. Dead means no longer living. End of discussion. The only contact the living have with the dead is that brief period during which the survivors spend thousands on monuments to impress friends or to assuage their guilt over things not said or done. Millions of dead lie decorated with great wealth, while the world over millions of near-dead are allowed to starve.

Adam recklessly made his way across cold hardwood floors, and darted down the hallway before switching on a light. He shook off his depression and the guilt that always attacked him when he thought of Franci. He made a mess digging through drawers searching for a sweater, and dragged out a wool crewneck ten years out of style.

Quickly, he exchanged it for his jacket, and dashed to the kitchen for a cup of tea. He cradled the hot mug in his hands. The steam rising in twirls from his first cup felt good on his face. Carefully, he tested the temperature before taking a sip, and jumped when the doorbell rang. He didn't bother to answer. When the door opened, Adam listened and the heavy footfalls confirmed what he already knew.

"In the kitchen, Bulldog. Want a cup of tea?" Adam searched for the instant coffee. He always offered tea, and his best friend always said, "Yes," but both knew that coffee would be served.

"Yeah, that would be great." Bulldog filled up the kitchen entrance. "Had a drug bust earlier. I'm freezing." He surveyed the counter top and laughed.

"What's so funny?"

"You, man. You can't even make a cup of coffee without peppering the whole kitchen. No bigger than a gnat yet you're like a bull in a china shop." It was true. Adam couldn't argue. His mind was usually preoccupied. Bulldog glanced back toward the living room. "Christ, it's like a morgue in here. Why don't I start a fire?"

"Good idea. You still playing detective or do you want a little brandy in your cup?"

Over his shoulder Bulldog answered, "No, hot as hell and black as my ass, thanks."

Finally warming up, Bulldog took his cup of coffee from the mantel and sat down across from Adam. As the fire had sputtered then caught hold and roared to life, nothing much was said. Best buddies since childhood, both knew that Bulldog dropped by as he had done every January fourteenth since Franci's death to check on Adam. Both knew that Bulldog would not mention their mutual friend. Over the years, the two had poured out their grief and argued the well dry. Adam believed that he pushed Franci over the edge, and Bulldog couldn't convince his friend otherwise.

"How's Trace (Adam was fond of truncating names) and Bulldog II?" asked Adam, feeling more human now that the fire had overpowered the cold.

"Great. I just can't explain what it's like to hold that little guy and know that he came from Tracy and me. It's such a miracle man; it brings tears to my eyes. Course, you tell anybody that and I'll break every bone in your scrawny body."

"Then I won't tell."

"Where you been anyway? Tracy gets bitchy when she hasn't seen you in a while. Misses your bullshit."

"You can't blame a lady for being starved for intellectual stimulation when she's married to the last of the Neanderthals."

"Well, at least now I know you and Tracy haven't been having an affair." Adam's expression questioned his friend. "Otherwise,

Terry Jr. would be a runt," said Bulldog. He twisted in the chair, and rubbed his side.

"You'll never know for sure unless he turns out to be brilliant." Adam studied his friend. "How's the wound?"

"Healed, but I still feel it sometimes. Like a rookie I let a little sniveling piece of shit stick me. I can't get over it."

"Even John Wayne occasionally took it on the chin. You're human."

"In my business, being human will get you killed."

Adam propped his elbows on his knees and stared into the teacup that he held with both hands. The dark brew reflected the flickering fire light like a crystal ball, but revealed nothing. Absently, he quoted,

"And ever near us, though unseen,

The fair immortal spirits tread;

For all the boundless universe is life; there are no dead!"

"What?"

"Sorry, just thinking out loud. The ending of a poem, *Resurgam*, attributed to Bulwer Lytton. My mother used to say, 'People don't die, they just switch channels." Adam absently shook his head from side to side. "Everybody's entitled to their opinions I guess."

Bulldog grinned but didn't comment. The thought was right, but Adam's behavior never reflected the sentiment. The detective said, "What did she mean?"

"That we watch only one station at a time, but all the channels broadcast simultaneously. Everything exists at once, but at different frequencies. Psychics can tune into other channels. You know, all that baloney, hopping back and forth from the present to the past and to the future." Adam looked up toward Bulldog, but he focused on his memories. "She claimed psychics could contact those who have passed on by tuning to the dead person's frequency, or vibration, or some such nonsense."

Without thinking first, Bulldog said, "Maybe they can."

While trying to sit the cup down, Adam spilled his tea and stared at Bulldog. "I can't believe you would say such a dumb thing. An afterlife is just an invention of the privileged and you know it."

"Damn it, Adam, how do you know there's no life after death? And what are you talking about anyway?"

"Talking about? *What am I talking about?*" Adam chopped the air with both hands. "Since the beginning of rational thought, the powerful have controlled us peons by insisting that behavior during life governs the quality of life after death. Don't make waves here, and life will be better there. That's crap." Adam kneeled down and used his handkerchief to soak up the tea. "Truth for the masses is merely the point of view of the powerful. Period. Franci no longer exists anywhere except in our memory."

"You know, you get worse every year. You hate people with narrow minds, but when someone holds an opinion different from yours, they're wrong. How can you be so sure that you know all the answers?"

Adam glared at his friend. "How? How can I be so sure? I'll tell you how. Do you think that if Franci still existed in some way, she wouldn't let me know? Do you think our Franci wouldn't tell even God to fornicate Himself if it meant contacting me?"

"Damn it, man, maybe she's got better things to do than to hang around you. We were just stupid-ass teenagers. Let it go."

"Let it go!" Adam shook his head in disgust. "That's easy to say, but then you didn't kill her."

Both men fell silent. Adam fiddled with his wet handkerchief before throwing it in the almost empty cup and splashing more tea. Bulldog sipped his coffee then cleared his throat. "Adam, we're best friends, brothers really, but you're becoming a Jekyll and Hyde. What the hell is really gnawing on your ass?"

Adam opened his mouth, but hesitated. "I don't know," he finally said. "No, that's not true." He fingered through the magazines that littered his coffee table until he came to the latest issue of *News and Views*. He studied the cover picture for maybe the tenth time, applauding abortion protestors celebrating a burned out clinic. Adam figured that for the revelers the incompatibility of their cause with the violent solution was buried just as the magazine had been a moment earlier. He shook his head. Some people just don't see the inconsistencies between their beliefs and their actions.

Adam stuck a finger between the pages to mark his place.

"Remember Joey from my article on teenage suicide in America? His mother called today all excited. Said she talked with Joey through some fraud who calls herself a psychic. Bills herself as Phoenix, no less. Joey's mother wouldn't tell me how much she had to pay for this miracle, but a penny would be too much." He sailed the magazine across the room. "She's dirt poor, uneducated, and vulnerable."

"So that's it."

"That's what?"

"I know you *think* you hate all that psychic shit, but deep down, I think you're jealous."

"Jealous? Of what?"

"Maybe somewhere in the bowels of that one-thought brain of yours, your mother's beliefs are more a part of you than you think. You—"

"Bulldog, you know—"

Bulldog held up his huge hand, "I'm sorry, I know, I know. You believe that your mother died because she believed in faith healers and you couldn't convince her otherwise, but maybe because of her teachings deep down you believe that there is a possibility of life after death. You would like to try contacting Franci, but over the years you've raised such a stink that now your pride gets in the way."

"So all of a sudden you believe in God? You believe in an afterlife, and that people can talk to the dead?"

"Yeah, Adam, to all three questions, as a matter of fact I do, but I've never admitted it for fear I would have to kill you. A lot of police have used psychics on murder cases and missing persons cases. Murder victims have actually fingered their killer through psychics. Granny says we all have guardian angels who once lived just like us, and she has seen her mother as clear as day several times. She even tells me that I am psychic, and that's what makes me a good detective." Bulldog set his cup down, and leaned toward Adam who gripped the chair arm. "If Granny believes it, I believe it. You know what she's always told us, 'Talk with your mouth, but listen with your heart.'"

"Well, it's crap, Bulldog. I love and respect Granny too, but it's intuition, buried memories and delusion. Joey's mother is being conned."

"Uh oh, smells like trouble brewing."

"I'll keep calm."

"That's a lie, and you know it. You're not happy unless you're in somebody's face. Without a cause you don't exist."

"When something's wrong, you fix it."

Bulldog measured his words. "Adam, I know you help people because you care. The first time we met was when you got my ass kicked just to help a cat, remember, but now, ah, well, nothing you do will make you feel less guilty. You—"

"Franci's death has nothing to do with this."

"You know damn well it does. You keep looking for absolution."

"So, I should let this con artist take advantage of helpless people like Joey's mother?"

"No, I'm just saying why be so damned eager to read trouble into everything someone does that doesn't square with what you believe?"

Adam walked over to the fireplace, and with a poker stirred up the fire. Sparks flew in all directions. "Because they're wrong," he said.

"Every day I'm on the streets, man, I wish I could snap my fingers and fix all the shit, but I can't. I can't save the world, and neither can you."

"I can try."

"One of these days, Adam, you're going to bite into a mess too big for both of us to chew." Bulldog's handy-talkie interrupted. "Sorry, gotta go," Bulldog said. "There's been another shooting in the Oven."

Adam heard the call too, but only recognized static, a few numbers, and the word "oven". Bulldog put on his hat and coat, and hurried to leave. "Lock this door behind me. I don't want to come over here some night to investigate your murder."

Adam grinned and spread his hands, palms up. "Who would want to murder me?"

"Only about half the people in this town you've stuck your pen into." Bulldog rushed to his car, and sped off to investigate another drive-by shooting. He headed for the Oven, an ethnically mixed neighborhood of subsidized housing where the decent poor barricade themselves in at night like frightened rabbits in a warren. Pimps and drug dealers rule the night. Shootings are frequent.

Adam knew that Bulldog was right about one thing; he had always protected Adam, and so had Franci before she died. A good thing too. Adam never thought about how much he might be expected to chew before biting into trouble, and he would lose a fight with billowing sheets on a laundry line. His advantage was his courage, and if he was helping you, he might be more a hindrance than an aid, but you absolutely loved him for trying. Conversely, if he disagreed with you, you wanted to swat him.

★

The cold air bit into Dr. Huntley's face as he rushed to the old Ford. He wondered if his wife's murderer was cold in prison. Fardy could be released in three years, but even after an eternity Jean Huntley would still be dead. Dr. Huntley had visited Phoenix, hopeful to find a link to the spirit world. He would expose her as a fraud if not, the only thing he enjoyed doing lately. He hesitated only after a crazy but delicious scheme, enriched by hate, sprouted within the fertile folds of his brain.

Weak people such as that corpulent excuse for a human killing themselves for a better life after death appealed mightily to Dr. Huntley's embittered soul, and the prospect of seeing one particular piece of white trash commit suicide especially excited him. It seemed perfectly logical now that the idea had securely coiled its roots in and around his convoluted mind. Clarence Fardy killed Dr. Huntley's wife, now Clarence Fardy would kill himself. The perfect murder couched behind the veil of a public suicide.

Anxious for a bath and decent clothing, Dr. Huntley turned the rented clunker around and headed home. He reached for his CD of Beethoven's Symphony Number Nine then he remembered that his Mercedes sat unused in the garage of his palatial home on Bay Shore Boulevard overlooking the Upper Hillsborough Bay.

★

Adam knew about the Oven and he worried for his friend. In his mind, being a policeman and playing Russian roulette for a living were equally unappealing. Even kids had guns, and they would shoot you for an insult, imagined or otherwise. He used his last tea bag to brew one more cup; the caffeine helped defend against fatigue. As much as he disliked the cold weather, he realized that a trip to the market was necessary. Better tonight while charged up than tomorrow morning without a jump-start.

Adam retrieved the magazine containing his latest article, and fanned the pages to the six-page spread. Five suicides were investigated, and he interviewed thirty survivors. Since Franci's death, Adam had aided a number of people who had lost loved ones to suicide, and had probably helped several potential suicides to escape that irreversible solution to their madness. He would never know for sure, however, because they may have regained control of their lives without his intervention. Nevertheless, that didn't lessen his resolve to help whenever he could. Bulldog was wrong. Adam had always helped anyone in need, even before Franci's death. He was in control. He had not become a fanatic.

He couldn't save his mother or his girlfriend, but maybe he just didn't try hard enough. Oh, to have another chance, but that is not possible. The evening of Franci's death he had approached the tree in time to hear the splash. Darting forward, he ripped off his jacket and jerked off his shoes, but under a cloudy sky, the dark water revealed nothing. He dived in anyway and raced downstream, screaming her name. She popped up only a few feet away, gasped, "Adam" and went under again. He clawed at the water, but Franci disappeared before he could reach her. Adam tossed the magazine aside and went to get his hat and coat. He never thought to lock the front door to his house.

Later, after paying the cashier, Adam hurried from the store to his Chevy. Before zipping from the parking lot, he cranked up the heat, and tuned in the late jazz broadcast from WUSF public radio. He fondly remembered how Franci used to sit next to him, shifting gears and eating peanut butter cups. He drove with one hand, and used the other to hold his girl. The thought calmed

Adam. Her lips always tasted like peanut butter and chocolate. He imagined that he could smell her favorite treat.

A stoplight forced him to reign in his imagination, his reverie shattered by the clicking of valves as a beat-up old Ford station wagon pulled alongside. In the faint green glow of dashboard lights, Adam studied the bearded driver. The man appeared battered like his car, but smiled broadly. Adam considered himself to be fortunate, and he often reflected on that good fortune when noticing others with greater burdens. The grizzled old driver looked as if he had hauled a few. The man appeared in deep thought, but he was definitely grinning. He held the steering wheel with his left hand and used his right to stroke a pointed beard.

Adam concluded that his fellow sojourner had been knocked around by life. Because of the man's familiarity with hardship and temptation, the gent would not harshly judge others for their misdeeds and failures. He was a decent sort who could hold his head high because he had bent but not yielded. He smiled because he was heading home to a warm house with a loving and supportive wife. Adam laughed at his presumptuousness. He knew nothing about the old man. Adam could be dead wrong.

June, 1993

For six months Clarence Fardy, a thin, shy, little guy with Hubble-thick glasses, had followed the same routine. It became habit. You lined up when told, moved when told. To avoid trouble, you followed orders. An experienced order-taker, Clarence obeyed easily. It had always been easier to take orders than to argue, first from his bitter and domineering mother then later from his disappointed wife. Sometimes he had wanted to stand up to his mother, then later to his wife, but he never did. Instead, he became a drunk.

All the doors rattled opened simultaneously and every prisoner on Clarence's row stepped into their individual cells. Clarence never even looked up. If he met you one day, he would never recognize you the next unless you were wearing the same pair of shoes. In jail that didn't help because all the shoes were the same. His eyes rested on the barless rectangular design reflected before his feet in which his shadow lay. The clear spot broke up the image of steel bars that partitioned the cold concrete floor, and Clarence passively watched the pattern complete itself as the door banged shut behind him.

He heard the familiar click as the steel bars locked him in, just as long ago he had locked in his emotions. Moving aimlessly toward his bed, he spotted a yellow tear sheet. It had not been there earlier. Perspiration beaded on his forehead, then trickled down his nose. Clarence pushed up his heavy glasses. He managed to read the note although his hand shook terribly.

> Thou shalt not kill.
>
> For the remainder of your stay here, you are going to do everything I say exactly as I say. You are going to dedicate your life to God. Do as I say, and no one here will harm you. Disobey, and every lover boy here will pop a puddle in your shit locker and pump it dry. That will be a blessing of sorts to help keep your mind off your wife and children who will suffer horribly as they burn to death. Tomorrow, we start your conversion. Right now, you eat this note.

Clarence mopped sweat from his brow, and struggled to control his bowels. They were boiling. He had not meant to kill. Aggression and violence were alien to his nature. He avoided confrontation. Careful to keep his head down, Clarence peeked across at the other cells he could see. No one appeared to be watching, but he couldn't be sure. The fat guy reading the book glanced up a lot, and when he looked up again, Clarence quickly averted his eyes. Clarence had been doing OK so far by keeping his head down and challenging no one; he didn't dare chance another peek. He briefly eyed the tear sheet then ate it as directed.

After choking down the note Clarence paced his bare cell trying to reason its meaning. Hours later he fell asleep while still trying, and woke up sick with fear, exhausted. Later, during the recreation period, he wandered zombie-like about the sandy Florida prison yard until startled by a muffled warning. Clarence sensed that the words came from well above his head. Shifting his eyes, he stole a glance at his shadow. It was dwarfed by the black reflection of a giant.

"Don't turn around, partner. Just keep looking at your feet and you won't get hurt. Got a picture here of your family taken just last week, your three kids playing out front, and your wife standing in the doorway. Nice looking kids. Your wife's got beautiful long black hair, but she's too skinny for my taste. To each his own, huh? Be a shame if anything happened to them."

Clarence stiffened, and the deep voice warned, "Easy now, partner. Ain't nothing gonna happen as long as you follow instructions, see? Ain't nothing gonna happen to them, and you're gonna be safe as a virgin in a room full of queers." Clarence shifted uneasily.

The voice continued, "It's real simple. You're gonna start seeing the shrink, and you're gonna join that Bible study group. You're gonna be a model prisoner, get converted, and be paroled early. Understand? Don't matter if you hate Jesus and would eat shit for a drink of whiskey. You better make everybody believe the opposite. If you don't, if I even think that you squealed about this to anybody, if I see you stray from the trail, partner, your family will accidentally burn to death." Clarence almost turned around. "No! Don't even think about it, amigo. Comprende?"

"No, I – I mean, yes, but what…? Why?" Sweat flooded from Clarence's pores and drowned his shirt. With a shaky hand, he pushed up his heavy glasses.

"Now, partner, part of the deal is, you don't get to ask no questions, see? Besides, I'm just a hired hand; I don't know nothing anyway. I was hired to get that note to you. I get paid to give you instructions when I'm told, and report if you don't follow them, savvy? But I smell money, partner, enough to buy whatever it wants. For what it's worth, you're very important to some jasper with deep saddlebags who will do whatever it takes to have his way. If you don't want your family killed you better play by his rules. That's the only advice you're gonna get from me so don't ask no more questions."

As the voice continued, Clarence swallowed bile that boiled up from his stomach and burned his throat. Every muscle tense, his body shook. "You just need to know that every day you follow instructions, you're keeping your kids alive, and that's good, ain't it, partner? Just look at this as doing your fatherly duty. But, and this a real big but, Clarence, the first fuck up by you, and you will spend the rest of your life hearing your kids scream as the meat burns off their bones."

Clarence lost control and watched helplessly as a puddle formed briefly in the sand. Transfixed, he considered the damp pattern between his feet. An image of a beaked Lucifer swooping toward unsuspecting prey, his razor sharp talons extended, popped into Clarence's mind. He shuddered.

"That's good," the voice said. "You stay scared for your family's sake. I'll be contacting you again whenever I'm told to. I'm gonna back away now and ease into the crowd, but I'll be watching, see. If I even think you look around your kids are gonna be barbecue."

Clarence felt the photo being stuffed into his hand. "I know the cinch is tight, partner, so keep this where you can see it so you don't forget," the deep voice said, then disappeared.

★

Kyle Keysor sat on his bed and rapped the loose end of his stick in the palm of his free hand. After years of handling, the bark was smooth to the touch, the balance friendly. Kyle gripped it like a pit bull on the attack. In two hours he would marry his high school sweetheart. The wedding party would be small; mostly his new wife's family and friends. Still, he should have been happy; instead he was angry. "Why?" he asked again. "Why?"

His oldest brother breathed deeply. Through clenched teeth, he said, "I've told you three times already, we couldn't afford to have another child. Reg getting pregnant was a freak accident, a statistic that wasn't supposed to happen."

"But to have an abortion. To murder your own baby."

Kyle's brother stomped toward the door, hesitated, then turned and glared at Kyle. "I'm sorry this has upset you, especially today of all days, but Reg and I don't see it like that. She could have had another baby, but we chose not to. We chose to terminate the pregnancy so that we could afford to care for the four children we already have." Before Kyle could respond, his brother marched from the bedroom and slammed the door behind him. The impact knocked over a pistol on Kyle's gun rack, and rattled the picture of the Last Supper providentially placed next to it.

Kyle stared at the copy of Da Vinci's masterpiece ingloriously imposed on a crosscut section of redneck pine. The glossy finish had yellowed with age, and sections of bark were missing around the edges, but it had been his mother's favorite picture of Jesus. She explained that the Savior was God's conduit, the left hand held palm up to receive the Almighty's blessing, and the right turned palm down to pass that love to the faithful. A pose envisioned by Leonardo, it was symbolic of the life that Jesus would soon sacrifice, a life surrendered while hanging between God and man. After his mother's death, Kyle had resurrected the keepsake from the garbage where his father had tossed it.

Had the butchered remains of Kyle's niece or nephew been similarly discarded in a dumpster somewhere? You don't kill babies. Kyle remembered the Bible lessons learned at his mother's knee. He knew the story of Abraham and his son, Isaac; God stayed Abraham's hand. Then there was the helpless baby, Moses, set afloat in a river infested with crocodiles, but protected by the Lord. And later the Master, Jesus, an infant refugee hidden by the

Creator's shield from Herod's treachery. God's word is clear. You don't kill babies. You can invade, rape, kill and conquer, but you don't murder babies. Kyle leveled the picture, then set the 357 Magnum upright, wiping off all fingerprints before doing so. As he scrubbed his hands, Kyle decided to never speak to his brother again.

February, Three Years Later

Late again, Adam rushed from his house. As usual, he forgot to lock the door, but he didn't forget his big briefcase that his friends had labeled lethal. As often happened, Adam didn't sleep well. He experienced a recurring nightmare where he fell over a waterfall, and steadily drew nearer the dark river below where he knew that a mound of water would rise up to swallow him in a cavernous maw. Adam shook away the depression that always rode in on his nightmare and dumped the black case on the passenger seat. He speeded toward Bulldog's house for dinner with a few friends and family. The case was especially heavy since he had stuffed it with autographed copies of his first published book, *Suicide, The Unpardonable Sin*.

Adam had gathered information for the work ever since Franci's death, but realized it only after the publication of his article on suicide in *News and Views* three years ago. He frequently volunteered his time to man the suicide hotline and realized that instead of one-on-one in a crisis situation, he could reach both those in trouble as well as others around them who might be able to help. The book wrote itself, and now his friends were having a dinner in his honor. The literary effort did not resurrect Franci. It did not purge Adam's guilt. It did make him happy, however. Being able to help others while at the same time earn a living has a lot going for it.

He switched the radio from WUSF Public Radio to a local talk show. It was time for, as Adam called him, The Mouth. Adam liked to listen in case he needed to insert his opinion as a member of the human race that The Mouth managed to vilify daily. Adam had not called in a while because he could no longer get through if anyone recognized his voice. The Mouth loved to trap deer, but he disliked being cornered by a badger.

"Listen bozo, Kyle, or whatever you said your name is," The Mouth said over the air, "I can solve the abortion issue. Outlaw all abortions then pass a special tax for all you pro-lifers. You people will pay for raising all unwanted children. What do you think of that idea?"

"Abortion is already outlawed by God," Kyle said. "There would be no abortion problem if people followed God's law."

"Go back to sleep, Rip. Maybe you'll wake up in the real world." The Mouth cut Kyle off. "Can you believe that clown? Man, you should go drown yourself. Good idea. All you Bible-toters go jump off the Sky Way Bridge. Leave the real world to those of us with the brains to run it. Next caller. Who's this?"

Adam braked hard then snatched the Chevy into the right-hand lane. Ignoring the blaring horns and squealing tires, he wheeled over to the first pay phone he spotted. He knew the number from memory. As with clocks, Adam had no use for cell phones.

"All right, next caller, you're on the air," said The Mouth.

"Telling people to kill themselves is socially irresponsible," said Adam, "but typical of cretins like you."

"Oh, people! Do you recognize this voice? It's our old friend, Adam Eden, the guardian angel of the oppressed, the daddy of the downtrodden. What's your beef, Father Teresa? Didn't you write in your book that it's OK for people to pop themselves?"

Taken aback, Adam didn't immediately respond.

"Surprised, huh?" continued The Mouth. "I read your book about suicide, bozo. I like to keep up with the fairy tales you clowns are spinning." Adam started to answer, but was cut off the air. The Mouth continued, "That's enough of that jerk. Next caller. You're on the air…"

Adam stared at the receiver as if trying to figure a way to reach through and grab The Mouth by the neck. It's true, people suffering from accidents, disease, or the old who have already died but are kept alive artificially, should have the right of choice. Otherwise healthy individuals who are diagnosed as suicidal can be helped. Depression is treatable. Adam kicked a rock across the parking lot, and with a loud bang it ricocheted off a wheel hub. He didn't notice where it finally stopped. A special tax for pro-lifers? As if there wasn't enough lunacy in that quarter already. Adam should hurry, he was running late.

★

As The Mouth continued his evening harangue, Dr. Huntley maneuvered the old rented heap to the curb two houses down from the one belonging to Phoenix. He would purchase the book about suicide by Adam Eden. A frequent listener to talk radio, Dr. Huntley had heard Eden spar with the host several times, and Eden's humanist naiveté never failed to amuse. Now Dr. Huntley wanted to know more about the combative author of the book about suicide. The populist idiot might prove useful.

The ratty old house appeared the same as it had three years earlier when Dr. Huntley had first visited Phoenix and conceived his scheme. Again in his disguise, he counted the people attending the séance, and gasped when he spotted a provocative brunette. He calmed himself. There appeared to be five other guests, plus a shriveled old lady who offered punch. She obviously knew her way around the house, but failing eyesight slowed her down. She acted as host and attempted a second time to get Dr. Huntley to take some punch. Still, he declined.

Several people were chatting, including the seductive brunette who looked to be thirty years old. A flashy, overly made-up woman, she obviously lacked depth. If a product lacks quality, neon lights can help attract attention.

Dr. Huntley's eyes kept clicking back to watch her. He was disturbingly stimulated by the woman's beauty while simultaneously repulsed by her commonness. Obviously a tease, she apparently found herself unable to resist toying with a shy young man who couldn't look her in the eye without blushing. She talked with him about her deceased husband, and the young man shared memories of his grandmother, recently deceased. A piano teacher until she died, the young man wanted to know that she was OK. Dr. Huntley stole another lingering look at the heavily perfumed brunette then resumed his search for peep holes and listening devices. Everything appeared innocent, but after years of experience he knew better.

The hostess disappeared, but soon returned. In a shaky voice she announced, "Phoenix will be with us shortly. She is working to center her consciousness." The woman rubbed her gnarled and knotted hands as if to emphasize the struggle. "As you know, alignment is not always easy. Phoenix says you can help too. Sometimes just talking with others about your needs helps break the negative barriers that separate us from our departed loved ones. Expectation can draw them nearer."

Dr. Huntley studied the old woman and labeled her a believer. Careful to mask his contempt, he continued searching. Nothing obviously amiss struck him except the rickety rectangular-shaped table placed in the center of the living room. Simply constructed with a thin top and spindly legs, the table weighed very little. He glanced at the leg tips set in an old mustard-colored carpet that covered the living room and hallway floors. Matted from lack of care, the stained shag carpet looked disgusting and smelled like a damp basement, but it served to envelop the leg tips. He searched again and discovered a right-angle reduction in leg size just above floor level.

Other methods were also common, but this one worked well. The carpet helped to mask the design. A skillful con artist with hands clearly visible on the tabletop needed only to slide a foot over next to a leg, hook the sole of a shoe beneath the lip and lift. Result? Instant table-tipping guaranteed to amaze and satisfy the gullible.

Dr. Huntley eased away from the table, and discovered a huge mirror and two other strategically placed smaller ones in the hall. Briefly, he and a curly-haired redhead studied each other, he from the living room and her from a bedroom. Phoenix had chopped off her hair, and changed the color. She made the sign of the cross, and Dr. Huntley stepped to a corner of the room secure from observation through the mirror. He didn't doubt that Phoenix could read lips skillfully.

Later, the elderly hostess seated everyone around the shaky table, and Dr. Huntley noted that the attractive brunette sat at the opposite end of the table from Phoenix. She caught him looking and flashed a coquettish smile. He forced his eyes to look away, but couldn't escape her overpowering scent. He fought an erection.

Phoenix, in her late forties with a frumpish figure topped with short, tightly curled hair, presented a comical appearance. Mottled skin and heavy makeup completed the image. She sat under and slightly in front of a low wattage wall light that produced a halo effect, and served to cloud her facial features. Her smoker's cough was irritating, but her deep gravelly voice aided to suggest an otherworldly origin.

After the séance began, he noted the feedback of various bits of information that even he had picked up while waiting. Pleased, he grudgingly admired Phoenix's skill at gleaning even more knowledge from a participant's body language as well as verbal responses. She didn't miss the most subtle movement or simple gasp, displaying a sixth sense for the unspoken. Considered objectively, Dr. Huntley accepted Phoenix as much better qualified to participate in his scheme than he had remembered.

An experienced hustler, Phoenix revealed nothing spectacular to the first two people on whom she centered her attention. She served them just enough information to reinforce the faith that had made them gullible in the first place. Again, she examined all the participants then abruptly, in a singsong voice, said, "Oh, I feel so gay." Lifting her hands and swaying back and forth, she said, "I want to play the piano." Suddenly, the table tipped toward the shy young man.

Dr. Huntley stole a glance at the young brunette. The strain wasn't noticeable, but he knew that it existed. Phoenix obviously pulled on the tabletop with her arms and hands that were laid flat while the younger woman pushed with hers. The brunette would also be tilting her end with one foot hooked under a table leg. Obvious proof of those in the spirit world manipulating objects trapped in the physical. A convincing demonstration of life after death.

Phoenix continued in her singsong voice, and fed the young man facts to prove that his grandmother still lived. Dr. Huntley had overheard some of the information told to the brunette by the boy, and Phoenix skillfully reasoned other responses from the kid's reactions. Survivors can be so gullible, but the young man got his money's worth. The grandmother was well and happy.

Quiet for a time except for breathing heavily, Phoenix seemed to search around the table through closed eyes. Her head rolled back and forth as if she were spastic until Phoenix settled on the attractive brunette. With her eyes still closed, the psychic slowly began to groan and twist her head from side to side. The groaning grew more intense and she began to squeeze and twist and pull at her face with her hands. Her eyes popped open and she jerked her head around as if shocked by her whereabouts. In a deep voice but with whispered words, Phoenix said, "What's happened to me? It feels like I'm in a phone booth here. Flo, Flo, help me!"

"Oh, my God! Walter! Is that you, Walter?" the attractive brunette screamed. The wrinkled old hostess pulled on the young woman to keep her seated then patted her on the back to calm her.

"Where am I? I'm trapped in here, Flo. Help me! Oh, God! Please help me!"

"Tell him he's not trapped," the hostess said. "He's just speaking through another person. Tell him he needs to let those on the other side help him."

After this was conveyed, Phoenix began jerking wildly. She said, "Flo, they are helping me get out of here. They are going to take care of me... Mother? Oh, my God, Flo, Mother has come to get me."

"Walter, I miss you so much. Don't go. Please don't go."

"They are going to help me, Flo," Phoenix said again, then her head snapped back and she struggled to breathe.

"Walter!" Flo screamed, "Oh, Walter, I need you." She began to wail and the hostess led her from the room.

Everyone but Dr. Huntley sat stunned. They unconsciously allowed their breath to become irregular and willed the gasping Phoenix to regain control of hers. The hostess returned and began massaging Phoenix's neck and shoulders. The old woman said, "Often times a loved one will become trapped in the earth plane. Sometimes it's because they don't believe in life after death, and other times it's because they are emotionally tied to a person or hooked on alcohol and other drugs."

Dr. Huntley and Phoenix locked eyes. She touched the old woman's hand, who immediately said, "I'm sorry, but that will be all for this evening. The link is broken, but wasn't it beautiful? Phoenix rode Flo's faith to Walter then led the teachers on the other side to him. He will be all right now. He has followed the light. I need to take Phoenix in to rest so please visit a while if you wish then let yourselves out." It was a convincing demonstration that would bring back those faithful who would pay again for the chance that their loved one would get through.

Dr. Huntley waited impatiently as he watched all the guests but Flo exit the house and drive away. Finally, Flo strutted out and darted off in a red late-model Toyota Camry. He closed his eyes and imagined her sweet-scented and heavily applied perfume that had tempted him all evening. The woman would be beautiful if she had any class and half the makeup. The door opened again, and Phoenix and the old woman picked their way across the yard to a faithful old Dodge Reliant.

Cautiously, Dr. Huntley tailed Phoenix as she drove the woman home, and he continued following to a high rise overlooking the Gulf of Mexico. He stroked his bearded chin and smiled as Phoenix parked next to a red, late-model Toyota Camry. Dr. Huntley's man, Lee, was right. Phoenix had a partner now, and the sultry brunette called Flo at the séance was actually a fellow con artist, a beauty named Barbara.

★

Except for occasional reminders that the giant still watched, Clarence tended to forget that someone had dictated his prison routine for some unknown purpose. His imaginary trips home sustained him as he waited for freedom day. One more sunset, one more sunrise, and he could go home. He owed his children. He owed his wife. He owed God. Anxious to regain his liberty and pay his debts, Clarence grunted when a familiar whispered warning startled him: "Don't turn around, Clarence."

"Oh, it's you," said Clarence.

"No, it's Paul Harvey."

"What?"

"It's time for the rest of the story, partner. Damn strange too. Seems you've drawn the toughest bronco of them all, so for your kids' sake hold on tight. Looks like you're gonna die." Clarence stiffened. The giant continued. "That's the breaks, huh? You're being told now so you got time to prepare yourself, see? Whoever's pulling your strings don't want to shock you when you get back with your family."

"The way I understand is this. You're supposed to go home, convince everybody you been born again, and because you love your family and Jesus, you can't live with guilt no longer. You gotta die to clean away your sin. You want to do that so your fellow man might find, ah, what was it he said? Oh, yeah, so your fellow man might find respite on the other side. Then you're gonna soak yourself with gasoline and strike a match."

Clarence trembled. The inmate continued. "Yeah, it's kinda like getting bit by a rattlesnake in the badlands, but I been watching you. You're a better man than when you came here. Whoever's holding the reins gave you that, and I'm supposed to remind you to keep looking at the photo of your family. Don't pull iron against this jasper. If you go to the cops, you'll eventually bite the dust anyway, but then so will your family." The man stuffed a newspaper photo into Clarence's hand. "Better take a look at this, Clarence," he said. "I been told to tell you that you will be watched and then contacted when it's time. Guess this is where we part trails, partner. Don't turn around."

The man ambled off. Clarence heard the shoes squeaking against the sand, but he didn't need to look around. There were several inmates who wore a shoe big enough to make the prints Clarence had examined so often, but only one of the men counted. Clarence observed them all until the obvious seized him: western novels. Billy Tuttle was the man's name, but he answered to Cowboy. He spent his time reading cheap cowboy stories.

Clarence watched Cowboy closely, and learned that the man landed in prison for everything from passing bad checks to murder, depending on who told the story. Cowboy, forty and balding, had a big rounded nose and acne-scarred features crisscrossed with what appeared to be two knife wounds. The man who decorated Cowboy's face died, beaten to death by the bare-fisted Cowboy. At least that was one story Clarence heard, and certainly the inmate looked mean enough and tough enough. Now, all Clarence's watching amounted to nothing. He was going to die.

The next day, after three and one-half years behind bars, Clarence Fardy, sober and ten pounds heavier, fidgeted while he waited for the remaining gate to rattle open. Freedom lay less than ten feet away. Well, not really freedom anymore, although within minutes the jail sentence would end. It was the other sentence for which no pardon came, the sentence that began with the yellow tear sheet.

During the first year in prison, Clarence changed little. He routinely followed the voice's instructions. Although his conversations with the psychiatrist, the minister and others revealed nothing of his dilemma, his general countenance suggested depression. Treated thusly, Clarence gradually began to be coaxed into discussions during Bible study, and he learned that as a shy, verbally abused child his escape into books had sharpened his mind.

He developed a knack for grasping concepts and perceiving symbolism. Other members of the study group began to first welcome then later solicit his input. After a few months of prolonged study and consideration, it seemed to Clarence that insight often came from a part of himself that he didn't know. The information didn't develop through his normal thought processes; instead it leaped into his mind. Did it come from his subconscious? Could it be an epiphany? Clarence didn't know, and it didn't matter. Even when the visiting minister corrected Clarence's interpretation to comply with accepted dogma, Clarence knew that there was more to the Bible and Jesus' ministry than the accepted dogma.

Thusly armed, but managing to spare his humility, Clarence literally talked his shyness to death. As a kid he had rushed through the pages of many wonderful books, including the outdated but still exciting Jules Verne classics. They took him on exciting journeys, and often he became depressed when he reached the last page in his refuge. In prison, he rejoiced upon learning that the story of God is a never-ending adventure.

Clarence marveled at the faith of Abraham, trembled before the Commandments, commiserated with Job, and found himself in the Beatitudes. He embraced the Gospels with open arms and faith changed him. By first learning to love Jesus, Clarence learned to love himself, and then he grew to love his fellow man. As a child who was told that he brought nothing but misery to his mother, he had thought of himself as unlovable, but as he accepted that God loved him, Clarence necessarily accepted that he had to be worth loving. With that simple revelation, Clarence Fardy escaped the most confining prison of all; self-loathing. He became born again.

The gate rattled to a stop and Clarence's thoughts returned to the present. He stared at the opening. It must be akin to birth. You're secure in familiar surroundings, awash in all the ingredients for life, then suddenly the gate opens and you are flooded into uncertainty. "Fardy, are you going or staying?" a guard growled.

Clarence looked around and briefly eyed the guard. Three years ago Clarence couldn't have done that. He would have lacked the courage. He didn't remember changing, but he had. Prison had been a frightening place. On the surface it seemed peaceful enough, but like a bat after a bug, violence could hop in a man's face in a flash. It happened to Clarence but only once, because the next day you couldn't recognize his attacker.

Afterwards, Clarence labored many hours pondering his explosive neighbors, studying the Bible and contemplating the healing words of Jesus. He identified fear as the culprit, the root of all evil. Fear is Satan. Love is God. Although direct correlation could not always be determined, Clarence became convinced that every negative act stemmed from fear. Fear of rejection makes a man uncompromising. Fear of lack encourages selfishness. Fear of weakness drives ruthless behavior. A fearful man cannot love. Jesus loved everyone. Jesus was not fearful.

Clarence grew to believe that every act of kindness toward his prison mates was an act of kindness toward God. Love your friends. Love your enemies. By adhering to the peculiarities of a particular faith, all the points amassed by an individual in the eyes of his religious peers amount to nothing on God's scoreboard compared to a simple act of kindness shown by one neighbor to another. Love is the key to understanding; understanding is the door to salvation.

Gradually, a man long dead in a bog, his cells reproduced by minerals due to metasomatic replacement, is granted a new existence. Clarence, long dead in a bottle, his fear replaced by love due to the acts of giving and serving, became born again. He made friends, he made converts. He gained the silent respect of hardened men around him too fearful to be more then they were. Clarence Fardy the drunk died, and Clarence Fardy the believer was born. Clarence gave the guard a friendly smile. "Sorry," he said, and he stepped out to the sidewalk. Prison was history, but now so was Clarence Fardy and all that he had become.

March 13, Monday

Adam literally skated across the newspapers and magazines splattered over the floor as he searched for a clean shirt. The phone call had been strange. Dr. Huntley had insisted on no facts over the phone. They must talk in private about an "important, urgent and unique experiment". The voice had sounded strained, the tone demanding. Adam had not appreciated the man's manner, but a writer's curiosity made him accept an "immediate audience".

Unable to drag a face from his memory, Adam recalled that a few years ago Dr. Luther Huntley had made network news with some radical views on world population control. Adam threw back the bedspread and found his laundry; his maid was taking the week off. He selected a plaid shirt, one not without wrinkles, but at least it was clean. Dr. Huntley lost his post as the head of some population thing for advocating sterilization of people on welfare. Probably now he wants to surgically implant sex-inhibiting electrodes into the brains of every person down on their luck.

"Humph," Adam grunted as he rushed out the door, "This could be interesting." Running late as usual, his audience with Huntley wouldn't be so immediate after all. He grabbed the newspaper on the way to his car, and waved to Mrs. Stein who was sweeping her brick walkway.

Once downtown Adam dogged the Chevy into the empty parking space nearest his appointment. He reached the revolving door of the Citrus and Commerce Bank building on the run, and burst into the lobby while trying to read the headlines. Swinging his big inexpensive briefcase, Adam stalked toward the elevators. A female voice warned, "Watch where you're going!" but too late to prevent Adam from banging her knee with the case.

"Oh! I'm—" Adam began, but with his mouth still open, he stopped, dumbfounded. A schoolboy grin captured his face.

"What's so funny? You almost break my leg and find that

humorous?" The young woman balanced on one foot and rubbed her knee.

"I'm sorry," Adam said and searched the lobby. "Let me help you over to a chair." He got her seated and glanced at the lobby clock. Running late, he should hurry. He looked back at the woman. Maybe three inches taller than Adam, tan, but not the crusty burn of sun worshipers, she had the healthy glow of one who enjoys the outdoors. Probably a health freak, but Adam wouldn't hold that against her. Comparatively ghostly, Adam figured why sweat in the sun if you can stay cool in the shade? His victim, a shapely, long-haired brunette, wore only a hint of makeup. She was a walking, breathing fitness ad, the building material for fantasies.

"Honest, I wasn't smiling at your pain, but I couldn't help being pleased with my good fortune."

"Good fortune?" the woman said, still frowning. She continued to rub her knee.

"Yes, but it does require your cooperation." Adam hesitated, but the woman committed nothing. "I need you to help me keep a promise. You see, this morning I vowed to take my first victim to lunch." Slightly disheveled and grinning disarmingly, Adam waited as the woman stopped rubbing her knee and stared at him.

"Of all the dumb stunts. You almost cripple me to get me to have lunch with you?"

"No, no, of course not. I'm just without a doubt, no questions asked, unbelievably lucky, that's all. I mean, most guys owning an attack briefcase would collide with a female wrestler or Whistler's Mother." Adam shrugged, and threw open his hands. "You know what they say about God and his special relationship with drunks and fools." He plastered a little boy grin on his face.

Still staring, she cocked her head slightly as if wanting to shake it from side to side, but finally decided against it. "You don't look like a drunk," she said. Her voice had calmed.

Adam glanced at the clock again. "Your implication may be clinically correct, but let's debate that over lunch. I owe you. How about The Creek's Place at 12:30?"

"Thank you, but—"

Adam cut her off. Orchestrating with his hands, he said,

"There's no time to argue. I admit that I'm not a candidate for Hollywood, but I do have sound teeth –" he flashed a smile – "and a solid character –" he held up crossed fingers. "I've been known to tell a white lie or two, but absolutely never, on my Boy Scout honor, cross my heart and hope to die, have I ever broken a promise to a dying man."

"A dying man?"

"Yes, if you make me break my promise, I know I'll do something desperate. I – I'll eat my own cooking." She didn't look convinced and started to speak. Adam threw up his hands palms forward, then picked up his briefcase, and started backing away. "Please, save it till lunch, I'm late for a meeting." Slowly backing away, and raising his voice as the distance grew, Adam said, "Look, I have a confession to make. I'm scheduled to be executed at sundown. I have already killed three people with this thing," he lifted his briefcase, "and today is your absolute, your only last chance to have lunch with me." He had attracted the attention of everyone in the lobby. "Even the vilest prisoner gets a last—"

"All right, all right, I'll be there," she interrupted, her face showing a hint of pink. The response lacked enthusiasm, but no anger remained in her voice. Adam wriggled backwards into a crowded elevator, and called, "Hey, what's your name?"

"Kelly," she said.

"Adam," he called out. The doors tried to gobble up his briefcase, but Adam reacted quickly. He saw Kelly laugh when someone immediately behind him groaned. He shrugged and grinned sheepishly.

Kelly threw up her hand in a slight wave. Adam wore gold-framed glasses over hazel eyes that spoke of intelligence and energy. He was short, but not unattractive. Kelly rubbed her knee again before standing up. A pushy little guy, but refreshingly imaginative.

★

"Sterilization is the only effective solution," Dr. Luther Huntley stressed. "Educated people don't have litters; it's the aimless masses that drop babies like dung. The inferior are being allowed to breed mankind to extinction. Each year man's overall level of ability, the intellectual capacity to meet challenge, decreases. Chaos approaches."

Adam eyed the older man suspiciously. Lean and tall, Dr. Huntley easily reached six feet three inches. He had a thin face elongated out of proportion by a sharp chin that he habitually stroked. Honing it to a cutting edge, Adam figured. The man's eyes, which he rarely blinked, were green beady slits that stared through a man. Adam subconsciously added the horns and goatee, and couldn't believe that he had rushed away from an angel like Kelly to meet with an elitist devil.

"OK, Dr. Huntley, let's scatter the fog. I'm familiar with your theories. I know that a few years back you were head of the, ah, WC—"

"The WPCC, the World Population Control Center."

"Yes, you were a respected futurologist—"

"I am a respected futurologist."

Unfazed, Adam continued, "Yes, well, I believe your dire predictions are simply a camouflage to cover elitist prejudices." Although calm, Adam talked rapidly as was his custom. He sat on the edge of his chair as if expecting foul play, but it was really because of his restless energy. "Besides, due to birth control, education, and improvement of the economic status of women in third world countries, people are responding to thwart your Chicken Little warnings of over population. Now, Doctor, rehearsal is over. You invited me here under the pretense that I might find a story. Start talking."

Dr. Huntley stroked his chin, and slowly rocked in his high-backed leather chair. Through the window behind his host, Adam could see ships plying the channel in Upper Hillsborough Bay, going to and coming from third world countries. Dr. Huntley said, "I'm coming to the story, and you may label me as you wish, but liberals have evolved an unnatural environment where those who can't make it are supported by those of us who can. Under natural circumstances the weak perish, but today we sustain such individuals, and by doing so we dilute our gene pool and deplete our capital."

He leaned forward for emphasis. "Pardon the vulgarity,

Mr. Eden, but the United States is literally fornicating herself into a third world country. Fortunately, there are positive signs. Kicking illegal immigrants off the dole, the right-to-die movement, and welfare reform come immediately to mind. Unfortunately, each faces long court battles with judges who have long forgotten the difference between adjudicate and dictate."

"The story?" Adam said again. He sensed that his interruption irritated Dr. Huntley, but the man's patrician expression betrayed little.

"I'll be blunt. A mysterious Mr. X, a faithful Christian, has volunteered to commit suicide in order to prove the existence of life after death." Adam gasped. His attitude hardened as it always did at the mention of religion. Dr. Huntley continued, "I have here a letter, which you may read later, that explains everything. He signs himself Mr. X, and claims that he knows there is life after death. The writer wants his own death to count for something. He—"

"Intends to end his misery, find eternal bliss through resurrection, and ship us a nugget from the Golden Gate as proof of his arrival," said Adam.

Dr. Huntley cleared his throat, and Adam figured it helped the man control his irritation. Obviously, he objected to interruptions by inferiors. "No, he envisions less dramatic evidence, but more, ah, complex. He intends to deliver a message to the world through some psychic; mediums, I believe they are called."

"Get serious, Huntley." Adam dropped the doctor. Titles and courteous honorifics should stem from respect, not custom or requirement. "Don't you see all this is an elaborate joke? Or maybe some conniving individual is dying anyway, and has concocted a scheme to swing some sympathy money to his family."

"Perhaps, but I don't believe so. Shortly, I am to receive another letter identifying Mr. X, announcing the deed, and giving the location. The letter will also contain half of a message that will tie into the second part to be communicated to a psychic after Mr. X's death. I am supposed to choose one other individual whose reputation will lend credence to the evidence. Only you, uh, that is if you agree, only you and I will know the message which we must keep secret. Supposedly, we will recognize the second half of the message when we hear it. Bogus claims of contact by charlatans attempting to cash in will be easily dismissed. Mr. X, or what remains, if anything, of the gentleman, will prompt some medium to go public with the contact. We will match the communication, and have proof of life after death."

Adam didn't try to hide his disgust. "I think Houdini has already tried that trick. It didn't work."

"Humm, well, I'm not familiar with that, but it has nothing to do with this case. If this Mr. X is serious there is no way to stop him. The police can do nothing. All they have to go on is the typed letter dated one week ago and postmarked Tampa. They have the original, on which they found no fingerprints other than mine, but I made copies." Dr. Huntley stroked his chin. Adam imagined that he could feel the heat from the man's eyes.

One part of Adam had been listening, but another portion had been busy searching Huntley's stylishly decorated and richly furnished office. The old devil had money. The address overlooking the bay confirmed that. Adam eyed the several shelves of books about over population, immigration, welfare, militias, and other titles written by the country's leading conservatives. He reluctantly admired the Mont Blanc pen set, and noticed that it, a paperweight, and works of art on Huntley's desktop and credenza were meticulously arranged. The bookshelves, however, were suspiciously unbalanced, there were gaps.

A picture cube on the desk caught Adam's attention. Picking it up, he asked, "Why me?" All six sides of the cube contained pictures of the same woman but at different ages. She looked vaguely familiar, but Adam was certain that he had never seen her before. He returned the cube, deliberately avoiding its original place, but only slightly.

Dr. Huntley leaned forward and adjusted the cube's position. "Association more than anything, I think. I readily admit that my views make my participation suspect; therefore, I immediately thought of you and your recently published book about suicide. Later, thinking it through, the more logical it became. More than most, you understand the horrifying statistics of suicide. You have by-lines in the best magazines, and in the public mind you are to be trusted. If anyone can play down the sensationalism surrounding this suicide and present the sobering facts, it's you."

"OK, now, why you? Why did this Mr. X select you, and why are you pursuing it?"

"To answer your first question, he doesn't say. He merely explains that I will eventually understand. To answer your second, I'm no different from anyone else. I'd like to believe that there is no death. Well, no different from most, I should say. If I read correctly between the lines of your book, you don't believe in life after death, do you, Mr. Eden?"

Both men were momentarily thoughtful. Adam considered his book, surprised that he had allowed his attitude to bleed through. "No, I don't," he finally said.

"Well, our neighbors, the Christian faithful, do, so all the more reason to at least pursue this thing in honor of Mr. X if he goes through with it."

"In honor! Christ, can it, Huntley! You're out of character. Now, what do you really expect to get from this? Level with me or I'm walking."

Dr. Huntley stroked his chin, and with unblinking eyes, briefly considered Adam. He leaned forward, clasped his hands, and rested his arms on his desk. His face was a mask, only a slight upward tilt of the man's head revealed an inner contempt. Adam didn't trust him. Dr. Huntley said, "Consider the implications, man. What if X pulls it off and confirms the absence of annihilation? What if this claptrap debate over the morality of capital punishment and abortion could be laid to rest? What if he shows the old, the ill, the crippled, and the failures that death brings relief? What if he proves that suicide is conquest over the miseries of life? Would you continue to sleep in a refrigerator box after Mr. X opens the door to Nirvana?"

Adam couldn't believe that he hadn't realized it before Huntley's admission. "So that's it. You're so puffed up with illusions of superiority that you will latch onto the most bizarre and improbable scheme no matter the morality. You lick your lips over the desperate insane act of some troubled man, hoping it will help rid the world of your aimless masses." Adam rose to leave. "Count me out."

"Wait! At least read the letter first. If I judge your sense of honor correctly, you owe the man at least that," Dr. Huntley said. He allowed his contempt to surface. "Besides, perhaps you were instrumental to X's decision. You pointed out in your book that nowhere does the Bible expressly forbid suicide. That credit goes to St. Augustine. You wrote that the zeal of Christians to become martyrs concerned him. He feared that the ranks of the faithful were being seriously reduced. Maybe Mr. X places more importance on the word of God than the scribbling of saints."

Adam reluctantly took the letter and began reading.

Dear Dr. Huntley,

Please read this letter through before you judge me. I can't explain now why I have chosen you, but I believe you are a decent man, and I promise that you will soon understand.

I have decided to end my life because I am a burden to my wife and a failure to my children. I wish to do something to pay for a wasted life and to pay for the great wrong I have committed. I'm convinced that there is life after death, because my grandmother who is dead appears often to comfort me.

People will believe that I am crazy, but I know that my grandmother survives her death. Just as when I was a kid, I could tell from her look when I pleased her and when I displeased her. She is happy with this decision. I never did much with my life so maybe my death can mean something.

I have devised a plan…

Adam finished the letter that detailed what Dr. Huntley had already revealed. "Seems to me a lamb has mistaken a wolf for one of his own."

"You have made it abundantly clear that you don't approve of me, but what does it matter who either of us is or what either of us think? Here is a man who wants to die, and for good reason it appears, but has too much character to accept a meaningless demise." Dr. Huntley leaned across his mahogany desk and glared at Adam. "Are you going to discredit this wretched man's death just because you disapprove of me?"

Adam's jaw twitched. Not for one minute did he believe that

X's efforts would be more than folly. Nevertheless, elitist rot like Huntley should not be allowed to even remotely benefit from the misguided act of a decent man. Besides, if it wasn't a hoax, somewhere there was a troubled man. Probably there were people who loved him who would have to live with the guilt.

"I'm in, Huntley. May I keep this copy?" Adam folded the letter and put it in his pocket without waiting for an answer. "Call me when there's news." Adam picked up his briefcase and stomped from the office.

★

Dr. Huntley glanced at the time. With a few minutes to spare, he turned his chair and admired the view of Tampa Bay. The city leaders were doing a credible job rejuvenating the downtown. Old rundown buildings that blighted the landscape were disappearing to be replaced by plazas and parks, and grand structures partitioned with colored glass. A new aquarium decorated the waterfront. There were problems as in any downtown, but what couldn't man accomplish if society were sensibly culled? If the burden of supporting the failures could be toppled and buried? Yes, society needed an earthquake that gobbled up structures made of flesh too weak to withstand the test.

Dr. Huntley turned and flipped the switch hidden under his desk top to the off position. He opened a desk drawer filled with books, itching to return them to their proper places, but suppressed the temptation. His new partner could not be relied upon for predictability, and might visit the office at any time.

Dr. Huntley considered the top book, a biography on Houdini, but didn't pick it up. "I was a sucker, Harry," he said to the picture on the jacket cover. "Death padlocked you in chains and boxed you up. Even the great Houdini could not duck the Grim Reaper's scythe. You're gone without a trace and so is my murdered wife." Huntley slammed the drawer shut. He was no longer a fool.

Psychics and mediums are all bloodsucking frauds. Nothing but vultures waiting to prey on the gullible and hapless grief-strickened whose reason has been clouded by despair. Untold séances had produced nothing but a dent in Dr. Huntley's fortune and further discoloration of his darker side until his fateful visit to Phoenix.

He buzzed his secretary and explained that he didn't wish to be disturbed. Again, he flipped the switch hidden under his desk. It allowed communication between his office and an adjacent bedroom and bath. A one-way bar mirror, which swung freely after first being pushed toward the wall, separated the two rooms. The racist Dr. Huntley was not a man without enemies.

The safe room was also accessible from a door located in the building's common hallway, but around the corner from Huntley Enterprises. From all appearances, the entrance led to a real business sarcastically named Search, Inc., but the door was never unlocked. It guarded a narrow passageway that led to the back of a bookcase designed to swing open when properly keyed, and allowed entrance to Dr. Huntley's safe room. LeRoy Lentz, his presence known only to Dr. Huntley, waited there now.

"Lee, did you hear everything? Come to the office." To ensure that his secretary did not disturb him, Dr. Huntley pushed a button that locked the office door. He leaned back and stroked his chin. LeRoy Lentz was another victim. After fifteen years on the police force, ten in vice, he was sentenced to prison for killing a drug dealer. He was punished for ridding society of a piece of dung. Another mockery of justice, but providential for Dr. Huntley. Lee truly was a gift. If there were a God, certainly giving Lee to Dr. Huntley would amount to sanction of Dr. Huntley's mission by no less an authority than the Almighty, Himself.

Lee, at six-three, weighed a hundred and ninety-five pounds and his physical condition matched that of most men half his age. Once jet-black hair now mostly gray grew thickly over clear cold eyes shaded by thick, bushy eyebrows. Several nasty scars on his face and a boxer's hands, marked him as a man of whom one should be wary.

Like a powerful tiger Lee quietly entered the office. He appeared relaxed but left no doubt that he would react to a threat swiftly and ruthlessly. Lee poured coffee for himself and Dr. Huntley. "I heard," was all he said in greeting.

Dr. Huntley smiled. He paid Lee well for services rendered,

but the man still dressed like an unkempt and overworked detective. Also, he had little need for conversation, while Dr. Huntley, on the other hand, craved feedback. "What do you think? Did it go well?" he asked Lee.

"A wild card. Sure you should bring him in?"

"Absolutely. Trite it may be, but the best watchdog has no loyalty." Dr. Huntley averted his eyes. It angered him that he could never stare Lee down. "Mr. Eden is the epitome of a bleeding-heart liberal. He's a do-gooder."

He opened a desk drawer and fished out a sheet of paper. "You're familiar with Mr. Eden's book of course, but his articles include 'The Plight of the Poor', 'Welfare Reform – Who Benefits' and 'Capital Punishment Is a Crime', and many others of the same disgusting ilk." He leaned forward and slapped the sheet of paper down on his desk. "The prize, however, is a little article he wrote while still a teenager, just after his mother's death, I believe. The title? 'Psychic Flimflam'."

"Christ, if he doesn't believe in psychics won't he try to queer the deal?"

Dr. Huntley tightened his jaw over Lee's crude language, and he briefly spoke through his teeth. "Precisely. I'm counting on the controversy. Eden is an atheist, or at least an agnostic. His views are at odds with the views of the helpless who want to believe in life after death. When one's beliefs are attacked, the more cherished those beliefs tend to become. Mr. Eden's outcry over communication with the dead will attract the press, which will serve to render the gullible more gullible. Many others, however, who now only *wish* to believe, will pick up the banner and join forces with fools."

Dr. Huntley leaned back in his chair, and traded stares with Lee. "Besides, you will ensure that there is no tangible evidence of fraud to expose."

Lee sat back with one leg resting on the other, sipped his coffee, and didn't respond. Dr. Huntley continued. "And Phoenix, are you still comfortable with her?"

"She's solid. She's so afraid of losing her sassy little lover, Barbara, that she'll do anything. As you learned when you recently scouted her out, her new partner, Barbara, is a prime piece. She's as big a con as Phoenix, but Barbara has the T&A that Phoenix can't resist. That's Phoenix's biggest weakness that we can take advantage of, but it's also our biggest risk."

"What's our defense?"

"Phoenix is laying low like I told her."

"Good, over the past three years she has developed a loyal following. After she announces contact, many will come forward and testify that Phoenix is a great psychic, that her predictions helped save their marriage, or fortunes, or some such nonsense. All of it imagined or coincidental, but there also will be others who will help certify Phoenix's ability with all sorts of fraudulent claims." Dr. Huntley shook his head. "Fools will do anything for their fifteen minutes of borrowed glory. See to it that Phoenix stays out of trouble."

"With a promise of a lot more, I've given Phoenix a wad of money to take her tasty girlfriend on a vacation to the East Coast," said Lee.

"I noticed the amount, but I agree. Keep her happy and out of trouble."

"Phoenix is no dummy," Lee continued. "She recognizes what this scheme will do for her business. The money and the trip will seal her lips, but like all hustlers, she has a big ego. I'll watch her." Lee leaned forward and set his empty coffee cup on the desk. Dr. Huntley was grateful for a man like Lee, but one day the man would have to pay for his impertinence.

For the third time, Dr. Huntley straightened up a stack of mail on his desk. "Tell me more about this Barbara, Lee. Of course, I remember her from the recent séance, but only vaguely. I think she called herself, Flo, that night." He studied Lee for any sign of insight, but the man had long ago encrypted his emotions and reactions into an unbreakable code.

"With Barbara, Phoenix knows that she has fallen into her own trap. I promised her that all competition for Barbara's attentions will be, ah, discouraged. Barbara is a tease, and plays around to keep Phoenix off balance. Phoenix would kill for that to stop." Lee locked his hands behind his head, and stared at Dr. Huntley. "Barbara's a good-looking piece. She attracts a lot of attention."

Dr. Huntley lowered his eyes. "Yes, I presume so. Now, how is our mousy little leech, Clarence Fardy?"

"Under surveillance. Funny thing though, he actually found religion while following our instructions. He's not the same shy little guy we started with. I had my prison contact slip him a reality booster just before his release. It'll keep Fardy in line." Dr. Huntley quizzed Lee with a raised eyebrow. Lee said, "Slipped him a newspaper photo of a fire. Three kids died in the blaze."

"Excellent, Lee. We don't want difficulties when we're this close."

★

Lee left without comment. He didn't like the lowlife that he had spent so many years fighting while with the Tampa police department, but he disliked even more rich people such as Dr. Huntley who think they shit apple pie. Mostly, however, Lee listed as enemies some of the same pariahs as did Dr. Huntley, and Lee was learning to enjoy the money.

As a policeman, money had never tempted Lee, but prison had locked him away from much that had been decent in his former character. Such a long separation virtually ensured no reconciliation; besides, Dr. Huntley had shown Lee what a man with enough money can do. The rich bastard had managed to have Cowboy, Lee's prison contact, paroled along with Fardy.

Lee, the man, contemptuous of his fastidious employer, had never cared for a man who perfumed himself up like a woman. Still, Lee, the tiger, exercised caution. He understood that even the puniest of men walking in the jungle is not alone if he carries a rifle. In Dr. Huntley's office, Lee had wanted a cigarette with the coffee, but he could always sense how far to push a man.

When Lee pushed free of the revolving doors to the street, he lit up an unfiltered Camel, took a deep draw and smiled at Dr. Huntley's camouflaged query about Barbara. Lee definitely disliked the man, but didn't blame the bastard for wanting to check her oil.

★

Dr. Huntley took time to make certain that no one lurked in the shadows before rushing to his car. The stifling heat and unpleasant odor of oil and gas that permeated the parking garage always displeased him. With time still available, he drove across town to relax. Lee's intentional goading and disrespect angered Dr. Huntley, but without the crude ex-detective, the plan for Fardy might never have come together. Dr. Huntley slid a CD of Beethoven's Symphony Number Three into the guide, and as he listened, he couldn't keep his mind from straying to the memory of Barbara.

When the red light changed, he shook his head to dislodge the lingering thoughts, and checked the time. A call from the boss would help insure Phoenix's loyalty, although his identity would remain a mystery. Spotting a pay phone outside a Quick & Easy market, he pulled in and parked his silver Mercedes next to it.

★

After the disturbing meeting with Huntley, Adam went shopping to buy a gift for his sister. He also picked up a decorative jar and filled it with Reese's peanut butter cups as a peace offering for Kelly. Franci couldn't eat enough of them. Somehow, Adam had to find this Mr. X and stop his madness. It would be wonderful if death were not really death, if we did just switch stations, somehow existing invisibly in another reality.

Adam suffered no delusions; Franci had not bridged the gulf. The absence of that contact alone was proof enough of annihilation. Adam dodged a potted plant and juggled the bag containing the candy jar before using his briefcase as a battering ram to deflect closing elevator doors. The Greek's Place was six blocks away. He should hurry. He was running late.

Twenty minutes later, he and Kelly ordered lunch. "Will that be all, sir?" the corpulent waitress asked.

"Yes, but coffee and hot tea now, please," Adam looked at Kelly for confirmation. The waitress whisked away writing, and Adam centered his attention on his guest.

"I'm glad you came, Kelly, and I am really sorry that this man-eating briefcase of mine attacked you this morning. I believe the leather is genuine tiger hide." Adam kicked the case. "Settle down fellow," he said and winked at Kelly. "Did you hear it growl?"

"Yes, and your bribe of peanut butter cups aside, you should know that I consulted my attorney. It's illegal to keep a wild beast without a special permit. I could have you locked up." She grinned. "Maybe committed would be more appropriate."

"But who would take care of Claw? He's just a pussycat at heart, my character barometer. Normally he limits his hostility to jerks, and this is cross my heart and hope to die absolutely the first time that Claw has erred." Talking with his hands, Adam almost knocked over his water glass.

"How do you know he's wrong? Maybe I'm an animal trapper hired to capture this loathsome flea bag that's taking up all my leg room."

Adam shoved the case out of the way. "Move over, Claw. We're going to have to walk softly here, she's tough."

"Your order will be right up," the waitress interrupted. She served Adam's tea, and poured Kelly's coffee.

"Thanks," said Adam. The waitress hurried off, and Adam followed her progress. He marveled as she gracefully maneuvered her bulk between tables while carrying a hot pot of coffee and skillfully balancing a serving tray. He muttered, "Disgustingly agile."

"I can see where that would disturb you, but don't sic Claw on her."

Adam stirred sugar into his tea. "I'm not that cruel, he wouldn't stand a chance."

"Pass the cream, please," Kelly said. They sipped their beverages and made small talk. Adam again offered a sincere apology for banging up her knee, but reasoned to himself that her presence indicated all was forgiven. Besides, she had seemed impressed with the gift. All women must like peanut butter cups.

Kelly waved off the apology. "It was an accident, and I'm OK, but I am curious. What do you carry in that trunk?"

"Camera and recording equipment, essential toiletries, and a couple changes of shirts, socks and stuff."

The waitress returned and served their lunch. "Enjoy," she said. "I'll check back."

"Thanks," Adam said.

"You a photographer?" Kelly began to explore her Greek salad.

"Naw, I literally scratch out a living. I make enough to eat doing it so I guess that qualifies me as a professional writer."

"A writer! Adam who?"

"Uh oh, our first hurdle. I'll tell only if you promise not to laugh, smile, twist uncomfortably in your chair, or ever mention it again."

"I promise," said Kelly. She crossed her fingers in plain view.

"An honest woman. Memory log that."

"Impatient too, now give."

"It was my mother's idea to name me Adam. My old man says that she insisted because of some quote, prophetic, unquote, my father's word, sense of my destiny. She was a, ah, a religious woman." Adam was embarrassed to disclose that his mother was a Spiritualist. "But she didn't force her beliefs on me or on my father. Said God's will would be done, and that she 'loved her devilish husband too much to saddle him with a burden alien to his nature'." Adam paused, then declared, "My name is Adam Eden."

"Why, of course! I read your book about suicide. That's why I went to the Citrus and Commerce Bank Building this morning. I, ah, well, your book made me remember that I had not checked on my uncle in some time. I went there to see him."

"What do you mean?"

"Almost four years ago, my Aunt Jean died in a terrible car accident. A drunk, a sad little man named Clarence Fardy, ran a stop sign and sent Aunt Jean's car flying. It flipped over, slid across the intersection, and careened into a utility pole that broke in two. Gas spilled, and somehow with all the loose wires, the fuel ignited." Kelly played with her salad. Adam waited. "Pinned in her car, Aunt Jean—" Kelly didn't finish.

Continuing, she said, "Given credit for time served, Mr. Fardy got paroled maybe four weeks ago. You would, ah, have to know my uncle, but I think that my Aunt Jean was his only true friend; she loved him in spite of his faults. He became violent at first, then depressed because Clarence Fardy wasn't executed, but a few months later he seemed to have it all together again. No anger, no depression, no anything; he acted very controlled, fake, smug actually, but that was about three years ago."

"Fake?"

"My opinion. He always fawned over me, and Aunt Jean's other friends and relatives. Even though the words were appropriate, when I got older I sensed them to be insincere. The smile was too broad, the handshakes too ambitious, and the hugs, well, nothing." Kelly sipped her coffee and Adam sensed that nothing really meant something, but it was her business to tell or not to tell.

"I believe his pain is a monster locked away that someday will break free. You see, the drunk had three prior DUIs, and he survived on welfare, unemployment, food stamps, whatever. My uncle hates—"

"The picture cube!" Adam said. "I thought I recognized the woman pictured on the cube, but now I see that it's only because she resembles you. Is your uncle, Luther Huntley?"

"Why, yes, but how—"

"He's also the reason I went to the Citrus and Commerce Bank Building."

"Then maybe you can explain his high spirits today. I was close to Luther only when I was a child. Born wealthy, he did spoil Aunt Jean, and me too, at first." Adam saw Kelly's eyes sparkle. "He taught me to sail, you know. Bought me my first sailboat, a sunfish." Kelly sipped her coffee, then set the cup down rather loudly. "I quit staying with them so often after I got older."

Adam waited until Kelly continued. "Anyway, I think Luther is too smug maybe. But Aunt Jean favored me over my cousins. She treated me wonderfully. After reading your book and remembering that the anniversary of the accident is near, I decided – no, I felt strangely compelled – to check on Luther. He acted peculiarly, but he seemed jolly, more up than at any time since the accident. He was disgustingly full of himself."

"I think I can explain," Adam said, and he proceeded to relate the events of his meeting with Dr. Huntley.

"Committing suicide to prove life after death? This is not an uncommon claim, but why would it please Luther so?"

Adam studied Kelly. Her deep feelings were reserved for her Aunt Jean, not Huntley. Saying that she felt compelled to check on Huntley struck Adam as an odd statement, but he decided to tell her exactly what he believed. "I have a theory, but it's not pretty." Kelly expressed no objection. "Huntley is an educated man so I'm certain that he doesn't believe in this medium hocus-pocus, such chicanery has been too frequently exposed." Kelly almost choked on her coffee, and Adam, concerned, waited politely.

"I'm all right," she said. She used her napkin to clean up the spill around her coffee cup that she had banged down. "Sorry. Please go on."

"I don't know why, but I believe Huntley intentionally removed books from his office for my visit. I would like to know what they are. I think he is betting on publicity, and that somewhere someone will claim to be in contact with Mr. X. Many innocent people will fall for it, an age-old human fallacy, because they so desperately want to believe in something that's an improvement over what they have here." Adam sipped his tea. "You know how it is; the better the economy, the weaker religion and vice versa."

Kelly didn't respond. She appeared to be considering what he had said so Adam continued. "Statistics dictate that there will be an increase in suicides. It's what's known as the contagion effect, and it affects others in two ways: the glamour of the act, and the mechanics. This case has the potential to be highly publicized because of the lofty motives, thereby elevating Mr. X to folk hero status. He will become the envy of many depressed individuals who see a similar sacrifice on their part as infinitely better than their current despair. They will crave the attention, the notoriety.

"Mechanically, I don't know what Mr. X has in mind; however, the more sensational the technique of suicide, which I am certain will be published to the smallest detail, the greater the potential for copycats. Eventually, it will blow over, but in the meantime Huntley will have derived some ghoulish satisfaction that your aunt's death is somehow vicariously avenged." Adam considered what he had said. "At least that's what I think. I intend to prevent publicity if possible, and maybe even help whoever wrote the note."

Both finished their meals without talking, partly because both were occupied with their thoughts about what they had been discussing, but also partly because of two young heavily tattooed white males who had been seated near them. The men were making racial slurs against blacks with the obvious intention of upsetting an African American couple seated nearby.

When the skinny tattooed man used the insult "nigger", Adam excused himself and walked over to the innocent couple. He couldn't just sit and do nothing. He apologized to the couple for their discomfort, and begged them to take heart in the fact that the only pariahs in the restaurant were the two lowlifes making all the noise. Other diners applauded, and the couple thanked Adam. The two young men lowered their heads and shut up. Kelly grinned at Adam as he returned to the table. He might be short, but his guts have to duck to enter a room. Maybe the finest gifts do come wrapped in small packages. The man was proving to be quite a treat: witty, intelligent, caring, and courageous

Adam threw up his hands. "I've really botched it. Claw attacked you and I felt duty bound to make amends, to heal you with gaiety."

Kelly smiled. "So, you still owe me. You brag about keeping promises, how are you at paying your debts?"

"Hmm, depends. How are you at last-minute invitations? I'm not good at planning ahead. In fact, I don't even own a watch or have a clock in my house."

"Somehow, for you to be otherwise would be disappointing. I might make exceptions."

"Good, but for now I gotta go. Oh, by the way, what's your last name?"

"Dorsey."

"Kelly Dorsey, I like that. You in the book?"

"K. L. Dorsey, Shore Drive." Kelly and Adam prepared to leave. She excused herself and went to the rest room while Adam paid the check. She exited the ladies' room at the same time the skinny young punk who had used the insult swaggered from the men's room. One step ahead of her, he stopped and blocked the hallway. He said, "Lady, you better tell that nigger-loving runt to keep his nose out of other people's business or he might get hurt."

Kelly stepped back in a karate stance for balance, then punched the guy in his solar plexus. He doubled over and she gave him a sharp chop to his neck followed by a powerful knee to the chin. He collapsed at her feet. She stepped over him, and said, "You should heed your own advice."

At eleven years old, when she first realized that Dr. Huntley often hugged and touched her differently when in the presence of her Aunt Jean than when not, Kelly became depressed. Precociously developed and shy about it, Kelly painfully accepted the realization of what the hugs and touches implied. Instinctively she blamed herself for looking as she did, but contradictorily, she felt violated. While Kelly remained quiet, because she didn't wish to hurt her Aunt Jean, her will to survive cried out for protection.

She had always been physically active, a tomboy who loved sports, the rougher the better, and with the change in her uncle she became even more determined to defeat her blossoming womanhood and her helplessness. Ironically, her Aunt Jean produced the answer. Kelly had no way of knowing, but she grew to believe that her Aunt Jean perceived what Kelly would not talk about. The cure came as a Christmas gift placed within a card, a gift certificate for one full year of karate lessons. That experience sparked a love that never dampened.

Her breath even, she rejoined Adam and never said a word. They walked out into the warm sunshine. Adam took her hand. "I'm glad you came, Kelly," he said. "I'll call you."

"Do, and thanks for lunch." She turned and started toward her car.

Adam watched for a few steps, then called out. Kelly turned and waited while he approached. "Kelly Dorsey, I must tell you that without a doubt, may I burn in hell and freeze in Buffalo if it's a lie, you have the prettiest ass I have ever had the privilege to admire."

Abruptly, Adam turned and rushed up the street toward his car. He didn't walk in a straight line, but rather gradually gravitated toward the side on which he carried his case. When he approached too near the street, Adam shifted the case to his other hand and trudged obliquely forward. Fellow pedestrians gave him a wide interval.

Kelly held a hand on her flushed cheek and watched Adam round a corner. The little squirt had balls. He would be a great sailing partner. Kelly ran and caught Adam as he reached his car. "I know you said you must go, but I still have a little time. Want to take a walk?" she said.

Adam thought about his young sister. Glory wouldn't expect him to be on time anyway. He glanced from Kelly to his briefcase. "Claw, I owe you a side of beef."

★

At precisely 12:30 P.M., Dr. Huntley alighted from his Mercedes, dug in his pockets for change, and dialed a pay phone in St. Petersburg across Tampa Bay. The sun shinned through a cloudless sky, and Dr. Huntley quickly became hot in his tailored suit. He had never accepted the less formal dressing concession most residents make to the Florida climate. After examining the receiver, he wiped it with a handkerchief.

A deep but feminine voice answered, "Hello, Phoenix here." She coughed, and Dr. Huntley heard her exhale smoke. A disgusting habit.

"Hello," Dr. Huntley said. "Have you followed instructions? Barbara is not to know of our plans."

"Sure, I haven't told a soul. No pun intended."

Dr. Huntley ignored the feeble humor. "Be certain that you don't. We will go as planned when you return from your vacation."

"You can count on me, and thank you for the money. It will, ah, help with Barbara, you know."

"Yes, and don't worry, she's all yours like my man promised. I generously reward loyalty, Phoenix, upon which I place great value. My people always get what's coming to them. Do you understand?" Dr. Huntley didn't wait for a reply. "Goodbye for now." He hung up thinking of Barbara, and cursed the desire he felt between his thighs. At a reasonable time after Phoenix's performance, the psychic would suffer a fatal accident. It would be a shame for Barbara to be a victim too, but weakness leads to a loose tongue.

He returned to the cool comfort of the Mercedes that he had left running. St. Petersburg and its flock of elderly people, the retired from Canada and New England who flocked to the Sun Coast; God's waiting room, some people joked. How prophetic.

★

Phoenix had maintained her cool while talking with Dr. Huntley, but she was furious. Barbara had not come home last night, but now the red Toyota was in its parking space. Phoenix parked her car and rushed upstairs. She slammed the apartment door behind her and stomped into the living room shouting, "Barbara! Barbara! Damn it, Barbara, where are you?" No answer came. She slung her purse onto a chair and marched into the bedroom.

The clothes that Barbara had worn littered the bed, and the lingering fragrance of perfume reached out and grabbed Phoenix's attention. Like a magnet, the silky satin black chemise drew her. She held it to her nose, closed her eyes, and breathed deeply. Her mind was filled with a picture of Barbara's voluminous breasts, and she sensed the saline taste she craved. Like opium, the scent dulled her anger. Phoenix walked over and opened the bathroom door.

Barbara looked up from drying her shapely legs. "Oh, hi. I didn't hear you come in. Guess the water was still running." She extended a towel to Phoenix. "Would you dry and brush my hair for me? You know how much I love when you do that."

Barbara's ruse did not fool Phoenix. A manipulative tease, Barbara had scattered the sexy lingerie and conveniently showered as a distraction, a setup to dampen the anger. Phoenix knew it, but accepted the towel anyway. Barbara impishly brushed her bare bosom against Phoenix, first one breast then the other as she moved toward the bedroom. Phoenix followed mindlessly, and began to dry the glistening droplets of water from Barbara's shoulders.

"Sweetheart, you know how this angers me, and I told you that we must stick together. Our ship has come in."

Barbara reached up and rested her fingertips on Phoenix's hand while watching her in the mirror. "I'm sorry. It won't happen again. Why don't you brush my hair now and later you can make love to me." Barbara leaned back and thrust her breast upward as she used Phoenix's finger to massage a nipple. The nipple stiffened. "See," Barbara said, "it needs your attention."

Phoenix gave up. She had lost again. End of sermon. She had never touched anyone as beautiful as Barbara, and she knew that she never would again if the younger woman walked out. Secretly, Phoenix longed for a normal relationship, a mate who would love Phoenix as Phoenix would love her. Although a consummate hustler, Phoenix suffered a weakness for beauty. Barbara was her nemesis.

When down, Barbara's hair reached the small of her back. Her dark complexion and brown eyes made her appear Hispanic, while her tousled hair and pouty lips made her sexy. Five feet five inches tall, one hundred fifteen pounds, at thirty years old she had the flat tummy and waist of a teenager. All that, complemented with the finest sculptured breasts and dimpled ass that God had ever designed, made Barbara irresistible. Readable to anyone who might choose to open the book, Barbara read clearly as fiction, but her uncommon beauty and raw sex appeal hypnotized the reader into accepting her as fact.

The séance room became a stage that Phoenix knew her young partner couldn't resist. Phoenix encouraged Barbara to develop various characters. When the lights were dimmed, Barbara easily became the bewildered young widow, distraught daughter, pining sweetheart or grieving mother. She would work the believers as they came in, and during a trip to the bathroom she would report interesting items to Phoenix.

By twisting a small decorative picture out of the way, a hole, cut through the wall that separated the bathroom from the bedroom, provided the means for Barbara and Phoenix to talk face-to-face. The two had also worked out at least a hundred signals by which to converse during the séance. Phoenix understood that Barbara's vanity fed on the deception, and although she would often stray, so far Barbara had always returned. Whatever Barbara required, Phoenix did, always.

★

Kyle Keysor, driving his red four-wheel drive Ford Ranger pickup, rounded the curve then braked hard to miss a young girl and an older woman and man who darted across the street.

"Watch where you're going!" he shouted. His wife Sandy rubbed her neck.

"What's going... Oh," Sandy said, noticing the gauntlet of abortion protesters jeering at the trio racing to their car.

Kyle noticed too, and he rolled down his window. In his rather high-pitched voice, unusual considering his size, he called out, "Hey!" and the frightened, white-faced young girl and the older woman looked up while waiting for the car doors to be unlocked. "You murdering bitch!" Kyle shouted at the girl. "I hope you die!"

"Kyle!" Sandy said, "What are you saying?"

The man, dressed in a suit, appeared to be approaching forty, and looked to weigh no more than one hundred sixty pounds. He quickly unlocked the car and jerked around to face Kyle. With his face puffed and boiling red, he clenched his fists and lunged for the pickup. His quickness almost took him to the truck's satin brite running board before Kyle could react.

"Shit!" Kyle said, grinding the truck into first gear. The color poured from his face, and with every one of his two hundred twenty pounds Kyle stomped the accelerator. The pickup squealed to a start, and fishtailed down the street to safety.

After Kyle wrestled the truck under control, Sandy said, "Honey, how could you say such a thing?"

"What? Huh?" Kyle said, while trying to calm his shaky voice. He dug a package of Tums from his pocket, and chewed up two of the chalky tablets. He wanted to wash his hands.

"How could you say such a cruel thing to that girl?"

"How? Why not? We want a baby and can't have one while she has one she's going to kill – or maybe it's already dead."

"Honey, we don't know anything about that girl. We shouldn't judge her." Kyle gripped the steering wheel more tightly and clenched his jaw, but he didn't respond verbally. Sandra continued hesitantly, "Honey, don't worry. We'll figure something out. Dr. Russel said that I am a good candidate for artificial insemination. I'm sure—"

"Yeah, why don't you just say it. I can't make you pregnant so you and the doctor will do it artificially."

"Baby, honey, don't act like this. I know it's been stressful having sex by a thermometer, and now to find out that it couldn't have worked anyway. But that's not important. What's important is that we still can have a baby."

"Maybe it's not important to you, but what am I supposed to tell my brothers? Yeah, we're going to have a baby, Sandy's doctor knocked her up."

Slow swimmers, the doctor had said of Kyle's sperm. Like his fourth grade teacher had described Kyle; a slow learner. He almost ran a red light and screeched to a halt amid blaring horns. A guy in a BMW seemed glued to his horn. Kyle honked his right back and let fly a few birds along with appropriate epitaphs. Rich people; they only get that way by walking all over everybody else.

Sandy started crying. "Jesus, don't start that," Kyle said. "I'm just upset, that's all." With no one else present, Kyle could be a tender and loving husband. He reached over and took Sandy's hand. Tiny compared to his, it looked fragile, almost like a baby's hand in comparison. The perfect wife, at least until they started trying to have a child, Sandy had changed. Kyle had always initiated sex until the doctor gave her that thermometer. Now after all that, Kyle would have to fuck a bottle.

He stared in the rear view mirror, past his gun rack, and watched the abortion protestors picketing the clinic. Kyle had not thought about his brother and sister-in-law in a long time. Now he wondered if his little helpless niece or nephew had been murdered right back there just around the corner from the hospital. He belched and dug the roll of orange flavored Tums from his pocket again. One more wouldn't hurt. He and Sandy drove the rest of the way home in silence. The only communication came from his mud flaps that pictured Yosemite Sam, pistols ready, telling everyone within reading distance to, "Back off!"

★

Gloria Eden came in from school and changed into shorts and a T-shirt. She glanced at her watch. Adam was to arrive by four o'clock. She smiled. It was now 5:30 P.M. so she could begin to expect him.

Adam may often be late, but he had always been there for her when she needed him, especially since their father had died when she was fifteen. He even paid her tuition and other bills while she pursued an accounting degree, but Gloria insisted on working part time at a dress shop in the mall. "If you insist on working," he had said, "we'll let that be your fun money." Gloria loved her stepmother, Judith, but she figured God didn't manufacture a better model when it came to brothers.

She jumped when she heard Adam drive up. Driving fast was his only fault, but then he did everything in overdrive. Gloria opened the front door to the suburban ranch-style home that she shared with her stepmother, and watched as Adam climbed from the faded car. Maybe Adam, like his wheels, could use some sprucing up, but always both could be counted on to not leave you stranded.

"Hey, Glory," Adam called, after looking up and seeing her studying him. "What, have I got a stain on my tie?"

She laughed. "Do you even own a tie?"

"Probably not one that I should wear in public. Sorry to be so late, but I had a debt to pay this afternoon."

They walked inside and sat down. "It takes all afternoon to pay a bill?" she asked.

"Not always, but this time I wasn't sure how much I owed. I wanted to make certain that my debt was one hundred percent satisfied."

Catching the glint in his eye, Gloria asked, "Are we talking about the same thing?"

"You pay your bills your way, and I'll pay mine my way. On second thought, you make sure that you always pay with money."

Gloria lost her smile. "That advice is too late, I'm afraid." She put her bare feet on the sofa, pulled her thin legs up tight and locked her arms around them. She rested her chin on a knee and continued, "I'm in trouble, Adam."

Adam, already on the edge of his seat, leaned forward. "Trouble as in pregnant?" he asked, hoping that it wasn't true. Adam knew that if Gloria answered "Yes," it didn't mean that she thought she was pregnant, it meant pregnancy was a fact.

"Yes, Adam. I'm sorry." He started to speak, but she held up her hand. "Before you say anything, I know that I acted incredibly stupid. I've checked negative on an AIDS test, by the way, so that at least is good news. I've been so critical of girls getting pregnant, and risking their health." She raked a hand through her short blond hair. "If anyone should know better than to have unprotected sex, Adam, I should. I don't know what to do now."

Adam moved over to the sofa and put his arm around her. "Glory, knowing better and always doing better just isn't human. Even our gods have always had their foibles. What's done is done, so no need to dwell on that. First, I, ah, didn't know that you were seeing anyone on a regular basis. What about the father?"

"After the pride comes the fall, I guess. I've always considered myself so smart, too smart to fall for the wrong guy, and I wound up choosing the worst." Gloria lowered her eyes. "It was like if I insisted on protection, I didn't love him. It sounds so stupid now, but at the time it made perfect sense." She returned her gaze to Adam. "He no longer has anything to do with this."

Adam took her hand. "We'll talk this through, and when you make a decision, I'll be by your side all the way."

She laid her head on his shoulder. "How could I have been so stupid? And what about Mother? I can't let her find out, Adam, I just can't." For the first time since she knew for sure, Gloria cried.

"All right, Glory, it's all right. I know that you're embarrassed and that you don't want to hurt Judith, but she needs to know." Gloria shook her head in protest and Adam began stroking her hair. "Not immediately, OK, but she does need to know. If you prefer, I can talk to her first." Gloria didn't respond, and Adam took that as meaning yes.

Later, after staying to eat, Adam and Judith talked over another glass of the bottle of Chardonnay begun at dinner. Gloria had excused herself to study. Adam gave Judith the facts as far as he knew them, and waited for her to cry and talk out her frustration and fear.

"Oh, Adam, how does a person know what to do? On one hand I'm telling Gloria that she should save sex for her marriage, knowing how difficult that is for a young girl these days. On the other if I tell her to take birth control pills it's like I don't trust her. I knew that I should have told her, I knew it."

Adam paced, his hands orchestrating his thoughts. "Judith,

each person does what they think is best at the time. This is just a new crisis that we all must deal with in the best possible way." Adam sat next to Judith and took her hands in his. "You've done a wonderful job raising Glory. You have been a real mother to her, she doesn't think of you in any other way. My father was very lucky twice, first to have found our mother and second to have found you. All of us were lucky when Dad found you."

"You've never said that to me before, Adam."

"Well, I should have. You took on the responsibility of a two-year-old daughter and a dumb teenager, whose intelligence obviously hasn't improved, and you never complained. Even after Dad died you have been a rock. If there's a Heaven and you don't qualify, then it's got to be a lonely place."

Judith wiped away the tears again. "Thank you, Adam. I love you too."

Adam stood up again. "Well, now that we have that settled, let's see where we are. Glory is very confused, and so am I for that matter. Hmmm... you know, I have a friend, a psychologist, who is a rape counselor. I bet she could help us put this in perspective, help Glory decide for herself the best course to follow."

"Adam, are you talking about abortion? How could Gloria live with an abortion? How could I?"

"Judith, if I have learned one thing from the various articles I have written, it's that trained professionals can often help solve problems by introducing and helping to prioritize all the ramifications and options. I believe that you and I must and should want Glory to do what is best for her. Obviously, this includes Glory considering your feelings and mine." Judith shook her head slightly in agreement. "Now, first things first," continued Adam. "You let Glory know that you aren't disappointed in her and that we are all in this together, OK? I will talk to my friend tomorrow, and see if she will help."

Judith went in to talk with Gloria and Adam called Bulldog. "Bulldog, it's me."

"Hey, man, where you been?"

"Busy. How's Trace and the kids?"

"Great. Terry Jr. is growing into a lineman, and we got Fran potty trained in one week."

"Now if Trace could only housebreak you, huh?" They both

laughed. Adam continued. "I need a favor." He explained the bizarre story of the promised suicide, and Huntley.

"All right, I'll check it out. I've heard about the suicide note, but don't think it's being taken too seriously at the station. You know we've got too many people dying who don't want to die to worry too much about someone who does. Still, I agree, it's strange this character Huntley is involved. A certified asshole. Charmin should recruit him for research and development."

Adam laughed. "What's with the jokes? I'm supposed to be the funny one."

"Yeah, I guess assholes have that effect on me. Anyway, because of his behavior he was watched closely during the Fardy trial. None of us would have put murder beyond his options. Hates the little people, and anybody who is not lily white. Besides, radicals always operate close to the edge. I'll get back to you. Drop by for dinner. Tracy gets bitchy when she hasn't seen you in a while."

"Her fault for marrying a dumb jock. Kiss her for me, hug Bulldog II, and don't scare the baby with that ugly mug of yours. See you," Adam said and hung up.

He let himself out. The humid Florida evening, which was unseasonably warm, coupled with the wine made him feel a little woozy. The Chevy's tires squealed a tad when he took off from a traffic light, and as he brought the car under control he passed a hospital sign which made him think of Kelly.

Kelly was twenty-eight, divorced from a surgeon, and had no children. She taught a women's self-defense course, and worked as a rape counselor at Tampa General Hospital on Davis Islands, an island community just a bridge away from downtown Tampa. She had been too polite at lunch to interrupt as Adam explained the motives of suicide, but as a psychologist she understood them intimately. Adam grinned. The day sure hadn't been all bad. He drove home and crawled into bed. He was exhausted.

Did he bring misery and pressure on himself by always trying to help others? First, it was his mother, then Franci, and since then too many to count. How many had he lost? If there were a benevolent god somewhere, the wine would help Adam sleep.

Soon he found himself struggling to swim ashore before the

swift current dumped him over the falls. He knew it was hopeless, however. He had been there too many times before, but still he kicked his feet and clawed at the water with his hands. He screamed for help and struggled to breathe. Shortly, he would tumble over the falls and drop toward the swirling basin waiting below like a serpent coiled to strike. Adam would wake up as soon as the water swallowed him, but not before fighting to stay and search for Franci. He never could though.

As Adam fought against the current he almost accepted his fate, but the familiar anger that had been his companion since Franci's death wouldn't allow surrender. How many must he lose? If there were gods gathered somewhere they had no right to interfere in a man's life. Still, a god with human frailties one could understand, but not the God marketed as being all knowing and beneficent. That God is a myth. Franci's death proved that. Death, disease, destruction; all are proof that there is no omniscient benevolent god pulling strings. Mother Nature is in charge, and she operates on the principle of random circumstance and survival of the fittest. Planned coincidence is an oxymoron. A coincidence may suggest a causal relationship, but it is pure accident. A welcome circumstance is not God at work answering prayers.

Adam twisted and tumbled, searching for something, for anything to grab onto. There must be a way. As the water sloshed in his face, Adam ceased to struggle and thought of escape. His eyes clicked first one direction then another. I refuse to go over the waterfall. Maybe he could dream up some help. After all, he created the nightmare, so why not create someone with a lifeline?

A disembodied voice agreed. "Why not indeed?" A bright ball of light appeared before Adam and he automatically floated toward it. By the time Adam realized that he was no longer tumbling toward the falls, he found himself in the tree house where he and Franci made love the first time. Adam had never escaped the water before. As he tried to reason why, he gradually became aware of another presence. He stared at the light until it faded into a human form. "Franci!" Adam shouted. "My God, am I dead?"

"No, more alive than ever, I would venture," his companion said.

Adam stared. The voice was that of a stranger. Adam was sure that he had seen Franci, but the person eyeing him now was a wrinkled white-haired Native American. The deep facial furrows that marked his weathered face suggested a past of great struggle while his knowing eyes testified that wisdom and love lay within.

"Who are you?" said Adam.

"An old friend. You asked for help. This is a rare pleasure." The old man grinned and settled himself cross-legged in a corner. His lively eyes belied the appearance of age. "Usually you are too stubborn to ask."

"I thought you were someone else."

"I apologize for the deception, but I didn't wish to startle you. Your friend is doing well, by the way. I have brought her near you many times, her concern for your well-being is great. You often respond by thinking of chocolate peanut butter cups, but you refuse to accept her presence." The Indian smiled but more with his eyes than his lips. "It's too bad that men don't reincarnate as animals, you would be a great mule."

"Very funny but not original." Adam studied the man. "You are not exactly what I envisioned when I thought about dreaming up a little help."

"You glimpsed the truth of life. As Mr. Dickens so cleverly wrote, a man forges his own chains, but fortunately, we also possess the power to free ourselves. However, I'm not the solution and you're not dreaming. Of course your conscious mind will jumble up this experience and you will wake with mixed memories of our encounter. The more often we meet, however, the more your thoughts will march in step with what actually occurs. Like the hard shell of an acorn simultaneously protects and imprisons the miracle that lies within, man's ego is very protective of itself and holds you in bondage."

"What are you talking about?" said Adam.

"Within the tiny acorn lives a mighty oak, but before that miracle can manifest itself, the hard shell must crack, give way, surrender in order to free the potential that lies within. You are spirit. You are made in the image of God. Indeed, you are a part of All That Is. The physical body comes with an ego designed for self-preservation. When you enter the physical world, the ego recognizes your free will. It becomes like the bride or groom that immediately begins to isolate their new partner from family and friends. Such an insecure personality seeks to protect itself by controlling the new mate.

"This is the true fall of man – the belief that he is separate from God. However, it is not the physical man who falls but rather your spiritual self. Spirit forgets that it is a part of All That Is and accepts the body's egocentric point of view. Instead of using the body as a tool, you, the spiritual self, wrap yourself in chains. The ego must crack, give way, surrender, in order to free the potential that lies within. To prevail against the flesh, the ego must be crucified and the spirit resurrected. Then you are born again."

Adam studied the acorns that littered the tree house. He picked up one and shot it across the floor like a marble, but it missed the intended target. "You tell me I am not dreaming, yet you expect me to believe that you are real and that Franci still exists. Not hardly."

"Not *yet* would be more precise. We have met before, and we will continue to talk on the occasions when you are receptive."

"I don't remember ever seeing you before, let alone talking to you," said Adam.

"No, you are an uncompromising empiricist and have chained yourself up like Mr. Houdini. Fortunately, also like the magician you have an escape available. Your ultimate resurrection is assured."

"Then I go to Heaven and sit on clouds all day playing a harp. No thanks. Dullsville."

The Indian smiled. "I quite agree. Existence without challenge is like a stagnant pool. Life and challenge flow one from the other as surely as night turns into day and day into night."

"So what do you mean that I will be resurrected?" said Adam.

"It means that you have a date with God. We all do. You have a destiny, one that you are creating yourself, by the way, as do we all, but you currently deny your power. One day you will grow to question why the tail is wagging the dog, why you allow the wagon to go before the mule. The Master Jesus revealed that man is limited only by his beliefs. All the power demonstrated by Jesus and other great teachers is man's birthright. You can do anything you wish once you free yourself of the belief in limitation. You are not the body. Life is forever. There is no death."

"Right! And after a battle soldiers play dead?"

"Ah, myopic hearing, it can be convenient." Many Faces smiled. He fired his own acorn and sent two others flying. "Indeed, man can and does commit many horrible acts. God is infinite potential and it is man's birthright to use this potential. The secret to life is to develop the wisdom to follow the higher will. In terms of scale, war is one of man's grandest achievements. It reflects the tremendous power man has inherited. Unfortunately, it also shows how foolishly you squander your bequest. To eat of the fruit of the tree of knowledge is to follow man's will. To enjoy the fruit of the tree of life is to follow God's will. Fight and lose, Adam. Surrender and win. The choice is always yours." The old Indian winked. "All you need is love."

Adam opened his eyes. He sat up and searched the dark corners. He snatched up a handful of his sheet and stared at it. Adam had difficulty accepting that he was in his bedroom. He knew he had been dreaming, but it seemed too real for a dream. Not the falling, of course, but the… What? What the dickens had just flashed through his mind? Adam ran his hand through his hair. Heck, he had dreamed of Franci, that's all. But dressed as a Native American? That was strange.

Adam remembered the familiar falling. The Indians lived in harmony with Mother Nature. They didn't try to control it. If a terrible storm destroyed the village, the people didn't complain. In the aftermath of tragedy they were grateful for the rain. Maybe the Native American garb was a psychological symbol that Adam beat the river because he ceased to struggle against it. He crawled out of bed and brewed himself a cup of tea. He padded to his office to catch up on some reading, but instead he called Bulldog.

"Yeah, who's this?" a groggy voice answered.

"It's me, Adam. What you doing?"

"Damn, Adam! Considering that I'm normal and it's two o'clock in the morning, I'm trying to sleep. You ought to try it sometime."

"Oh, is it that late?"

"The next time you wake me up in the middle of the night, I'm going to nail a clock to your scrawny ass."

"Sorry, Bulldog, but did you ever hear about the duke who inherited a vast estate? He was rich. He had it all. If he wanted one of the female servants he took her, married or not. He wantonly killed the animals on his land without regard for the meat or trophy. He enjoyed his power. He lived for debauchery. Then one day he died while still young.

"He was surprised to wake up in a palace with servants who attended his every need and desire before he could make demands. If he saw a female he desired, she made herself available. If someone angered him, the servant submitted to the punishment without a struggle. No matter how badly he treated the servants they waited on him as if he was the greatest master one could have. If the duke wanted to hunt for a wild boar all he had to do was step into the woods and there it was. He didn't even have to aim.

"At first, the duke couldn't believe his good fortune, but quickly he became despondent then depressed. He struggled to control his thoughts because he knew that whatever he might desire would be his. Eventually, one night the butler entered the duke's bedchamber to turn back the covers and said, 'You are not yourself tonight, sir.' The duke said, 'I'm confused. I am aware that I didn't live a Christian life, so I can't figure out why I made it to Heaven.' And the butler said, 'Why, sir, whoever told you this is Heaven?'"

Silence. Finally, Bulldog said, "Adam, are you alright? No, strike that. You ain't ever been alright, but is something bothering you?"

"No, why?"

"Alright, alright, I'll bite. What the hell are you trying to say?"

"I'm talking about Heaven... Don't you see? A Heaven without challenge would be hell." There was no response. "Bulldog, are you holding your breath?"

"No! I'm counting to a million. You know you really should try sleeping before I come over there and knock you out."

"Fight and lose. Surrender and win," said Adam.

"What?"

"Huh! I don't know. Sounds interesting though. I'll have to give it some thought."

"Good night, Adam."
"Night, Bulldog. I love you man."
"Yeah, me too."

★

Many Faces studied Franci as she leaned out a window of the tree house into the dark and watched the moonlight sparkle on the ripples below. As the black water crept by, various species of frogs competed with constant calls and warnings to one another. The splashing of water and an occasional grunt of an alligator punctuated their chorus. "You are healing," said Many Faces. "I sense no distress."

This was Franci's first visit to the tree house since her death in the water below. Many Faces was right. She was enjoying the beauty of the place and remembering the fun times, not her death. She turned and faced her mentor. "You did not tell him that I was here too," said Franci.

"To have revealed your presence would have convinced Adam that he was dreaming. He would have blocked my efforts to communicate," said Many Faces, who maintained his Indian body for Franci's benefit.

He experienced physical life many times in different aspects and in different ages. He took great delight in teaching his charges to review their alternate lives, and for each lesson he adopted a different look from his own experiences. To his students he was known as Many Faces and that pleased him; nevertheless, he preferred his life as a Native American holy man.

"I wish I could tell Adam to quit blaming himself for my death," said Franci.

"One day you shall, my child, but not before he is ready. You might say that currently he is enjoying his misery too much to listen."

"What do you mean?"

"Ignorance is bliss. A part of Adam calls to him, reminds him that he is spirit, a part of God; consequently, Adam denies God because he fears the responsibility that acceptance will bring," said Many Faces. "It's always easier to fight than surrender."

"I don't remember ever seeing Adam afraid of anything," said Franci.

"Consider two rivers. One meanders and plods slowly through farmland and plain as it nears the sea, while the other tumbles down the mountain range and plunges into the first. The lowland waterway is filled with sediment. It is dark and unappealing. The mountain water is clear and clean, its path swift and certain. After the point of confluence there are two distinct rivers following the same channel. One side is dark, dirty, and drifts slowly toward the sea. The other is clear, refreshing, and pulsates with purpose, driven by the energy gained on its ride down the mountain. In the middle of the common channel where the two waters collide, there is a terrific turbulence.

"When spirit enters flesh it can become as a swimmer in the muddy part of the river. Because of the ego, the eternal self soon forgets its true nature, and accepts the turbid waters as reality. Suffering and lack become accepted as inevitable until finally self calls out in the belief that there must be a better way. The swimmer begins to work his way toward the center of the river until he encounters the turmoil created by the confluence of the two estuaries. Here, the struggle becomes greater and more frightening than any he has ever experienced as it is always when one travels from the known toward the unknown. Life in the dark may be far from perfect, but at least the hardships there are familiar.

"Some swimmers, however, refuse to quit, and plow through the agitated waters like a mighty salmon swimming upstream to spawn. A part of them remembers, and that memory becomes an indefatigable belief that there is a better way. The divide between acceptance and understanding appears insurmountable at first, but once failure is tossed out as an option, the passage opens like the Red Sea," said Many Faces.

"Do you know what Adam is going to do?" said Franci.

"Causes, the patterns in Adam's life, offer suggestions, but these can only be graded as possibilities or probabilities because existence is fluid. We each have free will and that is the food of life. Without this sustenance we would cease to exist. It is a paradox. To exercise our free will may cause one to forget his oneness within God and that could condemn the lost soul to temporary damnation. Contrarily, to fetter our free will can prevent the lessons garnered from independent experience that leads one to understanding."

"I don't know what you mean," said Franci.

"As our mutual friend briefly remembered, man creates his own problems and subsequently, his remedies. The secret, however, is the wisdom to allow one's personal will to parallel the higher will," said Many Faces.

"But how can we know God's will?"

"Simple. One must surrender. How is this accomplished? By wanting with every particle of your being that your every thought, your every word, and your every deed will be that which is best for All That Is. To reach this state of grace, one must be saved. One must cast out Satan who is nothing more than common fear. Pray that love which is God will flood your being and wash away all fright," said Many Faces. "Learn to love."

Franci shook her head. "Will I ever understand? I still expect one day to meet God sitting on a throne."

Many Faces smiled and stroked Franci's long black hair. "I am reminded what my good friend Thomas Aquinas once said, 'God's center is everywhere, His circumference is nowhere'."

"I like that. I would like to meet your friend."

"Desire is the key. Hold that thought," said Many Faces. "But I am needed elsewhere. Come, we must go." Immediately, Franci found herself standing on the front porch of the home where she often stayed with her grandparents. One day she would learn to manifest a place of her own, but for now the company of loved ones comforted her.

★

"Honey? Baby, it's OK," Sandy said. "It's just the stress, trying to have a baby and all, and then today at the doctor's." Kyle sat on the side of the bed with his back to her. Sandy sat up and tried to put her arm over his huge back, but he stiffened up. Allowing her hands to fall to her lap, she said, "Please, honey, this can happen to anybody. It's no big deal."

"No big deal! I'm only twenty-four years old and can't get a hard-on. First, I can't get you pregnant, now I can't even fuck you. That's no big deal?" Kyle had been swilling beer since they had arrived home from the doctor's office. He checked the can on the nightstand. It was empty. Sandy started crying, and pulled the sheet up to dry her eyes.

Kyle collapsed the empty beer can and dropped it in the trash next to the bed. Naked, he stomped into the kitchen, punching his heel down first followed by a slap on the tile floor made by the ball of his foot as he worked to maintain balance. He freed another beer from its plastic noose and popped it open. Alley, Sandy's brittle-colored cat, scampered from his perch on top of the refrigerator and raced from the kitchen. Kyle laughed at the frightened cat and plopped down at the kitchen table. It was Sandy's fault that he couldn't get hard. She used to bathe before sex, but since she got that thermometer it was hop in bed and screw.

He had nine nephews and nieces. Certainly his brothers had no problems. Kyle and Sandy had been married for three years and he had always been able to blame her. What the hell would he tell them now? His brothers were always calling him limber-dick as it is, now there would be no stopping them.

He staggered over to the hall closet and retrieved his new seven-shot .357 Magnum, model 607 from Taurus. Kyle worshiped big guns. This one felt good in his hand, a trusted friend. He dumped the cylinder clear. The pistol didn't need cleaning, but that didn't stop him. Florida humidity was a relentless foe. He positioned his index finger to reflect light up the barrel. He searched for problems but spotted none.

Kyle could outshoot his brothers, even though the oldest two had served in Vietnam, and Chuck, just four years Kyle's senior, worked as a Tampa police officer. Kyle's father had taught all the boys to shoot and hunt, but Kyle had been a prodigy, the Beethoven of sharpshooters. During hunting trips, his brothers were always teasing Kyle. He plowed through the forest with the racket of a wild hog, he couldn't resist killing whatever crossed his path, and he couldn't butcher a kill without tossing his breakfast. His father forced him anyway, which caused more laughter. His ability to shoot, however, was sacrosanct.

Brooding, Kyle gulped the remainder of his beer. He sniffed the gun oil. It pleased him. It smelled clean, not like the odor of grease. When he thought of his fastidious mother, he remembered fresh laundered clothes. When he thought of his mechanic father Kyle smelled grease and grime.

He crushed the beer can, and tossed it toward the trash but missed. It ricocheted off a cabinet door, and tumbled loudly across the tile toward Kyle as he watched passively. He didn't bother to pick it up. When the rattling ceased, he just muttered, "Another dead soldier."

His two oldest brothers had sometimes talked about Vietnam and killing children who men had made into soldiers. Kyle plucked another beer from the refrigerator and popped it open. He threw the pull top in the trash. What do abortion clinics do with dead babies? Probably pitch them in the dumpster along with the rest of the garbage. He reassembled the pistol and aimed the empty weapon toward the bedroom. He squeezed the trigger, but nothing happened.

March 14, Tuesday

Kelly snaked her way through the serving line then found an empty table near the wall. The cavernous hospital cafeteria sounded less like a bus station with a nearby wall to help muffle the noise. She emptied her tray and slid it out of the way. Usually Kelly chose the fruit bowl with a slice or two of cheese added for protein, but this morning she also sneaked in a mushroom-shaped muffin.

More hungry than usual, she felt the change in her body and in her psyche like one senses a change in the seasons. She radiated energy generated by a nervous excitement. Kelly wasn't quite sure yet which one, but she blamed or credited Adam Eden for the sudden difference. This was not a safe unemotional involvement such as her current one with her friend and neighbor, Gil. Deep in thought, she jumped when her pal, Trudy, spoke. "Hey, girl, you should take your body with when you run off like that."

Kelly wiped strawberry from her chin. "Oh, my goodness."

"Sorry, didn't mean to startle you."

"That's all right. Daydreaming I guess. How are you, Trudy?"

"OK. Just dropped by to see if you and Gil might like to come over for dinner tonight. Joe just returned from his fishing trip, and I'm trying to get rid of as much as possible. Fish in a freezer are like clothes hangers in a closet, they multiply."

"Thanks, but I took some time off yesterday, now I need to stay late and catch up." Kelly studied her friend. They enjoyed each other's company, but not always around Trudy's choice of men. Kelly tried to help, but when Trudy got rid of one it seemed that the next one was worse. "Uh, Trudy, I thought that you were through with Joe?"

"I know I said I was, but at least I'm familiar with his faults. There aren't any good men, honey, so I might just as well stick with what I got." With her eyes Trudy asked permission then reached over and pinched off part of Kelly's muffin. "Friday then?"

"Uh, I... let me think about it, OK?"

"Hey, what gives girl? Are you and Gil having trouble?"

"Hum, not exactly. I just, well, you know we're just friends really."

"OK, let's have it. You've met someone haven't you?"

Kelly played with her fruit, as if searching for the best chunk. "Not really. Well, maybe yes. God, I don't know."

Trudy laughed. "Who is he? Tell me about him."

"He's a writer. Honest I think, but maybe not a one-woman guy."

"And what man is?" said Trudy. "That's why I may as well stick with Joe. What's he like?"

At first Kelly thought Trudy was asking about Joe, at least he worked and paid the bills unlike some of Trudy's other choices, but no, Trudy was asking about Adam. Kelly considered her breakfast. "He's like this blueberry muffin speckled with flecks of spinach."

"Girl, what does that mean?"

"It means that he's mostly pretty damned good."

"That's wonderful." Trudy reached over and laid her hand on Kelly's. "When you're ready, bring him around." Trudy shook her head. "I sure hope he likes fish. See you later."

"I will, I promise. Bye," said Kelly. She examined her muffin, flawed now with the pinch missing, and thought about the hole in her own life. Being deeply in love had been wonderful, but it only made the wounds deeper when she discovered that the man she had loved for seven years had never been faithful.

Emotionally devastated at first, it took time for the wounds of the heart to heal, and then the hate set in. The man she trusted not only brought home every nurse that he bedded, but, like the infinite reflection of a mirror in a mirror, he also brought home all of their partners and their partners' partners to a faithful wife who willingly but unknowingly parted her legs to receive them.

Kelly's anger turned to rage, and gradually dampened only because, by the grace of God, was she still alive and not dying from AIDS. Her gratitude for this blessing grew until there was no room for hate. She glanced at the time and realized that she needed to hurry. She wrapped the muffin in a napkin and rushed to catch the elevator. After glancing at her grinning image reflected on the shiny door, she felt a little silly and looked around hoping that no one had noticed.

She had caught herself grinning several times since meeting Adam Eden, but this time she grinned over how he had tricked her. Well, not a trick really, but still funny to think about. The walk along Bay Shore Boulevard after lunch had been entertaining and revealing. By the time the walk detoured from Bay Shore into Hyde Park, and ultimately to Adam's house, she had not known that he lived so close, she wanted to believe that Adam was what he appeared to be, a man who valued honor, his word, and a handshake. A contradiction, Adam was a man of heroic principles disguised in a body of lesser proportions.

Once at Adam's house, Kelly marveled at the fishpond as Adam had promised she would. A yardman maintained everything, but Adam enjoyed the pleasure his backyard brought to visitors. Landscaped by the former owners, the yard had been replaced with decks and pathways, sitting areas and a hammock, a spa, and the centerpiece, a fishpond fed by a waterfall.

Kelly learned that Adam did some of his best work on his laptop when writing by the waterfall. He had said that the flowing water seemed to encourage a current of thoughts and words as well as making him urinate fourteen and one-half times daily. How can one urinate one-half time?

Colorful butterflies fluttered about, and dragonflies darted and hovered here and there. Fish of all sizes and color combinations schooled in circles. Fluffy-tailed squirrels scampered about fighting and scolding one another over some invisible indiscretion, and birds stuffed themselves at several feeders. Kelly excused herself to discreetly remove her panty hose, and then she insisted that they sit on the oval bridge and soak their feet in the water. The setting, the energetic and entertaining company, the Chardonnay, all combined to make Kelly behave like a rosy-cheeked schoolgirl on a picnic.

After soaking and swinging their feet for a while, and sharing most embarrassing moments, Adam looked at Kelly and told her that she was a terrific person. He didn't call her a beautiful or an attractive woman; he had seen what lay below that and had chosen to express it. That impressed Kelly. The two of them locked eyes briefly until he leaned over, placed his hands on her cheeks, and they kissed tenderly. When they stopped, he took her hand and said, "When you leave here today, I want you to have only happy feelings. I don't want you to worry that you did something foolish, so let's go inside where I can get protection."

The elevator raced to Kelly's floor, and she giggled then turned red as her two fellow passengers eyed her. She laughed at her response to Adam. She had stared at him at first, then said, "Thank you, I would appreciate it." Just like that. If Adam had asked her to go to bed, or to make love, or to have sex, or even if he had continued to get more familiar after that first kiss, Kelly could have said no. She probably would have said no and would have indicated that it was too soon, but his question caught her off guard. She believed that he used those precise words because they most accurately described his concern for whomever his partner might be. He was definitely honest, a good man. One could just tell.

At her desk, Kelly sipped a fresh cup of coffee, and considered the muffin as she unwrapped it from the napkin. She glanced at the time. Her first appointment was due any minute. Adam had been the best lover she had ever been with. Not because of some exotic technique, but simply because he unselfishly occupied himself with pleasing her. He cared.

It was obvious now that she thought about it. She always told herself that she didn't want an emotional relationship, no more commitments for her, but deep down Kelly knew that she did. Her friend Trudy, however, accepted that she could do no better than Joe, although he was never faithful and perhaps worse, he did little to hide the fact. Trudy's belief chained her to the relationship. Contrarily, Kelly believed that she deserved a good companion, and now maybe she had found him. She examined the spinach flecks then gobbled down the mostly pretty damn good muffin.

★

Clarence Fardy had been on parole for four weeks, and he did exactly as instructed. A legal requirement, he had the rules of his parole to follow. His anonymous instructions, however, and the unbearable consequences if he failed to follow them, forced Clarence to guard his every word and action. He rejoined his wife and three kids in Tampa. They lived in a subsidized housing project, but it seemed to Clarence that Marvel, his wife, had managed to improve things considerably during his absence. He immediately recognized that she acted more like the nine-year-old girl he had fallen madly in love with and later married than the shrew he drank to.

He never understood why someone as full of hopes and dreams as Marvel, someone as confident of her future, could care for him. Even as a child, Marvel would talk for hours about how they would grow up, get married, raise babies, and live in a mansion. Except for the years that he lived in a bottle, Clarence had always recognized Marvel as his salvation. He, on the other hand, had disappointed her.

The family still depended on welfare, but Marvel babysat four children and had several customers for whom she did the washing and ironing. Clarence praised her success, but even talking about such unrestricted subjects proved difficult. Mounds of neglected bitterness and disappointment remained to be sifted through and discarded.

The long separation had served to smooth some of the jagged edges that kept them from fitting securely together again; nevertheless, enough barbs remained that Clarence felt like a stranger. At first, his youngest child, Melissa, had even occasionally called him Bob instead of daddy. He didn't ask questions though. Almost four years in prison was a long time, and even before that he had not been much of a husband to Marvel. The bottle had been his mistress. He had no right to judge.

The four children for whom Marvel babysat had been dropped off, and her own three were ready for school. "May I walk you to the bus stop?" Clarence asked.

Ten-year-old Tommy, the oldest, shook his head vigorously. He stubbornly refused to have anything to do with the father who had abandoned him. The youngest, six-year-old, Melissa, said,

"Oh, yes, Daddy," and grabbed his hand.

Tommy, leading his brother David, bounded out the door and walked fast enough to stay well ahead of his father. Melissa felt pretty important to have her father in tow to show her many friends. In this neighborhood, fathers were a sometime thing. Marvel took a minute from her demanding schedule of cleaning and caring, and lingered in the doorway. She watched the scene with amazement. Aware of how fit Clarence had become, stirring memories were freed from the recesses of her brain. The extra weight looked good on her husband.

Later, Clarence returned to the apartment and poured himself another cup of coffee. On TV, cartoon characters blew each other away, and the violent images blasted the four children Marvel babysat. Clarence asked if the kids would like for him to read to them, but the animated heroes won out. Marvel was busy changing a little girl, but her thoughts were on Clarence. She almost dropped the baby powder when he spoke. "I could do the laundry if you like," Clarence said.

"What? Oh, if you want to." It had been this way ever since Clarence had returned. He was thoughtful, attentive, and helpful, but not ingratiating. At first, Marvel resented his efforts until she realized that Clarence gave simply because he wanted to. She had forgotten that he had always been unselfish with her, and now he appeared to be that way with everyone. What Marvel or anyone else might do or not do in return was not part of the equation.

She finished with the baby and laid her in a scarred old crib that had been passed around the neighborhood. Who originally purchased it and later left it no one knew. Marvel got busy cleaning up the breakfast dishes, but kept glancing at Clarence as he separated the clothes. She smiled when he pushed up his glasses. Such a simple gesture, yet so familiar, it made his presence more natural now that she had noticed it. He glanced up and briefly they regarded each other. Marvel instinctively brushed a strand of long black hair from her face. She felt warm.

"Am I doing this right?" he asked, resting his eyes on Marvel. She had encountered considerable difficulty remembering Clarence as anything but a drunk, and had intentionally avoided eye contact since his return. She appraised him now, and accepted that he was admiring her, not just as a woman, but as a special woman. She experienced a tinge of guilt, and realized that it had been years since he had noticed her that way.

She recalled their giggles when just kids while comparing their anatomical differences, and later their wonder as awkward teenagers exploring the pleasures of sex. She felt unattractive as a tall reed-thin teenager, her breasts were just bumps on her chest, but Clarence had loved her madly and passionately. His attention brought her breasts to life. Shy as he was, he had even named them.

In the early years he frequently reminded her of what a prize he had won. Along with tender words, Clarence's ministrations taught her nipples to grow long and ridged when kissed. With the surge of excitement the memory generated, Marvel's nipples swelled. She forced the feeling away, and studied the two piles of clothes in front of Clarence.

"Well, first thing..." she started, but checked herself when Clarence's expression changed. Not an angry look, but rather one of patience, a willingness to learn what she preferred. Marvel found it uncomfortable because before prison, except when talking about a book he had read, Clarence had always been too shy for much eye contact even with her. "Yes," she said instead, "That's OK." She darted around the kitchen, making a lot of noise as she nervously piled the sink with dishes. She was well aware that Clarence appeared to be sorting clothes but actually watched her.

"Marvel," Clarence said. She turned her face but kept her hands submerged in the hot dishwater. Clarence eased up next to her. "I'm sorry I turned into such a loser. I understand now how I made you and the children suffer." She stared at him with her mouth open. Unable to speak, Marvel turned back to the dishes. Clarence touched her arm. "I just want you to know that, Marvel. I don't blame you for anything. Any man would be lucky to have your love." He moved back to the pile of laundry.

Tears began to pour until Marvel willed them to stop. Once the kids had started coming, she had begged Clarence to ask for a raise. She pushed him to look for a better job, to stop letting people walk all over him. Raised by a demanding father who expected and enforced complete obedience from his wife and children, Marvel had fallen in love with Clarence because of his gentleness. Later, she resented his lack of aggression. She longed for something in between. Clarence's letters from prison hinted at such a man, but Marvel remained unsure.

She blamed herself for Clarence's collapse even though he didn't. Clarence had been seven and Marvel nine when he and his mother moved into a garage apartment on the alley behind where Marvel lived. Clarence's father had run off and left Clarence trapped with a mother who blamed him for her loss. She constantly reminded him. She began to drink heavily, and only on her best days, which were rare, did she have a kind word to say to Clarence. He in turn responded by trying harder to please her. He worked patiently for the scarce compliment, for the rare gesture of approval.

It didn't help much at home, but a kindly old neighbor, a white-haired widower, befriended Clarence, as did Marvel. The widower was a bibliophile who had spent a lifetime reading and collecting books. In that sense, the mother's drinking became a blessing. The more she drank the less time she spent abusing her son, and the more time he spent reading. Marvel never learned to enjoy books, but she did sit transfixed when listening to Clarence repeat a story for her. Always the most animated when sharing an exciting novel, Clarence's insight enthralled Marvel, and she would listen without interruption.

She also enjoyed the fact that Clarence never made demands. She always led. When they grew older, she was the first to plant a kiss, and later she was the first to suggest more than kissing. Clarence had been hesitant, but Marvel led the way. Now, as she remembered, Marvel suddenly realized that she and Clarence had been happy together as long as she led the way. Things soured only when she stopped leading and started pushing.

Through the years, Marvel learned to bitch and berate just like Clarence's jilted mother, and Clarence learned to drink, also like his mother. Marvel rinsed a glass and placed it in the drain rack. "You've changed," she said without looking around. "Like when we got married, but stronger." She wiped away a tear. It would be so wonderful to give in and cry. She hurried to the bedroom to regain control.

Clarence eased into the room. "Excuse me. I know that you may not want me too, and I will understand if you don't. Sometimes, though, it helps just to have someone hold you." He spread his hands slightly in invitation.

Marvel stared at him indecisively, but finally stepped into his arms. Clarence had been home a month and until now they had not touched. He had accepted sleeping on the sofa as probably best anyway, so as not to disturb the life Marvel had built for herself and the children. Now, Marvel felt her resolve pushed aside as Clarence grew partially erect. Happier memories marched to the surface of her mind, vanquishing everything that had taken place in between.

Clarence's interest grew, and Marvel's nipples stiffened. Clarence's letters, which increased in frequency as he changed, had again revealed to Marvel the sensitive, loving little guy she had married. They also introduced her to a stranger, a confident man, a man with opinions, a man with beliefs. Both now held her tightly. One calmed her frazzled soul while the more familiar of the two called out to her flesh.

Seeing Clarence healthy and sober had taken her by surprise. It left her confused. She felt her wetness, and forgot the fears that Clarence might slide back into the bottle. She wanted this, and had to admit that she wanted it with Clarence. Marvel eased free from his arms, and peeped at the kids. The baby was in the crib, the other three had plenty of juice and cookies, and the TV babysat. It would take only a minute.

With the need so great, and the rekindled feelings too demanding, foreplay was unnecessary. Later, when the children were tucked in for the night, there would be time to touch, time for whispered endearments, time to remember, time to recommit. It was over quickly. They caught their breath, and both of them laughed and both of them cried. Amid giggles and laughter, Clarence wiped away Marvel's tears and she dried his.

The baby cried out, and Marvel jumped. Everything would be OK now. Time to get back to work. She took his face in her hands. "I know you didn't mean to hurt us," she said, "and I ain't no saint either. Welcome home." She kissed him mightily, threw on her clothes, and rushed to check the baby.

Clarence had not intended for this to happen. He just didn't want to leave without apologizing. How could he leave his family hurting that much more because they thought he didn't care? But he was only human. When Marvel moved into his arms he lost control. The familiar warmth and scent of her reminded him of happier times. A wayward strand of her long hair tickling his face, the memory of her body, long and agile, the taste of her tiny breast, and the warm moist folds of flesh between her thighs summoned Clarence and he responded.

While listening to Marvel singing in the kitchen, Clarence sat up and leaned against the headboard. It would have been better if he had not returned home, but what choice did he have. His instructions were to convince everyone that he had been born again, that he loved his family and Jesus, that he suffered great guilt, and that he wanted to die.

Ironically, this was easy for it was all true, except for the last part. Clarence no longer wanted to die. After discovering Marvel and his children again, he desperately wanted to live. Even knowing the horrendous consequences if he failed to follow instructions, he didn't want to die. Unfortunately, he didn't have the slightest idea how not to.

Clarence found his glasses and eased out of bed. He retrieved the newspaper photo that had been stuffed in his hand at his last meeting with Cowboy. The photo showed a house destroyed by fire. The headline read, "Three Children Die In Flames". Finally, Clarence placed the clipping back in his wallet, but froze when Marvel abruptly stopped singing. He snatched on his trousers and discovered Marvel in the kitchen, shaking. "What's wrong?" he asked, taking her in his arms.

"Probably nothing. It's just that there's so many dangerous people in this neighborhood. I worry about the kids all the time."

"What happened?"

Marvel nodded at the window over the sink, "See that man limping down the alley pushing the shopping cart? I swear I seen him hanging around before. He walks with a limp, that's why I first noticed him, but he don't walk like he belongs here. He seems, well, he's too interested. Will you meet the kids at the bus stop later?"

"Sure, but I think he's harmless." Clarence hugged her. "Don't worry." He breathed deeply to calm himself, and hoped the words sounded more confident than he felt.

Clarence stared out the window and watched the man push the Kash 'N' Karry grocery cart up to the dumpster in the alley. The cart, piled with assorted clothes, cardboard, and all manner of other things, had bags filled with aluminum cans hanging from every available hook like ornaments on a Christmas tree. Busy talking to himself, the man started flipping trash about in the dumpster as if oblivious to the world. He looked up and grinned at Clarence.

The man's face was freckled and filthy, and tufts of red hair escaped from under an old orange Tampa Bay Buccaneer football hat now shapeless and caked with dirt. The lips parted in a grin, and the man tipped his cap to Clarence while bowing slightly. He limped over to a discarded pile of broken up furniture, and plopped down on a mostly intact nightstand. Fishing a brown paper bag from inside a ragged jacket, he took a drink and wiped his lips with his sleeve. He said something to himself, and leaned back against a utility pole. It appeared to Clarence that the man planned to stay awhile.

Almost whispering, Clarence repeated himself, "He's a harmless idle-headed drunk, but I'll meet the children."

★

Nigel Hunttington, currently posing as a beggar, and better known as King Red because of his regal name and blood red hair, enjoyed life. From his perch on the nightstand, Nigel considered the trash heap that surrounded him. It held all that he required. There was cardboard to protect him from the damp ground, broken up furniture to fashion a fort, and a perfect view of his target. He smiled. He enjoyed planning a fire almost as much as watching it. He laid his head back against the utility pole and enjoyed the warm sunshine on his whiskered face.

The warmth reminded him of his first fire. Even though only ten at the time, the boy could still hear his father's frantic screams. Nigel fondly recalled that first spontaneous ejaculation as the flames escorted his abusive father to hell. Yes, indeed, fire was the indisputable god of pain and pleasure, and a man couldn't have one without the other.

He didn't recognize at the time that his arson was readily apparent, but they were poor people in a small town. No one cared that Nigel's quarrelsome and abusive father burned to death. Except maybe his creditors, but truth be told they were probably relieved never to have to deal with the man again. No one said goodbye when Nigel's battered and defenseless mother packed up her brood and moved back to her native Canada.

He lifted his head from the utility pole, opened his eyes and checked for problems. Seeing none, he sipped the bitter cheap wine, and allowed it to stream down his whiskered chin. He wiped it away with a filthy sleeve. Accustomed to better, he raised the bottle skyward anyway. "Father, we owe our success to you." Nigel always used the collective reference to himself. Buried deeply beneath tons of painful memories, he thought of himself as two people, King Red, the one he was, and Nigel, the one he might have become had there been a benevolent god. He continued, "May your black-hearted soul fuel the fires of hell forever."

It would be a long day and night, but Nigel would keep busy studying the rhythm of the area. He would watch Clarence's neighbors to see when they went out and when they returned. He would be alert for police patrols. He would observe the drug deals. He would listen to whatever tidbits of conversation trickled his way and glean any usable information. He would interpret the arguments that might pierce the night. He would consider the nightlights, note the ones that were burned out, and record those that would best be burned out.

Nigel would please his god. He would watch and plan the strategy for this next fire. It wouldn't be easy. His employer for this job wanted it to appear to be the suicide of a distraught widow and her three children, a suicide that gets out of control and burns the whole building, and hopefully others too. No, not easy, but Nigel had time to plan.

The building wasn't to be torched until after the third of April for some reason. That gave King Red plenty of time to sit on his nightstand throne and think. Plenty of time to visualize the flames climbing the clapboard walls that currently protected the Fardy family. Plenty of time to close his eyes and imagine the intense heat. Plenty of time to hear the roar. Plenty of time to savor the smell of burning wood, and appreciate the beauty of billowing smoke. Plenty of time to play with himself.

★

"We got a problem," Lee said.

"I don't appreciate problems," Dr. Huntley said.

Lee ignored the threat, and helped himself to a cup of coffee. From an angle, he watched Dr. Huntley. "Seems your niece, Kelly, spent yesterday afternoon with your Mr. Eden."

Dr. Huntley's face flashed anger. "What do you mean by 'spent the afternoon'? I was not aware the two of them were acquainted."

"One of my men watched as Eden literally bumped into Kelly yesterday after she left here. Later they met for lunch, took a walk on Bay Shore, and wound up at Eden's house."

Dr. Huntley's eyebrows moved together. "She bumps into a total stranger then goes home with him?"

Lee didn't miss a thing. Not only was Huntley hard for Barbara, the old pit viper wanted to warm his blood between his niece's thighs. The guy must be hard up, and with all that money? Not that Lee could blame him now though. Kelly was a looker. "The important thing," Lee stressed, enjoying the sarcasm, "is what my tail overheard during lunch. Kelly told Eden about your, ah, the late Mrs. Huntley and about Clarence Fardy." Dr. Huntley rocked slightly and fidgeted with a pencil. This was the first crack in the normally cold, confident Dr. Huntley that Lee had noticed.

Dr. Huntley stopped rocking. "Do you think he suspects anything?"

"Don't know. From the questions I asked I think Eden accepts the story as you told it. Still, I've alerted everyone in case Eden contacts Fardy. One thing though, knowing about Fardy, Eden may start digging. It may be wise to move up the target date."

"No!" Dr. Huntley said too quickly. Lee remained expressionless, and watched as his benefactor calmed himself. "Fardy dies on April the third, the anniversary of the day that he killed my wife.

Besides, doing so will make his suicide more plausible." Dr. Huntley leaned back and stroked his chin. "I think it's time that Mr. Fardy and I have ourselves a little tête-à-tête."

"You think that's wise?"

"You say that the little leech has become a Christian. Well, he may think that God has forgiven him his sins, but he needs to know that with me it's still quid pro quo. He may be frightened now, but after he visits with me, being born again will assume a completely new meaning."

The pencil that Dr. Huntley had been twisting between his hands broke, and the man let the two halves drop to the desktop. Both men were surprised, but Lee didn't allow his to show. Wiping lead from his hands with a tissue, Dr. Huntley got up and walked over to the window. With his back to Lee, he said, "Arrange a meeting." Lee left via the bar door.

Dr. Huntley buzzed his secretary. When she came in, he stood in front of the window, and he didn't turn around or speak. She cleaned away the broken pencil and wiped the mahogany desktop clean. Dr. Huntley watched a developing thunderhead gallop in from the East. He peered through the cloud-covered morning toward Davis Island and the Tampa General Hospital where Kelly worked. He would do whatever became expedient to prevent rain on his carefully crafted parade. His secretary jumped when he suddenly spoke. "Get my niece on the phone."

Later, Ms. Parks put the call through. "Hello, Kelly, I wanted to call and thank you for dropping by yesterday. You are just like your Aunt Jean, thoughtful and kind to everyone."

Even over the phone Kelly could sense the masquerade, the phony salesman smile, the feigned friendliness. "You're welcome," she said.

"I miss the times you, your Aunt Jean and I spent together. We had fun didn't we?"

"Yes, we had some good times." Until you became too free with where you put your hands.

"Why don't we have dinner tonight and talk about old times? I get very lonely without Jean. Also, I've got an exciting but sad secret that I wish to share with you. I value your opinion, you know."

The glib explanation didn't fool Kelly. She didn't want to have dinner with the man, but she did want to learn more about the suicide. "Yes, we can have dinner, but it would have to be tomorrow night, Wednesday."

"Wonderful. I'll pick you up at seven."

"That would be too much driving for you. Let's meet at The Treasure Cove around seven, OK?"

"It's really no trouble for me to pick you up. Besides, these are dangerous times; a young lady shouldn't be driving alone at night."

"I'll be fine. See you then. Bye."

"Goodbye," Dr. Huntley said, failing to mask his annoyance.

★

Adam answered the knock on his front door. "Bulldog, come in."

"Afternoon, Adam. Got the information you wanted. Since I was in the area thought I would see if you were home." Surprised, Bulldog searched the room. "You alone?"

"Just us roosters. Anything interesting?"

"Not sure. Huntley's clean. He's been busy heading up a nonprofit organization that he started three years ago. They publish a racist newsletter about over population, welfare, falling educational standards as well as stuff on morals and ethics." Bulldog sat down, and looked around again. "Couldn't convince some babe that you were the stunt man in *Deep Throat*, huh?"

"Turned them all down. Now get back to Huntley."

That was odd. Adam must have been joking, but he didn't sound like it. Bulldog said, "The various editions contain scientific studies that prove conclusively the intellectual and moral superiority of the white man. Never heard about you, I guess. Claim to have about three hundred thousand members and growing. Kind of an elitist hate letter. Minorities and poor people are what they are because they are inferior. Same old shit, in other words."

"Sounds like Huntley all right. What about Fardy?"

"Maybe, man. Seems he became a Christian in prison. Changed his whole personality. Warden thinks the guy is truly a reformed drunk, and his probation officer says Fardy is staying straight so far. Says Fardy is just a guy with a drinking problem who had the bad luck to kill someone. Should have never gone to prison he says. Me, I say sounds like prison helped him."

"A Christian, huh? Have you read the suicide note?" Adam didn't allow Bulldog time to answer. "Mr. X seems the zealous type."

"A big coincidence all right, Huntley getting this note just when Fardy gets released. Still, Huntley reaches a lot of people through the mails. Could be any of the crazies that read his garbage."

"Bulldog, people who hate don't normally kill themselves, they kill other people."

"Probably right. I'll run it up the flagpole down at the station and see if it flies."

"Good, and I think I'll pay Mr. Fardy a visit. Got an address?" Adam wrote it down as Bulldog recited it. "How about a phone?"

"Sorry, no pot, no phone."

"Some things are easily taken for granted."

"Ride with me one day, and you will never take such things for granted again. There's a lot of sorry slime out there who don't deserve the time of day, but some damned decent people are caught in the crack too."

"Sounds like this Fardy and his family may fall into that category. I'll let you know after I meet him. By the way, how's Trace and the kids?"

"Great, just great. Terry Jr.'s going to be a football player just like his old man."

"That's OK as long as he has Tracy's looks."

Bulldog picked at the armrest on his chair. "Yeah, I admit it, Adam, I'm lucky as hell."

The banter had been quick and relaxed, but Adam had known Bulldog long enough to know something was eating at him. "What's wrong, Bulldog?"

Bulldog shifted and crossed a foot over one knee. "Tracy never complains about my work even though I know she worries, but I never really worried until now. Now, with Terry, Jr. and the baby, I can't seem to stop thinking about it. What would happen to the kids if I, well, you know. That's why I appreciate you agreeing to be their godfather. Tracy and I have our families, but we both agree that you're the one who would be a real daddy."

"Hey, it's natural to question one's mortality as your responsibilities grow, but it doesn't mean something bad is about to happen to you. Just make sure you don't take stupid chances."

"It's a two-edged sword, man. You think of your wife and kids, and you want the world to be safe for them. At the same time you can't stop thinking about the possibilities of getting hurt or killed. We have to be so careful now because of brutality claims and wrongful shootings, some unfortunately justified, but it's too easy now to hesitate too much at the wrong time. Besides, as you know, I've already brought one piece of dung down to room temperature."

"So? It was ruled justifiable homicide. The guy refused to surrender. When he brought his gun up you fired in self-defense. You were exonerated."

Bulldog's eyes rested on a collage hanging on the living room wall. Surrounding it were pictures of himself, his wife, and his kids, as well as pictures of Adam's family. Bulldog and Adam weren't kin by any biological or legal sense, but psychologically they were brothers.

The collage revealed that. Adam's sister, Gloria, put it together, and depending upon which artifact hampered her progress, she ripped, sawed, and sliced it in half. She framed both halves, and presented one to Bulldog and the other to Adam. To understand the whole story of their friendship required a visit to both halves of the collage.

A cookie dough cat symbolized the beginning of the relationship, and Gloria had centered the feline in the collage thus allowing the friendship to be presented radiating unrestricted in all directions. Adam got the cat's head while Bulldog wound up with the tail. Wisely, each half of Gloria's handiwork had been wrapped the same, and each was labeled with both names. Bulldog still accused Adam of somehow manipulating the choice to insure that Bulldog received the ass end of the cat.

Adam followed Bulldog's gaze. "What are you smiling about?"

"Oh, I was just thinking about all the times this battered and bruised body of mine has cashed checks written by your mouth. I still think that you goosed Lady Luck into giving me the shit end of that cat."

Adam studied the collage. "Hey, it's my job to stir things up, and yours to jump in and smooth the ripples," he said. Bulldog grinned as he remembered that damn cat incident.

★

With mixed emotions, Terry watched from the sidewalk, wanting to leave, but deciding to stay. He watched three boys struggle to stick masking tape to the feet of a frantic Siamese cat. Clawing, hissing, and howling, the feline tried to bite its way to freedom, but six hands were too many to combat. The boys, including Terry, were all about ten years old, but Terry wasn't one of the cat's tormentors. New to the ethnically mixed neighborhood, Terry had no intention of getting involved.

His mother had given him fifty cents to blow at the corner store owned by a rotund, no-nonsense Cuban widow named Mrs. Rios. Half the time you might not know what she said, but all the time you knew she meant it. The three boys were on the front porch of the house that sat next door to the store. Terry wondered if the house belonged to Mrs. Rios, and if so were one or more of the boys part of her family. He doubted the latter; she was a nice lady. She gave him a soda to welcome him to the neighborhood.

With only two pieces of tape in place, the cat managed a healthy swat across the arm of the largest boy, the biggest of the three, the one as big as Terry. The cat screamed and plowed three nasty furrows down six inches of the boy's unprotected arm. The boy yelled and let go of the cat that started to scamper to freedom until it realized that something didn't feel right. It hopped as if the porch were a heated grill. It howled, and bounced, and twisted; it scratched feverishly at the menacing tape on its feet.

Holding his bleeding arm, the boy shouted to his companions, "Catch that cat. He scratched the shit out of me." The two boys did as ordered, and the torment got meaner. The big kid was pissed. He peeled off a long strip of tape and tightly wrapped it around the struggling cat's midriff, and then managed to tape the other two feet. They set the cat free and howled at its misery, as it twisted and spun around clawing and tearing at the tape.

The three boys found the cat's struggle hilarious, and at first, Terry did too. He laughed at the cat's comical gyrations, but the piercing screams changed to plaintive groans of desperation. Terry realized that to the cat it was not a game. An emotional part of Terry begged him to stop the torment, but a practical side warned him to keep his nose out of it. He turned to leave when a geeky-looking little guy wearing glasses, and a tall dark-haired girl ran up.

"Stop that," shouted the new boy. He darted past Terry and leaped up the steps. He caught the cat and ripped tape from two of its feet before the biggest boy grabbed the geek and slung him against the wall. The gangly girl screamed, "Adam!" and ran toward the porch. The two other tormentors blocked her way, but she gave as good as she got. The girl had guts. Adam ignored the big kid, and again lunged for the cat. The big kid grabbed Adam's shirt collar, spun him around, and hit him on the chin. Adam's glasses flew off as he again bounced off the wall. Adam fell and the big kid straddled him, throwing one punch after another.

Embarrassed that he had not stopped the torment earlier, Terry had seen enough. He barreled up the steps, moved the struggling girl aside, and waded through the two boys to get to the one beating Adam. With both hands, Terry collared the kid, jerked him up, and threw him across the porch. "That's enough man," he said.

Screaming, "Get that cat!" the kid bounced up and rushed Terry. The two smaller boys collected themselves, and joined in. Like a redwood battling chainsaws, Terry stood his ground. As his father had taught him, Terry made each punch count. There was no wild swinging from his quarter.

The action moved swiftly, but Terry saw Adam try to tackle one of the tormentors only to be kicked back on his geeky ass. More effective, the girl managed a couple of stout kicks to the shins that doubled the recipients over. It helped, but the boys weren't finished. Terry dropped the biggest kid, and hoped that the boy wouldn't get back up, but he did.

All three of the tormentors hit Terry just as Adam struggled to his knees. Terry stepped back for balance, but tripped over Adam.

Mayhem ensued at that point because the girl jumped into the fray crying, "Adam, oh, Adam," as she kicked and clawed his attackers. Fists flew, the biggest tormentor cursed, the girl cried, Adam screamed, "Help the cat, help the cat!" and Terry growled like a dog as he sank his teeth into somebody's leg. Pissed off and getting tired, Terry became desperate.

It didn't matter, however, because Mrs. Rios, rattling off admonitions in Spanish, waddled up on the porch and placed her impressive bulk in front of the pile of kids. She grabbed two of the tormentors, one in each hand, and threw them aside like logs tossed by a flood. Terry didn't understand what the woman said, but the three tormentors were out of sight before she had finished saying it. Terry looked around and saw that Adam, blood pouring from his nose, was already working to free the tormented cat. "Let me help you man," Terry said.

Later, Terry learned that Adam Eden performed Sir Lancelot's role. Francesca Rojas, a tall, thin, dark-haired girl with huge expressive eyes, a girl who had beauty, and unfortunately tragedy, in her future, played Guinevere. Terry became Bulldog, and the three of them became inseparable.

★

Still examining the collage, Adam asked, "You're not planning to close the bank are you?"

"No, you've got a lifetime protection guarantee, but a little help occasionally taking care of your scrawny ass wouldn't be unwelcome." Bulldog searched the collage, and saw himself represented by a tiny ceramic bulldog, a piece of his football jersey, a badge, and a picture of boxing gloves. He saw Adam represented by a tiny fuzzy bumblebee buzzing around a picture of a bonnet, and also there was a miniature oil, painted by Gloria, of a hummingbird flitting from flower to flower.

The one Bulldog liked the best, however, was at home on his half; a cut out photo of his and Adam's faces, Adam's placed over a suit of armor and Bulldog's over a chubby body holding a knight's lance. A windmill filled in the background.

Terry examined further and spied Francesca smiling back at

him. To her breast, she held a pasted-on cutout of a romance novel. "I miss Franci," he said before thinking. "Sorry, it's just that I, well, things can happen so quickly. All your hopes and dreams…"

Bulldog sat quietly for a minute then slid to the front of his chair. He leaned toward Adam. "I've never told anyone this, but that's not what happened; that's not how the creep I killed died. I had him pinned down while waiting for backup. To escape the alley, that man had to come through me. He couldn't escape.

"Protected, crouched behind my car, I needed only to wait. Taunting me with insults, he gave himself up, but laughed at me when I cuffed him. In a uniform back then, I wore a nameplate. The piece of garbage looked at my wedding band, then at my name. 'Got an old lady, huh, Officer Wright?' he said. 'I'll be out on bail before you get off duty, and you're gonna regret ever fucking with me, nigger.' He laughed, and I saw hate reflected in his eyes like the reflection of a burning cross on a windshield. Tracy was three months pregnant, and I realized that I would live in fear for her as long as that sleazy son-of-a-bitch remained alive."

Bulldog eyed his friend. "The police have a saying: 'I would rather be fired by one than carried by six.' The rules give creeps like him the advantage. If someone is out to get you all it takes is patience. The police can't protect you from a determined killer, no one can. I could play by the rules and live in fear for my wife and unborn child, or I could make Tampa a safer place to live while ridding myself of a nightmare. I followed my instincts, and shot the bastard." Adam sat gape-mouthed, until he realized that his best friend needed a response.

"Terry, you work in an environment that requires instant decisions and quick action. You did what you thought you had to do. Me, I probably would have wanted to do the same, but doubt I would have had the guts. Were I in your shoes, my wife would probably be dead or a rape victim. I've told you a million times, I wouldn't do your job even for a roll in the hay with the Playmate of the Month." Bulldog smiled. He knew that even with beauty a long way off, it didn't take much to get Adam in bed.

"Don't know why I told you that. Guess it's just been harder to leave the house since the baby was born."

"Bulldog, you've never been afraid of anything. Now you see

your daughter so tiny and helpless, it makes you fearful for her. Once you learn that she bounces pretty good you'll bounce back yourself."

"Maybe—" Bulldog started, but got interrupted by a call from dispatch. He rushed to the door. "Time to earn your tax dollars."

"Bulldog," Adam said, "there is not a better cop anywhere than you. I love you man."

"Yeah, Adam, I love you too." They hugged goodbye, and Bulldog bolted for his car. Over his shoulder, he yelled, "Lock your door."

Adam watched the unmarked car speed away, and sensed that he was running late for his appointment. He raked through the contents of his briefcase and hurried to the Chevy. Thoughts of Gloria's pregnancy and his meeting at an abortion clinic occupied his mind, but he did take time to speak to his neighbor, Ms. Stein, and ask about her health. She assured him that all was well. He revved up the Chevy and tore down the street. Without looking, he could imagine his neighbor shaking her head in bewilderment.

★

Bulldog had grown to hate the Oven, and as he drove there now from Adam's house he could feel himself growing tense. Every time he knocked on a closed door he got the willies. He could feel a bullet tearing through his belly, grabbing and ripping as it traveled deeper until it burst free beyond his shattered spine.

The fear, the pain, the suffering; all were real to Bulldog because he had experienced them. He didn't know where his familiar bed went, or his wife's warm body that lay next to him. The hum of the central air conditioner was also missing. Bulldog knew only that during the dream he wiped real sweat from his brow. He could smell the urine-soaked hallway, and he could see the graffiti-covered walls. His knuckles felt the impact of knocking on a badly abused wooden door, and he heard the rap, rap, rap. He supposed he jumped when the pistol fired. He wasn't sure. However, he did feel the searing fire in his stomach until his spinal cord snapped in two.

The chilling events of that dream sparked Bulldog's current

fear of the streets. No one would ever convince him that those events were any less real than the time he searched a subject and found nothing only to be knifed in the gut a minute later. The pain from both events, the dream sequence and the one that made the morning news, were permanently etched in his memory. Both brought chills. Both taught valuable lessons. How could one be less real than the other? Bulldog had a family now, and he intended to be careful.

★

One block from the abortion clinic, Kyle Keysor radioed in to the auto parts company for which he made deliveries, and reported a mechanical problem. He hated the grease and grime, but the extra money earned by repairing the company vehicles came in handy. Now when he asked for no assistance, there were no questions. He would radio back if he couldn't get the truck running again. Wrappings from three biscuits and ham lay wadded up on the floorboard but he still sucked on a large soda. Slowly, he drove by the abortion protestors.

Kyle counted six protestors, four women and two men, ranging in age from teenager to grandmother. Two carried gruesome color posters graphically depicting bloody butchered fetuses after suction-aspiration, and the more common dilation and curettage, D and C. Somewhere, the protesters played a tape of babies crying.

Kyle stared in horror, but only for a second. He swung the door open and violently tossed his breakfast. Dry heaves continued long after his stomach purged itself, but he pulled himself up just in time to see Adam Eden speed around the corner in his old Chevrolet. Kyle, although blessed with perfect vision, leaned forward as if it would help him see better. He watched Adam expertly and quickly back into a curbside parking space. Adam exited the car clutching his black case, and stalked into the clinic seemingly oblivious to the protestors and the little woman hanging in effigy from a car antenna.

The cocky little bastard with the big bag had to be going in there to do an abortion. Kyle's eyes were lured back to the posters.

They were pictures of what once had been human beings, living breathing babies. Now they were chopped liver. People who do that ought to be shot. Kyle got out of his truck and stomped up to Adam's Chevy.

The tag depicted the almost extinct Florida panther. It was a special tag sold to Florida residents who wanted the extra money to go into efforts to save the endangered cat. The asshole obviously thinks killing babies will make more room for the doctor panthers. Kyle memorized the license number and returned to his truck to wait. He dug his roll of orange flavored Tums from his pocket, and wiped his hands on his shirt.

★

Inside the clinic, Adam met the director, Susan Barrett. A friend who followed the health beat for the newspaper had made the appointment, and based on an accurate description the clinic guard opened the door as Adam approached. The door, made of an opaque bulletproof glass darkened so that the guard could see everything occurring outside, allowed no one to see in. The brawny guard, armed with the lightweight but incredibly strong Celayaton police baton, and a Glock 17 automatic pistol, looked formidable.

Adam surveyed the facility as he was quickly ushered in to see the director. Once past the guard, one couldn't miss the striking contrast. The clinic, smelling strongly of disinfectants, looked like every other medical facility Adam had visited. The director's office impressed Adam as clean, neat, and modestly furnished. A vase of freshly cut flowers, mums of lavender and white, helped to subdue the odor of antiseptics. Adam reasoned the arrangement also served as a homey anchor for patients tossed about in a stressful sea of conflicting emotions.

The walls supported a couple of nature scene prints and the shelves, crowded with journals and medical texts, held pictures of family. Adam deduced three young adult children, two girls and one boy. The husband and father struck Adam as professional, friendly, and capable. He looked as if he would be a good friend.

Adam studied the director. A petite woman, fiftyish, with

brown hair streaked with gray, she had a ready smile that let one know that she could be a friend, while her steel blue eyes warned that she didn't push easily. Twisting uncomfortably in his chair, Adam said, "I'm embarrassed to admit that I haven't really followed the abortion controversy. I, ah, I've been stuck on other things, but now I wish to help my sister. What exactly happens when, ah, when a person comes in?"

"We do a social history, determine the support system. Is there a father, a job, school? What are the living arrangements? We stress that abortion is not a form of birth control. We present options. The patient views a video of the changes that occur during pregnancy. It explains the details of what an abortion is, of how it is accomplished." Adam's surprise must have shown.

The director leaned forward and placed her arms on her desk with her hands clasped. "Mr. Eden, you may visit two lawyers, two mechanics, or two of anything, and one may be mercenary while the other may be ruled by a higher morality. My point? I, and many others like me, provide abortion services because we believe in what we do. I am running a business, and if it starts to lose money, then I will necessarily have to earn a living another way. Nevertheless, I would still work in every way possible to aid women who choose abortion."

Adam caught himself shaking his foot, and uncrossed his legs, embarrassed that he had not come better prepared on what to expect. The director probably had her reasons. She continued. "I pray for the safety of all women and young girls who may become victims of rape and molestation. I would prefer that all females practice birth control to prevent unwanted pregnancies, but that will never happen. Women will always get abortions, and I would rather the service be as medically and psychologically safe as possible.

"If your sister chooses to make an appointment, we will try to help her decide what is best for her. Contrary to what my placard-waving friends outside would have you believe, the several women currently in our waiting room are not viewed as paychecks. They are patients."

Adam liked the director. She impressed him as a capable businesswoman, but also as an impassioned care giver. He didn't doubt that she spent many anguished hours being loyal to her beliefs while outside the front door she hung in effigy. They discussed a few pros and cons on abortion, and agreed that opposing moralities didn't have to result in violence.

"Abortion is an issue of puzzling contradictions," she said. "It's a set of stairs that create a different group of contradictions for each individual depending upon on which step the person finds herself during the process. It's the intransigent extremists on both sides who cause unnecessary agony for the rest of us."

"Yes, some people can't see both sides of an issue," said Adam. He thought of Huntley stroking his chin in his plush office. He and the director talked more, but briefly. Adam thanked her, and she insisted on walking him out. It would give him a chance to see the protesters in action.

When Adam and the diminutive director stepped outside, the protesters immediately started shouting their favorite names. One struck the director's likeness that hung from the antennae. The ripped-up body parts of a baby doll, tossed by someone in the crowd, fell at the director's feet. Adam watched as she steeled her back, but he could still see hurt in her eyes.

"I see what you mean," he said. "Why don't you go back inside." Never thinking that she might not appreciate the familiarity, Adam leaned over and kissed the director on her cheek. "The world could use more people like you."

As the door closed behind the director, Adam glared at the protesters, and shouted, "Who appointed you God? Everybody's got a right to their beliefs." Several protesters hurled heated responses back, but already concentrating on his next destination, Adam ignored them. Some people just can't see the inconsistencies between their beliefs and their actions.

★

Only thirty minutes passed before Adam returned to his car, but Kyle had spent it applying a negative slant to everything that had ever happened to him. The last of four brothers, nothing unique remained about another baby boy. He grew up taken for granted by his busy father and bullied by his brothers. He should have been first string on the football team, but Douglas Arnold's mother fucked the coach into favoring Douglas over Kyle. Sandy had become a filthy whore, and at age twenty-four, impotence strangled Kyle's balls.

Kyle sat up when he saw Adam exit the clinic, and then Kyle noticed the director. She was tiny, just like Sandy. Wore her hair the same too. And look at that. Kissing in public. They were either married or the little murdering doctor was dicking the woman in between killing babies.

"Who appointed you God?" Kyle repeated. He shook his head. For a baby butcher to mock the Lord was unforgivable. Kyle cranked his truck and pulled out to follow Adam, who wasted no time reaching the first intersection. "That murdering bastard thinks he owns the road," snapped Kyle. The fear of getting pulled over again in the company truck gripped him. He didn't want to face his boss again.

Which Kyle added to the list of things that he didn't like. A married couple who had been in business for twenty years owned the company. The business currently had three locations, and all operated under the wife's orders. She had big sagging tits and bulldog jaws to match, and she constantly barked orders to Kyle. Called him lazy. Obviously she didn't like him because he wouldn't hose her. Even a stupid moron could figure that out.

Kyle sweated and his cheeks chewed up the seat as he speeded behind Adam down Hyde Park Boulevard and across the bridge to Davis Islands. When Adam bore to the left leading to Tampa General Hospital, Kyle stayed to the right. He drove to the first street and turned around. As he fumbled for the radio, Kyle mumbled, "I knew he was a doctor." Kyle popped another Tums and radioed in that he was on the road again finishing his deliveries. As he crossed the bridge leaving the island, a black thunderhead broke open and began a deluge that was unusual for the season and for the time of day.

★

Adam located the information desk and asked where he might find Kelly Dorsey. Although given specific directions, he still managed to get lost in the sprawling hospital complex that had served Tampa for more than six decades. Along the way, he passed a vase filled with red roses sitting at a nurses' station. He did a quick search, found no one looking, and lifted a stem. After finally locating the right office, he claimed that he was indeed Dennis Conner, the world famous sailor. With much hand waving, he insisted to the secretary that he did have an appointment. If it wasn't listed, there must be some mistake.

The flustered secretary eased into Kelly's office that resembled a nautical museum. She reported the strange little fellow carrying a long-stemmed red rose between his teeth and a big, ugly black briefcase. Said that if he wasn't one of the doctor's patients he should be. Kelly laughed. "Send him in," she said.

"You bought a flower for me? Thank you."

"No, it's more exciting than that. I lifted it from a vase down the hall." Adam held the rose out and Kelly accepted it.

She smiled. "You gambled more than you know. If Nurse Ratched had caught you, you would be in a straitjacket by now." Kelly smiled. "Altogether, not a bad idea when one considers public safety." She smelled the flower then found it a home in a vase on her window ledge. She turned back to Adam. "Dennis Conner, huh? I bet you don't know port from starboard."

"Of course I do. Port is a sweet fortified red wine that goes well with chateaubriand. Starboard is one of the many financially strapped little mom-and-pop tourist attractions that still dot the Florida landscape. This particular attraction mimics the Hollywood Walk of Fame; however, the stars' names and handprints are painted onto a boardwalk that winds through three acres of swamp. It is also famous in that none of the handprints shown there are authentic with the exception of Chevy Chase's. He was the only star generous enough to honor the invitation and visit the park."

"You are so full of bs. How do you come up with that stuff?"

"I'm deeply offended," Adam said, placing a hand on his heart. "God strike me dead if a lie ever forces its way through my virgin lips."

"There's nothing virgin about you buster, and you know it. Sit down and tell me what brings you to the hospital on such a rainy day."

Both Adam and Kelly sat in front of her desk, her crossed legs attracting most of his attention. She wasn't muscular, but she was firm, her legs shapely. Most important, however, she had a quick wit. She was fun. Dressed in a fashionable navy blue business suit, pink blouse and a striped blue and wine bowtie, she looked like a professional one could trust. Adam said, "I thought maybe you could recommend a good doctor to transplant a set of gills into my lungs."

"Is it raining that hard?"

"No, it's just that being this close to you again I'm thinking about growing six more arms."

Kelly smiled and placed her hand on Adam's. "You do quite well with the two you have. Any more might get in the way."

He took Kelly's hand. "It's good to see you. Sorry about barging in though. It's a bad habit of mine."

"I told you I might make exceptions. I'll let you know if it becomes a problem."

"Speaking of which, I do have a problem I hope you can help me with." He got up and began to pace. "My sister, Glory, I told you about her. She's twenty-two, she, well, I won't bother you with a lot of details right now, but Glory's pregnant, not married." Adam stopped in front of Kelly's trophy case. It appeared that she had been modest about her sailing ability. "I don't know how you feel about – well, I know that you are a psychologist, a trained counselor..." Adam's eyes asked for help as he continued to search for the right words.

"You want to know how I feel about abortion?"

Relieved, Adam turned and faced Kelly. "Yes, and I'm sorry. I know it's a highly personal matter so if you prefer we can drop it right now."

"As I told you, I specialize in dealing with rape victims, and occasionally rape victims become pregnant. Every situation is unique because the individual involved is unique. The dilemma is compounded when the child could possibly be the husband's or a boyfriend's. There are no easy answers, but the one thing I never do is knowingly impose my own morality." Adam sat back down, fully engrossed with Kelly's explanation.

"Adam, many factors are involved. I try to get the patient to make a decision based on her own morality and other contributing circumstances with which she must contend. Her husband's feelings, relatives, religion, economics, the considerations are endless. Nevertheless, in order for the patient to live a productive, happy life, the final decision must be one with which she can live.

"Experience has taught me that most women can better deal with knowing that a child is alive somewhere rather than aborted. In their imaginations, a healthy individual can fantasize a happy life for that unknown child. When the fetus is aborted the imagination cannot escape that finality. I encourage women to carry to term and give the baby up for adoption, but only when I honestly feel that is the best choice for the individual. If my analysis points to abortion as the best solution, I recommend it without qualm. Me, personally, I say that I could never abort a child, but I have never had to face carrying a baby conceived by a rapist. Now, how do you feel about abortion?"

He smiled. "Tit for tat, a fair question. Humm, I've never concerned myself with the question to any significant degree. I guess if there were a God, I would consider it wrong for women to be treated as mere chattel. Where is the free will in a morality that holds a woman in bondage to an unborn human?" Adam scratched his head. "Course, I don't believe in gods, so I say it's the individual's choice. Everybody is entitled to their own opinion." Adam searched Kelly's expressionless face.

"I'll be happy to talk with Glory if you like."

"I'll let you know. By the way, this is some collection you have here." He pointed to a picture hanging on the wall. "Is that one yours?"

"Yes. Say, would you like to go sailing this weekend?"

"Humm. Is there a place where we can sail in the shade?"

Kelly thought a minute. "As a matter of fact, yes. It's called Moonlight Bay. Meet me Saturday around 5:30 P.M. at the Island Yacht Club. Ask anyone where *Perpetual Debt* is docked."

"*Perpetual Debt*? That sounds like a boat that's going under."

"The only thing you have to fear is the captain, and then only if you don't perform precisely as ordered."

"And if I disobey?"

"You get flogged."

"Is that a promise? This is sounding more like fun every minute."

Kelly shook her head as if disgusted, and nudged Adam toward the door. "Get out of here. I've got work to do. I'll see you then – that is unless I see you earlier."

"I'll bring dinner then – that is unless I bring it earlier." Adam winked and kissed Kelly on the cheek. "See you."

"Oh, Adam, I almost forgot. I'm having dinner with Luther tomorrow night. I think he wants to tell me about Mr. X."

Adam briefly filled Kelly in on Bulldog's report. "I'm going to pay Mr. Fardy a visit. I believe he's Mr. X."

Kelly agreed. "Shall I call you after dinner tomorrow to compare notes?"

"Sorry, my phone will be out of order. You'll have to deliver the news in person."

Kelly grinned. "It was bound to happen. In this technological age running out of gas is too low tech. I'll see you then. Now scat before I call the bug man." Adam turned to leave and Kelly stopped him. "Adam, are you alright? You look really tired," she said.

"I'm fine. Lately, I have been having a little trouble sleeping that's all."

"Is there anything I can do?"

"No, no, I'm OK, really. Sometimes I wake up thinking that I stayed up all night talking. Just can't seem to get my mind out of overdrive, but it will pass." Adam looked around her office to change the subject. "Of course, if you want to have a quick session on the couch with me?" Kelly shook her head from side to side and shoved him out the door.

★

With pleasant thoughts of Kelly still tempting him, Adam aimed the big Chevy from Nebraska Avenue onto a side street. In the ethnically mixed neighborhood crowded with poor people, Adam found the address he wanted. Three old wooden buildings sat in a row like building blocks. Each contained eight apartments, four up, and four down. Fardy lived in the middle building.

Junky cars and trucks of various vintages, with two on concrete blocks, filled up the curbside parking in the front. Patches of grass passed for a lawn. Trash, in the form of newspapers, paper bags, and fast-food packages littered the area. Small children ran and played in the dirt while out-of-work adults sat around talking. Adam turned the corner, then took another left to follow the alley to the parking area behind the apartments.

The back, littered worse than the front, twice forced Adam to guide the Chevy around broken bottles as well as several potholes. He parked behind apartment number three, the downstairs unit where Clarence Fardy lived with his family. As Adam climbed from the car he grabbed his briefcase then grabbed his nose. The stench of urine, sun-baked garbage, and the smell of old oil embedded in the pitted asphalt assaulted him.

Near the dumpster, King Red lay sprawled out on a cardboard mattress under a lean-to of discarded furniture. He appeared dead. Adam watched until he detected movement, then avoiding the rubbish, Adam walked up and knocked on the back door. Someone there cared enough to sweep the concrete landing. The remains of a fall garden ran under the rear window.

He watched Marvel draw aside a curtain and peek out. She appeared concerned until she spotted his briefcase, then she opened the door. Adam said, "Hi, my name is Adam Eden. Are you Mrs. Fardy? I'd like to talk with Mr. Fardy please." Adam learned that Clarence had gone to meet his children at the bus stop and would return soon. Honest with Marvel, Adam convinced her that he believed Clarence was in trouble. Adam didn't elaborate, but a couple of magazines with his by-line and his book, convinced her to invite him in.

The furnishings were cheap and worn and the carpet threadbare with well-worn paths leading from room to room, but everything was orderly. It smelled of old carpet, and the walls desperately needed paint, but Adam noticed no excessive dust or dirt. Begonias on the window sill brightened up the kitchen. He turned down coffee but accepted a glass of Kool Aid, drinking half of it before setting the glass down. They sat at the kitchen table since the living room bulged with her four charges.

"Have you noticed anything odd about your husband's behavior? Does he seem depressed?"

"It, ah, it's been rough. We been apart so long you know, but Clarence seems OK." Marvel remembered the morning and smiled. "I think everything's gonna be all right now."

"What do you mean, now? Has he been having problems?"

"No, ah, well, it's just that we had trouble talking at first." Marvel twisted her hands. "You know what I mean? It seemed like Clarence wanted to be with me and the kids, but he didn't know how to go about it. Me neither, I guess. We both held back. Even when he had nightmares I didn't go to him, uh, he, we, we didn't, you know, sleep together at first."

"I understand, Mrs. Fardy. It takes time for trust to return." Adam saw Marvel's eyes tear up. He continued, "I'm glad things are working out for you, but I'm concerned. Can you tell me anything about the nightmares?"

"Humm, not really. Mostly I just hear Clarence moaning and groaning in his sleep. Once I heard him shout, 'Run, run, it's on fire!' and twice I heard him say the word 'cowboy' just clear as day."

"Does that mean anything to you?" Adam asked, but before Marvel could answer, she heard Clarence and the children breeze through the front door.

The children raced into the kitchen for Kool Aid and cookies, followed by Clarence whose face drained of color when he saw Adam. Adam stood up and Marvel introduced him as a writer. She appeared disturbed by Clarence's white face. She picked up one of Adam's magazines and said, "See kids, Mr. Eden is a real writer, and look here, he wrote this book, too. I just met him today."

"Mr. Fardy," said Adam, "I'd like to talk with you. Maybe we could go out back?"

Clarence didn't say a word. He just turned and walked out the back door. Adam glanced at Marvel, who looked concerned. "Don't worry, Mrs. Fardy. I'm here to help make sure you two make it."

Adam joined Clarence by the Chevy and noticed King Red sit up and take a drink. Adam explained his concern that Clarence planned to commit suicide, and was surprised to see the color return to the man's face. Like a good interviewer, Adam said his piece then shut up. The silence would force Clarence to respond.

Clarence fidgeted with the Chevy's antenna. Relieved to learn that the time had not come, he nevertheless had long suspected that Dr. Luther Huntley may be behind the misery, and felt relieved to have it confirmed. Otherwise, he remained frightened for his family. Unable to control the quiver in his voice, Clarence said, "Mr. Eden, I don't know what you're talking about. Yes, I killed Jean Huntley, and I will never forgive myself, but I am not going to commit suicide. All I want to do is take care of my family. They have missed out on too much already because of me. Besides, Dr. Huntley is a well-known man. A lot of people could have written that note."

"I believe you wrote it, Clarence, and I am going to report that to the police. There are people who can help you come to terms with your guilt. You would not be the first to commit suicide under the guise of proving life after death, but that's just a cop out and you know it. Do you really want to kill yourself, and leave your wife and those three beautiful kids with the guilt? You'll be dead, no more problems, but your selfish act will sentence your family to a lifetime of suffering. That is a horrible burden to saddle a person with, especially your own children."

Clarence had been rolling a cigarette butt around with his shoe, but jerked his head up at the word "saddle". Adam stared at Clarence until the man returned his attention to the cigarette. The butt became trapped in a crack in the asphalt, and Clarence looked again at Adam. "I told you. I am not your Mr. X. Now, please, please go away and leave us alone."

"All right, Clarence, I'll leave, but something stinks. You don't act suicidal, and you don't sound like a religious zealot, but you sure act frightened of something." Adam fished a business card from his shirt pocket. "Call me if you decide you want my help. Don't do this to your family, Clarence. Your wife and kids are innocent. They don't deserve such cruelty."

Adam backed up the Chevy and as he started forward, he spotted King Red studying him. The man's eyes were clear and alert, his skin too healthy. This man was no drunk. Adam glanced back at Clarence and noted that he too eyed the redhead. Again, fear gripped Clarence's blood-drained face. Adam saw the man wad up the card, hold it up for the drunk to see, and toss it aside before retreating to his apartment. Goosing the Chevy, the last thing Adam noticed was King Red grinning with a set of healthy teeth.

*

"Nigel, old boy, I do believe that we are the beneficiary of some very valuable information." He limped over and retrieved the tossed card. "Adam Eden, eh? An unusual name and vaguely familiar. Ah, of course, the writer. Writes a lot of stuff for the opinion columns in both the *St. Petersburg Times* and the *Tampa Bay Tribune*. May come in handy, but the real prize of course is the name of our dear benefactor, Dr. Luther Huntley."

Like for most jobs, Nigel didn't know who banked the payroll, a man called Dr. Justice, Nigel had been told. With Eden's story, however, it only made sense that this Dr. Huntley was the bank. The odd request for this job, a grieving widow killing her kids then herself, meant that there had to be a dead husband somewhere. Only the owl-eyed spouse appeared to be alive, scared shitless, but alive nevertheless.

Obviously his death was scheduled for the third of April since the fire could not take place before then. Nigel grinned. With benefit of the banker's name he could renegotiate the fee for this job to include a lifelong residual. He would have to be careful of course to ensure that he didn't become a target, but that obstacle could be overcome. Nigel limped back to his blind, gathered his belongings, and trudged back up the garbage-strewn alley the way he had come. He did not like Adam's scrutiny. A writer would be a skilled observer.

March 15, Wednesday

Careful not to look at the posters, Kyle parked near the abortion clinic to eat his lunch. His mother had dressed him in fresh clean clothes and taken him to Sunday School when he was little so Kyle knew about God. Kyle also knew about what God did to people who pissed Him off – Sodom and Gomorrah for instance. Kyle searched, but didn't spot the '57 Chevy.

Midway through the first greasy cheeseburger he noticed a young, attractive, short-haired blond idle by in an old maroon colored Mustang. Within the next ten minutes, she drove by two more times, and Kyle decided to follow her. She left the neighborhood and drove to Hyde Park. Kyle couldn't believe his luck when the girl parked her Mustang behind the familiar '57 Chevy.

Obviously she had been looking for the creep at the clinic, but he didn't show. Now she drives to his home with Kyle following as if God willed it so. But if she just wanted an abortion and her doctor ran late why would she know where he lived? Unless, of course, that creep is the one who got her pregnant in the first place. Nothing else made any sense. She had probably been his patient for something else, and he knocks the little whore up. A first-class jerk. Later, Kyle would stop when no cars were around and check the guy's mail for a name. No sense calling attention to himself by having a friend run the license number.

★

Gloria sat in her car for a while. Adam had told her about the director of the abortion clinic, about how nice she acted, and about her concern for her patients. He had also told Gloria about Kelly and how easy she was to talk with. In fact, Adam had spoken in great detail, and with a lot of animation about how Kelly impressed him, until Gloria realized that even Adam was unaware of his underlying feelings.

That pleased Gloria. She knew of his childhood friend and sweetheart, Francesca Rojas, but Adam would never talk about what happened. Bulldog wouldn't tell either. He said it was Adam's secret to reveal if he ever chose to do so. Now, Gloria hoped that Adam had found someone to help cure whatever hurt still pained him.

Gloria's problem loomed more immediate, however. She had been having dreams. Well, some were dreams, but others were visions. If you are wide awake, briefly shut your eyes and rub your temples to help get you through a tough accounting assignment, you're not asleep, right? Then, if a television turns on in your head, you're not dreaming, right? There is no sound, but a motion picture unaided by any part of you that you are aware of, superimposes itself across your mind screen. Like a star, the image shoots into your head from out of nowhere. It has to be a vision.

Is it an omniscient subconscious that is riding herd on an intellect stampeding in the wrong direction? Is it Universal Mind? Is it guardian angels? None of that matters really. The important thing is validity. Is the information received relevant to a part of one's life? If so, shouldn't the message be heeded?

Gloria desperately wanted to talk with Adam about her new experiences. He had always been her Father Confessor, her counselor. He had always answered her questions without beating around the bush, even questions about sex. She did not listen closely enough to his admonitions in that regard, however, and now she must endure the consequences.

Adam had always been available for Gloria except when it came to questions that leaped beyond the empirical. She knew that her biological mother had been a Spiritualist, but neither her father nor Adam would give details. "That psychic nonsense is just a crutch for people who don't want to face their problems," her brother would say, and he would hear no more.

Their mother believed in psychics and in mediums. Gloria knew that much. She had read that mediums were psychics who could also communicate with disincarnate beings, and Gloria believed that such people did exist. She didn't know why, but she did. She often fantasized that her mother would visit during sleep, especially when Gloria was little. The child would feel warm and snug, just like being embraced by a quilt on a cold night. Lately her dreams seemed especially real.

Her mother believed in faith healing, and doctors too, but she died of cancer. Adam blamed the faith healers, or as Adam called them, the fake healers, for his mother's death. He didn't talk about it much, but Gloria collected pieces of conversation and put them together. In fact, Adam hated anything that had to do with religion period. Gloria knew that much.

She also knew that she must not waver. Alternately depressed and sobbing about her condition, then euphoric and bubbly over the visions, Gloria's agitated state of mind made her difficult to rebuff. She had to make a decision soon, and she needed to share with Adam the images she experienced. She would not accept no for an answer. She alighted from the Mustang and marched up to Adam's door. Once greetings were expressed and they were seated, Gloria recited her lines.

"Adam, I am not here to argue. I love you, and I owe you more than I can ever repay. You have always supported me financially and psychologically. You march by my side, vanquishing my fears and encouraging my dreams. You have explained away my failures and cheered my successes. Now, I want to talk with you about some things that I don't understand, but things that to me seem a blessing, maybe a gift. I am going to visit a psychic."

Gloria watched Adam's face turn red and his mouth drop open. She quickly said, "If you say anything, anything at all, I am walking out right now." Adam started to speak, but his sister quickly stood up. "I mean it, Adam." Her plan appeared to be working. She had never seen him so puffed up, and would not have been surprised if blood spurted from his crimson cheeks. Nevertheless, he remained mum. She continued. "I want you to go with me, but if you refuse, I am going anyway. You think about it after you have a chance to calm down, then call me."

He started to speak, but Gloria restrained him with the palm of her hand. "I also wish to meet your friend, Kelly. I am leaving now. I love you. I hope you call." As she drove away, she giggled. Adam looked so funny, all pink and puffy. Such a one-sided conversation had to be a new experience for him. She glanced back and he was still rooted to the doorway, dumbfounded.

★

Kyle didn't understand why the girl had not stayed longer, but it pleased him that he now had more time to follow her. After Gloria pulled into her driveway and went inside, it tickled Kyle to think about leaving a note in the mailbox addressed to her father. It would read:

Dear Sir:

I know who has been snaking your daughter. He is a cocky little baby killer who drives like a maniac. Not to worry, though. After I cut off his offending hands, I am going to shoot the son-of-bitch.

Yours truly,

Moses

P.S. Your dirty little whore daughter is pregnant. I may have to smite her too.

★

Kelly had always enjoyed dining at The Treasure Cove, but now she regretted her selection. The restaurant was hot and the smoke stifling. Every scrape of silverware across china, every scrap of conversation, every clink and bang of the busboys clearing tables joined into a relentless annoying attack on her nerves. Even the occasional laughter, although gay as it should be, seemed ominous as if generated from the sound track of a B-grade horror movie. Never this way before, it had to be the company. She thought of Adam and wondered if the reverse were true. Would being with Adam make spinach taste better? She smiled.

"What's funny?" asked Dr. Huntley. "Kelly, what's so amusing?"

"What? I'm sorry. Listen, thanks for dinner, but I really do need to run."

"But you haven't had dessert. I seem to remember that you love the chocolate mousse here."

"Hmm, yes, but I have a trying schedule tomorrow. I need to do a little homework tonight."

"I don't understand why you waste yourself—" Dr. Huntley started, but stopped when anger flashed across Kelly's face. "Of course, I understand," he said.

Once outside, Dr. Huntley insisted on walking Kelly to her car. "Remember how you, your Aunt Jean, and I used to travel? I'm going to Paris in April. Why don't you come with me?"

"Thank you, but I really can't get away. More people need help now than I can reach as it is."

With his hand on her arm, Dr. Huntley stopped Kelly and moved in closer. He brushed her hair behind her ear. "You are a beautiful woman, Kelly. You resemble your Aunt Jean more than your own mother."

Kelly backed away. "Thank you. My Bronco is just down there." She nodded her head. "I'll be fine now."

He held onto her arm. "Kelly, didn't we have fun when you were young? Remember how you used to enjoy staying with us when you were a child? The delight you took from opening gifts? I want to take care of you again the way I took care of you then."

"Luther, when I was very little life with you and Aunt Jean was special, but I'm grown now. That time is only a memory. What you want from me now, I can't give. I'm sorry."

Luther tightened his grip on Kelly's arm. "Your Aunt Jean would want us to be friends. She never got over how you treated us!"

"How I treated you? What do you mean?"

"I had to explain to her how you tried to tempt me. I understood that you were just a young girl blossoming into a woman, that it didn't mean anything, but it hurt her deeply that you avoided us."

"You what? You insufferable ass! You know it was you who wouldn't keep his hands to himself. You thought I would say something didn't you? That's why you told Aunt Jean that lie."

Luther released Kelly's arm. "I'm sorry, Kelly, I'm sorry. I didn't really tell her that. I just said that because you hurt me. There's been no one since Jean, don't you see that? Don't you see how we are meant for each other?" He gripped each of Kelly's shoulders and leaned in to kiss her.

"Stop it!" she said, raising her two arms between his and

thrusting outward with lightening intensity. It broke his grip.

Surprised, he studied his hands as if they had somehow stopped working. He glared at Kelly. "I'm not good enough for you, but you wallow like a sow with that weasel Adam Eden after just bumping into him."

Balling her fists, Kelly asked, "How do you know that? Have you been spying on me?"

"Uh, no, no, of course not. I, I just saw you two at lunch through the window at The Greek's Place. Jean, ah, Kelly, I'm sorry. Please, forgive me. It's just that you remind me so much of Jean."

Kelly glared at Dr. Huntley. The anger that she thought she had released years ago broke free from somewhere deep in her mind where she had anchored it. The anger that she had been combating all evening as Dr. Huntley fussed and fawned over her rushed to the surface. She took a step back. If he touched her again she would explode. Kelly didn't want that.

Clenching her teeth, she glared at the man who had once been her favorite uncle. "How did you know Adam and I bumped into each other? How did you know I went home with him?" Although constructed as questions, Kelly's words, paced evenly and equally accented, left no doubt that they were demands.

"Ah, the guard, the guard in the lobby told me about your mishap. Eden was late. I asked the guard to let me know when Eden arrived. He is easy to recognize, you know. And I didn't say anything about you going to his home. I didn't know. I made a careless remark for which I am deeply sorry. Can't we start over? All I want to do is make you happy."

"Then stay away from me. If you ever touch me again, I'll break your body into so many pieces the devil won't find enough of you to burn."

★

Thirty minutes later, Kelly's anger still smoldered when Adam invited her in. "Uh oh, looks like your dinner with Lucifer was overcooked," Adam said.

Plopping down on the sofa, Kelly said, "I can't talk about it yet," but continued to talk anyway. "I am so angry, Adam." She picked at a button on a throw cushion. "What an asshole. Why are there assholes in the world?"

Adam handed her a brandy, walked behind the sofa and started slowly massaging Kelly's temples, neck and shoulders. His fingers were strong and experienced. She moaned and began to relax. "It's a religious thing," Adam said. "In His infinite wisdom, God decreed that all souls must meet and learn to deal with at least fourteen and one-half assholes during their sojourn on earth. Like exercise builds the muscles, friction shapes the soul, that sort of thing, you see. However, God being all good, He began to feel a little guilty about what Eve referred to as His tendency to overreact. 'Cruel and unjust punishment,' I believe she said after her disastrous encounter with the grand dragon of assholes, Lucifer. As an incentive to keep man from switching allegiance to a golden calf, God decreed that in the end, all assholes will be wiped out."

Kelly shook her head as if disgusted, then reached up and took his hand. She enjoyed another sip of brandy and closed her eyes to savor the sweet, thick taste. As soothing warmth accompanied the liquid to her stomach, she got up and led Adam to the bedroom. Slowly, between sips of brandy, they undressed each other. They touched, they kissed, they caressed. Between sips of brandy, they took their time.

Afterwards, Adam held her tightly, methodically massaging her head, her back and her thighs until she climbed down from the peak. He guided Kelly to lie on her stomach, as he positioned himself cross-legged next to her. Lightly, he ran his fingernails up and down her moist back, encouraging her to relax and drift off to sleep. Adam admired her for a few moments, then returned to his work in the bedroom that served as his office.

Almost an hour later, Kelly found him. She wore his maroon and green paisley bathrobe. It had been a gift, his taste wasn't that developed. Adam stared at her unkempt hair, matted in places, and at her face bare of makeup. The woman was beautiful when she shouldn't have been. "How much do I owe you for that?" she asked.

"A lot of patience. At least fourteen and a half tons."

"That's within my budget. I'll even throw in a cup of cof— a cup of tea. Want one?"

"I'll show you where everything is."

They headed for the kitchen. Kelly asked, "By the way, what happened here? Did your housekeeper return from vacation?"

Adam surveyed the living room that he had cleaned up earlier. "No, I figured you might appreciate a little less clutter."

"I'm surprised that you recognize clutter, Mr. Eden."

"I'll admit that once I finish with a magazine or paper it no longer holds much interest for me."

"Well, it's more comfortable, but I appreciate the fact that you thought of it more than the deed itself."

After the kettle whistled, Adam asked about the dinner with Huntley. Kelly said, "He repeated what he had told you about Mr. X, but what made it so unbearable was his insufferable elation, his self-possession." Kelly tapped her spoon against the saucer, repeating one of the sounds that had so annoyed her earlier in the restaurant. She sipped her beverage. She could begin to enjoy tea and cream. "He's over the edge, Adam. In Luther's mind, I am Aunt Jean's surrogate. He's obsessed by me." Kelly looked up at Adam. "He knows about Monday."

"Knows what about Monday?"

"Everything," she said, and then smiled. "You almost maiming me to trick me into a lunch date, and the fact that you forced me to come here with you." With her foot, she rubbed Adam's leg under the table. With his mouth open, Adam just stared at her. "I'm just joking, you jerk. You know I wasn't forced," she said.

"No, no, it's not that. How does he know?"

"I inadvertently told him I came here with you. He caught me off guard with some snide remark made because he spotted us having lunch together."

"Oh, I thought he may be having you followed," Adam said. He proceeded to tell Kelly what he had learned from Bulldog about Clarence's time in prison, and his religious conversion. He told her about the visit to Fardy's and about how likeable Mrs. Fardy was as well as how scared Clarence had been. Then Adam described the redhead in the alley.

"Kelly, that guy didn't look like a bum or homeless person. He was watching Fardy's place for some reason, and Clarence knew it. He made it a point to let that guy know that I wasn't welcome. Later, Bulldog personally drove over to check the creep out, but he had skipped with no trace.

"Bulldog questioned the residents, but people in that area aren't cooperative with the police, it can get them killed. He questioned Fardy, who said he had never seen the guy before, but Mrs. Fardy spoke up and claimed that she had seen him at least three times. She was very concerned, because she didn't think that he came from the streets either. Fardy just sat there ashened-faced, silent as a spent volcano."

"But why? If Clarence Fardy is not suicidal, why is he being followed, and who wrote the note?" asked Kelly.

"Getting out of prison and starting over is tough. Clarence may be depressed. I think Huntley is paying Fardy, who sees this as a way to financially take care of his family."

"Paying him? To kill himself?"

"Yes. Bulldog thinks so too, now. The police are going to watch Fardy and his neighborhood closely, and Bulldog is going to question Huntley about the note. The hope is that the increased interest will force a crack somewhere and turn up some hard evidence."

"So, we just wait?"

"My meeting you and learning about Fardy didn't figure in Huntley's plans. If that guy in the alley was no bum, then Huntley knows by now that I visited Clarence, as have the police. I think he's a mad man and mad men get reckless when they see control slipping away. He's bound to get nervous and make a mistake."

Adam poured himself another cup of tea. Kelly declined. "Huntley disliked me from the beginning, and judging by his fixation on you, I would say that by now his urine has reached boiling point. I'm going to see him again and turn up the heat." As Adam drank his tea, they were silent for a while.

Kelly placed her hand on Adam's arm. "How's Gloria?" she asked.

"Not good." Adam slowly shook his head. "Craziest thing. This afternoon I talked with her, well, actually I only listened. She said that she'd like to talk with you, but, and I'm embarrassed to say this, she wants to visit a psychic. Can you believe it?" Adam looked at Kelly, but she said nothing. "I mean, you're a psychologist, you could set her straight."

"Adam, why are you so against psychics?"

"You're not?" he said, throwing up his hands. "You mean you believe all that palm-reading tripe? My God, Kelly, you're a psychologist!" With a lot of racket, Adam slid his chair back, stood up, and started pacing. He gesticulated wildly and talked so fast he was difficult to follow, but Kelly just sat there grinning at him. With no words bouncing back to fuel his argument, he finally caught on. "I just called you stupid, huh?" he said.

"Oh, the little man is smarter than he sounds. It's obviously a subject you feel very strongly about. You still haven't answered my question."

After some thought he decided against mentioning his mother, and said, "A few years back, a friend, a poor simple woman whose son committed suicide, got hooked on a con artist who billed herself as Phoenix. My friend got angry when I became involved. I told her that talking to the dead is nonsense. I tried to help her.

"She warned this Phoenix character who then immediately claimed to receive transmissions from the ether that I was to be avoided at all costs. Phoenix basically told my friend that I was on God's shortlist of bad guys just below the antichrist. I could do nothing after that, but I haven't forgotten. One day I'll get another crack at Phoenix."

"Strong belief in anything can make one gullible, Adam, but conversely, strong disbelief can be equally blinding. When I was in undergraduate school I took a course in parapsychology. To do research, several of us visited a psychic. No one, absolutely no one of my friends was as skeptical as I. The psychic confirmed this, which would have been obvious to any observant person, and told me very little else. However, she did tell me that I would see a sock in a tree. My girlfriends and I laughed over that one all the way back to the dorm.

"That weekend, several of us visited Disney World. We were riding the People Mover in Tomorrow Land. Suddenly, while moving along above the buildings and trees, I spot a white sock draped across the branch of a tree. It reminded me of a Dali painting. I couldn't believe it. No one else saw it until I started shouting, and pointing, and grabbing them." Bewildered, Adam sat back down.

Kelly placed her hand on his arm. "I have an idea. I have a dear friend, a Spiritualist, whom we can visit in Cassadaga over near Daytona. This will give Gloria and me a chance to become acquainted. Also, this will show your support, that is very important to Gloria right now. It will give the three of us a chance to talk, for you and me to listen really, and that is what Gloria needs most right now." Kelly took Adam's hand. "I believe this will be beneficial for us all," she said. "Will you trust me?"

Adam admired Kelly sitting next to him in his bathrobe. A disturbingly domestic scene, but he had never met a woman so easy to get to know, so comfortable to be with. He had never met a person with less guile. The psychic nonsense was a problem, but now he could solve that for Kelly and Gloria at the same time. Adam knew of Cassadaga from his mother: it was a Spiritualist camp. "Yes," Adam said. This time Adam led Kelly to the bedroom.

As they crawled into bed, Kelly asked, "Fourteen and one-half A-holes, huh? Where does the half come in?"

"Simple, that one is only an asshole when he's awake."

March 16, Thursday

There was a faint knock on the door and Marvel answered it. A small neighborhood boy said, "Man at the store told me to give this to your husband. Gave me five dollars, see?" He flashed the five then took off.

Marvel looked at the card. It read, "Is your fire insurance up to date?" A phone number followed, along with the words, "Call immediately." As Clarence walked into the living room, Marvel laughed.

"What's so funny?"

Marvel held the card up. "Is your fire insurance up to date? Call immediately." Clarence froze and his mouth dropped open. Marvel continued, "That's all that's on this card other than a phone number." She turned it over. "And this awful picture. I sure ain't interested." She passed the kitchen garbage, and tossed the card.

Speaking louder, she said, "It shows some poor man watching his house burn, and there's four bodies laying in his yard covered with sheets. There should be a law. Besides, ain't nobody in this neighborhood can afford insurance anyway." Still shaking her head, Marvel started cleaning up lunch. Her four charges were down for their naps.

Clarence slipped into the kitchen, and poured himself a glass of Kool Aid while he watched Marvel from the corner of his eye. When she kneeled down to put away the sandwich meat, Clarence quickly leaned over and fished the postcard from the trashcan. He stuffed it in his pocket and retreated to the bathroom.

Marvel was right. The card was brief and the picture grim, but unlike his wife, Clarence recognized the deadly significance. He returned to the kitchen, and told Marvel that he wanted to take a walk unless there was something that he could do for her. Without looking around, she indicated no by shaking her head. Clarence was thankful that Marvel had been busy. Otherwise she would have noticed how he shook, and how utterly white he had turned. Clarence rushed outside.

Marvel dumped the remains of lunch in the trash. It wasn't until she piled the dishes in the sink that it struck her. She walked back over to the garbage can and looked. She reached in and shifted the napkins and sandwich remains around. The horrible postcard had disappeared. At first she couldn't reason why Clarence would be interested in insurance, then it struck her.

Clarence had not been convincing when he waved off the suicide story that writer fellow kept pushing, and then later that detective. Two men in one day saying Clarence had a problem. Still, seeing the changes in Clarence, Marvel had accepted his denial. Now, behind her back, he ups and digs an insurance card from the trash. If he was going to commit suicide maybe he wanted insurance for his family... She couldn't figure how Clarence hoped to pay for a policy, but she had to be right, especially since Clarence just up and took a walk out of the clear blue. As soon as he returned, she would find out for certain. She just got him and more back. She would not lose him again.

★

Clarence pulled out the card and hurried up to a pay phone hanging on the outside wall of the nearest convenience store. He dug in his pocket for a quarter, and jumped when startled by a high-pitched voice behind him. "Hey mister, you looking for fire insurance?" a female voice asked. Instinctively, Clarence continued to face the wall. "Hey mister, can't you hear? I said, are you looking for fire insurance? I see you got the card."

Clarence slowly turned around. The voice belonged to a young black woman, maybe twenty, hair styled in cornrows. She struggled with a chubby baby boy resting on her hip. "Yes," he said.

"Then point or something to act like you giving me directions. The man say you probably being watched."

Clarence looked around and pointed a couple times. "What man? Where?"

"You supposed to go in the store and out the back door. Climb the wall to the alley, and the man's waiting there. You supposed to get in the back seat and lay down. That's all I know." She turned and walked off in the direction Clarence had pointed.

Clarence watched her switch the child to her other hip, then he entered the store. He lingered in front of the magazine section and checked to see if anyone followed him in. Several people, men and women, were hanging around outside, but no one approached the store. Clarence worked his way to the cooler section and slipped into the foul smelling storeroom that reeked of cleaning supplies, old produce, and a sour mop. He spotted the back door.

Once outside, he climbed the dumpster to scale the gray concrete-block barrier. The six-foot drop to the alley proved too much, however, so Clarence hung on while sliding his feet over the edge. His grip weakened, and he scraped his hands as he fell. It drew blood, but he was too scared to care. He fumbled with the rear door of the Buick, but finally managed to crawl inside.

"Keep down until I tell you otherwise," said Lee, and not another word was spoken until Lee ordered Clarence out forty minutes later in the middle of a dusty orange grove. He sat up and looked out. Leaning on his Mercedes, arms akimbo, his tan Bally loafers sinking into the fine Florida dirt, Dr. Huntley glared back.

Strangely calm, reconciled to his fate now that the moment had arrived, Clarence slid out of the car. He closed the door, and waited. Dr. Huntley stared, rarely blinking as was his habit, but Clarence didn't avert his gaze. "You don't appear surprised," said Dr. Huntley.

Clarence shrugged. "I always believed you were behind everything. Besides, that redheaded man in the alley has already told you that Mr. Eden came to my house, and then that detective. I didn't tell them anything, though."

Dr. Huntley blinked and glanced around at Lee, but read nothing on the man's face. Staring at Clarence again, and angry at his composure, Dr. Huntley said, "You don't seem concerned. Maybe you believe this is a joke?"

"I know this is serious. I've thought about the police, I've thought about taking my family and running. I even thought about trying to kill you, all the while knowing that I could not." Dr. Huntley raised his eyebrows but didn't say anything. Clarence continued, "I only care about my family, and the only way that I know for certain that my wife and kids will be safe is for me to trust the will of God. I will do exactly as you say. Please don't hurt my family."

Dr. Huntley clapped his hands. "Bravo, bravo. Did that midget-brained degenerate Adam Eden write that speech for you? You don't sound like the pickled-brained drunk I heard in court."

"You hate Clarence Fardy, the man who killed your wife, and want him dead. You have already killed him. I live with the guilt, but my sins have been forgiven."

Dr. Huntley marched forward and slapped Clarence so hard he fell back against the Buick. His glasses flew off and landed at Lee's feet. Warm blood trickled down his chin. "You impertinent piece of garbage," shouted Dr. Huntley. "The man who killed my wife is standing in your shoes even if you have bought into that Christian poppycock of absolved guilt. Do you believe God is going to save you? Is that why you stand there feigning condescension?"

Clarence said nothing. Dr. Huntley slapped him again, but Clarence suffered in silence, his expression blank. Enraged, Dr. Huntley slapped and backhanded Clarence half a dozen more times while Clarence reeled under the onslaught. Only the Buick kept him on his feet. He said nothing. He never even clenched his fist, although blood flowed heavily from his nose.

Dr. Huntley, his beady green eyes ablaze with anger, screamed, "You insufferable little leech, you don't even have the backbone to fight back." Dr. Huntley breathed deeply and shook his head, and spoke more to himself than to Clarence. "Unless men such as I reverse the slide, you are America's sad destiny."

Clarence slowly collected himself from the car fender and licked the warm salty blood from his lips. Quietly, but with a steady voice, he said, "I am sorry that I killed your wife. I am sorry that I am the cause for your anger. My death will not bring you peace, but the only sure way to protect my family is to do as you say. I will give you no reason to hurt them."

Dr. Huntley turned abruptly and pulled a Smith & Wesson .38 caliber revolver from his Mercedes. With Clarence watching, he dumped the cylinder, catching the bullets in his left hand. Locking his eyes with Clarence's, and pleased to see the fear, Dr. Huntley slowly reloaded the weapon. He brought the pistol up and pointed it at Clarence's face. His pleasure obvious, he cocked the weapon. When Clarence closed his eyes, Dr. Huntley fired.

Clarence grunted and stepped back. When he opened his eyes, he saw that the pistol was pointed down the row of orange trees. Dr. Huntley fired again, and twenty yards away, dirt flew up when the bullet burrowed into the dry, powder-like soil. Clarence's heart pounded in his throat. He tried to swallow, but could not. He spit blood on the ground.

Dr. Huntley grabbed the pistol by its barrel and extended the handle toward Clarence. "Take it. Take it now." Clarence didn't move. "I said, take it now." Gingerly, Clarence reached out and took the weapon. "As you just witnessed, it's loaded," said Dr. Huntley. "You may shoot me if you wish."

Clarence stared, first at the gun and then at Dr. Huntley, who said, "Go ahead, pull the trigger. You admitted that you have already thought about it." Clarence looked again at the gun then let it drop to the ground.

"You made the wise decision, Clarence. I wanted you to understand that even if I die, you and your family will die too. Do as I say, and only you will depart this world. You killed my wife so it is only justice that you kill yourself. If you had pulled the trigger, my last thought would have been that now you would know the pain of seeing your family burn to death. My dying expression would have been a smile.

"You will do exactly as I say, when I say, or your family burns." Clarence flinched at the word. "So the Christian soldier is not as brave as he would have me believe." Dr. Huntley smiled with satisfaction. "When I contact you again, you will be wired with what will appear to be dynamite, to ensure that the police don't interrupt your plans.

"You, your meddling Mr. Eden, and I will drive to the intersection where you murdered my wife. We will accompany you at your request. You will convince Eden and the world that you are in control, that the plan is yours. With the world watching, you will douse yourself with gasoline, strike a match, and end your miserable existence." Dr. Huntley grinned sadistically. "You will correct the court's oversight, and your selfless demise will be a beacon for others to follow."

Dr. Huntley handed Clarence a copy of the suicide note, but Clarence couldn't read it. He couldn't even see well enough to find his glasses. Lee obliged, and Dr. Huntley didn't bother concealing his delight over the alarm that registered on Clarence's face as he read. Shocked by the revelation, Clarence stared in horror as Dr. Huntley took the note back. Dr. Huntley continued. "Your message to the psychic will be, 'Yea, though I walk through the valley of the shadow of death.' The message which Mr. Eden and I will open together, will read, 'I will fear no evil, for God walks with me.'"

"But why? How does this—" Horrified, Clarence could only stare at Dr. Huntley.

"Because with enough publicity, hundreds of your ilk will follow you to God's embrace."

"But only I killed your wife."

"Society killed my wife. A society that has allowed parasites such as you to breed. You can go to your death pleased that for the first time in your miserable existence you are contributing to mankind rather than feeding at the community trough. If this nation is to survive, it must rid itself of beggars."

With the toe of his shoe, Clarence kicked at a dirt clod and watched it crumble. Without looking up, he said, "Beggars like my family?"

"What? Uh? Oh, your family will be safe as long as you do as you are told." Dr. Huntley paused and collected his thoughts. "Actually, they will probably benefit. There will be a lot of financial offers for interviews. Someone will probably write a book about your tortured life, your miraculous redemption and your selfless suicide to prove life after death. Ironically, you will be more successful dead than alive. Your family will be better off without you than with you." Dr. Huntley stared at Clarence, and asked, "Don't you agree?" but Clarence said nothing.

"The important thing is that I know a man who likes to enjoy little girls, and little boys too, before he burns them. If you want to protect your children, you will do as you are told. Everything is in place. If I am murdered, if I am arrested, you will die anyway, but your family will die first. It's not God's will but mine that should concern you. You do understand?"

"Yes," Clarence whispered.

"Make sure he is watched closely, Lee," Dr. Huntley said, pleased with Clarence's submission. "Any hint of rebellion, grab his daughter for security."

Lee picked up the revolver, and offered it to Dr. Huntley. "Clean it," Dr. Huntley said. He crawled into his Mercedes and sped away, showering Lee and Clarence with dust.

He slid a CD recording of Beethoven's Violin Concerto in D Major into the player and began to relax. Would the world ever again see the master's equal? Very doubtful unless men such as Dr. Huntley checked the incessant breeding of the inferior masses. More men of reason must shake free of their fear and join the cause. It was war, after all, and one needed to be prepared to die. If necessary Dr. Huntley would, but a man worthy of the adjective intelligent need not worry about that consequence.

Unconsciously tapping his fingers in time with the music, Dr. Huntley grinned. He imagined the scene: thousands of mesmerized TV viewers, a host of anxious police, and a flock of pesky reporters. Dr. Huntley would appear to be fighting to save the life of a distraught Clarence Fardy, while in actuality, he would be killing the man. The perfect murder.

The only catch; the puppeteer must not fear the fate planned for the puppet. But there was no danger, really, the weak such as Fardy would never have the guts to fight back. Dr. Huntley concentrated on Beethoven's mastery of composition. The maestro manipulated the strings of his violin in a faithful performance of the piece as Beethoven had so beautifully composed it. Like a puppeteer, the maestro controlled his instrument. For it to be otherwise would be disastrous. Mishandled, the poor puppeteer would be the one to flip, flop, and die.

★

Clarence lay in the back seat of Lee's car watching the power poles fly by. At the speed the car was traveling, the poles reminded Clarence of the bars on his prison cell. He labored over the conflict of saving his family, and how his death possibly would be used to encourage others to die. He didn't consider himself an Abraham or a Job. Still, like the two biblical icons, Clarence didn't doubt that faith, trust in God's will, was the only path to follow. What did he know of power and money?

He had been frightened at first, and that fear remained, but added to it was the sorrow Clarence felt for his tormentor. Clarence understood hate. All his life he had gingerly made his way along webs of hate spun daily, first by his bitter mother and later by fellow inmates. Now, however, Clarence fought his troubles armed with the vision of love, while Dr. Huntley faced his burden with the blindness of hatred. Clarence said a silent prayer for his tormentor.

Later, Lee pulled into a Stop 'N' Shop for cigarettes. Before returning to the car he already had a Camel burning, and he savored a couple of deep drags before entering traffic again. He struggled with his thoughts and had forgotten about Clarence until he spoke. "I know you, don't I?" asked Clarence.

"Huh?" Lee checked the back seat through the rear view mirror. "Maybe," he said.

"You were in prison when I first went in. You were a policeman who killed a drug dealer for selling to your daughter."

"Something like that," Lee said, exhaling smoke. He had been having troubling thoughts. When first contacted by Dr. Huntley, it seemed simple enough. Revenge. Fardy killed Huntley's wife, so Fardy dies. You do what the courts will no longer do. Even the thought of multiple suicides as predicted by Huntley didn't bother Lee. If people wanted to pop themselves that was their business.

Feel Good Freddy, the drug dealer, had been a product of the system. Culling the losers seemed a good idea. Huntley's comments about the little girl surprised Lee though, because he never figured the threat to kill Fardy's family a real one. If Fardy didn't play along, Lee figured that Huntley would take Fardy out and be done with it. Fardy's little girl? That bothered Lee.

"You came to Bible study a couple times didn't you?" Clarence asked.

Although usually quiet, after a silence, Lee said, "Once. Watched you face down that bonehead Malone. He was throwing his weight around as usual, picking on that Brantley kid. You confronted him. Anybody else would have met with a bad accident. I watched Malone study you, and I watched you stand there nonthreatening and, it seemed to me, unafraid. Something about you made him walk away, and the next thing I know you become his teacher. Your power interested me."

"It's God's power; man is only the instrument."

"The preacher asked the group to comment on Job. Dullsville, until you stood up." Lee took a pull on his smoke. "Remember what you said?"

Clarence thought a minute. His face still stung, and his swollen lips throbbed. As he considered his answer, the pain faded. "Each of us is a part of God but free will allows us to mistakenly believe that we are separate. It's like amnesia. You don't know who you are so you begin building a new life. Within you there remains a light. Every time you acknowledge the light it brightens. Each time you deny the light it dims. The individual controls the degree of light, but it can never be extinguished."

"If you say so." Lee lit another smoke with the one he was about to extinguish. He picked tobacco flakes from his lip.

"The important lesson in Job is that even God can't destroy the light. He is the light. The light is faith. A man may choose to nurture faith until it produces fruit to feed the man, or he may choose to ignore faith and continue to be spiritually malnourished."

"Yeah, yeah, I get it, but before, in prison I mean, you said something about power?"

"Power?" Clarence unconsciously ran his fingers over his purple lips. He still bled a little. "Well, faith is power. Even God can't kill a man's faith because faith is that speck of light. As I said, that spark may grow to illuminate every particle of a man's being, or the individual may deny it and live in darkness. No matter what emotional, material, or physical loss a man may suffer, in gravity, it can never equal the loss of faith."

"Yeah, that's what you said. I like the part about faith being strong as God. Maybe that's all God is anyway. Maybe belief is power. You know, positive thinking."

"No, God is the generator, and faith is a part of God like electricity is part of a power plant," Clarence said, although he had difficulty talking. "We can't see electricity, but it's there for each of us to use – for good or evil actually, depending upon our heart. Jesus became the Son when His faith took Him through death to resurrection, the reward for each man who grows to fully recognize his oneness with God."

"Whoa, Fardy. I may not be a Bible toter, but even I know that Jesus is the Son of God. Course, ain't no virgin ever dropped a kid."

"Physical laws change with belief, that's why we have miracles. Jesus was a man who nurtured faith. He believed and allowed every particle of His being to become irradiated with faith, the Holy Ghost, the Spirit of God. We are all one within God, but we see ourselves as fallen. We see ourselves as separate. Jesus taught that He and the Father are one, and that we are in Him just as He is in the Father. Jesus knows that He is truly the Son of God, but then so are you, and so am I."

Lee exhaled smoke. This Fardy sure was different than the one Lee remembered. This little guy could talk, but Lee didn't pretend to understand what the hell he was talking about. Still, Fardy must know something, though, because for some reason, the little mouse sure learned to roar.

"Whatever, Fardy. I admit I thought a lot about what you said, about power I mean," allowed Lee, shrugging his shoulders to indicate that he had reached no conclusions, "but I try to keep my thoughts on more practical stuff. Tell me about the redhead you saw."

"You mean the man who's been watching me?"

"Yeah, him."

"I don't understand."

"Uh, well, he's supposed to watch, not be seen."

"Oh. Marvel, uh, my wife, noticed him first. He's dressed as a street person, and he walks with a limp. Marvel's always been very watchful of our kids. I guess she had to be because I was never much help." Clarence paused briefly, and lightly ran his fingers over his eye. It might turn black. "Now I guess I never will be."

"Well, nothing personal, Fardy, but you screwed the golden goose. Now you have to pay."

★

After dropping Clarence at a bus stop and giving him the fare, Lee stopped at a rundown hotel to see Cowboy. "Got a job for you, Cowboy. I want to know who else is watching Fardy. Some pecker head who dresses like a street person and walks with a limp has been nosing around."

Lee noticed Cowboy's eyes roll slightly back. For a man like Cowboy the first instinct is to lie, to extend his plate for a bigger helping. That didn't surprise Lee. Information always has value. "Do you know something?" asked Lee, his eyes cold and threatening. Given time to think, Cowboy would remember that some people you pushed and some you didn't.

Cowboy said, "Don't have to hit the trail on this one. Your man's known as King Red. He's a torch." Cowboy waited briefly, but Lee said nothing. "He's not yours?" Cowboy asked. "That don't make sense. If torching Fardy's family is the threat to keep Fardy in line, you got a torch right? Why would there be a second man?" Lee looked at Cowboy, and let him know that questions weren't welcome.

"Thanks," was all Lee said, and he turned to leave.

"Wait, a funny thing happened Tuesday you ought to know about. Your man Eden went to an abortion clinic. While he's in there some hombre, a big kid, takes Eden's tag number. When Eden hits the trail, the kid follows him."

"Where did Eden go?"

"Tampa General Hospital, and that's where the kid ups and takes another trail."

"Maybe Eden's working on an article about abortion. Course, he could have visited the hospital for another reason. Did you follow him inside?"

"Went to visit the woman he porked on Monday, and again last night. The same looker who visited Dr. Huntley."

"Christ, she was at Eden's last night?"

"Yeah. Got there around nine thirty, and stayed the night. For a runt he must be able to lick his eyebrows, huh?"

Lee didn't comment. "Be careful and let me know if you see the kid again."

"Already have. He showed up at Eden's house yesterday, following a short-haired blond driving a Mustang."

Lee nodded and left. Cowboy returned to reading *The Left-Handed Gun*. He had difficulty concentrating, however. King Red watching Fardy and Lee not knowing about it, and then the kid trailing Eden. None of it made sense. Still, Lee was a man to be trusted as long as you did right by him.

Unlike a common thief or con, Lee wasn't amoral, and he wasn't mean. He didn't fear violence coming or going, but he would use it when it fit the circumstances. Even prison had not robbed him of his basic integrity. The man may be operating outside the law, but basically he remained a white hat. Cowboy liked working for white hats. Working for men of character always gave a man without any an advantage. He would worry only if Lee told him to.

★

Clarence climbed onto the bus, and from the stares of the driver and passengers, he realized that he probably looked awful. The driver said, "Hey, man, you all right? Looks like somebody worked you over good."

Clarence dropped in the fare and examined his reflection in the driver's rear view mirror. The left eye was a deep purple, as were his swollen lips. His cheeks ached and bore several cuts caused by Dr. Huntley's jeweled ring. Blood lay caked on his chin. "I'll be all right," Clarence said as he searched for a seat.

He arrived home hoping to sneak in and at least wash away the blood before Marvel spotted him. He heard the children laughing in the living room about something on TV so he circled around back and peeked in the window. Marvel stood at the sink cutting up a chicken for dinner. Clarence breathed deeply and opened the door. Marvel looked around, and shouted, "Oh, my God, Clarence, what happened?" She cleaned her hands on her apron and rushed to aid him.

"I'm all right," he said. Marvel led him to a chair. "Really, I am," Clarence said. "A guy wanted to rob me and got mad when I didn't have anything for him to take."

"Did you call the police? I've been worried sick. You left here and you been gone all – wait a minute! I ain't sure what's going on, but you left here with that insurance card, and now you come back all beat up." She put her hands on her shapeless hips. "Clarence Fardy, I want to know what's going on right now."

Clarence looked down at the floor and struggled to think of something. He remembered one of the many schemes that he had learned about in prison. "It's two guys from prison. They want to start a mission with me as the minister. They will con donations to run the program, but most of the money they will pocket. All they want from me is to add a religious appearance. They tried to convince me that although they will profit, I will be doing good by ministering to the homeless and poor. That's supposed to make the crime OK. When I refused, they beat me up."

Marvel hadn't changed positions. "What is this business with that awful postcard?"

"Uh, just a signal that they wanted me to call them. They've been planning this for a long time, waiting for me to get out." Marvel shook her head. "Marvel, please, I need a bath and rest – and maybe an aspirin. There's nothing more to this. I wouldn't cooperate so they will do something else. They'll probably be back in jail soon so there's nothing to worry about."

Marvel sat down at the table and took his hand in both of hers. "Clarence, we need to call the police."

Clarence studied his wife before responding. He needed the time to search for the right answer for her and for himself. "Marvel, God gave man intelligence so that he could help himself, but sometimes, no matter how much you twist and squirm, you can't find a way out. You turn it over to God. As He tested the faith of Abraham and Job, so is the faith of each man tested according to the light that he has been shown. I committed the greatest of sins, but Jesus lifted the burden from me. He gave me a voice, and enabled me to minister to others as greatly in need as I. I owe my new life to Jesus."

Clarence took his free hand and clasped Marvel's as she continued to squeeze the hand that she held. "Please believe that I know the will of God to be right and just. Never question it. Accept it always, and you will be rewarded. These are confused men who want me to do their bidding. The police can't protect me from them, and I have turned my problem over to God. I accept His judgement. I once failed you and our children. I once failed God. I won't fail either of you again."

Marvel wiped tears from her eyes. "How do you know what God's will is? Nobody knows that."

"I always had a hole in me that I couldn't fill up. A part of me was always unhappy until I gave my life to God." Clarence looked up at Marvel. "If I wasn't doing God's will, I wouldn't be happy."

"So just 'cause you think you know God's will, you are happy with men beating you up? Are you happy being poor too?"

"I mean I am happy with myself. Besides, is it better to live without hope? Is it not preferable to be poor and happy than to be poor and bitter?" Clarence stood up. "I am going to bathe now."

Marvel stared out the window. She had trained herself to see only the beauty that surrounded her. She loved the determined pink and white periwinkles that established themselves no matter how lacking the hospitality. She admired the jasmine that struggled to survive on the fence across the alley. She never tired of watching the stray cats that streaked back and forth across the alley between naps. She envied the children when they laughed. She couldn't see any of that now, however. Clarence's words seemed to wrap around the truth, but somewhere within lay a lie. Something was dreadfully wrong.

Marvel decided not to push further until later. Clarence hurt and his wounds needed attention. Afterwards, she would get the truth, then look up that writer fellow's name in the magazine and call him. She didn't doubt Clarence's faith in God, but the story of the beating rang sour. He had never been able to lie convincingly.

★

Unfamiliar with the busy supermarket, Nigel maneuvered around slower shoppers while he searched for the aisle containing pesticides. Dressed in jeans, a plain white T-shirt and wearing a wig of sandy brown hair, he spotted the aisle marker he wanted. Midway down the aisle on his left, Nigel tossed two cans of pesticide fogger in the cart. Mixed in with the half-dozen other items such as fruit and toilet paper that he had already selected, the canisters would go unnoticed.

In the sixth busy supermarket, Nigel completed his purchases of twelve canisters of pesticide. No one would notice a man buying only two foggers. A distraught widow wishing to kill herself and her children by fire could turn on the gas, allow the room to fill, and strike a match, but she might chicken out at the last minute. By using highly explosive canisters, activated and piled in the living room, she could light the gas stove, take a few sleeping pills and never wake up. This method would also give Nigel plenty of time to exit the scene and return as a spectator. The explosion would start a fire that would spread quickly through the wooden building.

In the event the police might stop him, Nigel never liked to carry fuel to the scene. Resources were usually available at the targeted site, but in this case the price was right. Nigel couldn't suppress a grin as the cashier slid his purchases over the reader. His benefactor's identity was no longer a mystery. He envisioned a surprise face-to-face meeting with Dr. Huntley to mutually agree on an annuity, but he didn't intend to be greedy. If both men acted reasonably, conflict need not surface. The cashier spoke and startled Nigel. "You must be having a great day, sir," she said.

"I beg your pardon?"

"You're grinning from ear-to-ear as if you just won the lottery."

"Hmmm, yes, perhaps we have." He paid and left the cashier busily scanning the selections of her next customer.

★

It pleased Adam that he could detect Dr. Huntley's discomfort. The man remained disdainful and condescending. Nevertheless, a hint of venom seeped into his conversation, attesting to the increased hostility he felt toward Adam.

"I am pleased that you dislike our newsletter, Mr. Eden. Indeed, it would disturb me greatly if a bleeding-heart liberal such as you found any redeeming qualities in our humble publication. I expect that you find the discourse on morality especially disturbing."

"Anal retentive, actually."

"Cute, Mr. Eden, cute."

"Maybe if people like you spent more time and effort helping the less fortunate learn to take care of themselves, there would be fewer unfortunates for you to hate."

"I assure you, no amount of time and effort can combat the misfortune of poor breeding. In the animal kingdom only the fittest breed. The beef you eat, the pork, the chicken, even your vegetables are the result of careful selection. A farmer will not jeopardize his future by planting inferior seed, yet the misguided such as you are blind to the perils of indiscriminate human procreation. It is my hope that our Mr. X will at least to some extent alter circumstances by his selfless demise."

"What if he changes his mind?"

"Why should he? He's obviously someone with a backbone too weak to face life, someone who suffers from too much religion. His death could not delight me more."

"I see that you're enjoying yourself, Huntley, but I believe Mr. X is Clarence Fardy, and that you're pulling his strings. How much are you paying him?"

Dr. Huntley raised his eyebrows. "Clarence Fardy? Pay him? An interesting theory, but I'm afraid that little twerp wouldn't have the courage no matter the sum. And even if Mr. X turns out to be Fardy, why would I pay that murderer to kill himself? Indeed, if I were inclined to spend money it would be money to have that pathetic excuse eliminated by a professional."

"I wouldn't put murder beyond your morals, but only Fardy's suicide holds the promise of copycat deaths. Fardy feels guilty about Mrs. Huntley's death, and that his family has suffered because he hasn't taken care of them. I think his torture is great enough that your wealth is a powerful lure. His death would end his suffering, his family would be financially protected, and your ghoulish pleasure would be placated over Fardy's death as well as the deaths of others who might follow."

"My, my, you certainly have it all figured out, but you forget; without any contact from the beyond there are not likely to be other suicides."

"Oh, there would be others. The attention that Fardy's death would generate, no matter how foolish his quest, would most certainly encourage some distraught individuals to seek the same notoriety. I don't know how much you're paying, but I'm sure that you consider it money well spent."

"You do have an active imagination, but then you are a writer. Still, in the spirit of debate, let's concede that you are right. If I am moved by the plight of Mr. Fardy and his poor family, and I wish to demonstrate my forgiveness as well as my compassion by a generous largess, what harm has been done? None, and certainly no law has been broken. If the unfortunate wretch turns around and commits suicide that is not my fault, is it? Actually, the press would probably venerate me as a savior of sorts. A wronged man aiding the family of an individual he should hate." Dr. Huntley grinned broadly as he stroked his chin. "That would be a headline worth reading, wouldn't it?"

"I'll find a way to stop this, Huntley."

Dr. Huntley sighed. "No man can stop a suicide. You might delay it, but I assure you, if Mr. X's reasons are important enough, he will persist. Unless of course you are capable of watching him twenty-four hours a day for the rest of his life."

Dr. Huntley rested his elbows on the arms of his chair and placed his palms together. Over his fingertips, he stared at Adam. "I have read that once a great composer begins a piece it's akin to punching a small hole in a dam. Momentum takes control and the composition literally writes itself. Mr. Eden, once set in motion, some things are unstoppable."

The two men glared at each other. Huntley's confidence was unshakable, and that frightened Adam. He decided on another tack. Picking up the picture cube filled with photos of Jean Huntley, Adam said, "Kelly resembles your late wife enough to be her daughter." He set the cube down on the opposite side of the desk from its original position, and waited for Huntley to return it to its proper place. "No matter what, Huntley, I will always be indebted to you. If you had not invited me here in the first place, I wouldn't have met Kelly."

"An unfortunate occurrence, I assure you. Sadly, Kelly is still young, and her profession corrupts her judgement. I'm afraid she is vulnerable to the pearls of swine such as you. Fortunately such relationships are tenuous at best." Dr. Huntley drummed his fingertips together. "You are not a wealthy man, are you Mr. Eden?"

"Money-wise, no, but I do have Kelly." Checkmate. Adam rose and strolled from the office without further conversation. Once he closed the door behind him, he punched the air and said, "Yes!"

★

Lee left Cowboy's and unconsciously made his way to The Stake Out, a popular bar for off-duty police. An old friend, forced to retire from the department when a gunshot crippled his right leg, owned the place. Lee rented an apartment above the bar. His speech slurred after several drinks too many, Lee said, "Another one, Floyd." He pushed the empty glass toward his friend, and toppled it along the way.

"What gives, Lee? I haven't seen you drink like this since you were on vice."

"How long I been coming here, not counting prison, I mean?"

"Years, Lee."

"You remember Lee, the twenty-one-year-old who just wanted to make Tampa a safer place? He's dead, you know."

Floyd set a fresh whiskey on the bar and removed the used glass. "You're not making sense, Lee."

"Me, Floyd, the kid who joined the police to make things better. He's dead, kaput, gone, out of sight. The Lee sitting here on this stool is not the same man. Do you understand what I mean? All those things that I thought were important, they died with the kid when he went into vice." Lee looked down at the bar and mumbled, "Just like Clarence Fardy the drunk died. You can't kill him cause he's already dead, and killing Clarence Fardy now, well, that's a lot like murder."

"Lee, you're not making a lot of sense, but if you're talking about Feel Good Freddy, nobody blames you for wasting that creep. Hell, he not only got your young teenage daughter hooked on crack, but a lot of other kids too. What man could find his own daughter in a prostitute sweep, learn that she was dying of AIDS, and not kill the son-of-a-bitch responsible?"

Lee tossed back the fresh drink. "That's just it, Floyd, *I* was the son-of-a-bitch responsible. I didn't see it at the time, but I was responsible. Yeah, I blew away Freddie, but before that I blew away my marriage. I blew away my family. Should have been there for my daughter. Should have been there. I couldn't give up the street, man. I told my wife that somebody had to do the job, that I couldn't just walk away, but in truth, I was nothing but a adrenaline junkie myself." Lee lit up another smoke, and struggled to focus on Floyd. "I killed for my daughter, but would I die for her?"

"What are you getting at? You were just doing your job, Lee, and you were good at it. Lots of families adjust, but your wife couldn't. Besides, if you had been just Joe Citizen you probably would have gotten off with probation, but being a cop and hunting Freddy down – well, people tend to not recognize that police and preachers are human too."

Lee struggled to his feet, and pushed himself away from the bar. "Yeah, well, gotta go. Later, huh?"

Floyd called Lee back to the bar. "There is still some life left in that twenty-one-year-old, Lee. If there wasn't, you wouldn't be getting shit-faced over whatever it is that's bothering you tonight."

Lee found thinking difficult. "Yeah, maybe," he said, and then he staggered upstairs to bed. He had more money than he had ever dreamed of. Stonewall Huntley had started to crack. Huntley's niece, Kelly, dropping in out of the blue to see the old man was proving to be more important to Huntley's instability than Lee had expected. Moving on sounded better every minute. He would think about it when he sobered up.

March 17, Friday

Adam considered research essential for battle, and after an extensive search he found several books with passages on Cassadaga. Choosing a remote corner of the library, unnecessarily cooled to an uncomfortable temperature, he learned that in the Seneca Indian language, Cassadaga is a word meaning "rocks beneath the water". It is also the name of a Spiritualist community located near Lily Dale, New York.

Cassadaga, Florida, is named after this community, and was envisioned as a retreat for Spiritualists from the harsh New England winters. On December 18, 1894, the parent organization granted a charter to form the Southern Cassadaga Spiritualist Camp Meeting Association on thirty-five acres of land deeded by its founder, George P. Colby. Today, the camp encompasses fifty-seven acres.

Of a population totaling three hundred or so residents, more than half are involved in mediumship as psychics or healers. To work within the camp requires certification which may involve four to six years of study and practice, and the ministerial program usually requires an additional two to four years of preparation. Ordained ministers may use the title reverend or doctor, and fulfill any or all of the duties normally expected of a minister in any Christian church, as well as give spiritual advice and messages from the beyond. Certified mediums, however, may perform only mediumship. Adam shook his head.

Although there are many Christian denominations, the belief that Jesus is the Son of God and personal savior of mankind is the common denominator. Spiritualist groups also vary. The common thread is the belief that the living can communicate with those in spirit, those who have passed on, and the belief that each individual is responsible for his own salvation. They do not commonly believe in vicarious atonement or eternal damnation.

The difference between mediums, also known as spiritual counselors, and ordinary psychics is that mediums, although psychic, are also able to communicate with spirit entities. Psychic or mediumistic ability does not correspond with character, good or bad. Reportedly, however, the purer the medium is in character, the higher, or more spiritual levels of being they can tune into to. The more amoral the character is of one open to spirit communication, the more mischievous, misinformed or even evil the likely contact. Like attracts like.

Depending upon the medium's motivation, his or her purity of heart, he or she is able to receive or sense information of a more constructive nature beneficial to an individual's soul growth or spiritual progress. Others most often communicate facts and data of a more material quality. The information may be important or mundane. When will I get paid? When will I get laid? Seekers should choose wisely when desiring council.

Adam outfitted for battle with whomever Kelly might introduce him. He did not intend to die behind enemy lines, and psychics or mediums – it was all the same to Adam – were the enemy. Kelly referred to her friend as a medium, but despite the euphemism, people believing themselves to be fortune-tellers, and especially people who claim to talk with the dead, are either frauds or they suffer from delusion.

Like a shadow-hugging drug dealer, psychics spread venomous escapism. That such beliefs are drugs, Adam had no doubt. Educated and trained as a psychologist, Kelly's interest in the occult proved its addictive power. Adam would save Kelly, and free Glory from her interest in this nonsense once and for all. A doctorate in mediumship, how preposterous! Probably all were graduates of the state penal system or candidates for the loony bin.

*

Singing along with a Garth Brooks tape, Kyle looked at his watch. At ten thirty A.M., it was a Chamber of Commerce day. Taking a day of sick leave, plus the weekend and his vacation starting Monday, put Kyle in high spirits. He systematically searched an ethnically mixed neighborhood in Ybor City, the old Latin quarter of Tampa.

Home originally to a host of cigar manufacturers and

hardworking *émigrés*, and more recently an eclectic haven for artists and host to a few ethnic clubs, Ybor City had experienced hard times until lately. Perhaps the recent proliferation of bars frequented by tourists and local youths spurred a new confidence in the area, or perhaps a new confidence accounted for the bars. Whichever, shops, apartments, and refurbished housing were experiencing unprecedented growth. Kyle searched for one of those houses now.

Several days ago, he overheard a firing range acquaintance telling a friend about an upcoming trip to Houston. The man asked the friend to drop by and check on the cat every couple of days. Said he would leave the key hidden in the pot containing an aloe vera plant.

As part of a group, Kyle had once been invited to the man's home after a day on the firing range, and after a short search he found the house again. Kyle had rented a clunker for the day and salted the open trunk with a couple of rolled-up carpets. Once he found the house he confidently parked the car in the empty driveway. The owner's truck was parked in long-term parking at Tampa International Airport. Kyle popped a couple of Tums to settle his stomach.

Feigning confidence, he strolled up to the one-story clapboard home and searched for the thorny aloe vera as he approached. Red geraniums and pink pentas decorated the porch, but no aloe vera. As if he belonged there, Kyle walked around back and spotted the plant at the door. Once in, he noticed a slick gray cat, but only once. When the cat woke up and spotted Kyle, it bolted to hide.

Kyle discovered a spare set of truck keys dangling on the back of a kitchen cabinet door then began his search for guns. Knowing that the man had an extensive collection and that its location wouldn't be obvious, Kyle didn't concern himself with the ordinary places. Quickly, but clumsily due to nerves, Kyle pushed and pulled on mirrors and walls until he finally discovered a built-in bookcase that swung away from the wall. He discovered a sizeable storage area filled with knives, guns and ammunition.

He gaped at the collection then whistled. Facing such a magnificent arsenal of weapons, and smelling the gun oil, Kyle calmed down and grew more confident. He assessed each item then selected the Remington 700-P sharpshooter long rifle, .308 caliber, bolt-action. Reverently, Kyle took the rifle and ran his hand along the hammer-forged barrel then along the smooth synthetic stock. The weapon radiated power.

Unlike the staff of Moses, it couldn't turn into a serpent, but it could definitely kill a snake. Hell, with a clear line of fire a sharpshooter could drop a man over in the next county. Kyle also lifted a Colt 45 semiautomatic pistol. With one in the chamber and seven in the magazine, that gave a man eight shots. For balance, he added a couple of Benchmade survival knives and closed the bookcase. Everything combined equaled a pretty good staff.

Kyle grinned as he recalled the story of Moses. He never talked about it to anyone when he was a kid, because most boys dreamed of being GI Joe, or Superman, but Kyle ached to be Moses. His magic stick that he stored under his bed at night gave him power. After his mother died he never went to Sunday School again, but he didn't forget the lessons of God's avengers. Kyle was never happier than when wielding his magic stick to smite bugs, lizards and occasionally a sleeping cat.

Exhilarated, he rolled his treasures up in a five-by-eight carpet, strolled to the car with it on his shoulder and stuffed it in the trunk with the other two salted there. He had not noticed anyone, and hoped that no one had paid him any attention. Burping several times, Kyle dug in his pocket for a Tum. He wiped his hands on his shirt. He regretted not washing them before leaving the house.

He drove to where he had parked his red Ranger and transferred the carpets. Careful that no one noticed him, the guns were moved to behind his seat. He returned the clunker to the rental agency and hiked the several blocks back to the Kash 'N' Karry grocery store to his pickup. He didn't know if the hike caused him to perspire so profusely or if adrenaline could be blamed. He only knew that he and his sweat-soaked shirt smelled. He wiped his hands on it anyway.

He drove to the airport and wheeled up to the long-term parking entrance where the machine promptly spit out a ticket. The arm lifted, and Kyle drove through. He quickly located his victim's pickup and transferred his treasures. After explaining to the cashier that he had mistakenly driven into the wrong lot, Kyle exited the airport without paying because there was less than fifteen minutes on his ticket. It would be exactly seven days before the truck's owner returned and reported the theft of his gray Dodge Ram pickup and the stolen weapons. A competent hunter needed less.

★

As Lee walked into the office from the hidden room, Dr. Huntley pressed the button on the intercom. He told his secretary not to disturb him for any reason. Lee studied the older man. He appeared disdainful as usual, and Lee looked forward to baiting him. "I checked with Cowboy yesterday after I dropped Fardy. Seems that Eden had a visitor late Wednesday evening. Around nine thirty P.M. I believe," Lee said.

"A visitor?" repeated Dr. Huntley. Lee wanted to smile. It wasn't readily apparent, but Lee could see that Dr. Huntley struggled to control himself.

"Kelly, your niece. All dressed up, too, like maybe she was coming in after a date. She stayed the night with Eden. For a little guy, he must swing a pretty good stick, huh? Seems they got a hot romance going." Lee held up his fingernails, but actually examined Dr. Huntley.

The man's self-possession momentarily melted, his eyes narrowed and his face appeared ready to spurt blood. Lee watched his employer's hands curl to fists and thought Dr. Huntley might actually throw a punch, but then the patrician expression that Lee always found so amusing reasserted itself. Dr. Huntley sat down behind his desk. "They are adults, Lee. Our concern is what damage has been done to our plans for Mr. Fardy."

"Fardy's not going to take any chances. He knows you have the power to harm his family if he doesn't play ball, but Eden has managed to interest the police so we've got to be careful. They are watching Fardy. They are watching you. Spotted them when I came in, but they took no notice of me. Still, I think I need to stay in touch by phone. They have only suspicions at this point, but someone may recognize me and start asking questions."

"It is regrettable that Mr. Eden and my niece met; nevertheless, the most important thing is that Mr. Fardy understands that there is no escape. Next is Phoenix. It is imperative that she stay out of trouble. I want you to drive to Fort Lauderdale, and ensure that she conducts no phony séances or psychic readings. Once she claims to have received Fardy's message from the grave, we want no unfavorable publicity. In the meantime, I will contact the press and TV. I will set up a news conference tomorrow. It should hit the evening news on TV and make page one Sunday morning."

"With the police nosing around, April third is a long way off. Maybe you should move up the target date."

"Mr. Fardy dies on the anniversary of my wife's murder. You control Phoenix and her wanton little strumpet, I will control things here."

"You mean Barbara?" Lee said. He didn't like hypocrites. The thing they badmouth the loudest is usually the thing they want the most. Besides, any man, even a saint, would allow a thought or two about hosing Barbara, at least any man who wasn't cold-coded to begin with. "She needs a real fuck," he said.

Dr. Huntley clenched his jaw, and Lee watched the man's temples swell. "Of course I mean Barbara. Agreed, Lee, she is a tramp, but even such a common woman deserves a degree of respect. Just be certain you keep her out of trouble."

Lee shrugged. "No problem."

Dr. Huntley leaned forward. "By the way, when I had my little visit with Mr. Fardy, what did you make of his comments about a redhead watching his house? Is he one of your men?"

Lee suppressed a grin. "No, just some alley bum I would guess. Fardy's understandably jumpy. There is another wrinkle, though. Cowboy spotted some kid following Eden. Eden visited an abortion clinic, and when he left, the kid followed him. Showed up again Wednesday at Eden's house. Doesn't smell good to me."

Dr. Huntley leaned back in his chair and stroked his chin. "Interesting. Perhaps Mr. Eden's liberal libido has gotten him, or more precisely, gotten some woman in trouble. No, on the contrary, he is a womanizer, but understanding him as I do, I'm certain he considers abortion murder."

Dr. Huntley looked at Lee. "Of course abortion should be required by law for any tramp pregnant out of wedlock, and women on welfare... " He didn't finish the thought, and due to his angry expression, Lee deduced that Dr. Huntley's thoughts centered on his niece, Kelly. With his eyes rolled back, Dr. Huntley muttered, "Perhaps this kid following Mr. Eden is a religious zealot. Perhaps he will shoot the deviant bastard."

Lee, surprised, smiled at the rare expletive. "Would that be convenient?"

"What? Oh, I, no, no, of course not." Dr. Huntley evened up an already neatly stacked pile of papers. "Just a figure of speech. All writers of his ilk should be shot, but not Mr. Eden, at least not now. It would draw too much attention too close to our plans. He is probably doing research for a bleeding-heart article about the crime of abortion, so why would one of their own harm the little crusading angel?" With a wave of his hand, Dr. Huntley dismissed Lee. "Make sure your men know how to reach you in Fort Lauderdale."

When the mirrored door closed behind Lee, Dr. Huntley turned and stared out the window at Tampa General Hospital. The thought of Kelly, wet with sweat, wallowing in bed like a common trollop with a man who championed everything anathema to reasonable belief went beyond acceptance. Dr. Huntley caught himself holding his breath. He never thought he could hate a man more than he hated Clarence Fardy. Adam Eden shattered that belief.

★

Always alert to possibilities and careful of leaving trails, Phoenix waited in Barbara's Camry while the younger woman checked in at the rental office. Lee had reserved a lighthouse replica as lodging which overlooked the beach on the outskirts of Fort Lauderdale. He had promised four floors, including the lookout with a partial wall four-feet high and the remaining wall, including the ceiling, paneled with tinted glass. The room, circled by a balcony, housed a huge Jacuzzi plus a wet bar. The other three floors contained a kitchen and den on the middle level sandwiched by bedrooms above and below.

Arriving at the lighthouse, located one mile down the beach from the rental office, both women loved it immediately. Landscaping and sand dunes afforded the unit a sense of privacy that especially appealed to Phoenix. Relatively secluded, since it was lined with single-family housing and single-family rental units, the beach was beautiful. Use would be light. A perfect spot to vacation. Lee had promised to discourage competition, but Phoenix wanted no distractions or temptations for Barbara.

March 18, Saturday

Soon after driving through Orlando, about midway to Daytona Beach, Adam spotted the exit to Cassadaga. He had spoken little during the trip, but Kelly and Gloria behaved like sisters who had been apart too long. That pleased him. It also eliminated the initial awkwardness that had threatened to ruin the day due to his obvious agitation over visiting a psychic. He steeled himself for the worst.

The old Chevy hummed as it tried to outrun County Road 4139, and enjoying the thrill, Adam stuck to the curves and sailed over the hills like a Formula One driver. He began to relax, and that's when the oddity struck him. Florida had suddenly become hilly. He speeded around a curve and met a Cassadaga city limits sign.

Shaded by mammoth oaks, towering pines, and several varieties of the ubiquitous palm tree, the quaint little town seized Adam's attention. Built mostly before the 1920s, the up-and-down hamlet consisted of one- and two-story cottages wrapped with picket fences. Each home was harmoniously placed within a grid of narrow lanes that invited one to stroll the grounds. Other common buildings as well as parks, wooded areas, and small lakes complemented the village. Except for the palms, Adam imagined that he had been plucked from central Florida and plopped down in New England.

Following Kelly's directions past a little store, a gas station, and a hotel, Adam uncharacteristically eased the Chevy past two blocks of homes, identifying their owners as either Doctor This or Reverend So-And-So. He shook his head, remembering the tripe that he had read about earning a doctorate in mediumship. He stopped when Kelly pointed and excitedly said, "Here we are. This is the house." She had her hand on the door handle.

Adam couldn't help shaking his head over her enthusiasm. He wheeled the old Chevy into the dirt driveway only to have Kelly start climbing out even before the engine was turned off. The screen door screeched open and slammed shut, followed by hurried footsteps across the old wooden porch. He switched off the Chevy and looked up to see Reverend Doti Meeks bounding down the front steps, her arms open wide and her face mostly smile. She wore a lavender floral-print dress, beautiful and lively, but Adam could see that it failed to match the wearer's effervescence. This was not what he expected.

An eighty-two-year-old, ninety-eight-pound lightning bolt of joy, her enthusiasm struck out and charged everyone and everything around her. Spotted with age marks and furrowed with wrinkles, Reverend Meeks spoke with a faint vibration matched by a slight shakiness in her hands, but she attacked life as if death had been outlawed. Anyone sharing her space for long quickly forgot that statistically Reverend Doti Meeks was an old woman.

Kelly climbed from the Chevy and managed to meet her friend as she reached the picket fence that corralled the front yard. They hugged tightly until Reverend Meeks pushed Kelly away and said, "Let me look at you, child. What's this? A sparkle in your eye?" Reverend Meeks glanced knowingly at Adam and then smiled before returning her attention to Kelly. "It's wonderful to see you happy, and thank you so much for the birthday gift." Reverend Meeks pirouetted then curtsied while holding out the hem of her dress. "It fits beautifully. I wear it every chance I get." She took Kelly's hands. "Now, dear, introduce your friends?"

"This is Gloria and Adam Eden. I'm afraid that I have brought you an angel and a devil, but I will leave it up to you to guess where the labels apply."

Reverend Meeks took both Gloria's hands and studied her. "It is a pleasure to meet you, child, and I don't have to be psychic to see that you are the angel in this duo." Without looking at Adam, Reverend Meeks nodded her head in his direction. Although her hands shook, her grip was firm as she continued. "Gloria, do you know what I see?"

Reverend Meeks didn't wait for an answer. "When I look at you, I see the foundation and framing of what is to become a beautiful house. I see a team of building inspectors examining every inch of the structure, the foundation, the plumbing, the wiring, the materials used, and the quality of workmanship. They are all smiling and nodding their heads up and down, obviously very pleased with what they see." Reverend Meeks squeezed Gloria's hands. "Welcome to my home, child, welcome indeed."

"Thank you," Gloria said. "Will I live there someday?"

Reverend Meeks laughed. "No, dear, the house is you in progress. You're already living there." She patted Gloria on the cheek and turned to Adam.

"A devil, huh?" she said, eyeing her guest.

Adam shrugged his shoulders and grinned sheepishly. With a twinkle in her eyes, Reverend Meeks continued. "There are two types of devils, one is the doer of evil deeds, while the other brings excitement." Reverend Meeks winked at Adam. "If Kelly wasn't like a daughter to me I do believe that I would try to steal you away. I like your energy." She embraced Adam's arm. "You will let me know if she doesn't treat you right, won't you?"

Caught off guard by the charm, Adam laughed. He pretended to whisper in her ear, "We could slip around and Kelly would never have to know."

"Only if you promise to pick me up in your Chevrolet. It takes me back to a time when I wasn't such a wrinkled old prune." She looked from Adam to the car and back again to Adam. "You're kind of short though. You would have to sweeten the deal and wash some of the grime off that buggy first."

Everyone laughed, and Adam said, "Be happy to. I prefer a prune to a date any day."

After boos and groans from Kelly and Gloria, Reverend Meeks leaned over and whispered in Adam's ear, "Glad you're smiling. I am not really your enemy, you know." She tugged him toward the steps. "Come inside everyone. I've got tea and cookies. You do prefer tea to coffee do you not, Mr. Eden, sweetened with sugar?" Adam stared, his mouth open, and Reverend Meeks patted his cheek. "You can close your mouth now, child. It is tea is it not?"

"Uh, yes, yes, thank you." He delivered Reverend Meeks over to Kelly. "You go on inside. I want to get my briefcase." Again, Adam heard the front screen door screech open as everyone else went inside. It made his skin crawl, but he couldn't help thinking how inappropriate the chilling sound was. Prepared to do battle, Adam's intentions were in full retreat. Such a lovely, but obviously disillusioned old woman, he had no desire to attack her and be seen as the enemy himself. To regroup and listen would be wise. Later, he would reason a response.

He retrieved his case and looked around. The one-story cottage, currently painted a pale yellow and connected to a matching picket fence by a brick walkway, rested beside a narrow asphalt lane with no curbs. Grass grew sparingly in the oak-shaded yard. Nevertheless, what was there had been neatly cut, and the bare areas recently swept clean.

Perennials, already showing some blooms, among them azaleas and gardenias, bordered the house. Partially shielded as they were from the unrelenting Florida sun, pentas and periwinkles bloomed in abundance practically everywhere else. Ignoring the pull from three inviting rockers shaded by a honeysuckle vine, Adam took the four steps to the porch in two strides and hurried inside.

★

Parked at the corner, Kyle shook his head and cursed under his breath. They were acting so ordinary. How could a man kill babies for a living then visit Grandmother like decent God-fearing people? And what about the other woman who had shared the front seat with Eden? If the skinny blond in the back was Eden's knocked-up girlfriend, was he poking the other woman too? Probably. A baby killer would have zero morals.

Kyle dug a Tums from his shirt pocket. He was generally hidden by several of the huge gnarled live oaks draped with Spanish moss that dominated the hilly landscape of Cassadaga, but he left the motor running just in case. He observed Adam retrieve his case and sprint up the steps to the house.

Kyle glanced around. Small towns overflowed with nosy people, and he didn't expect Cassadaga to be different. Detection was certain if he continued his surveillance from the corner. Driving slowly back the way he had come, Kyle wondered why Adam needed his medical case.

Studying the tired old houses as he passed, he thumbed out another Tum and drove toward the little store. He craved a beer, and something to eat wouldn't be bad either. As he rolled past the hotel again, Kyle noticed the service station and checked his gas gauge. He pulled up to the pump and by the time Kyle got out of the truck, a skinny, greasy-faced kid wearing a hunter's camouflage hat had started twisting off the gas tank cap. The kid never looked up. "You want regular?" he asked.

"Uh, yeah, yeah, that's good enough," Kyle said. The register started clicking in rhythm with the advancing numbers and Kyle looked around. He shook his head. "I've been to a lot of backwaters, but this place takes the cake. You live in a weird place, man."

The kid kept watching the numbers spin as if only his vigilance gave them momentum. "Never thought much about it," he finally said.

"Well, hell, look around, boy. I mean where *is* the town? You got this little hotel sitting over there like this is a resort, this service station here, a little store over there, and a hole-in-the-wall bar down there, and that's it. Where's the bank, the hardware store, the lawyer's offices? You got all these spooky old houses, half of them with signs out front saying Doctor So-and-So, or Reverend This-and-That, but where's the people? Where do they work?"

This time the boy glanced around before turning back to the dial, but never made eye contact with Kyle. "You don't know where you are, do you?"

"What's that supposed to mean?"

"It means you're in Cassadaga. This is a Spiritualist camp. Most of 'em only come down here in the winter, but others live here all the time."

"What's a Spiritualist?"

"People who talk to dead people," the boy said as he hung up the gas nozzle.

Kyle handed the boy a five and ten ones and twisted on the gas cap. "Very funny. I suppose you talk to dead people too, huh?"

"Not me, but them Spiritualist do." The boy counted the bills, and made change from his pocket.

"Then what you mean is these people, these Spiritualist, are devil worshipers."

"I don't know nothing 'bout that, but they talk to your dead relatives. They tell you all about your future and stuff. They can cure people, and they can make you sick too, by God. Best not ever try to mess with one neither, 'cause they can get a ghost to cause you all kinds of shit."

Kyle laughed at the boy who used a greasy rag to wipe his hands. "Yeah, like what?"

"With my own eyes I seen 'em make this rich Yankee eat cow shit like it was ice cream. Never touched him. Did it with their minds. And if you're married you better not bring your wife 'round. They can dry up her insides so's she can't never have babies. I've heard it told they can even burn your baby in your belly if you're pregnant. My daddy told me that."

Kyle didn't say anything. He surveyed the town again and climbed into the truck. His instinct had been right, this was a bad place. It made sense though. That's why that butchering bastard Eden is here. He's a devil worshiper. And that old woman? She's a preacher for Satan. She's a witch who kills babies with her mind, and all these doctor signs on the gates, this town is an assembly line for abortions. That's what going on. That short-haired whore is getting an abortion from a witch. The whole town ought to be burned to the ground. He glanced back at the lumber scraps in the truck bed.

Kyle stopped at the store and purchased a couple of six packs, some ready-made sandwiches, and a roll of Tums. The sandwiches were delivered daily from Daytona, the talkative old man with white eyes said. Amid questions and misplaced expectorations of tobacco juice, he had offered Kyle a plug. Kyle shook his head to both the questions and the tobacco, paid, and left. There was no place to wash his hands.

He drove past the city limits sign and turned onto a dirt road. Within a mile an overgrown jeep trail punched into the woods and stopped among a stand of oaks. Kyle cut the engine and popped open his second beer. He switched off the radio in case someone happened to come his way, then he inhaled a turkey sandwich. He had eaten worse.

His hunter's eyes examined the oak hammock that was spiked with towering slash pines and sprinkled with assorted palms, shrubs and wild plants. Ubiquitous grapevines sprawled snakelike up the massive oaks and along powerful branches. Leaves, pine needles and rotted deadfalls blanketed the ground with a springy layer of mulch. Birds flew in and out of the trees searching for food or rest. Butterflies fluttered about the plants for nectar, and lizards scurried over the ground-cover snagging ants and other unlucky insects. In the distance two squirrels scolded one another like noisy children. After a loud sulfurous fart, Kyle flicked the wadded up wrapper out the window.

★

During refreshments Reverend Meeks and Adam continued to spar, but it was clear that they were evenly armed with wit. Stories were told and Reverend Meeks especially enjoyed Kelly's description of how she and Adam had met. Adam felt obligated to clear up a few inconsistencies.

Kelly intentionally rammed her knee into his briefcase, but Adam admitted that he was used to pretty women attempting all manner of contrivances to meet him. He explained that one had even claimed to be a movie director who could help him break into the movies as an action adventure hero. "A logical ploy," Adam said, pumping up an imaginary muscle, "and the casting couch is always a powerful temptation. Only my high ethical and moral standards saved me."

"There is a term to describe drivel like yours, Adam. I wish I could bag it up for my garden," said Reverend Meeks. They all laughed then grew quiet, enjoying the tea and cookies as well as the comfort of friendship. Reverend Meeks examined her three guests and smiled. Mischievously, she winked at Kelly.

"What?" asked Kelly.

"I look at you three and I see a closet full of tangled clothes hangers." She addressed Adam. "Did you know that you are the main reason for this visit?" With a raised hand she stopped his objection. She said, "There are things that you need to know, so relax." Adam started to speak, but again Reverend Meeks signaled him to silence with her tiny but commanding hand.

"Yes, yes, I know what you think, Adam, but Gloria already

knows the answer to the question that you think she came to have answered. She is a very strong person with a deep sense of responsibility. There is only one path acceptable to her and she has already chosen it."

Reverend Meeks turned to Gloria. "Yes, the vision you saw of yourself holding your son is a real, a viable probability for you. Not because it is preordained, but because you make it so. You have been raised to believe in yourself and your abilities. Because you have been so blessed with a wonderful mother who filled in for your biological mother, you have always had an inner determination to be just as great a parent. Being an unwed mother is a challenge that you have chosen. Matter moves in concert with mind, child. Do you understand?" Reverend Meeks didn't wait for an answer.

"Think about it, dear. You have always dreamed of being a mother, but have you ever dreamed of being married? However, this is not to say that you will or will not marry someday. Do you understand? There is much more that could be said here, but you have plenty of time to learn."

Reverend Meeks nodded toward Kelly and continued. "Kelly can be a great help to you, Gloria, for you see, she also is developing her psychic insights." Adam had been resting with one foot across a knee, but he brought that foot to the floor with a thump as he sat up straight. Reverend Meeks again put up her tiny hand, but it was her invisible will that demanded restraint.

She continued. "Kelly's sensitivity is a great asset to her as a psychologist. When I saw the tangled hangers, Kelly's sensitivity was part of the reason. Both of you know that our naughty Mr. Eden here has a closed mind to all paranormal phenomena. If he can't see it, touch it, taste it, smell it, or hear it, then it doesn't exist as far as he is concerned.

"He is prideful of his open-mindedness, and does not realize that when he is against something he locks up that opinion tighter than Ebenezer Scrooge guarded his money. On this subject his mind is closed to contrary thought more securely than the cap on my pill bottle. Both of you considered it important that Adam learn your secret feelings within the context of this demonstration. You both hope that he might become more supportive or at least less hostile toward your beliefs."

Reverend Meeks turned and smiled at Adam who sat with his arms akimbo and his jaws tightly shut. He had become uncharacteristically still and sullen. "First, my devilish friend, you should at least breathe," she said. That brought a blush as well as a slight smile and she continued.

"We will try to get you to question your current attitudes. I believe that you agree with John Stewart Mills that truth attacked becomes stronger if it is indeed truth, and if it is a falsehood the attack will free you of the burden? The problem is you are blind to your own provincialism." Reverend Meeks didn't wait for confirmation.

"It seems I met your mother once, by the way. She visited Cassadaga as part of a group retreat. She is a beautiful soul." Reverend Meeks faced Gloria, "Child, do you sense anything?"

"Sense? Why, I – yes, yes, I do. I feel very warm, hot actually, burning up on my left side. What's happening?"

"Does this feeling alarm you?"

"Humm, no. I feel happy, wonderfully happy as if I am in a wonderland where nothing can go wrong."

"It's your mother letting you know how much she loves you, and she is very pleased that you are able to sense her energy. In the future she will contact you in this same fashion in order that you will know she is aware of your joys and sorrow, or whatever happens to draw her to you at the time. Do you understand?"

Reverend Meeks gestured over the tea service and asked if anyone would like more. Kelly helped herself and Gloria asked to be excused. While they waited, Adam got permission and turned on his tape recorder. Reverend Meeks noticed that he took his time while Kelly and she talked.

★

Kyle gobbled another sandwich then finished off his third beer. "What a screwed up mother-loving world," he said. He cocked his arm to throw the beer can out the window, but stopped when he heard something moving irregularly through the brush. He grabbed the stolen Colt 45 from his tote bag then sat up and concentrated. The movement came from his left rear. He searched his side mirror for movement, but as the sound grew stronger he stopped looking. He recognized the familiar scraping and rooting of a hapless armadillo.

Although normally nocturnal, the armored little critters frequently leave the protection of their burrows to roam the brush during the day in search of roots and bugs. They are harmless, as well as cute in a robotic way. They help farmers by eating tons of harmful insects.

None of which impressed Kyle, of course, and that made the armadillo's poorly developed sense of smell and hearing that much more a burden. The solitary creatures are squat and quick, however, and one can plow its armored body through the thickest tangle of thorns with impunity. Kyle tossed the colt back in the bag and used his fingers to search behind the driver's seat for the tire iron. He touched steel and wrapped his fingers around it.

Kyle eased the truck door open and placed his booted feet on the running board. He swallowed a belch, but held the tire iron steady. The innocent armadillo continued foraging and rooting for tasty grubs. It wandered out of a cluster of palmetto palms then froze. Obviously the truck presented a dilemma. The animal was poised to flee but no threat came. Without breathing or blinking an eye, Kyle stared at the armadillo with anticipation. Finally, hunger won over caution and it wandered near the opened door then beyond.

Watching the armadillo, Kyle eased out of the truck and took one step off the rail. A twig snapped and the creature bolted for the nearest burrow. Cocking the tire tool, Kyle screamed, "You're dead meat!" He burst after the armadillo that began plowing through the underbrush. Swinging the tire tool like a machete, Kyle hacked through several yards of branches and bramble until he became hopelessly entangled. "Shit!" he said, as he fought his way back out the way he had entered.

Finally free, Kyle listened, but there was nothing to hear. The armadillo, safely catching its breath, rested in a familiar burrow. Kyle kicked a termite-shredded deadfall that disintegrated, which increased his rage, and with a powerful throw he sent the tire tool whistling through the trees. Still breathing hard he stomped back to the truck to kill another beer.

★

Reverend Meeks could sense the rush of vitality as spirit moved closer. She closed her eyes and focused on the stairway built long ago in her mind. At the top of the steps, she pushed open a door that led to the universe, much like an astronaut opening a hatch and stepping out into the magnificent void. She had never looked, but Reverend Meeks imagined that her body glowed at such times.

The charge that leapfrogged throughout her body generated the light and sensitized every fiber of her being. No longer fully focused in the physical world, but not wholly in the spiritual, she knew only that sweat would pour from her hands. Words would rush from her mouth. She was grounded enough, however, to wonder what Adam would think of the transformation.

She returned her attention to Adam. "Your efforts to understand as well as educate people about suicide is a good pathway for you if you choose to continue down it. It is no accident that you and Kelly met and that she is similarly involved. Your current research into abortion, your visit here and other, I want to use the word sensational, circumstances in which you are currently involved are all part of this pathway concerning life and death. If you think back, you will see that you have always been moving in this direction. You can help spread understanding if you so choose."

Reverend Meeks used a tissue to pat sweat from her palms. "Adam, before we continue, you must know that your reason for researching suicide in the first place is due to a mistaken belief. The death that concerns you was not your fault." Adam's mouth flew open, and Reverend Meeks waited while he stared at her in disbelief. "Do you wish to know more?" she asked.

Speechless, he glanced at Gloria and then at Kelly. Leaning forward and clasping his hands in his lap, Adam wanted to resist. Helpless, he turned again to Reverend Meeks. "Please," he whispered.

"Your girlfriend," Reverend Meeks put a hand to her head, "I don't get a name, but I sense that she was Hispanic... anyway you grew up as neighbors. You loved each other desperately as teenagers are wont to do. She is a beautiful soul, but is not here with us today. All the souls gathered here who love and watch over you know that if I said, ah, Francine, no, I get the name Franci... If I said that she was here today you would bolt back to Tampa believing me to be a charlatan like others you have confronted in the past. Still, I can sense that Franci wants you to know that the problems she died to escape crossed the threshold with her. Her suicide merely added to those conditions that she had to face, but she is learning. She is well and happy, but concerned for you.

"You were just a youth, and all your buddies participated with the other young girl who made herself available to the group. You were intoxicated. You didn't think of what you were doing as cheating on your girlfriend. It was a male thing, a manhood ritual. A part of you did not want to, but the sex drive is very powerful, especially in an undisciplined youth. Also, to have objected or not participated would have put you outside your group.

"That is why today you work, albeit unconsciously, at being independent, even to the point of sometimes alienating those closest to you. No matter the consequences, you never sacrifice your principles to curry the approval of others, and you have never been drunk since that fateful night. Indeed, you often go overboard to prove your independence, thereby alienating some who would help you. Do you understand?" Adam nodded his head as Reverend Meeks continued.

"Your girlfriend discovered the truth, but if you will think back you will remember that she suffered with many other problems. Significantly, her brother was an innocent victim in a shooting incident, her parents were divorcing, and her grades had subsequently fallen. She suffered from depression. You did your best to help her, but she believed in fairy tale romances and happy endings. You were her white knight, yes, her Lancelot, I believe." Adam stopped twisting his hands and looked up at the mention of the name.

Reverend Meeks paused before continuing, and watched Adam glance at Kelly. "When Franci found out about your escapade she felt that her world had collapsed. She went to a favorite spot. I see a tree, by the river. Contemplating suicide, she sat crying for such a long time that her legs went to sleep. When she tried to stand, her legs cramped, she simply let go and plunged into the river."

Reverend Meeks watched Adam until he looked up at her. "Adam, as painful as the memory has been, your friend's death – call it accidental or call it suicide – you did not cause it. Many pressures sent her to that tree, her life pattern, if you will. You were each a brief part of the other's pathway and as insensitive as this may sound, her death made you a better person.

"You are honest with others and very caring of their feelings. You have avoided permanent relationships, but you always are quick to help if someone appears in need. You don't worry about rejection, and again, you never go against your principles to curry acceptance from others. These traits have served to make your adult life a happy one, even though you have suffered with the sadness of loss and guilt. Do you understand?

"Before we move on, however, there is one more thing." Reverend Meeks wiped her hands again. "Franci has heard your apologies and felt your grief. She wants you to forgive yourself, for only you can unlock the chains with which you have fashioned your prison. Do you understand?" Adam didn't respond, but Reverend Meeks could see that he was too choked up to say anything.

After a long pause, Adam's eyes questioned Kelly, then Reverend Meeks began again. "There is more, and this is very important. I see you inching your way through a minefield. Danger surrounds you." Each of her guests registered their surprise at the sudden negative turn in the reading, but all three remained quiet. "Normally, I do not talk of such things, because mistakes can be made, or indeed, some predictions may become self-fulfilling. Do you understand? In your case, however, I feel a great urgency to continue.

"First, I am seeing a tall thin man stroking his chin. He is herding a group of souls, yours included, as you would herd sheep. He has a destination, a goal if you will, and intends to have his way. This person with whom you are involved is determined that nothing will stand in his way. Adam, this man has the heart of Lucifer. I don't know why you are involved with him, but if you can, get out of that situation now.

"Next, two men are following you. One is a giant and the other is a big young man. I feel that you will learn about the giant soon, but I get nothing on the younger man except that he is very dangerous. Indeed, he is the doer of evil deeds." Reverend Meeks shook as her skin crawled. She wiped her hands in an effort to rid them of the negative energy that tried to coil itself around her.

"I can sense him today, now, but I can pick up nothing in the future. His future is a blank canvas, and this disturbs me greatly." Reverend Meeks closed her eyes hoping to discern more. She shook her head. Almost whispering, she said, "Be very careful – be very, very careful of this man."

Reverend Meeks remained silent. With her eyes closed, she said, "There is nothing more that I can sense here, but you must remember that we have free will. What I have shared with you about the current danger are probabilities. The equation that equals each life is constantly changing because we have free will. Matter moves in concert with mind. The universe is a great musical composition constantly changed by individual improvisation."

She allowed the energy that had kept her elevated to dissipate, and slowly she opened her eyes. It was always sad to close the door through which she communicated with spirit. She desired more, but understood that spirit would not – indeed, could not – live another's life. Spirit could not interfere with one's pathway.

★

Clarence Fardy sat quietly in the rear of the little white neighborhood church. He would have donated his labor, but the preacher insisted on paying him to clean the Lord's house each Saturday for Sunday services. Now, however, the work completed, Clarence sat alone, worrying over his dilemma. What choices did he have? He knew of none. What did he know of evil ambitions and power among men? He squeezed the Bible that he held in his hand. That was the only power he understood.

As he had done many times during his developing relationship with God, Clarence randomly opened the Bible and began reading at the point that first caught his eye. This time, God directed him to the Book of Hebrews, Chapter 11, Verse 1. "Only faith can guarantee the blessings that we hope for, or prove the existence of the realities that at present remain unseen." Before he could read further, the door flew open, and Brother Abraham Lincoln, a robust black man with kindly eyes and a tender heart, burst in.

"Brother Fardy, I hoped you would still be here." With one massive hand on Clarence's back, Brother Lincoln gripped the hand reluctantly extended by Clarence, and began to pump. A clear cool spring aside a dusty trail frequented by weary travelers, the old oval-eyed preacher miraculously shared his vitality with all who stopped to drink. "You have worked miracles, you know. The grounds look like a fresh haircut, and the dust bunnies have all run off to the Methodist church down the street." He looked knowingly at Clarence. "Take care of the Lord's house, and He will take care of yours."

"I enjoy the work. I just wish—" Clarence started, but grabbed the thought before the words could escape and reveal his plight.

"You seem troubled, brother. Can I help?"

"I'm just, ah, a little overwhelmed with... Well, God has opened my eyes, and brought me joy beyond my wildest dreams. I just hope that I don't let Him down."

"Return to the bottle, you mean?" Brother Lincoln said. Clarence shrugged. That was not what he meant. He never thought about alcohol except in the context of a horrible memory. What worried Clarence was the loss of faith. A man, no matter how parched, should protect and save his final drop of moisture to nurture faith. To die with your trust in God intact is the only way to inherit "...the realities that at present remain unseen".

"No, that's behind me," said Clarence. "It's failing to follow God's will that worries me."

"Brother Fardy, light shines from your eyes. You're a teacher. Doubt that and you doubt God."

"I would like that."

"You're a beacon, brother. Your faith will lead others to God." Clarence flinched as he thought about others following him in suicide to find God, and Brother Lincoln embraced him in a bear hug. "Can't eat your peas, Brother Fardy? Put 'em on the Lord's plate."

"Yes, I will."

"Good, and again I thank you. I'll see you at services."

After Clarence had time to relax, and his conversation with Brother Lincoln ceased to echo in his head, he reread the passage from Hebrews. "Only faith can guarantee the blessings that we hope for, or prove the existence of the realities that at present remain unseen". He bowed his head and prayed.

"Dear Father, I want to live, I want my family to live. I desperately want these things, but they are the wishes of a spoiled child compared to the longing that shouts from the core of my being. My every cell vibrates with the cry, 'Your will be done.' It is only in ignorance of Your plan that I humbly pray, if it is Your will that I should die, I ask that I die with dignity. If it is Your will that I should die, I ask that You sprinkle my family with Your blessings. If it is Your will that I should die, I ask that You forgive Dr. Huntley for I have wronged him grievously. If it is Your will that I should die, and others will follow me into death, I ask that You guide them to Your door. If it is Your will that I should die, I ask that I die with gratitude for the life You gave me. Your will, not mine, be done. Amen."

★

Adam unclasped his hands and picked up a napkin. Wiping his palms, he shrugged. "I don't pretend to understand all that has been said here today, but I do admit to an interest in suicide and lately abortion." Adam looked at Gloria, then turned to Reverend Meeks. "I'm curious, is abortion moral?"

"Ahh, maybe it is your destiny to determine that for the rest of us. Food for thought? Do you believe in life after death?"

"No!" Adam blushed at his abruptness. "Ah, at least I didn't. Most people do, however."

"If they are right, if there is life after death, then why not life before birth? Well, I suppose I should qualify that to reflect current debate. If there is life after flesh, why not life before conception? And if there is life before birth and life after death, can a baby, a fetus, be killed?"

"As we know it, yes."

"Certainly flesh can be eliminated as a functioning organism, although matter cannot be destroyed, but can the soul be vanquished? Is the immorality that flesh is slaughtered, or is it that a trust between two souls, mother and child, has been broken? Or perhaps is it both or neither? There is the concept of karma that may also be considered."

"You reap what you sow?" Adam asked.

"An eye for an eye," Reverend Meeks said.

"A belief that disintegrates without the existence of multiple lives or continued existence after death, because some people never seem to get what they deserve."

"Precisely," said Reverend Meeks. "If there is life before birth and life after death, perhaps our sojourn here is short indeed compared to eternity."

"I've never believed in life after death. This is difficult to digest."

Reverend Meeks smiled. "Confusion swirls about you, Adam, as you ponder these things, but I see it as a calling to teach, if you will forgive the use of a phrase from organized religion. Maybe this will help. Do you believe in abortion?"

"I believe a woman should have the freedom to choose that option."

"Yes, but do you believe in abortion? If Gloria, or a close friend asked you for five hundred dollars to pay for an abortion would you give them the money?"

Adam squirmed in his seat. "Well, I, ah..." He cocked his head back and rolled his eyes. "I don't believe that I would. I don't believe that I could. Still, I wouldn't legislate that restriction on others."

"That's your position then. It is impossible to have direction in your life without first knowing the starting point."

★

A six-pack after Kyle had begun his vigil he became sleepy. He fought the drowsiness but lost, until an hour later a pressing need to urinate woke him. He jerked awake, looked from side to side, and then remembered where he was. Honing in on a crushed beer can, he stumbled over and soaked it. A man always likes to have something to piss on. He looked at his watch. He should have already checked the house.

★

Adam finished another cookie. While his leg bounced ninety miles per hour, he said, "You've given me a lot to think about. You're not what I expected."

Reverend Meeks winked. "I put away my cards and hid my crystal ball when I heard you were coming. Seriously, dear, psychics are people like everyone else. Indeed, we are all psychic, but few of us have developed the potential.

"Just remember that even the most hardened criminal can be a highly developed psychic, detectives too. The most successful criminals and policemen have spent years developing their sixth sense, if you will. My advice is to never consult a psychic unless you feel friendly toward the person. Like attracts like. Do you understand?"

"Makes sense. I won't listen to a lawyer or accountant or anyone else if I don't like them."

Reverend Meeks smiled. "I don't think listening to anyone has ever been your strong suit." As everyone laughed, she closed her eyes for a moment. "I don't know why, but I feel compelled to talk with you about possession. You were speaking of listening to people, of seeking advice, and I saw Lucifer again, the man in the red suit. Any time someone seeks help the potential for exploitation exists."

Reverend Meeks sat quietly, looking toward Adam, but not aware of him. "Problems can arise any time a patient visits a psychologist, a parishioner visits a priest, or a student seeks help from a teacher. Any time one person accepts another as an authority with the power or ability to help, the potential for exploitation exists. Hypnotism depends upon the trust of the subject in the hypnotist, and counseling can be a form of hypnosis.

"If the need of the subject and a weakness in the authority figure are juxtaposed under the right circumstances, exploitation results. It is a form of possession among the so-called living, one mind controlling the mind of another. One will dominating the will of another. Sometimes this happens by design, but mostly the parties are not consciously aware of the devil in their relationship. Do you understand?"

Adam nodded and Reverend Meeks continued. "The same thing can happen between an incorporeal being and a corporeal being, the living and the dead, but much more easily. People with little or no confidence, people under great stress crying out for help, lonely people; all open their minds to possession by confused, unscrupulous, or even demonic incorporeal beings.

"In every culture man has been taught to pray and perform rituals to please the gods, but prayer can be dangerous. In prayer one often opens the mind in desperation; unfortunately, many entities tied to the physical plane by human weaknesses such as hate, strong sexual desire, a chemical addiction, and most importantly fear, are eager to jump in and start making decisions for anyone who will open the door.

"Indeed, the recently deceased, especially those who die unexpectedly, often aren't aware that they are dead. We each take our habits and fears with us; therefore, many who cross over are highly susceptible to strong habits or desires, say a weakness for drugs or sex, and are confused by the new circumstances. The personality does not die with the body, and that is one reason why I am against capital punishment.

"Consider a controlling personality; they control because they fear rejection, and death sets them adrift from all their defenses. When they die they may immediately latch onto an available anchor. As Kelly can tell you, there are valid psychological conditions such as the development of multiple personalities that also occur, but do not be mistaken – possession does occur."

"So, not only is prayer useless, it is dangerous?" said Adam.

Reverend Meeks winked at Kelly and smiled. "He only hears what he wants to hear." Everyone laughed except Adam, who turned red and grinned like a boy caught with his hand in the cookie jar. "Adam, as I have said, one cannot *not* pray! Matter moves in concert with mind. The esteemed teacher, Dr. Emmett Fox, once wrote, 'You better look where you are going, because you will invariable go where you are looking'."

She continued, "Our habitual thoughts lead, but taking time to pray allows one the chance to relax and take charge of the rudder rather than allowing the currents to dictate direction."

Adam said, "But you said that prayer can also open one up to possession."

"There is a fail-safe, my dear. Prayer can help people plot their course, but it can also result in two other conditions: possession and the creation of multiple personalities. Just as the personality can bury traumatic events, it can also create other personalities when it feels powerless to act. Say the child is being abused. The child is supposed to love the parent; therefore, it feels powerless to protect itself. A new personality can be conceived that has the courage and freedom to act."

Adam stopped shaking his leg and leaned forward. "So what is this fail-safe?"

"Love, dear. Simply love. When you pray make sure it is for the right reasons." Uncharacteristically, Adam remained still and quiet. Reverend Meeks continued, "Read the Gospels. Possession does occur. Jesus recognized and routed unclean spirits. Be wary, Adam."

★

Dr. Huntley wandered aimlessly through his spacious mansion. He was immune to the beauty of ornately carved wood that enhanced the interior and the polished walnut staircase that seemed to float upward and never failed to garner comment from impressed visitors. He drifted, examining first this artifact and then another. Each one was an expensive souvenir or valuable piece of art; the things one can buy with money, collected by his wife during their extensive travels.

He had encouraged her to spend money. It delighted him that she never became accustomed to his wealth. Until the day of her death she remained a little girl with a key to the candy store. Intellectually she understood that there was no limit on her purchases, but psychologically, she always felt guilty, a weakness of her middle-class conditioning.

Dr. Huntley married beneath himself, but Jean had been beautiful; therefore, beyond the reach of most men. From speakers in each room, the soulful strings of a violin concerto accompanied Dr. Huntley on his lonely inspection. There was a gardener, a cook and a maid on the grounds somewhere, but these were non-people really. Only gaudy opulence kept him company. In the library, he revisited a photo collection of Kelly that Jean had arranged.

A fascinated child staring at the Crown Jewels of England; a smiling ten-year-old waving to the city from atop the Eiffel Tower; a wide-eyed girl viewing a three-thousand-year-old mummy; all greeted Dr. Huntley, and his eyes moistened. Distorted by the tears, he examined a picture of Kelly proudly clutching her first-place trophy from a sailfish regatta. He knew the glowing child occupied the photograph, but all he could see was Kelly being seduced by that decadent worm, Adam Eden. He tossed the picture and it smashed into an assemblage of his life's memorabilia that flew apart like pins struck by a bowling ball.

★

After visiting a while longer, Kelly got up to clean, but Reverend Meeks insisted that the job was small. She said that she enjoyed as well as needed the activity. With she and Kelly walking arm in arm, Reverend Meeks accompanied everyone outside. Goodbyes were expressed, and Kelly, Gloria and Adam climbed into the Chevy. Adam had his hand on the ignition key, but hesitated. He looked again at Reverend Meeks.

"You have a question?" she asked.

"Uh, yes. Now, I'm not saying that I believe it, but if there is life after death, what happens to, well, what happened to Franci?"

Reverend Meeks thought for a moment. "This is just an image mind you, symbolism, but I see people gathered around a casket. Each time they pull the lid open an arm from the inside pulls it closed again. It was an ongoing struggle until she finally accepted that there is no death.

"Please understand that my explanation earlier of why Franci chose suicide is a simplification, like looking at a highway on a road map. The map shows you direction, but it does not detail all the things you will see and do along the way. One is simply the route taken, the other is the trip experienced.

"On one level Franci believed that death would bring nothingness, release from torment. Spirit, her guides and relatives who had passed over, told her that she was not dead, but she insisted that she was. Eventually, Franci accepted her continued existence and began to work out her problems." Reverend Meeks stepped closer and placed her hand on Adam's cheek. "Be careful, dear."

"I will," said Adam. "I need to start digging into this, ah, these things. May I visit you again?" Reverend Meeks gasped and her face turned white. She put a hand to her gaping mouth. "What?" asked Adam.

"Nothing. Nothing that I can touch." She squeezed Adam's arm. "Be very, very careful, Adam."

"Don't worry, I will. Bye, and thanks again."

After her guests had departed, Reverend Meeks, hugging herself against a sudden chill, trudged up the steps and went inside. She felt old. During the reading she had sensed that danger stalked Adam. The feeling had been worrisome, but when Adam asked to visit again, she became stunned with the revelation that she would never see him again. Now, trying to view the future, Reverend Meeks could sense nothing.

She wrung her hands to dampen the sinister energy that accompanied her thoughts. Unable to shake the negative feelings bombarding her regarding the two men following Adam, she found herself especially anxious about the younger man. Kelly's happiness pleased Reverend Meeks, but it also intensified her concern with the danger that swirled around Adam.

She picked up her appointment book. She had lined through the whole afternoon, and penciled in both Kelly's and Adam's names. By Adam's, she had written "Tampa", but next to Kelly's, Reverend Meeks had drawn a smiley face. The doodle seemed inappropriate now, but recognizing that each person has free will, she forced the dilemma from her mind. She began cleaning up the tea service and cookie dishes. Her friend, Reverend Sykes, would arrive soon for their evening walk, and Reverend Meeks would consult with her.

★

As soon as Kyle turned onto the street to Reverend Meeks' house the empty driveway pissed him off. He hit the steering wheel with the heel of his hand and cursed. Clear headed enough to know that he couldn't speed down the highway in a stolen truck, Kyle decided to stop and see if he could find out what time Adam had left. Besides, he wanted to see the inside of a devil-worshiping abortion house anyway.

Kyle pulled on the screen door and his skin trembled when the door screeched open. He tried the doorknob. It turned freely. It disappointed him to see that the place looked like a prim old lady's home is expected to look; clean and orderly with lots of ornaments, and generously splashed with family photos. Also, it didn't smell of alcohol and other disinfectants, or even incense and blood; it smelled deceptively like fresh-baked cookies.

From the kitchen Reverend Meeks called out, "Mae, is that you? You're early." Drying her hands, she stepped from the kitchen into the hallway. She spotted Kyle and dropped the dishtowel. Her hands flew to her gaping mouth. "It's you!" she gasped, and turned to run.

Her reaction caught Kyle off guard, but sensing trouble if she got away he caught her as she grasped the back doorknob and pulled the door open. With one arm wrapped around her neck, Kyle stifled her scream with his huge hand. He pushed the door shut and looked to see if anyone watched from the outside. He kneeled down below window level and forced Reverend Meeks to a sitting position.

His heart pounded in his throat. Scared and confused, and trying to think, it took a while before he realized that his captive was clawing away strips of flesh from his arms as she struggled to free herself. Reverend Meeks kicked her feet up and down, scuffing the highly polished floor while trying to break Kyle's grip.

"Stop it! Are you crazy?" he said. He slapped her with his free hand and tightened his grip over her mouth. Still trying to concentrate, Kyle crawled on top of Reverend Meeks to stop the kicking, and that's when he noticed her eyes. She struggled to pull away his hand that covered her mouth and prevented her from screaming, while simultaneously her eyes shouted fear. Kyle experienced the awesome sense of power that always seized him when he found his prey on the business end of his stick or on the fatal side of a scope's cross hairs.

Kyle relished the power of complete control. He stared at his captive and laughed. As she struggled to free herself from beneath his huge bulk, Kyle thought how the woman was no bigger than his wife Sandy. He grew hard. It was his first erection since the night before he and Sandy visited her doctor.

Kyle reached down and jerked up the dress that Kelly had given her friend, and snatched down Reverend Meeks' panties. He unzipped his jeans and freed his penis. He forced himself into her, ignoring the initial pain, and not caring about her muffled screams as dry skin resisted dry skin.

Once in he looked into her eyes again, and her fear fed his excitement. "You murdering bitch!" he screamed. He began trusting violently, and the more Reverend Meeks' eyes screamed her panic, the more he tightened his hand over her mouth and under her nose.

At first, Kyle grunted like a pig. Then he began to moan way down in his gut. When Reverend Meeks' eyes rolled back and announced her death, Kyle's body spasmed and he exploded with a wail. Sucking in gobs of air, he collapsed on top of her. Finally, his breath came more easily and as it did his rage subsided. Reverend Meeks no longer struggled beneath Kyle so he raised up and studied his victim. Sex had never been so awesome.

He got to his knees and, feeling the sting of a cut on his penis, wiped himself with the lavender dress. The injury caused by the forced entry was tiny, but it stung like a paper cut. He glared at Reverend Meeks' lifeless body. Maybe he would get a purple heart. There was no remorse. In fact, he had never felt so great.

Kyle tried to reason who Reverend Meeks had thought he was when she first saw him. "It's you," she had said. Then Kyle recalled that Reverend Meeks had been expecting someone else. He didn't panic, however. He couldn't remember feeling so alive, so powerful, so in control. He thought about a murder his brother, Chuck, on the police force had once described. Kyle easily scooped up his diminutive victim and carried her into a bedroom.

He searched the deep closet and found a huge soft-sided suitcase hiding behind the hanging clothes. Softly humming 'Onward Christian Soldiers', Kyle pulled the green bag out and easily folded his victim's small body into it. Toppling a bowl of pot pourri, the fresh scent pleased him as he stuffed underwear, shoes, dresses, blouses and coats around the body. The smell of flowers seemed appropriate.

He found the bathroom, took time for a piss, and arrogantly left the toilet seat up. He gathered up a sampling of toiletries. Grabbing her toothbrush, Kyle spoke to his victim. "Lady, it's like those Egyptians who enslaved the Jews. You're going to the other side with everything you need to look your finest when you meet the devil face-to-face."

For added emphasis, Kyle scattered a few garments about on the bed and left a couple pairs of shoes strewn near the closet. He locked the back door and wiped away fingerprints. Retracing his steps, he wiped every surface that he may have touched. He hefted the suitcase and started for the front door, but noticing the phone, took time to cock its position enough that anyone calling would get a busy signal. All prints were carefully wiped clean.

Easing the front door open, Kyle searched the streets. Seeing no one he opened the door wide and pushed on the screen that voiced its objection. The loud screech alarmed him so he didn't take time to lock the front door. Hastily, he crossed the porch and lugged his burden to the Ram truck.

When he pitched the bag into the open bed of the truck the scrap lumber loudly adjusted itself to the intrusion. This racket, like the screech of the screen door, seemed to be shouting to anyone who might hear that a heinous crime had been committed. Forcing himself not to look around, Kyle hopped into the truck, but he remained careful not to drive so fast that it would attract attention.

★

Kyle's clandestine efforts were to no avail, however. Alerted when the screen door opened, Cowboy looked up from the Bible that he had been reading. Cowboy had remained behind Kyle as he followed Adam to Cassadaga, and Cowboy had watched the joyful arrival at Reverend Meeks' house from the vantage point of the street corner above the house.

He followed as Kyle gassed up and made his purchases at the little store. When Kyle steered his truck toward the woods, Cowboy drove back to town. He casually parked in the hotel parking lot and picked up the western novel he was slowly working his way through. Reading had never been easy for Cowboy, but he had learned in prison that it gobbles up time.

After he worked his long legs out of his rusting white Oldsmobile and stood up, Cowboy noticed several Bibles and pamphlets splattered over the front seat of the adjacent car, which was unlocked. Accomplished thieves are careful, but never hesitant when an opportunity presents itself. A Bible is a good character reference in case of confrontation. He quickly opened the door of the maroon Plymouth and grabbed the nearest Bible.

Elated to be unrestrained by bars, Cowboy strolled off toward the scenic pond where he had noticed picnic tables. From there he would have a clear view of Reverend's Meeks' house. Nearing the water, he observed the majestic oaks, and they gave him a feeling of security. Like Cowboy, the trees were giants. They had been growing for years, and if you roamed among them their longevity might rub off.

Cowboy breathed deeply, relishing the fresh air, enjoying the pungent scent of pine and the musty smell of damp, decomposing leaves that squeaked under his big feet. He selected a shady picnic table with splashes of sunlight. If you had to waste a day watching, Cassadaga was a pretty good place to do it.

Cowboy had begun strolling to his car while goodbyes were being said at Reverend Meeks' house when he noticed Kyle's truck approaching from a couple blocks away. He waited within the protection of the oak stand and watched Adam speed away. Curious, he waited, then puzzled over Kyle's reasons for entering the house. A hairpin trigger, the kid should be watched. Cowboy sauntered back to the table and reopened the Bible.

Now, alerted by the screen door, Cowboy studied Kyle as he peeked out and searched both directions then shot across the porch and down the steps. Cowboy watched Kyle lug the big suitcase to the pickup and pitch it in the back where it made a hell of a racket. Cowboy knew it was time to make tracks before a posse was formed.

He stepped out of the park and stuffed the Bible under his shirt. When he approached the hotel parking lot he saw that the Plymouth appeared undisturbed. Deftly, he placed the borrowed Bible on the seat where he had found it, then contorted himself into the Olds. He wasn't particularly religious, but he was superstitious. It didn't make good business sense to keep a stolen Bible when you could easily give it back. He sped away to catch up to the amateur.

★

As Adam drove from Reverend Meeks' house, he said nothing to Kelly or Gloria, but he searched every parked car for an occupant trying to remain undetected. He drove slowly, watching for someone to pull in behind him. One car did, but it stopped in front of the little store.

It didn't make sense. OK, Huntley has him followed. That's logical. Huntley is a controller. He needs to know where all the pawns are, but why two men? Unless, one is a hit man hired just in case Adam gets too close. Too close? Maybe that's it. Huntley's wound so tightly, maybe he thinks that with Adam out of the way, Kelly will become his.

Adam reached the city limit sign, and a pickup roared over the hill behind him. Still driving below the speed limit, Adam watched the truck find a flat stretch with no curves and speed past. Later, after merging into I-4 traffic, Adam pushed the Chevy up to seventy and stayed there for several miles before again slowing to fifty. While continuing to alter his speed, he studied all vehicles that he passed for big male occupants traveling alone. The ladies never commented, but Adam knew that his preoccupation was obvious. They too were silent and alert. Adam dropped Gloria then drove to Kelly's. No one spotted anything suspicious.

Feeling safer as no one had noticed a tail, Adam's mind periodically returned to Reverend Meeks' caution about possession. He had read about murderers who claimed to have been commanded by a voice from within. Could there be a grain of truth? He had serious doubts, but it deserved some thought. Something beyond his ken had happened today, and if nothing more it at least implied telepathy. That in itself is one heck of a discovery.

In his youth, he benefited from Christian teachings by his mother, contrasted by the atheistic views of his father. Adam considered himself an agnostic. He did not believe in life after death, at least he had not before meeting Reverend Meeks, but now a crack marred that belief. Like a building listed for destruction, Adam's belief still stood, but the first blow by the wrecking ball had slammed into it hard.

How did Reverend Meeks know about Franci, his teen sweetheart? Only Bulldog knew about that. Reverend Meeks knew all the facts, Adam's disloyalty, his guilt, and Franci's family problems. Reverend Meeks knew everything. Did Franci still live? Did she hear the apologies? Had she forgiven him? Did it matter? Maybe she did have other problems, but it was still Adam's insensitive and stupid behavior that sent her to the tree.

He wanted to know more. Somehow Reverend Meeks had seen into the cave where he stored his deepest secrets. And what about that conversation with Gloria? Was his mother, or whatever one may become after death, really there? Or maybe there's a pool of consciousness where all thoughts go to swim, a place where people with special talents can gain access? Maybe that's where the myth of reincarnation began.

If men have souls, is the soul of each new child dipped into this pool, this miasma of thoughts, thus randomly producing child prodigies and madmen alike? Or is there a grand design? Is there really a God dipping newborns, purposely granting blessings or curses and dispensing punishment and reward as merited from past lives? With every question the wrecking ball struck another blow. Adam wanted some answers to shore up his battered belief system.

For years his sleep had been disturbed by the nightmare of Franci diving headfirst into the gaping black jaws of a menacing Hillsborough river. Now he wanted to believe that his girlfriend fell into a benign river simply flowing toward the sea as it had every day for centuries, and as he hoped it would continue to do. Changing his belief would not bring Franci back, but it might be comforting to believe that there is life after death.

Adam tightened his grip on the steering wheel. Comforting,

yes, but nothing could alter the fact that it was his disloyalty that sent Franci to the river's edge in the first place. Before Adam could prevent it, he choked up and several tears rolled down his cheek. Kelly put a hand on his neck. He appreciated her wisdom not to ask and her sensitivity to care. Maybe one day he would talk to her about it.

★

Phoenix, contented, sat on a towel as the sun went down, and watched her self-centered friend frolic in the waves rolling onto the beach. Several men of different ages had attempted to engage Barbara in conversation, but she had rebuffed each one. Phoenix was grateful even though she recognized that the men had not been Barbara's type. Barbara wanted only males whom she could manipulate. Phoenix hungrily admired her younger companion as she strutted from the water.

An emerald colored T-back complemented her tanned body. It teased anyone who might be interested. Her ample breast bounced as she walked and the inviting outline of her nipples could clearly be seen through their meager cover. Sex had been good since their arrival two days earlier, but Phoenix suddenly wanted more.

Sundown quickly began to erase the water, and Phoenix struggled to control her hands in the semidarkness. Barbara leaned forward, away from Phoenix, and threw her hair over her head in an effort to dry it. In the T-back, Barbara's dimpled buttocks moved provocatively until Phoenix could stand no more. She said, "Baby, why don't we go back to the room and I'll shampoo your hair? We can take a long hot bath and I will give you a hot oil rub down."

"Hmm, sounds delicious," Barbara said.

Later, in their hotel room, the fake psychic's strong fingers flowed easily through the warm baby oil that coated her companion's voluptuous body. During their bath, Phoenix had brought her selfish mate to climax. Now, on the bed, as the older woman kneaded the muscles in Barbara's back and buttocks, small noises began again.

Phoenix's excitement budded and blossomed as her seductive playmate became more receptive so whatever excited her younger partner Phoenix did. Moaning ever so slightly, Barbara spread her thighs and began to rhythmically move her buttocks in a circular motion. While continuing the back massage with one hand, Phoenix slowly and softly started to excite her demanding girlfriend with the other.

As the rhythm increased, the older woman leaned over and began to guide her warm, moist tongue around Barbara's dimpled cheeks, which attention was greeted with a long, low moan of approval. The moans intensified and Barbara began to thrust and rotate her swollen clitoris in a dance with the familiar digit. The back lost its importance. Phoenix used her free hand to violently excite herself. Rearing back, muscles tight, she climaxed with a low growl that grew into a throaty string of affirmations.

Barbara joined her. "Oh, God, yes!" She flipped over and grabbed Phoenix's head, pulling the still contorted face to the spot that had been so masterfully manipulated. Breathing heavily, clinching a fistful of Phoenix's hair with one hand, and squeezing the life from a pillow with the other, Barbara gasped, "Slowly, slowly, oh, God, I don't want it to end." She slowed her movement to a sinuous circular pattern.

Barbara's nipples hardened as Phoenix tweaked them with her left hand while continuing to nimbly kiss the excited clitoris. The psychic again began to massage herself. Barbara began to shudder and Phoenix climaxed again, her whole body going rigid except for her tongue and hungry lips that suddenly made Barbara explode and her body convulse. Shoving Phoenix's head away, Barbara screamed, "No! Oh, my God, no!" She stuffed her hands between her thighs and protectively drew herself into the fetal position.

Both women, soaked and spent, lay quietly for a while until Barbara began to climb weakly from the bed. "Where are you going?" asked Phoenix, who was almost asleep.

Barbara leaned over and patted her exhausted partner on the forehead. "Go back to sleep. I'm going to wash away this oil then I will join you for a nap. Later, we can go for a nice seaside dinner, OK?"

"Yes, that would be nice." Phoenix yawned. "I do need a nap." Before sleep overtook her, Phoenix heard the shower start. Later, she thought she heard the door click, but sleep demanded her attention.

★

Cautiously keeping within the speed limit, and remaining obtrusively in the right lane of Interstate 4, Kyle enjoyed himself. He had the radio cranked up and he wailed along with Garth about friends in low places. Kyle felt great, alive, all his physical senses were tuned to a level never experienced before. The trees were greener, the traffic less threatening, his stomach sweeter. For the first time in his life, Kyle had direction. What he had done was right. Hell yes, it had been somewhat accidental, but that was to force him to see the truth. If it wasn't God's will, why did he feel so happy?

Enjoying the sensation of total control, Kyle could afford to be honest with himself. He admitted that he had never been very good at much except shooting and working on cars. Which made sense. If he wasn't chosen then why was he a born shooter? It was a God-given talent. Bathed with feelings of self-righteousness, all Kyle's doubts were washed away. Adam Eden must die. It was God's will.

Kyle exited I-4 at Plant City, a friendly little town between Orlando and Tampa. It is the home of the Strawberry Festival that celebrates the annual harvest each February. Popular Country and Western stars perform, and Kyle looked forward to going. He drove south through town and then past miles of fields planted with strawberries. Five thousand acres, one hundred million dollars of luscious berries, and rich farmers. After he buried the suitcase, Kyle would steal a few treats for the ride home.

Twenty minutes and several turns later, he reached a narrow back road. He turned onto a dirt lane and stopped before a stout metal gate. The five thousand acres beyond the fence was a water management area pricked with wells used for drawing water to be pumped to the thirsty Tampa-Bay area metropolis.

During season, a limited number of individuals could get permits to hunt on the preserve for deer, turkeys, and wild hogs.

Now, however, hunting season was over and, although one could enter the vast preserve for scouting and other legitimate reasons, Kyle had not registered to be there at all. He got out to unlock the gate and noticed a white car approaching. He decided to wait until it passed.

★

Cowboy easily followed Kyle from Cassadaga without being noticed. Certainly, Kyle had reason to be concerned, but Cowboy eased close several times and marveled as Kyle appeared to be singing. It was as if the boy was high on locoweed. Cowboy was highly skilled, however, and it is doubtful that a more determined effort by Kyle would have detected the shadow anyway.

Cowboy had orders to follow Adam Eden, but he reasoned that a man could never predict when a bargaining chip would prove useful. Police were big on dealing for the right information. As Cowboy neared the truck he slowed and rolled to a stop on the roadside, blocking Kyle from escape.

Kyle stood in the open doorway of the truck with his left hand on the cab and his right hand behind his back. You didn't have to be a Texas Ranger to know that he held a gun. Kyle waited and watched as Cowboy worked his way from the car. As colossal as Cowboy often seemed to strangers, he could see that Kyle was unafraid. Finally free from the car, Cowboy stood in his open doorway and leaned over the top. "Howdy, partner? Got a problem?"

"What do you want?"

"Want? Oh, nothing. Just thought you might be having trouble with your truck."

"No. No trouble. Just stopped to take a piss."

Cowboy examined the suitcase. There were a couple of bulges, but no recognizable outline. "See you got your suitcase. You on vacation?"

Kyle glanced at the bag. "Just some stuff for Goodwill. You know how women are. They give away perfectly good stuff just so they can go out and buy more."

"Yeah, women are kinda like horses, fun to ride, but I wouldn't want to own one."

"Own one?" Kyle said.

"Yeah, you know. If it flies, floats or fucks don't buy it, rent it. When you own a filly they're hard to get rid of too, don't you agree?" Cowboy smiled, but Kyle didn't join him. Cowboy continued, "Well, partner, if you don't need anything..." He squeezed back into his car and slowly drove away. He watched in the rear view mirror until he saw Kyle approach the gate. For an amateur the kid didn't spook easily. There had been no signs of nervousness, no squirming about, no tapping the foot, no hand wringing. Nothing gave the kid away except his eyes. In flop houses, back alleys, and in prison, Cowboy had seen a lot of eyes like the kid's. They were the malignant eyes of a lunatic masquerading as a zealot.

Just four days ago, Cowboy had watched Kyle stick to Adam and follow the man to Tampa General Hospital before peeling off. Lee reasoned that Eden probably planned to write an article about abortion. He cautioned Cowboy to be careful, to hang back and see if the kid popped up again. Well, like Texas whirlwinds, the amateur kept popping up again and again. Then there was King Red who Lee knew nothing about. It looked to Cowboy as if he was on a trail drive headed south.

★

Kyle fingered through his keys and found the one to his lock that helped form a chain of locks used to secure the gate. One belonged to the water management people, but the others belonged to the few individuals with permits to hunt the vast preserve. Having a cop for a brother did have its advantages.

Kyle found his family's lock and quickly drove deep into the well field that he knew like the back of his hand. He watched the sun go down, but he didn't turn on his headlights. He didn't need them anyway since the sandy two-rutted road he followed stood out like two white lines on a blackboard. The moon was almost full, and soon after sundown more light rained down on Kyle than he appreciated.

The trail crawled across overgrown fields, pushed through wooded areas, and in low areas hid under a few inches of water.

Kyle inched along, bouncing, slipping, and sliding deep into the management area. He drove to an area overgrown with saw palmetto, a ubiquitous native palm that can dominate the landscape. The trunks can run along the ground then twist upward where space is accommodating. Like any ground cover, the palm that grows to about five feet when upright, sinks its roots into sandy soil and snuffs out less hardy plant life.

Even without the rattlesnakes, a sea of saw palmetto is an unfriendly place. The trees crowd together fighting for space. The long, slender leaves grow like fingers from serrated stalks that sprout from around the tree trunk like pins from a cushion. They repeatedly slap and saw any man struggling to push through. Only a man with a strong reason would venture into a growth of saw palmetto.

Kyle spotted the area he wanted and pulled the truck into a stand of slash pine. He jerked the suitcase over a wheel well then grabbed a scrap of lumber to use as a shovel. He had spotted no other vehicles. Confident, he punched his way into the palmettos until he found a spit of bare ground. It was the perfect spot guarded by an old palm, which rose from the ground at an angle. It resembled a serpentine dragon with fan-shaped ears and a fuzzy snout of old leaf bases. Kyle jumped when he first saw it.

At first, Kyle struggled to work through the tangled mass of roots, but fortunately he had the stolen survival knifes to cut what he couldn't snap. Once beyond the top layer of roots, he quickly dug through two feet of sand and plopped the suitcase into the hole. No one would find that abortion witch in a million years. After quickly raking dirt back into the hole, Kyle stalked to his truck. Tomorrow was Sunday. He had only five days before his weapons theft would be discovered. Plenty of time. Adam Eden would be dead by then.

*

Phoenix woke up around nine in the evening and immediately sensed the emptiness. She fumbled for the light switch on the lamp between the beds and her eyes blinked wildly as they adjusted to the sudden light. She searched the room. Barbara was gone.

Later, Phoenix checked her watch for the hundredth time. It was eleven fifteen P.M., just five minutes later than the last time she had checked. She threw a pillow across the room. "I'm going to kill that whoring bitch. She knows what this does to me." She snuffed out her last cigarette, carelessly pushing other butts and ashes out of the ashtray as she did so. She crumpled up the empty package and threw it at the TV, which blared away impervious to her problems, then she froze.

The newscaster reported that a mystery man known as Mr. X planned to commit suicide in order to prove the existence of life after death. "Dr. Luther Huntley, the sometimes controversial…" the reporter droned on, but Phoenix no longer listened. She stared at the picture of Dr. Luther Huntley, or rather, to be more precise, Phoenix stared at his eyes.

Phoenix was a skilled observer, her living depended upon it. She knew those beady green eyes from somewhere but the face remained unfamiliar. Then she had it. She was looking at the fastidious guy who had dirtied his hands, pasted on a fake beard, and introduced himself as Herman. They had discovered each other via the hall mirror, and Phoenix had observed him closely throughout the evening. His bearing, his haircut, and his dirty but manicured nails had all broadcast the deception.

Throughout the evening, Phoenix had remained alert but finally decided that he wasn't a reporter or the police. More likely a society figure afraid of the publicity if knowledge leaked that he had attended a séance. She decided to try and root the man out later, but after Lee contacted her with a proposition of great financial reward, Phoenix quickly forgot less important matters. Now, however, the fastidious guy with the beady green eyes stared at her again, but this time from a television screen.

This was providential. Lee propositioned her to fake contact with some deceased guy, and now the news reports that the man is not even dead yet. She doubted suicide, murder made more sense. Lee's body language had told Phoenix that the proposition came with more than that presented, but she chose to act innocent in hopes of eventually generating a greater profit. This new knowledge put Phoenix in charge. The solution to her problem with Barbara could be solved with a simple phone call.

Phoenix dialed long distance information, but the number for Dr. Huntley was unlisted. She thought a moment, then remembered what the announcer had said, "Dr. Luther Huntley, famed futurist and president of Huntley Enterprises..." She tried the business, but a recording reported that the office was closed for the weekend. For now she would have to wait, but only until Monday. Then she would see if this Dr. Huntley would keep his promise about discouraging all competition for Barbara. If not she would make a date with a TV reporter.

★

Marvel couldn't sleep. The kids were down, and Clarence was sitting at the kitchen table studying his Bible. He still had not told her the truth about his beating on Thursday, and his silence disturbed her. She turned on the TV and was startled to see Dr. Luther Huntley staring at her. It was unsettling. Throughout the trial, he had stared at Clarence, then at her through those unblinking, beady eyes. She had nightmares of the man for months afterwards, and now there he was burning holes in her again.

She had thought the evil man was gone from her life until that writer fellow showed up at the backdoor. Clarence swore that he knew nothing about the Mr. X who the writer mentioned, and who Dr. Huntley was now talking about on TV. The scheme seemed more real now, and more threatening now that she was hearing about it on the television.

When Dr. Huntley made an appeal to the mystery man to abandon his plans and to seek help, Marvel laughed at the insincerity. Maybe people who didn't know Dr. Huntley might be fooled, but she wasn't. Instinct told her that Clarence was Mr. X, and that his beating had something to do with it. When the news went on to other events, Marvel shut off the TV, and joined Clarence in the kitchen. She would know the truth.

★

Adam switched on Kelly's TV for the evening news and smiled when he heard her remove a batch of cookies from the oven. She had decided to bake cookies for the sailing outing planned for the next afternoon. After postponing the outing in order to visit Reverend Meeks, the plans had been expanded to include Gloria and Judith.

Adam headed for the kitchen hoping to fleece a cookie, but froze when the doorbell chimed. Kelly stepped from the kitchen and stared at Adam. He checked the time as if he didn't already know that the eleven o'clock news was next. "Who could that be at this hour?" whispered Kelly.

Adam turned the TV off and they quietly made their way to the front door. Kelly peeped through the security hole. Her face turned white. "My God! It's the police." Adam looked and spotted Bulldog and a big man in a khaki uniform, wide-brimmed hat included.

Opening the door, he explained, "It's my friend, Bulldog." Adam motioned the two men inside.

"Adam, Gloria told me you were probably here. Sorry to disturb you."

"What's up?"

"This is Sheriff Riggs from Volusia County. He—" Bulldog started.

Kelly's hand flew to her mouth. "Volusia County! That's Cassadaga! What's happened?"

"I'm sorry, miss. A Reverend Meeks is missing. The sheriff thinks she's been murdered."

"No! No! That can't be. We were there just a few hours ago. She, she was fine. She…"

Adam put his arm around Kelly and led her to the sofa. After she was able to settle down a bit, he quietly asked, "Why do you think she's been murdered?"

"Sheriff Riggs would like to ask you and Miss Dorsey a few questions, Adam." Bulldog looked at Kelly. All color had left her face. "Miss, if you would like to lie down, maybe Adam could help us."

With lips drained of moisture, Kelly answered thickly, "No, no, I, I'll be all right. It's true. I sense it now, Adam. Reverend Meeks is gone." Kelly turned to Adam and gripped his free hand.

"He did it, Adam. The man she warned about."

"What man? Can you describe him, miss?" asked Sheriff Riggs.

Adam spoke up. "I have it all on tape. You should hear the part about the two men."

After the tape finished, Bulldog said, "I know who the giant is. You asked me to check if the word 'cowboy' had any significance at the prison; it did. Had a knuckle-dragging cretin there called Cowboy. He's six feet nine inches tall. Paroled same time as Fardy. Too much of a coincidence I'd say. Fardy calling the name during sleep, it belongs to a real person, and that person could easily be described as a giant like it says on the tape."

"What about Huntley?" Adam asked.

"Nothing. Haven't been able to tie Fardy or Cowboy to Huntley, but Huntley made the six o'clock news." Bulldog checked the time. The late news broadcast was finished. "You'll have to read about it in the Sunday paper. Huntley held a big press conference and told the world about Mr. X and his hopes to prove the existence of life after death. Put on a real show of concern, publicly pleaded for Mr. X to seek professional help. Huntley ended by declaring how wonderful it would be if life after death could be proven. Praised the unselfish heroism evident in a man who would even consider such a noble sacrifice." Bulldog shook his head.

Sheriff Riggs cleared his throat. "What does this have to do with Reverend Meeks?"

"Sorry, Sheriff," Bulldog said, who then proceeded to explain. After he finished, Bulldog said, "But none of that explains the kid who so frightened Reverend Meeks." Bulldog scratched his head. "What have you been working on lately, Adam? Have you been dogging someone?" He looked at Kelly. Was Adam's friend a psychic? She said that she sensed her friend was dead, murdered by the young man mentioned on the tape. This was too much.

"Adam, you of all people, what were you doing talking with a psychic?"

Adam sighed. "It's Gloria. She's preg— she's going to become a mother."

"Damn, I'm sorry Adam. Wait a minute! You went to Cassadaga because of that? You've got me really confused, you hate all that psychic stuff."

"I've been trying to help. I visited an abortion clinic, and I—"

"An abortion clinic!" interrupted Bulldog, and Sheriff Riggs grunted. "Sheriff, are you thinking what I'm thinking?"

"Good possibility. Aunt Mae, uh, Reverend Sykes, my aunt and Reverend Meeks' good friend, went to the house for an evening walk the two of them have been taking for years. Aunt Mae sensed the presence of a very confused young man. Also, a kid at the gas station sold gas to a stranger meeting the size description, but the kid didn't really look up at the man's face. Couldn't even remember what he wore except that he had on brown leather boots. Said he acted really weird when they started talking about psychics killing babies, red neck bull by the way, but it all fits. Except the truck. This fellow getting gas drove a gray Dodge Ram, but Aunt Mae, she works by psychometry, held an article of clothing that had been thrown across the bed by the intruder. She sensed a bright red truck. She was very upset at the time so the read on the vehicle may be a mistake."

"We're checking for all Ram owners," said Bulldog. "Now, we'll talk to people at the clinic and put the place under surveillance. If Adam did pick this kid up there, maybe the guy's a regular."

"One thing for sure," Adam said, "no one followed me from Cassadaga. If this fellow tailed us there, he didn't leave when we did." Kelly nodded her head in agreement.

"Adam, you stay here tonight, uh, I mean, ah…" Bulldog said, until Kelly helped him out.

"You bet he's staying here tonight. I'm not letting him out of my sight until this man is caught." Adam started to object, but Kelly stopped him. "Listen, my little Chihuahua who thinks he's a Great Dane, this condominium building is key entry only. You will be much safer here."

"My point exactly, and I'm going to post a uniform in the lobby just in case." Bulldog pointed a finger. "Now listen, Adam, you are not to go anywhere without the uniform. Is that clear? This is not idle threats from radio land, this is Broadway."

Adam grinned. He knew that his friend referred to threatening phone calls that resulted from on-the-air confrontations with The

Mouth. In conservative talk-show radio land, Adam was known as Father Teresa. Bulldog continued. "I mean it, Adam. No screwing around, you hear?" Bulldog caught himself and cleared his throat. "Sorry, Miss Dorsey."

"No problem, I like the stubborn little guy too." Her eyes teared again.

Bulldog said. "Like him? Hell I just feel sorry for him because God must have run out of enough dough for one more full-sized biscuit. You keep him here, OK? He has a nasty habit of not listening to me." Before leaving, Bulldog called in for a uniform to guard the condominium entrance.

Later, after watching Kelly finally stop tossing and go to sleep, Adam tumbled over the waterfall. "Indian, where are you?" he screamed.

"I am here, Adam, join me," said Many Faces.

Adam spotted the campfire and walked toward it. In the background he heard muffled drums sounding a hypnotic rhythm. Many Faces sat cross-legged near the fire that had burned down to mostly red-hot coals. He motioned for Adam to sit on a convenient log. "Reverend Meeks was murdered. Is she playing dead?" said Adam.

Many Faces placed a couple pieces of wood on the coals. Both men watched as timber began to smoke, pop sparks, then burst into flame. Many Faces said, "The ego always likes to blame something or someone outside itself when trouble brews. Man invented his gods as a scapegoat for this reason."

"That kid is to blame. I'm just telling you that Reverend Meeks is dead. She is gone," said Adam.

"Experience follows belief, Adam. Man needs to remember that."

"So Reverend Meeks believed that she was going to be killed? That's crazy!"

"A part of her did, Adam. You are a multi-dimensional being struggling to understand your existence using only your physical mind. You're trying to understand a book by reading just the cover."

"Don't talk in riddles."

"Learn to meditate. Accept that we are all interconnected, that understanding is universal; therefore, it is available to anyone who seeks," said Many Faces.

"Mumbo jumbo." Adam slid from the log to the ground and leaned back. He picked up a piece of pine bark and began scratching designs in the dirt.

A fuzzy raccoon ambled from the foliage and eyed the two men. Sensing no threat, the animal continued its nightly hunt for sustenance. "Indeed, Adam. It was good enough for the one who became known as the Christ and the one who became known as the Buddha, and the untold millions who have benefited from their enlightenment."

"So, should I go into the desert or just sit under a tree for forty days or whatever it is reported to have been?"

"Well, those facts may be just symbolic." Many Faces held out his hand and an egg materialized. He stretched his arm toward the masked intruder that hesitated briefly before easing up, taking the egg, and scurrying back into the brush. "You know, Adam, the number forty has great significance for man. First, the gestation period for a human is about forty weeks, and in what are known as prehistoric times, a man who reached forty years was often wise and respected as an elder.

"Later, we have the story of the flood that lasted forty days, plus the liberated slaves of Egypt who gestated forty years in the wilderness before being born in the promised land. Then along comes Prince Siddhartha who meditated for forty days and gained understanding followed by Jesus about five hundred years later who meditated in the desert for forty days to achieve cosmic consciousness. The prince became the Buddha, the Enlightened One, and Jesus became the Christ, the Anointed One. And, of course, the kicker of them all, Jesus ascended to Heaven forty days after the resurrection."

"Just coincidence and a succession of historians writing for effect," said Adam. "Just like the ghost always goes thump, thump, thump, or the infamous knock on the door is rap, rap, rap, never two, never four, always three."

Many Faces poked in the fire and the flames shot higher. The light penetrated the surrounding dark, and Adam spotted the masked bandit eagerly licking the eggshell under the brush just beyond the clearing. Nothing nourishing would remain unclaimed.

The old Indian smiled at Adam. "Individual claims and their proximity to fact are unimportant. It's the hidden revelation that yields results; the point here is solitude. The emerging child floats in solitude as it prepares for birth. The man who becomes venerated as a wise elder earned wisdom by considering causes and effects, by turning inward and contemplating life after much experience. The ark and its inhabitants never hailed a passing ship. They had time to contemplate their circumstances.

"Sometimes man requires great tragedy before he will consider the results of his actions. Wars end when those affected become sick of the carnage. Man then works harder for peace to prevent history from repeating itself. The Israelites, after much suffering, escaped slavery, the ego surrendered. They then survived isolation in the wilderness, the spirit was resurrected. When they were spiritually ready they entered the promised land, they were born again. And the great teachers sought solitude in order that their spiritual nature could assert itself over the demands and weaknesses of the flesh. Jesus and the prince wondered the earth seeking answers, but both stopped searching the physical world for understanding and located it within. Finally, Jesus ascended. Metaphysically, the number forty stands for completedness."

Adam shook his head in disbelief. He tossed the piece of pine bark in the fire and sparks flew. "Any more fairy tales?"

"Actually, now that you ask. Today, at around forty years of age many individuals find that they change. They begin to be grateful for their blessings and seek to give something back. They become more active in giving of their time and material wealth. You become less self-absorbed. The physical demands of providing for one's self becomes less onerous; therefore, the ego relaxes. The spiritual nature can more easily assert itself."

Many Faces stirred the fire again. Flames leaped up and battled back part of the darkness. He locked eyes with Adam. "You'll be forty in a few years, no?" he said.

Adam glared at Many Faces. "Reverend Meeks is still dead, and so is Franci."

"You will see them again. Perhaps they are close now." With his head, Many Faces gestured toward the distant drums. "Listen to the beat, Adam. Man's oldest musical foray imitates the heart. Learn to relax the ego, to crack the acorn." Many Faces flipped a hot coal from the fire. "A burning love for All That Is will light your choices, Adam. Stop allowing the tail to wag the dog."

Adam opened his eyes. He was totally awake. His mind was churning. An image of Indians dancing to a primitive drum beat around a fire popped into his mind. Adam didn't understand why he thought it, but the Indians were celebrating the death of a great chief. The leader was now like the wind. No matter where his people may travel individually or as a group, the chief would always be available to them for help. Adam glanced at Kelly. Good, she still slept.

March 19, Sunday

Kyle struggled to guide his mount without the benefit of a bridle. He finally gave up and hung on as the ass galloped headlong, choosing its own path across the rocky desert. A flock of blue vultures pecked relentlessly at both animal and rider, all the while repeating Kyle's name. Kyle opened his eyes, saw the policeman standing over him, and screamed. His brother, Chuck, put his hand on Kyle's shoulder. "Hey, it's only me, calm down. What gives, boy? I've been trying like hell to wake you?"

Kyle said nothing. Confused, he looked around. Then he remembered. He had dropped the Ram pickup at the airport and driven his Ranger to a buddy's house where he had been staying for a couple of days. He rubbed his face and checked the time. It was eight a.m. He had been sleeping for only four or five hours.

"Sandy called me," his brother said. "She's been worried. What gives?"

Kyle sat up and leaned against the headboard. "Nothing. Just a little spat. I'll call her and go home in a couple days."

"She says you been acting strange. She wouldn't tell me why."

"Strange? You said Sandy didn't tell you why?"

"She wouldn't tell me. Said you would have to."

Kyle breathed deeply and relaxed. "We wanted a baby, but, ah, Sandy can't have one. That's all."

"I'm sorry, Kyle. I know that must be really disappointing, but, hey, you guys can adopt. Give yourselves some time to get used to the idea then talk about it." Chuck sat on the bed. "Don't blame Sandy, OK. This is nothing she can help."

"Yeah, I know. Thanks for looking for me."

"That's what brothers are for. By the way, be careful when you go out today. Seems some old lady was murdered over near the East Coast, and the murderer is believed to live in Tampa."

Kyle felt the blood drain from his face, but Chuck fiddled with his hat as he sat on the side of the bed and didn't notice. "What's that got to do with me?"

"Nothing really, except they are searching for the owners of all gray Dodge Ram pickups. It's believed that the guy was driving a Ram, but there's evidently some confusion. At first the interest centered on owners under thirty driving a red pickup. Big guys like you and me, by the way. Anyway, cops on patrol will be looking for drivers of gray Rams on suspicion of kidnapping."

"Kidnapping? I thought you said it was murder."

"Well, some psychic, a friend of the victim, says it's murder, but no body has been found. She also claims the murderer drives a red pickup, although a possible suspect was spotted in a gray Ram. Anyway, right now it's officially considered a missing person case. A guy named Adam Eden is connected somehow and is under twenty-four-hour uniform protection. Funny name, huh? I wonder if he's inventoried his ribs lately?"

"Is he locked up?"

"No, he's staying over at the Normandy Condominiums. If you go out, be careful and cooperate if pulled over. Don't break any laws."

"Don't worry, I won't. I'll also call Sandy, but first I need some sleep. You get out of here. Go catch that guy."

Chuck shrugged. "I start guarding an abortion clinic today. They believe this fellow is a religious fanatic. Guess they're afraid he might blow up the place." Kyle's brother stood up. "You call Sandy, OK?" Kyle shook his head in agreement. "By the way, where the hell did you get all those scratches? You and Sandy must have had more than a little spat."

"Uh, no, I, ah, I spent the night in the truck down at the well fields. I was really upset, you know, about the baby stuff and all. Started walking, got lost. Damn palmetto bushes cut me up before I found the truck again."

"That's my baby brother. Better put something on them," Chuck said, and let himself out.

Now wide awake, Kyle continued to sit up in bed. He had returned the Ram to long-term parking at the airport as near as he could remember to the spot where he had found it. He had carefully wiped clean all fingerprints in it and the old witch's house. Certain that no one had spotted him at the house, his only problems were the kid at the service station and the old man in the store.

The stupid kid didn't really look at Kyle, kept watching that dial, and the old white-eyed man couldn't even see to spit his tobacco juice straight. Kyle smiled. He wasn't a religious fanatic. God obviously protected His avengers so not to worry. Police protection or no, Dr. Adam Eden had better start trying to figure out how to live with a bullet hole through his head.

★

Adam saw his neighbor, Mrs. Stein, put her hands up to her mouth when she spotted the police cruiser pull into the driveway. He hopped out and waved. "Hey, don't worry, it's me," Adam said.

"Oh, my goodness, I thought the police were here to arrest you for speeding."

"Speeding?" Adam said, throwing up his arms. "I don't drive fast. It's just that your husband drove so slowly my driving seems fast."

"Oh, this wind," Mrs. Stein said. She struggled to keep her pile of leaves from blowing back over the driveway. March was living up to its reputation.

Adam looked at the patrolman. "Can you help her bag those right quick? I'll only be a minute." He needed a few items of clothing and his laptop. He stuck his key in the lock and turned, but felt no resistance. After stepping into the foyer, he realized that maybe his carelessness might not have been wise. Adam turned to signal for the policeman, but hesitated. Silly to be frightened because of an unlocked door. It was often unlocked.

Adam turned around again and marched over to his answering machine. He would pack and listen at the same time. First there was a message from Gloria saying how much she liked Kelly, and thanking Adam for the trip to Cassadaga. She looked forward to sharing her recent psychic experiences with big brother. The message had probably been recorded earlier, before Adam had called from Kelly's and told Gloria about Reverend Meeks' disappearance.

Several other messages of no consequence followed, and Adam paid scant attention until the panicked voice of Marvel

Fardy jolted him. He stopped packing and listened. "Mr. Eden, me and my children are in danger. Meet me at eleven o'clock at the bus stop on Hill and Spring Street. If it's safe, I'll get in the car. Me and my children will be killed if he finds out. Don't let nobody know you're coming, especially the police."

The panic in her voice arrested Adam. Bulldog had ordered him to stay inside so the sailing trip had been postponed. He and Kelly planned to spend the day working on their individual projects: Kelly, her case load, and Adam his notes for an article about handicaps and what more could be done to aid them. If danger lurked, he didn't want her near it.

After erasing the recorder, Adam heard a definite thump upstairs. If skin could truly crawl his would be on its way out the door. He laughed at himself. God he was jumpy. Old wooden houses complain about this and that all the time. It had to be nothing. Besides, if it was something all he had to do was yell and the cop would be there in a flash.

He had to think. Marvel expected him at eleven o'clock so he had exactly one hour. The thump again, but fainter, maybe muffled? Call the cop? No. It would be embarrassing. Adam retrieved a hammer from a cabinet shelf and quietly made his way up the steps. His stealth was in vain, however, since several of the steps voiced their objection to his weight. He searched each room until he came to the back bedroom. Saliva stuck in his throat. He eased through the doorway and stared at the partially opened closet door, but it was motionless. He could have sworn that the door moved as he entered the room.

Squatting, he made certain that no one was under the bed. He eased closer, leaned forward, and gave the closet door a nudge. Nothing. He moved closer, and a gust of wind rattled an opened window. Instinct made him jump before his brain registered the cause. The closet door moved again slightly, manipulated by the March wind. Shaking his head and laughing, he hurried downstairs.

He quickly finished packing, changed clothes, scribbled a note to the policeman, and rushed out the back door. Across the alley and two houses down, Adam paid a neighborhood teenager fifty bucks for the loan of his bicycle. Downtown and several car rental agencies were less than two miles away. He would probably get there before his talkative neighbor freed the patrolman to search for him.

★

When Kyle heard the back door open and close, he fought his way through the clothes and stepped from the closet. He rushed to the front bedroom and peeped out. The policeman was still helping bag leaves, but Eden was not there. Kyle had leaped upstairs to the bedroom when he saw the cop car drive up. When Eden tiptoed in, the temptation was great, but killing the creep with a patrolman outside would have been crazy. One scream from the baby butcher, and Kyle would be caught.

He ran downstairs and looked out back. Nothing. Eden had disappeared. Confident that God would provide, and careful not to leave prints, Kyle exited by the back door.

★

Driving a rented Ford Tempo, Adam started searching for Mrs. Fardy as he neared the bus stop. He felt guilty sneaking away without calling Kelly, but at least she would be safe. When he reached Hill and Spring, no one stood at the bus stop. He stopped anyway. After a couple of minutes, Marvel darted from behind a sign and hopped in next to Adam, who promptly sped away.

"Oh, God, I hope I wasn't followed. We got to be careful."

"What's this all about?" Adam scanned the area. He didn't want to bring his troubles to this frightened woman. "If someone is following you, I'll lose them. Don't worry."

"You don't understand. It may already be too late if Dr. Huntley knows I'm with you."

"Too late?" Adam asked. Marvel told him the truth that she had finally been able to wrest from Clarence after seeing Dr. Huntley on the news.

"I can't take no chances with my children, Mr. Eden. Clarence believes that them and me will be safe only if he does what Dr. Huntley wants, but I don't know what to think. I don't know what to do." She started crying.

Adam comforted her as best he could. "We need to bring in the po—"

"No! No way. Clarence says the police can't protect us. If Dr. Huntley is arrested or killed, Clarence says we would all be killed instead of just him. I only know I want my babies to be safe. If me and Clarence have to die, all right, but not my babies." She grabbed Adam's arm. "You've got to hide my babies. Please hide my babies, then I can face whatever happens."

Adam looked into Marvel's pleading eyes. A man could love his children, a man could die for his children, but a man could never do either with the selfless devotion of a mother. Something Bulldog had said scratched its way to the surface of Adam's mind. "The police can't protect you from a determined killer." Adam scribbled Kelly's phone number on a card and handed it to Marvel. "So you can call me," he said. He took Marvel's hands and cupped them between his. "We'll do it your way."

★

Kyle drove to the airport and parked in the long-term parking garage. He grabbed his canvas overnight bag and went shopping for a new set of wheels. A black 1992 Oldsmobile caught his attention. The color seemed appropriate.

Thirty minutes later, Kyle observed the Normandy Condominiums about two blocks away when he spotted Adam exiting the rented compact. Excited about his good luck, Kyle eased over to the curb and hid behind a Bronco. Searching for possible witnesses, but spotting no one, he reached in his bag and fished out the stolen 45. What great fortune. He would force the little shit into the trunk and drive to the well field. After cutting off the bastard's offending hands, Kyle would send a bullet burrowing through the son-of-a-bitch's brains.

Kyle began to ease out into the street, but waited for an approaching car to pass. He watched as the car squealed to a halt and a big guy jumped out yelling, "Damnit, Adam, I told you to stay inside!"

Adam jumped, then ducked when tires started squealing. When he heard Bulldog's angry outburst, Adam wiped his brow.

"Jesus, Bulldog, you scared the hell out of me."

"Yeah, well you're lucky that it's me and not that crazy kid! Get in the fucking car, Kelly's worried sick." Adam climbed in and Bulldog continued his harangue. "The whole damn department has been searching everywhere for you, and I find you strolling down the fucking street like you're in the fucking Easter Parade. You—"

"Bulldog," said Adam, but his friend continued talking and slapping the steering wheel. "Bulldog," Adam tried again. "Bulldog, I'm safe now. I'm sorry I scared you. I wouldn't have slipped off had I a choice."

Squeezing the steering wheel, Bulldog stared at Adam. After breathing deeply several times, he said, "Can you tell me about it?"

"No, I promised."

Bulldog parked in front of the Normandy. He knew what a promise meant to Adam. "If your disappearance has something to do with Fardy, I wish you would tell me. I checked on Cowboy. Asked him why Fardy would call his name in a dream. He says he rescued Fardy from a beating. Adam, the man's not the type to get involved in another man's troubles, not for free anyway. I can't tie him to Huntley yet, but my guts tell me the string is there."

Adam massaged the back of his neck. "I don't know. Maybe we're on the wrong track completely. Maybe we should leave Huntley—"

"What? You don't believe that any more than I do."

Adam shrugged his shoulders and changed the subject. "What about the kid? Anything on him?"

Bulldog, his neck veins still prominent, pulsing, scrutinized Adam before answering. "Nothing yet, but we're still working on it. Anyway, you get your tail upstairs and let Kelly know that you're all right." Bulldog half smiled. "Course, when she sees that you're OK, she'll probably beat the crap out of you. Maybe I better go up and watch. Even a cop deserves some pleasure."

"She's capable. Teaches self-defense."

"She cares for you, Adam. Too damn good looking for the likes of you too. Did you tell her you're rich?"

"Unlike you macho types I never let a woman up until she's through."

"In your dreams, man. I'll let you know if something breaks. Oh, yeah, I told the uniform that if you go out to fart, he had better be able to tell me what you ate for breakfast." Adam grinned and got out of the car. He used the key that Kelly had given him and let himself in. He looked back and Bulldog waved as he drove away.

As Bulldog pulled from the parking lot, he searched his rear view and side view mirrors. He scanned every parked car and checked out the park across the street. Every time he thought about the kid killer, images of a rundown hallway flashed through Bulldog's mind. He remembered the searing pain of a bullet ripping through his guts. He had attended cop funerals. He didn't want his wife left with nothing to keep her warm but a funny folded flag.

★

It took him a while, but Kyle finally recognized Bulldog. When dropping by to visit his brother, Chuck, at the police station, Kyle had seen Bulldog a couple times. Kyle would have to be alert for unmarked cars. He had not thought about that danger until he recognized the detective.

Deeply perplexed, Kyle cranked the Olds and drove away. It puzzled him that Adam had been delivered so neatly then snatched away at the last minute. Kyle thought about Cassadaga. then he thought about the first time he had seen Adam strutting down the walk swinging his black butcher's bag. A cocky bastard, the man deserved to die.

Without thinking of a destination, Kyle drove to the abortion clinic. From two blocks away he spotted his brother's cruiser. Slowly turning off before getting too close, Kyle noticed the little woman who had walked out with Eden exit the clinic. Kyle pulled over to the curb. The woman stopped and talked to Chuck.

All the protesters had shouted at her. Kyle thought about his wife, Sandy, as he watched the tiny woman talking to his brother. He pushed it away. Even though it was Sunday, the woman was at the clinic. Killing babies on the Lord's day could not be tolerated. Kyle understood now. God intended that the little clinic lady die next, then it would be Eden's turn.

Kyle's brother opened the passenger door to the director's car and she dumped a load of files and a briefcase on the seat before walking around and getting in on the driver's side. Kyle held his breath as she backed out and drove up the street toward him. Quickly, he turned the corner and took an immediate right into the alley. Turning right again at the next street, he spotted his prey drive by. He gave her plenty of lead then turned left and followed. Later, the director had already entered the Albertson's supermarket by the time Kyle parked. He searched the trunk of the Oldsmobile and found a tattered blanket. He tossed it on the front seat and waited.

★

Thirty minutes later the director walked out carrying a bag of groceries that she had purchased for a single mother who had decided against abortion. The director shared her good fortune, her time, her counseling, and her help with many former patients with whom she had remained in touch. Never feeling more alive than when helping someone in need, she stepped lively across the parking lot.

She jumped when Kyle approached from the rear and put an arm around her shoulders. He shoved the 45 into her ribs and kept it hidden between his bulk and the bag of groceries. Before the director could grasp the situation, Kyle said, "One sound and you're dead." The director froze until Kyle forced her forward.

"Act natural or I'll kill you right here. All I want is your money. You're going to ride down the block with me and put all your money, rings, and watch in a bag. When it's safe, I'll let you out. You understand?"

Frightened, but also relieved, the director had known for some time that her choice to do what she believed in could cost her life. This was only a robbery. They were nowhere near her work. "I understand," she said.

They both entered the black Olds from the driver's side. Once in, Kyle pulled his knife and ordered the director to sit on the floor. She squeezed herself down and Kyle kept the knife tight against her throat. He fished a roll of duct tape from his bag. When the director saw the tape she realized that she had made a critical mistake getting into the car. Trapped with the knife at her throat she didn't dare yell or move.

As Kyle cut a piece of tape to cover her mouth, she forced herself to cry. Sniffing and with tears streaming down her face, she asked, "May I get a tissue please?"

"Don't start that. I don't like crying." He stuck the tape over her mouth and wrapped a piece around her wrists. With his head, he motioned toward her purse. "Stop the tears. I am not going to hurt you. I just want your money, but I can't let you go until we get outside the city." Kyle covered her with the soiled blanket.

The director corralled the purse and pulled out a tissue. She blew her nose for effect, then she worked a friend from her packed purse. A snub-nosed .38 caliber Colt revolver joined her under the dirty blanket.

★

It took forty minutes to reach the well fields where Kyle had buried Reverend Meeks. TV evangelists witnessing before millions used to make Kyle laugh, spilling out their hearts about how God had saved their wretched souls. Now Kyle understood the awesome power of God to transform.

Once a man sets aside his ego, once a man surrenders to God's will, that man begins to live. Once a man dedicates his life to God, that man is born again. Kyle remembered the fear that flashed in Reverend Meeks' eyes when she said, "It's you!" He relished her helplessness. He relived his dominance. By the time he reached the gate, euphoria gripped him. His dick was hard.

After he closed the gate behind him, the euphoria and the erection quickly faded. The Olds was not an all-terrain vehicle, and between bounces he cursed himself for not thinking ahead. He couldn't expect God to do everything. What if the car got stuck? He spotted a threatening mud hole and speeded up, hoping that momentum would take the car across. The sedan slipped first one way then another, but Kyle expertly kept control. The car slowed almost to a halt before the back wheels found some traction, and Kyle grimaced as he heard the spinning tires splattering mud under the wheel wells. Thankfully, rain fell sparingly during the month of March.

★

The director hurt. During the drive she had tried to move around to keep her circulation up, but the cramped space allowed little tolerance. She had tried to squat once, but Kyle forced her down and ordered her to stay still. Her butt throbbed. Her legs ached. She had a pounding pain where her head had smashed into the dashboard during the ride through the well field. Caught unaware, she almost blacked out from the impact. Blood trickled down her cheek and she was certain that her vision was blurred. She gripped the Colt tightly and held it to her breast. She willed herself to stay awake.

Finally, the car stopped. She heard Kyle get out, take a few steps through grass or weeds and then relieve himself, something that she was desperate to do. She leaned back against the door and toyed with the idea of removing the blanket. A risky idea; he might be watching. She decided that the best option would be to wait and let her captor remove the cover. Then she would shoot him immediately.

Kyle stomped around to the passenger side of the car. Too late to twist around and face him, she buried her hands and the pistol between her legs. Although her wrists were taped together, she still had mobility in her arms.

The door opened and Kyle removed the blanket as if unveiling a statue. "Get up," he said. The sunlight attacked the director's eyes as she struggled to comply. She couldn't use her hands or elbows for support without revealing the pistol. Also, her legs had no feeling and refused to respond. Scared, she looked around and saw her kidnapper grin. The image was blurred, but unmistakable. "I love your eyes," he said and he ripped the tape from her mouth.

Kyle reached down and put his hands under the director's arms. He easily pulled her up and out. Aware that only one chance stood between her and consequences she refused to accept, the director pressed the pistol to her chest. She had a devoted husband, children who needed her, and patients with no one to turn too.

Yes, she ran a clinic where abortions were performed, but she also did volunteer work at a home for unwed mothers. Over the years, the director had sent many of the young girls who came for abortions to the home. Some gave up their child for adoption, but a few could not break the bond once their child was born. These took their babies and did their best.

Kyle knew none of this, nor would he have cared. The director understood the type. God drove him. If God had wanted the director to live, He wouldn't have delivered her to judgement. When the director's feet hit the ground, she twisted at the same time that Kyle let her go. As she turned, her legs buckled. Sick with fear, aware only of the sadistic grin, the director aimed at the blurred white zipper between his lips. She squeezed the trigger. Kyle grabbed his head and fell backward at the same time the zipper opened. She heard an agonized scream until her head hit the car and she blacked out.

The director woke up surrounded by darkness. She scratched her cheek and realized that she itched everywhere. Then she noticed the dirty blanket on which she lay and wanted to scream. She tried to stand, but a numbing pain shot through her head. Rolling to her side, she spotted Kyle sitting on a log observing her. "You came close," he said, calmly. "My left ear's still ringing. My fault for not checking your purse. My fault for not thinking. It's God's punishment."

The director swallowed bile. Her wrists were still taped and now so were her ankles. She was in the hands of a religious fanatic. In spite of her courage, she began to cry. Kyle said, "I want you to say, 'It's you!'"

"What?"

"Just like I said it, I want you to say, 'It's you!'"

Kyle kneeled down beside her and put his knife to her throat. "Say it now."

"It's you!" she said, trying to move her chin away from the knife's razor-sharp edge.

Watching his captive's eyes, Kyle dropped his jeans and underwear. He took his knife and cut the tape away from her ankles first then from her wrists. That's when she realized that her jeans and shirt were gone. A dress covered her nakedness, but she had no way of knowing that just yesterday it had been worn by another human being who also did not deserve to die. But that didn't matter. Reverend Meeks had died anyway.

Kyle abruptly reached up the dress and grabbed her panties. The director screamed and Kyle placed his big hand across her mouth. He jerked the panties down, which slowed her kicking. He rolled his two hundred and twenty pounds on top of the diminutive director, who desperately scratched at his face. Grabbing both her hands in one of his, he guided his now hard penis to its mark. He rammed hard and the director screamed. Again, he placed his free hand over her mouth and began thrusting violently. "This is your punishment, bitch. Maybe you will give birth in hell."

The director continued to struggle and Kyle began a low, long, agonizing groan. He exploded, lost his breath, and collapsed, but he held the director tightly. She tried to move, but Kyle was too heavy, and she was exhausted. Kyle raised his head and watched her eyes. He squeezed her nose between his thumb and forefinger while continuing to press his hand over her mouth. Like God gave Samson strength through his hair, Kyle was replenished by avenging dead babies. He was a happy man.

He stripped the director, wrapped her naked body in the blanket, and laid the dress along with the underwear from both women aside. He threw the director's jeans and shirt on top of the blanket and buried her alongside the suitcase coffin containing Reverend Meeks.

Adam Eden would be next. Still, anyone could simply kill a person. Adam Eden, however, like the first two baby murderers, needed to be punished. He needed to suffer for his sins. With the women, the punishment was obvious.

Kyle studied the dress. He lifted it to his nose. It smelled musty, but the perfumed scent of his two victims mingled and still rested there also. That pleased him. He closed his eyes and pictured both his victims when they realized that they had only seconds to live. Kyle smiled and opened his eyes. He held the dress by its shoulder seams. It was small, but Eden wasn't a large man. Kyle would think more on it.

He searched through the junky trunk of the Oldsmobile and discovered a garbage bag full of rags. He dumped the rags and buried the dress and underwear in a shallow hole. He shoveled dirt into the hole then sat on a log. He had to figure what to do next. God doesn't like it when you don't think for yourself.

★

Kelly called Adam to the phone. It was Bulldog. "Adam, Dr. Susan Barrett is missing."

It took a minute for Adam to place the name. "The director of the clinic? My God, no!"

"Yeah. She's been missing since about five P.M. Found her car in an Albertson's parking lot, but not one witness to an abduction. Seems she called home before leaving the clinic, she had been doing some paperwork. Said she was going to stop by the store and take some food to a former patient. Her husband said this was nothing unusual. Said Mrs. Barrett often spent long hours with anyone who needed her, but that she always let him know where she was going. She always called him when she arrived and just before leaving."

"You think it's the same kid?"

"No way to know at this point, but we've got two missing women, both visited by you. Yeah, I think it's the kid. Maybe when people hear the news or read the paper someone will remember something and call in. We're going to put the pressure on known protestors. They may know or have at least seen this character.

"The clinic here and two others in Sarasota pay a guy to swing from one clinic to the other taking videos and writing down tag numbers. We're going through that stuff for the second time, but nothing has popped up so far. If he's a regular, he should be in that mess somewhere."

"She didn't deserve this, Bulldog."

"We'll do our best to stop him. Don't go out if you don't have to, and if you do, make sure you go with the officer. I'll keep you posted. By the way, did you read about Huntley's news conference?"

"Megalomaniac. Unfortunately, if you don't know him, he comes across as sincere."

"Exactly. You stay away from him, he's dangerous. That Cowboy character would pluck you like a chicken if paid to."

"I'm not going anywhere. Don't worry."

★

Adam needed to make plans. He told Kelly about the director, tried small talk to distract her, speaking about this and that until he asked Kelly about her childhood. She talked and Adam responded occasionally with a grunt or a nod. She said, "That's when my father had his sex change operation and ran away with the mailman. My mother had to prostitute herself to support my brother and me." Adam nodded.

Kelly stepped over and curled up on the sofa next to Adam. She took his hand between hers. "Do you want to tell me what's going on inside that head of yours?"

"What? Ah, nothing. I'm just concerned, that's all."

"Do you realize that we met just last Monday? I've known you for only one week, but sitting here with you, I feel like I've known you a thousand years." Adam nodded his head in agreement. "What I'm trying to say is that I know that your brain is working overtime. I believe you disappeared earlier because of Clarence Fardy, and I understand that. I think that you should leave it to the police, but I accept that you won't do that. You should stay here where you're safe, but I know that you won't do that either. You are a man with strong principles, and I find that terribly attractive, so I can't fault you for risking your life to help others.

"I can live with all that, Adam, but I won't accept you keeping me in the dark. Adam, look at me." Kelly waited until he did. "I would rather have six hours of pain knowing that it will end after six hours than to suffer thirty minutes not knowing when it will end. Now, what are you up to?"

Adam stood and started pacing. Kelly waited. "You must not tell Bulldog. You must not tell the police."

"I won't, without your permission."

Adam related the whole story. He even told her about Dr. Huntley handing Clarence the pistol. "Kelly, I believe that Huntley is prepared to die if necessary. I promised to help Mrs. Fardy get her children to safety."

"But don't you think that the police—"

"Kelly, think about it. Huntley is consumed with hate for Clarence Fardy and scorn for the lower class. He has concocted this elaborate scheme with some psychic con artist to get rid of Clarence and as many other gullible people who will believe that Clarence survived death." Kelly raised her eyebrows. Adam said, "I know, I know. I admit that Reverend Meeks has weakened my belief that death is the end of awareness. Maybe birth and death are no more consequential to existence than eating that second apple tart at a family reunion. Right now, I don't really know. I'm only certain that Clarence Fardy and his family need help."

"But, Adam, the police—"

Adam threw up his hands. "Let's say that the police believe Mrs. Fardy even though Clarence would deny everything. They somehow prove the scheme exists. Huntley is the mastermind. He gets arrested, but how long will the police guard the Fardy family, and how could they do it at all without making the family prisoners?"

"Yes, but Uncle Luther – ah, Luther would know that if anything happened to the Fardys he would be blamed."

"Ordinarily, but if hate is great enough that self-preservation is no longer a handicap to a murderer, how do you protect yourself? Clarence could have killed Huntley with the pistol. Huntley wanted to make that clear. More importantly, however, pompous maniacs like Huntley believe they are invincible. He is so cocksure of his superiority it makes him vulnerable."

"Won't moving the children result in the same dilemma?"

"If Clarence does as Huntley plans, maybe not. Mrs. Fardy has resigned herself to Clarence's fate, and she will not abandon him. She will join her husband if necessary to appease Huntley, but if Clarence follows orders, Huntley would have no reason to go further. Clarence will be dead and Huntley will be blameless as long as he keeps the children alive to threaten Mrs. Fardy into continued silence."

"You seem to have accepted Clarence's death as unpreventable," said Kelly.

Adam shrugged his shoulders. "It's like trying to diffuse a bomb without knowing how it works, unfortunately there's no time left to figure it out. You take a chance. I figure if we move the children from the equation, there will be less fear in fighting back. Also, Huntley hates disorder. He thrives on control. By changing the balance, we may get lucky and force him into a mistake. We know what that maniac is capable of, but he won't do the dirty work. He has someone in the shadows who is a mystery. That's where we need a little light."

"What is the plan? I want to help."

March 20, Monday

"I'm sorry. Dr. Huntley is not available at the moment. May I take a message?" the secretary said.

"Tell him it's Herman, the man with a fake beard, and I promise he will want to speak to me. If you don't tell him I am on the phone, when he finds out that you didn't put me through he will probably fire you," said Phoenix.

The reluctant secretary said, "Please hold, I will see if I can find him." She buzzed Dr. Huntley and relayed the message. After a moment, she said, "Sir? Dr. Huntley, are you there, sir?"

"What? Oh, sorry, yes, put the call through."

"Dr. Huntley," Phoenix said.

"How did you know...?"

"I am a psychic, you know, but it pays better to enhance my psychic abilities with a little practical flimflam."

"If you were truly a medium you would know that you have chosen a very unwise action calling here."

"All I want is what you promised. You said Barbara is mine, that you would see to it."

"What is wrong?" Dr. Huntley asked, but wondered why a problem existed with Lee on the job.

"Barbara is gone. She knows how it infuriates me when she messes around, and she does it on purpose. She's a no-good bitch, but I love her. If you want me to play along with your scheme, you had better do something."

A seductive image of Barbara flirted with Dr. Huntley's mind, forcing him to take a deep breath and slowly release it. It bothered him that he continued to think about a common trollop, no matter how lovely. There had been others who similarly captured his thoughts, even when he was married to Jean. Never, however, did he allow himself to surrender his principles and pursue or purchase the bait.

"All right, calm down," he said. "Soon you will have enough money to make Barbara behave as you like." Dr. Huntley stroked his chin and planned as he talked. He found Phoenix's concern with problems of the living amusing, considering that she would soon be dead.

Once she performed her little charade, he would ship her off to the Caribbean and have her killed. He wondered if Phoenix had told Barbara the plan. If he didn't have to kill Barbara too, what would the woman do? She did not realize the abundance of her beauty. His penis began to grow hard, and it embarrassed him. Such a common person, she was not his problem.

"You don't understand, damnit!" shouted Phoenix. "You've got to do something now. She's run off again. I'm going to kill her for this."

Dr. Huntley worried. Lee had never let him down before, and no one could reason with Phoenix in her current state. "Now listen closely," he demanded. "I will see to it that your problem is solved. Don't do anything foolish, do you understand?"

"I understand that the man I am to receive a message from is not yet dead, and that you are not an innocent bystander. If you want me to play along with your scheme you had better do something quick."

Dr. Huntley's face contorted with rage, but he gripped the phone tightly and managed to control his temper. The impertinent sow and a lot of other parasites would no longer be a burden to decent society soon enough anyway. "It will be taken care of. Do not call here again."

It was three P.M., and Lee had not checked in for two days. He stroked his chin and realized that he was sweating. He phoned the hotel where Lee planned to register, but found no one listed under an agreed upon assumed name. Dr. Huntley hesitated then asked if a LeRoy or Lee Lentz had checked in. Hearing the same negative answer, he slammed the receiver down.

★

At precisely 1:55 P.M., Adam, wearing a baseball cap, pulled the unmarked blue rental car into the line of other vehicles waiting for their children to exit Dr. Martin Luther King Elementary School. A teddy bear hung from his rearview mirror. On the other side of the school, where the Fardy children usually bounded out to freedom, a herd of yellow school buses waited.

Frightened, Adam scanned the area searching for anyone or anything suspicious. He understood that a dangerous maniac was stalking him, and he knew that an equally dangerous maniac tracked the Fardy children. It had been a dilemma. Adam did not want to endanger the children even more by bringing them into his own nightmare, but he had promised to say nothing to the police.

Besides, Mrs. Fardy probably had it right. Huntley had waited four years for revenge. He had invested a lot of effort planning the perfect murder, a suicide freely committed in front of live TV news. Undoubtedly, the man would have the patience to back off if necessary and wait to take the whole Fardy family together. The children had to be moved.

If Mrs. Fardy alerted the police, Clarence would never confirm her story. Clarence accepted without question that Huntley would have the whole family murdered if the suicide did not take place as planned. There wasn't much choice. Clarence intended to march to his death to save his family. At least this way the children would be safe temporarily, and maybe Huntley might allow anger at their disappearance to make him careless. It was a dilemma. How can one protect oneself from a determined killer? The question haunted Adam.

He thought of the policeman guarding the lobby at the Normandy. With no way around him and no way that he would allow Adam out of his sight again, Adam had no choice but to bring Kelly in on his plan. She was right. To keep her in the dark and worried was wrong. Kelly said, "I have the key to a friend's apartment on the second floor, just above the lobby. From the balcony you can climb down a magnolia tree to the parking lot."

Later, in the second-floor condominium, as Adam prepared to go from the balcony to the tree, he hesitated and stared at Kelly. "Once this mess is over, you know, ah, once our lives are sane again, maybe you would consider giving up the key to your friend's apartment." Adam studied the bicycle and gym shoes that occupied one corner of the balcony.

Kelly smiled and sandwiched Adam's cheeks with her hands.

"I've already decided to love you, Adam Eden, whether you love me or not." Adam nodded and Kelly kissed him passionately. "Please be careful," she said.

Adam heard the school bell ring and sat up to search for the kids. Mrs. Fardy was to explain to Tommy, her oldest son, that some bad men were trying to harm his father. Like in a movie they had once seen on TV, Tommy had to be brave and take charge of his brother and sister.

Marvel had packed a change of clothing for the kids to dress in before leaving the school. All three had worn colorful clothes to school that morning; the boys wore red shirts and the daughter wore a bright yellow dress. If Tommy did his part the three kids would be in drab colored clothes when they came out. Tommy would come first and his brother and sister would follow, trying to hide among the other children. Tommy had the job of spotting the blue Tempo with the teddy bear hanging on the mirror. Adam hoped the boy would get it right. He did.

★

After watching the children get in the car and lay down, Kelly breathed a sigh of relief. No way would she have allowed Adam to face this alone. As she had done before following him down the tree, she waited briefly, then tailed Adam to Gloria's house. Satisfied that no one else had, she said a little prayer. Maybe the children would be safe.

★

At six fifteen P.M. Lee still had not checked in. Dr. Huntley stepped into the phone booth and placed a call to Lee's number to check for any recorded messages. There was only one. "This is Bird Dog. The three birdies have left the nest. Waiting for orders."

Shocked by the message, Dr. Huntley had been confident that Clarence believed that only his suicide would save the children, now they were gone. The Clarence Fardy Dr. Huntley had slapped around in the orange grove would not have risked moving the children. Something smelled.

He fished a memorized number from his mind. When a man answered, Dr. Huntley asked to speak with Bird Dog. "You've got the wrong number, mister," the man said.

Dr. Huntley stroked his chin and thought a minute before placing the next call. Lee had obviously pulled his men and skipped to God knows where. Lee had been paid a lot of money for various jobs since starting to work, so Dr. Huntley had no fear that his accomplice would go to the police. A man like Lee who never had much money could quickly reach a comfort level. Mexico seemed a likely destination. After dispatching the Fardy family, Dr. Huntley would see to it that LeRoy Lentz also got what he deserved, but after Adam Eden, of course.

Dr. Huntley had his own connections, a side benefit to publishing his newsletter. He pulled another number from his memory and dialed. As expected, a recording instructed him to leave a message. Dr. Huntley said, "This is Dr. Justice and I am doubling your fee. I want you to be available at any time to complete the job. Complications prevent waiting until the original target date. The money will be wired to your overseas account tomorrow, Tuesday, March 21."

The time had arrived to have Clarence picked up. No longer certain of his foolproof plan, Dr. Huntley remained confident of one thing; no matter what happened, Jean's drunken murderer and his worthless family would burn. The phone rang. It was after hours and his secretary was gone for the day. "Huntley Enterprises," he answered.

"Dr. Huntley, this is Clarence Fardy."

"Well, well, well, Mr. Fardy. I'm surprised to hear from you."

"I didn't have anything to do with moving my children."

"Where are they?"

"I don't know. I've been trying to get my wife to tell me, but she refuses."

"And why would your wife move the children?"

"I had to tell her. She wanted to call the police the day I came in bruised up, then she saw your news conference. I tried, believe me I tried to make up something, but she believed nothing. It's because of that writer fellow. He made her suspicious and she wouldn't let things be. I thought if I told her the truth she would understand."

"Sad, but I warned you."

"But nothing's changed, Dr. Huntley. I'll still do it. It doesn't matter where my family is really. I will do as you demand. Please don't hurt my family."

"Then you will do it tomorrow, Clarence. You do as I say, and your family lives. If you make one mistake, they burn."

"I'll do it, Dr. Huntley. Don't worry. Please don't hurt my family."

"All right, this is the plan..."

★

Kyle Keysor didn't want to be bothered by his brother again, so he called his wife, Sandy. He explained that he just needed a few days to adjust to his problem. She needed to realize that his problem was a difficult thing for a man to accept. He promised to be home in a couple more days. She should not worry. Next, Kyle ran the muddy Oldsmobile through a car wash and drove to the airport. It was time for a trade. He parked the Olds as close as possible to the spot where he had stolen it and quickly selected a roomy van. He should accommodate his guests.

March 21, Tuesday

Adam explained to Kelly that he was going to burst in on Huntley and try to rile him up. Desperate as that seemed, anything was better than passively accepting the inevitable. Kelly insisted on going with him. The uniformed policeman drove, and after twenty minutes Adam confronted Dr. Huntley's secretary. She asked Adam and Kelly to please wait. Kelly said, "Thank you," but Adam opened the door and burst into the office without an invitation. Kelly, the patrolman and the bewildered secretary followed.

"We know your plan, Huntley. I am—"

"Ah, Mr. Eden, what a pleasant surprise, and an officer of the law, how convenient. I was just going to call you," Dr. Huntley said. With a wave of his hand, he indicated to his secretary to close the door.

"Skip the charade, Huntley. You're a common mur—" said Adam.

"And Kelly, too," Dr. Huntley interrupted, nodding to Kelly while ignoring Adam. "I'm delighted that you both are here as well as your friend, although I don't understand his presence." Dr. Huntley looked again at Adam. "I'm sure that Kelly informed you that I shared the story of Mr. X with her, and now I have sad news. Mr. X called me last night and said that he would be calling today with instructions."

Dr. Huntley looked at Kelly. "You will not believe who Mr. X is. You remember Clarence Fardy, the sad little man who caused the tragic accident that took your Aunt Jean's life? It's him." Dr. Huntley nodded toward Adam. "Your Mr. Eden here was right. I tried to convince Mr. Fardy to see a doctor, but he is determined that this folly is the will of God." Dr. Huntley flashed a pathetic little smile.

The secretary interrupted via the intercom. "I'm sorry to disturb you, sir, but there is a determined man on the phone named Clarence Fardy. He insists that I put him through."

"Indeed, indeed, put him through." Dr. Huntley picked up the receiver and covered the mouthpiece. "Kelly, you are a psychologist, maybe you can reason with him." He didn't wait for a response.

"Dr. Huntley, here. Mr. Fardy, as I told you last night, Mr. Adam Eden, the author of *Suicide In America* will be assisting me in validating your contact with a psychic. Ironically, he and my niece, Kelly Dorsey, unexpectedly dropped in. The police are here too. I am going to put you on the speaker phone so that we can all hear what you have to say." Dr. Huntley pressed the speaker button. After all the foul-ups, things had fallen into place quite nicely.

"Oh, hello. Uh, Mr. Eden, I, ah, I'm sorry that I lied to you, but I wasn't ready at the—"

Adam butted in. "Clarence, this is Adam. I know that Huntley is forcing you. I know that he has threatened your children. You don't have to pretend."

"I am not pretending. What I do, I can tell you truly is the will of God. I broke a commandment. I killed. I cannot bring Mrs. Huntley back to life. The only thing I can do that seems satisfactory is to take my own life, but that too is wrong. I worried about this until my late grandmother began appearing to me. There is life after death, and I was sent here to erase the doubt. I have been chosen, Mr. Eden. Please, please understand, I have no choice. If you interfere you will truly visit the sins of the father on my innocent family, my children."

Adam glared at Dr. Huntley. "Yes, Clarence, I understand."

"I want you to meet me at the intersection where I killed Mrs. Huntley. I am calling from the 7-11 on the corner. You say the police are there with you? Well, I am carrying a bag containing twenty sticks of dynamite plus a gallon of gasoline. I will keep my thumb on the detonator at all times. The police should clear the area, but make certain that they know I will use the detonator if interfered with in any way. Mr. Eden, you must believe me, and you must convince the police. I don't want anyone else to die."

"Clarence, your children are safe," said Adam.

After a long silence, Clarence explained, "Exodus, Chapter 20, Verse 5. '...for I the Lord thy God am a jealous God, visiting the iniquity of the fathers upon the children...' Mr. Eden, if you thought that my children were in danger, then you must have talked with my wife. You know that the only way to protect my family is to pay for my sin. Please don't interfere. Call the TV stations and newspapers. I want to announce my intention of proving that there is life after death."

"Mr. Fardy this is Dr. Huntley. I beg you, please reconsider. I understand that you have strong convictions and a pure motive, but if you do this thing, I will feel guilty. It's true that when my wife died I was very angry, but I have forgiven you. You told me that you discovered Jesus in prison, wouldn't it be better to live and to help others find Him too?"

"I have prayed over my decision for a long time, Dr. Huntley. I appreciate your kind words and concern, but I must submit myself to God's will."

"I admire your courage and selflessness, Mr. Fardy," said Dr. Huntley. "I intend to take care of your family, so don't worry about them." He peered down his nose at Adam, who was uncharacteristically subdued.

"Please make the phone calls and meet me here. I will allow only you and Mr. Eden to approach. Goodbye."

His eyes narrow with disgust, Adam glared at Dr. Huntley. "You won't get away with this, you know."

"Away with what? You heard the man, and I recorded the conversation just in case you wish to hear it again."

"Luther," Kelly said, startling the man; she sounded like her Aunt Jean. "This will not erase the loss or the pain."

Dr. Huntley allowed anger to flash across his face briefly, then brought it under control. "That's precisely what I have tried to convey to Mr. Fardy, but he is determined that he is doing the right thing. You heard him. He believes that he is chosen." Dr. Huntley stroked his chin. "Why, it's almost as if he believes that God will punish him if he does not commit suicide. Ironic isn't it, how people interpret the Bible to match their beliefs?"

Dr. Huntley questioned both Adam and Kelly with his eyes, but neither spoke. It pleased him, made him quite happy actually, that he could feign sadness knowing that his two guests recognized the masquerade, but the patrolman didn't know what to believe. Dr. Huntley wanted to laugh, something he had not done for four long years. He said, "We had better go. Why don't you two ride with me and I will make the phone calls to the media? The patrolman can contact his superiors."

★

By the time Dr. Huntley, Adam and Kelly reached the 7-11, the area had already been cordoned off and Clarence stood alone like a statue in the middle of the intersection. The policeman at the barricade motioned for Dr. Huntley to detour until he introduced himself. "I believe that we are expected," Dr. Huntley said. He drove forward and parked behind a line of police vehicles. Bulldog glanced up and motioned for the occupants to join him. He introduced everyone to his captain.

"Captain, this is Kelly Dorsey and Adam Eden who, as you know, are supposed to be under police protection at the Normandy." Bulldog scanned all the activity behind Adam and beyond the barricade. Danger from the kid didn't seem likely with all the police in the area. Kidnapping seemed the likely move so Adam should be safe. Bulldog looked at Dr. Huntley and frowned. "This is Luther Huntley. Folks, this is Captain Ansel."

The captain nodded to everyone. "I saw your news conference, Dr. Huntley. It would appear that this is no hoax."

"No indeed, as these two can attest. We tried to reason with Mr. Fardy, but he is riddled with guilt. He killed my wife you know, and he suffers from, well, too much religion in my opinion."

"He will not talk to us. The only thing he said is that he wants to talk with you and Mr. Eden and that he will blow himself and this intersection up if interfered with. He wants you to bring a microphone. I don't advise you to approach him."

"Thank you, Captain, for your concern, but I want to try again to talk him out of this folly. Because his guilt arises from the death of my wife, I feel responsible, although I should not." Dr. Huntley lowered his head. "One death is too many, and Mr. Fardy's will not bring back my wife. I understand too, that he has a wife and three children. I'm sure his death would be as devastating to them as my dear Jean's death has been to me."

"We need to keep him talking so I won't stop you if you are willing to try. He also wants you, Mr. Eden, but like I say, he's dangerous."

"I'll talk to him, Captain. Maybe there's still a chance that I can do something."

With his eyes, Dr. Huntley challenged Adam. "I doubt that, Mr. Eden. Clearly the man is deranged. He would rather face a horrible death than God's punishment for disobeying His will. But come, let's see what we can do. Captain, can you get me a microphone from one of the TV stations?"

★

With the conversation recorded live on TV, Clarence did most of the talking. Adam said little. Clarence's death seemed unpreventable. A man could risk his own life, but how could he risk the lives of children? And, if one thought about it long enough, there was a sense of justice, at least until you got to know Clarence personally. Maybe if Clarence was the same drunk who had been arrested several times for DUI and driving with a suspended license it would be justice or at least understandable, but killing this Clarence clearly equaled murder. Some people changed if given time. That's why capital punishment is wrong.

Desperate to save Clarence, and equally desperate to ruin Huntley, Adam felt helpless. He forced himself to remember that the lives of a mother and her three children were also at stake. Sometimes in spite of all you can do, life sucks, or at least your available choices do.

Speaking into the TV microphone, Clarence explained his intentions and his reasons while occasionally being interrupted by Dr. Huntley, who pleaded with Clarence to abandon his folly. Finally, Clarence announced that he was ready and that Dr. Huntley and Adam should move to a safe distance. Clarence doused himself with the bottle of gasoline and pulled out his lighter, all the while keeping his right thumb on the detonator visible in his hand.

★

Kyle Keysor slept in his newly acquired van that he had parked amid a collection of eighteen-wheelers at the Chat and Chew Truck Stop on Highway 301, East of Tampa. The big trucks had been pulling in and out all night, but exhausted, Kyle slept through it. The early morning temperature hovered at an invigorating sixty-one degrees, and oddly, the smell of oil and gas did not displease Kyle. The scent, coupled with the constant clicking of the big diesel engines as the huge rigs jockeyed for departure space, made the world seem especially alive.

Kyle admired the independence of the drivers, and he had enjoyed their stories the night before. Where there is an ear to listen, there are stories to be embellished. After Kyle finished God's assignment, he would give some serious thought to becoming a trucker. He showered and ate a big breakfast. When he paid, he checked his supply of Tums then realized they had not been needed for several days. Truly a sign that he was right with God.

He bought a cheap styrofoam cooler, iced down some beer and sodas, and added a couple of sandwiches. They would stay fresh sealed in ziplock bags. He hurried to the park near where Adam had conveniently parked the rented Ford Tempo down the block from the Normandy and away from the spying eyes of the police. Kyle waited several hours and finally relieved himself in a couple of soda cans that he emptied along the curb. Confident that today would be the day that God delivered Adam Eden to his judgement, Kyle had no intention of leaving for any reason.

He was disappointed when he spotted Adam and Kelly get into the patrolman's car, but his confidence remained high. God provided, and Kyle must be ready. He followed the trio to the Citrus Bank building and watched the cop pull into the parking lot beneath the building. Kyle drove around the block a couple of times until he found street parking that provided a clear view of the garage exit.

He tuned in a Country and Western music station, settled back to wait and almost fell asleep. He would have missed their exit completely if not for his hatred of wealthy people.

Dr. Huntley's Mercedes immediately caught Kyle's attention, and he surveyed the car's occupants. He hurriedly cranked the van and followed at a safe distance.

Later, Kyle almost panicked when two police cars, sirens screaming and their red and blue lights flashing, rushed up behind him. He sat up, steeled himself for the chase, but they flew right by. Then he heard other sirens and spotted two fire trucks turning onto the road a couple of blocks ahead. He wanted to flee, but something was happening and his prey appeared headed right toward it. God had done His part, now Kyle must have the courage to do his. He continued dogging the Mercedes.

Kyle spotted the orange-striped barricade ahead, beyond which sat a collection of fire trucks, rescue vehicles, numerous squad cars and TV news trucks. Electrical feeds snaked everywhere. People rushed to and fro, but the reason wasn't apparent. Traffic was being diverted at the next intersection, and Kyle was surprised to see the police drag the barricade aside to admit the Mercedes.

Horns started blaring behind Kyle, and finding no place to pull over, he slowly rolled forward. Looking around, he spotted a young woman standing at the head of a flight of stairs that led to an upstairs apartment. People were streaming in from every direction, heading for the barricades. Kyle watched the young woman pull her door closed and run down the stairs to join the others. She spoke to several people along the way.

The door had a dead bolt lock, but the woman had not used a key. Kyle managed to maneuver into the alley and park alongside the aging building. With everyone's attention riveted on the intersection ahead, Kyle casually climbed the stairs and looked. A huge leafy oak tree filtered his view.

Turning toward the door, he discovered a window to his left. A knock got no answer. He opened the door and entered without worry. The window was to a bedroom from which he could clearly see a small man standing alone in the middle of the intersection. The woman whose apartment he was now using had disappeared in the crowd, but Kyle did identify Adam and the driver of the Mercedes marching toward the little guy in the street.

Kyle estimated eighty yards between him and the action. He knew that his man Eden stood in the intersection, but Kyle didn't know why. He started to turn on the TV, but decided against it to prevent someone rushing in and surprising him. The scope on the Remington 700-P would help.

Searching the alley and streets below, Kyle saw that the stream of people pouring from the homes and businesses in the area had run itself dry. Cars were still backed up, but everyone was occupied searching the area ahead or behind, trying to find a way out of the jam that circled the huge cordoned off area in which his target waited.

Finding a bucket, a mop and a broom, Kyle picked them up along with a couple of towels. He walked down to the van and pulled out the rifle. He stuffed the butt of the weapon in the bucket and sandwiched it between the mop and broom. Carrying the bucket with one hand, he rested the barrel of the rifle and the cleaning tools against his shoulder, over which he threw a towel. As he climbed the stairs, no one noticed.

Through the scope, he studied the scene at the intersection and didn't like what he saw. The little guy gripped a detonator attached by wire to an overnight bag. He did a lot of talking into a microphone held by the driver of the Mercedes, who also spoke occasionally. Adam, who said little, distressed Kyle. The butcher was definitely scared.

Why did Adam continue standing in the middle of an intersection next to a fruitcake who looked like he wanted to blow a hole in the universe? Kyle held his breath when the walking bomb stooped and unzipped his bag. He produced a bottle of liquid and doused himself. Then he flashed a cigarette lighter.

Kyle cursed. Adam Eden belonged to him. God had chosen Kyle to punish Eden for his sins then kill him, but here Eden stood seemingly suspended in the middle of an intersection with a madman about to unleash an inferno. Was Eden nailed down, for Christ's sake? Maybe the little shit had killed the lunatic's baby. It didn't matter. God delivered Eden to Kyle and Kyle would not fail. He steadied the Remington and aimed for the head.

★

Clarence raised the lighter. He looked at Adam. "Please help my wife and children," he said. Adam understood the consequences, but he had to stop this murder. Deal with the imminent now, and handle the aftermath later. Adam lunged, Dr. Huntley jumped to stop him, Clarence screamed, "No!" and a shot was heard.

★

Kyle was pleased. Adam had moved and caused the others to move, but Kyle saw flesh and blood explode as the .308 caliber bullet found its mark. True, he had not meant to hit the other man too, but the target went down also as intended. Kyle never missed. It must have been God's will to make them move when they did.

Kyle replaced the screen and closed the window. He cracked the door and saw that people were looking around wildly, some stunned, some confused. Others, familiar with gunfire, had hit the ground and still lay there. It reminded Kyle of that brief instant between disturbing a fire ant bed when nothing happens, only to be quickly followed by the inhabitants' mass reaction to the intrusion.

He needed to take advantage of the confusion below, but running out with a rifle in his hand would be madness. Searching for a solution, he noticed that a window behind the bed overlooked another alley. Looking out, he spotted no one in the area, but directly below, weeds grew profusely from the crack between the building and the red brick alley. He quickly wiped the weapon clean then dumped it out the window. It landed almost perfectly, with only six inches of the barrel sticking beyond the weeds. Just as casually as he had entered the apartment a few minutes earlier, Kyle left.

★

Warm blood got Adam's attention first, then he became aware of a sharp pain in his chin, as well as a difficulty in breathing. Lying face down on the asphalt, bewilderment seized him. He twisted around and saw that Dr. Huntley pinned him down. Adam rolled free and examined himself. The blood poured from Huntley. The man looked dead.

Adam snaked over to the prone body of Clarence Fardy and looked back at Huntley. Blood coated Huntley's shirt above his heart. Adam looked again at Clarence. Understanding now what had occurred, Adam saw that a bullet had torn through Huntley's heart then scalped the left side of Clarence Fardy's head. Clarence still breathed.

Bulldog and then Kelly, who refused to be restrained, reached Adam at the same time. Each of them believed that the bullet had been meant for Adam. Other police and a medical team crowded in. Adam pulled himself up and spoke into Bulldog's ear. "Bulldog, they must report that Clarence is dead."

"Come on Adam, we've got to get you to cover."

"No! Listen! This is the only way to save his family."

"Damnit, Adam, let's go. Franci, help me."

Surprised by the mistaken name, Kelly looked at Bulldog then said. "Adam's right."

Bulldog literally dragged the two of them to safety behind a car before listening further. After hearing what Marvel had told Adam, Bulldog agreed that the ploy made sense. "Now," he said, "I'm going to take the two of you home and padlock your door."

★

Kyle strolled toward the barricades. He amused himself by watching the panic subside as people started getting up and stepping out from behind whatever cover they had found. The policemen at the barricade struggled to control vehicular traffic while trying to disperse the curious crowd of onlookers. Kyle approached one of the busy officers. "Excuse me, I'm Kyle Keysor. I need to see Officer Keysor, he's my brother. I was in an accident, and—"

The officer had been studying Kyle's scratches and bruises and motioned for him to go through before Kyle had finished explaining. The immediate concern of crowd control was too demanding. Kyle found his brother helping guard Adam and Kelly as they talked to Bulldog. Bulldog looked around. He wanted to get Adam and Kelly home. Captain Ansel shouted, "Bulldog, Keysor, the shooter's been spotted running down an alley with rifle in hand. Let's go!"

Bulldog said, "Adam, you and Kelly get in your car and drive straight home."

"I don't have a car." Adam rubbed his jaw as one of the emergency personnel cleaned away the blood.

"I can take them," Kyle said.

Everyone stared as Kyle stepped up. "Kyle, what are you doing here?" his brother asked.

"The guy at the barricade let me in. I wanted to make sure you were all right. I'm parked just past the barricade if these people need a ride."

"This is your brother, right?" Bulldog said to Officer Keysor.

"Yes," Chuck said. Bulldog stared at Kyle. Officer Keysor cuffed Kyle on the head. "My baby brother. He got himself lost in the woods."

"Keysor, Bulldog, get over here," the captain said, "I want a net around that lunatic now."

Bulldog said, "All right, you take them straight home. No detours, do you understand?"

"No problem," Kyle said. "I'll take good care of them."

★

Both Adam and Kelly crawled onto the middle bench seat. Kyle got in the driver's seat and asked for directions. He wanted to get away from the area as quickly as possible. Kelly put a compress to Adam's cheek. His face was scratched and badly swollen from his fall. Once free from the congested area, Kyle pulled over and parked next to the curb.

"Why are we stopping?" Kelly asked. She looked up and discovered the eye of the 45 automatic staring back at her. If she had not been preoccupied with concern over Adam, she may have sensed earlier what she now realized. Now it was too late. Kyle forced Kelly to place a piece of duct tape over her mouth and over Adam's. She then taped Adam's wrists together and his legs. She taped her own legs and Kyle taped her wrists.

He forced them to crawl around the seat and lay down in the back of the van. As added insurance, he taped them again and ordered that they lie still if they wanted to live a little while longer. It was a great day to be alive. Kyle had pondered how he would punish Adam before killing him, and now God had provided the answer. She was big, but she would have to do.

Under a cloudless sky, the sun had set before Kyle pulled the van under the pine trees near the stand of saw palmetto that guarded the lonely graves of Reverend Meeks and Susan Barrett. The moon was full and the stars bright. God had turned on the stage lights to enjoy the show. It was important that Kyle's performance be flawless.

He forced his way into the palmetto palms and dug up the plastic bag containing the lavender dress. He surveyed the area. There was little room, especially for three people. He decided that because no trails ran anywhere near he would be safe under the pine trees where he had parked.

Kyle pulled a blanket from the van and spread it under a towering pine. He dropped the dress on the blanket then dragged Adam and Kelly from the van, propping them against the vehicle. He fished a beer from the cooler and took a long drink. Needing to piss, he walked over to a pine tree and aimed for a prickly pear plant that sprawled around the base of the tree.

He turned and waved his penis to Kelly. "You'll be seeing more of this, bitch, but don't worry, you'll enjoy it after being screwed only by the piss ant there." He nodded toward Adam. Kyle turned again to piss and found that he couldn't. He stomped deeper into the trees where there was no audience.

Both Adam and Kelly were on their feet when Kyle returned, but both were still tightly bound. Kyle stalked over and punched Adam in the face. Adam careened off the van and dropped to the ground, his glasses lay somewhere in the weeds. "You better take care of yourself. You got a long night ahead of you, baby butcher." Kyle pulled Kelly over to the blanket. "You get out of your clothes and put that dress on." He pointed toward her feet.

Kelly screamed when she recognized the dress, but the tape on her mouth muffled the sound. Kyle saw the anguish followed by anger that filled Kelly's eyes. He watched her body tense. Adam had struggled to a sitting position. Kyle walked over and put his survival knife up Adam's nostril until blood flowed. "Listen you butchering bitch, you do as I say or I'll feed him his balls right now."

Kelly glared at Kyle, and he pushed the knife higher, forcing Adam to raise his head as far as it could possibly go. Kelly bowed her head. Kyle walked over and pulled out the 45. He aimed it at Adam as he cut the tape that bound Kelly's ankles. He stood up and cut the tape from her wrists. She started to remove the tape from her mouth, but he shook his head and pointed to the dress. "Put it on," he said.

Kelly slapped at the mosquitoes that were now gathering in mass. She slipped off her deck shoes and slowly unbuttoned her blouse. Her eyes rested on Adam, whose nose was bleeding. She didn't know if that was from the punch to his face or the knife wound. Without the glasses his eyes made him look wild. Kyle watched her nod discreetly, encouraging Adam not to do anything stupid. Kyle got up and found his beer that he had sat on top of the van. He finished it off, belched, and fished another one from the cooler.

Swatting at the mosquitoes to keep from being eaten alive, Kelly was kept too busy to undress. Kyle got up and pulled a can of Off from his bag. He sprayed himself first then he sprayed Kelly. She nodded at Adam, but Kyle just laughed. He dropped the can at her feet and said, "Finish up."

Kelly removed her slacks and sprayed her legs. She kept the can as she picked up the dress, but Kyle put the 45 to Adam's temple. "Roll the can over here. Be real nice about it." She complied.

Kyle stared at Adam and laughed at his helplessness. Kelly started to put the dress on, but Kyle stopped her. "Wait, take off the bra and pants first." Kelly almost started crying, but anger aided her control. She sniffed only once, then dropped her bra and peeled her panties.

Kyle studied Adam, who looked as though the slightest prick would send blood gushing from his already battered face. Kyle slipped his arm around Adam's shoulders. "Helpless as a baby, huh Doc? How does it feel?"

If stares were truly daggers, Kyle would have died looking like a pincushion, but Adam's anger served only to please Kyle. "Put your panties back on then the dress." Kelly retrieved her underwear and quickly covered herself. She tried to slip the size four dress over her head, but it wouldn't fit. It had looked lovely on the diminutive Reverend Meeks, and on the director too, but it would not fit Kelly.

"You goddamned sow!" screamed Kyle. "You've ruined everything." Still brandishing the 45, Kyle stomped over and grabbed the dress from Kelly's hands. She immediately brought her knee up, but Kyle was a tall man and the dress hid her target. She managed to connect with Kyle's thigh and testicles at the same time. It hurt him, but not enough to stop him. Kelly, barefooted and struggling to balance on a layer of prickly pine cones and needles, prepared to use the heel of her hand to shove Kyle's nose into his brain, but he managed to clip her on the head with the butt of the 45. Like a side of beef plopped onto a butcher's table, she collapsed to the ground.

Kyle heard Adam screaming through the duct tape. He turned and watched as Adam violently jerked and strained against his bonds. Kyle studied Kelly for a moment then walked over and vented his anger on Adam until a blow to the temple proved too much; Adam was unconscious. Further punishment would be wasted so Kyle taped his helpless victim to a slash pine tree.

★

Nigel Hunttington had frozen in Toledo for two days, and his return to Florida put him in a better mood. He preferred the warmer climate of the Sunshine State in which to pass the winter months. He clicked on the television and his phone recorder. A smile could not be suppressed when he heard the recorded message and the name Dr. Justice who Nigel now knew to be Dr. Luther Huntley.

The man wanted the job done now, and had sweetened the pot to seal the deal. Nigel got excited thinking about contacting Dr. Huntley to discuss an even sweeter arrangement. He hummed to himself as he unpacked and listened to the local evening news. The unpacking abruptly ceased when Nigel heard his benefactor's name. He sat and listened to the whole story, learning that not only did that pitiful Clarence Fardy die, but also the pompous Dr. Huntley. The police had no comment on the possible assailant.

"Nigel, my friend," he said to himself, "we have a delicious dilemma, a problem of ethics. My good benefactor, Dr. Justice, better known as Dr. Luther Huntley, is deceased. The now late doctor contracted for a fire, unfortunately due to circumstances beyond his or our control, he is no longer available to approve our performance. In other words, we can keep the money and no one will be the wiser, but is that ethical? Should we risk damaging a well-earned reputation of reliability? Ah, what to do, what to do?

"Perhaps another approach? Would we be happier performing as agreed or not completing the job? Ah, yes, an easier question indeed. Certainly we would be pleased to keep our end of the bargain. Toledo was a disappointment, just an old empty warehouse and some Jewish lightning." Nigel laughed. "A non-event, actually. No one hurt, not even a crowd to admire our handiwork. Nigel, old boy, we must do as agreed.

"After all, it's the humane thing. The poor grieving widow and her brood must be assisted in joining the father."

★

Bulldog was pissed at his stupidity. He should have told the captain to shove it. He should have taken Adam and Kelly home regardless of the consequences, but he had been trying to stay out of trouble with his superiors. He wanted a promotion. He wanted off the front lines before he got hurt. When he realized that they had cornered the wrong man, Bulldog called to check on Adam and Kelly. There was no answer. A little investigating revealed that Kyle owned a red Ranger pickup. A little more checking revealed that no one knew where Kyle had been the last four days or what he had been doing. That convinced Bulldog that he had made a serious error.

He reached the Royleston and parked next to the curb in front. It was an old rundown hotel that rented rooms by the month, by the week, by the day, or by the hour. It catered to the prostitutes and drug dealers who crawled over the area, night and day. Panhandlers worked the entrance.

If a man could afford a whore, certainly he could part with a quarter. It was always good business to keep the bums happy; that way they don't see anything. Bulldog wasn't a stranger there, but every time he entered the lobby he was reminded of old black and white cop and gangster movies. The movies were comical now. The reality was not.

He crossed the musty-smelling lobby and labored up the stairs to the second floor, and that's when it hit him. The narrow seamy hallway that stretched before him matched the hallway in his dream, even the marked up walls. He found room 217 and stopped and listened. Someone had scribbled on the wall next to the door, "The meek shall inherit the earth, because they won't have the balls to turn it down". He shook his head in disbelief and sweat ran down his ebony face. His shirt was soaked. Bulldog leaned up against the wall just to the left of the door and waited. He could hear a TV and a radio blaring from somewhere, but if any sound came from room 217, it was muffled.

He breathed deeply and exhaled slowly to calm himself. How could he dream of a place, an event, before it happened? As a precaution, he wiped the sweat from his hands and withdrew his Glock automatic pistol. Hell, his best friend needed help. Maybe Adam did accidentally pick the kid up at the abortion clinic, but it was also possible that Huntley paid the lunatic to go after Adam. The answer may be waiting just on the other side of the abused door. Bulldog hesitated. He was safe as long as the door remained unopened.

If the hotel was true, the hallway, the door, was it also true that on the other side a bullet waited with Bulldog's name on it? The fear brought bile to his throat. With the Glock in his right hand, Bulldog reached out with his left and knocked on the door. Expecting a shot, his stomach knotted. No answer came. Although Bulldog had not been able to discern any sound before the knock, the room seemed somehow more silent now. He knocked again. Still, no answer.

After a man has been on the streets for a while, he develops a sixth sense about things unseen. Cops wouldn't call it being psychic, but that's what it is. It's like being in a crowded room and suddenly realizing that you are being watched. You look around and find yourself staring into the eyes of a stranger. It's like that but stronger. Bulldog knew without seeing that Cowboy sat on the other side of the door to room 217. He even knew that until Cowboy had heard someone stop in the hallway, he had been packing.

Bulldog thought about his wife dressed in black; he had never liked her in black. He pictured his children. Then he remembered the scrawny ten-year-old Adam charging up the steps to rescue a cat from three boys, each bigger than Adam. "Fear is like giving money to a panhandler," his granny always said. "Give in once and the rest of them will see you coming." Bulldog stepped in front of the door, drew a deep breath, and kicked the goddamned thing in.

A surprised Cowboy found himself staring into the Glock's barrel before he could react. Bulldog had been right. Cowboy had been packing, and he had sat down to wait out whoever lurked in the hallway. An angry but confident Bulldog questioned him briefly, but Cowboy sat calmly, saying no more than he had to.

"Tuttle, I'm tired of this cat and mouse shit. I'm looking for a killer. A young kid, maybe twenty-five, two hundred twenty, thirty pounds. I believe you know something."

"I already told you, I don't know nothing about this kid, and I don't know nothing about this Huntley fellow either."

Bulldog aimed his pistol. "I may be too late to save my friend's life, but I sure as hell am going to catch his killer." Cowboy sat up straighter, his eyes bovine. Bulldog continued, "I'll go to jail for this you son-of-a-bitch, but I'm going to shoot off your fucking knee caps."

Cowboy cleared his throat. It was time to deal.

★

Adam was lost. He used a hand to wipe sweat from his eyes then plowed through more underbrush and saw palmetto. He crawled over a fallen palm tree and lingered to rest. Water ran somewhere ahead but nearby. Adam heard the roar of the falls. He worked his way toward it. Pushing through a tangle of muscadine vines that found sunlight high up in the branches of a towering pine, Adam reached the river. He was startled to hear Many Faces shout a greeting over the rush of the falls. "I've been expecting you. Please join me."

Adam couldn't speak. Many Faces sat in a lotus position immediately over the river where thousands of gallons of water poured over the precipice. With his hand Many Faces encouraged Adam to come forward. At first Adam just shook his head no then he managed to call out, "How can you do that?"

"Not only does a man create his own nightmares and solutions, you can do anything that you have the imagination to dream."

"Oh, yeah, I forgot; you're just a dream," said Adam.

"What? I can't hear you," shouted Many Faces.

"I'm dreaming you," returned Adam.

"If you put me here, then join me," said Many Faces. Adam stayed planted on the riverbank. "No? OK, I will join you. A walk is always pleasant."

As the two men traveled along the bank of the river, Adam said, "Could I have joined you? Could I have walked on water?"

Many Faces stopped to scoop up a drink of water. "All that is required is a little faith. Belief is the engine, Adam. What you generate is up to you." The old Indian allowed the remaining water to drip through his wrinkled fingers to refresh a fern struggling to grow within the rotting stump of a fallen palm tree. "Where there was once life, there is death. Where there is death, there is life," he mused.

"That's why I'm here," said Adam. "I didn't dream up this insanity. Why am I tied to a tree while a madman is about to kill Kelly and me too?"

"You've always been confrontational, Adam. You chose a slight physical stature to put yourself at a disadvantage, and you use defiance to test yourself. You are often blind to the opinions of others," said Many Faces, "and to their innate goodness. You can be a harsh judge of your fellow man because for you there is only black or white."

"You never answer my questions. Why am I tied to this tree?"

Many Faces shrugged. "You are fishing for an answer that can be as convoluted as a handful of bait, but trite though it is let's just say that the rock has met the hard spot. Look in the water, Adam. What do you see?"

Adam studied his reflection. "Myself of course."

"Precisely," said Many Faces.

"And?" said Adam.

"You have met someone who believes that he is just as right as you always do. Often during our life journeys we meet ourselves. Since we rarely see our own faults, it sometimes helps to recognize it in others."

"So I created this madman just to see myself? I don't think so."

"Yes, in a sense you created him. Monsters don't just create themselves, we all contribute. We all participate to make the world's tyrants and subsequently its saviors," said Many Faces.

Adam shook his head in disgust. "Reverend Meeks, Dr. Barrett, Kelly and myself, we're just victims here."

"Unfortunately, Adam, language can be limiting, but perhaps a word more acceptable to you would be to say that you attracted your demon. When we see ourselves it may be a caricature. An exaggeration if you please, so that even the dullest of us may recognize the resemblance." Many Faces grinned at Adam. "Some men spend their lives digging trenches, others build bridges."

"So, I'm supposed to get to know this guy, to build a bridge of understanding and he will let us go?"

"Oh, I'm not talking about you living or dying, Adam, I'm talking about something much more important. I'm suggesting that you get to know yourself."

"Well, I know that I want to get free and kill this guy."

"Do you really? But, again you miss the point. Fight and lose, Adam; surrender and win. The shell of the acorn must give way if God's loving light is to reach the potential that waits inside. As it is with you, your madman has not opened to receive the light, and it is your egos that blind you. It is your beliefs that have brought you together and now seemingly bind you beyond release. Ask for help."

"OK, I get it. When you religious people don't have an answer, you babble a few platitudes, tell people to pray, and then you wash your hands."

"Actually people pray all the time, they just don't realize it.

Analyze your beliefs, Adam. Consider what thoughts you produce in abundance. You are today what your habitual thoughts have made you. One thing, you believe that you are a failure when it comes to saving your loved ones, first your mother, then Franci, and now this new difficulty has developed. Prayers are always answered, but it is for your ultimate good."

Many Faces shielded his eyes from the sun and paused as he watched a young eagle test his new-found ability to fly. He nudged Adam. "Unlike you, our young friend harbors no doubts about his ability to fly. You live on a magical island in the universal sea. The beauty of it is that everything you wish for comes true. The horror of it is that everything you wish for comes true. The path to Eden, however, is to align your will with the higher will."

Adam shook his head. "Yeah, and how do I do that?"

"Love, Adam. The ego loves only itself. Universal love will light the flame that will illuminate your choices," said Many Faces. "Now, you should return. Your friend needs you."

Adam's head throbbed. He wanted to lick his lips but the tape prevented that. His drawn face told him that dried blood caked his cheeks. He blinked his eyes to clear his vision and saw Kelly bound with tape. Her back was to Adam, but he sensed that she was still unconscious. He searched, but saw no sign of the kid. The van was gone too. Adam surprised himself by wondering what suffering or loss had turned the boy into such a tragic mess. Had he lost someone too? Could he be helped?

Adam studied Kelly. Maybe she wouldn't wake up. Maybe help would come. Adam thought of Clarence Fardy and laughed in spite of the bark that dug into his back. Either there is a God or Fardy is the luckiest man to ever live. Adam tried to move his arms and remembered the tape that bound his wrists. He lost his mother. He lost Franci. Absolutely, he would not accept defeat again. He began to scrape his bonds as fast as he could across the bark that was already crimson with his blood.

★

Later, when Kelly awoke, she collected her thoughts and studied the sky. At least several hours had passed. She thought about Adam and tried to get up. Taped again, she rolled over and found Adam in the shadows sitting at the base of a tree. She started to call to him, but realized that tape still covered her mouth. He must be tied where he sat. In the dark she couldn't tell for certain if he was awake, but he seemed to be moving. She checked and saw that her legs were taped to her arms.

She tried to sit up, but a throbbing pain drummed in her head. The dress she had given Reverend Meeks was caked with blood. Her head had been laying on it. She looked but didn't see the van. She could only speculate where the kidnapper might be or what he might be doing. Digging their graves, she feared. She began to twist about and strain against the tape. She must escape and free Adam before the murderer returned.

★

As Kyle neared the clearing where he had left Adam and Kelly, his euphoria returned. He had been really pissed when the dress didn't fit. He had wanted everything to be perfect. He knew that the woman was taller, but he had not thought about the dress being too small. A mistake with the last woman had unleashed God's punishment. Kyle lost the hearing in his left ear. Then tonight he had made a mistake about the dress, and the butchering bitch had almost got him in the balls. God was good, but if you screwed up, God got really pissed. One had only to think of the flood and the Jews to know that.

At first, Kyle had been confused, but the blow on the head definitely put the lady out of commission. That's when he heard Adam struggling to crawl to her. Kyle beat Adam unconscious then taped him to a tree. Kyle sat down to think. He drank a beer and studied the dress. It didn't smell like a lady anymore. Although the witch had been no lady, she had smelled nice like one. The second one also smelled nice, but now the dress stunk of semen, blood and dirt.

Kyle finally understood. God wanted his sacrifices clean. That's also why Sandy never got pregnant. Nothing was wrong with Kyle, lack of cleanliness was the problem. Sandy had always bathed before sex until she got that thermometer, then they had sex without regard for bathing. Kyle understood then what he had to do.

He stopped the van and got out. "I see you two decided to stay. Now, we're gonna have a party." Kyle pulled out a couple of shopping bags. From one he delivered a couple of six packs of water, a sponge and soap. He dropped them on the blanket on which Kelly lay naked except for her panties, her ample breast outlined in white where they had been screened from the sun. He kneeled and stuck the 45 to her temple. With his free hand he cut the tape that bound her. "Bathe," he said.

He walked over and got a beer, but he never took his eyes off Kelly. "That means everything. God don't want me fucking unclean women." Kelly glanced at Adam who still struggled to free himself, and Kyle laughed. He said, "Yeah, bitch, he's gonna have to watch it all." She wet the sponge and began to wipe herself. "Soap, use the soap," Kyle said. "And bathe that blood out of your hair."

Kelly turned away from Kyle and removed her panties, revealing another white spot that accented her shapely figure. That didn't interest Kyle, however, he only relished watching Adam die from humiliation and helplessness second by second. Kelly bathed as ordered.

★

Bulldog used a tire tool to break one of the locks on the gate. If he had the killer located, Bulldog didn't want to spook him with a shot. There were too many directions to run. Five cruisers and twenty men to search the well field accompanied Bulldog. Moonlight lit up the night. He hoped for a little luck and a clear trail to follow. He didn't know what to expect. The sheriff who had jurisdiction suggested that all fresh tire marks leading off a road or trail be followed. Bulldog gave the order and the procession proceeded as planned.

★

Adam had long since rubbed the flesh from his hands. Warm blood leaked from his wounds, but he went beyond the pain and kept sawing the tape against the flaky bark of the slash pine that held him captive. He had never been a violent man, but now terror and fear for Kelly motivated him. Mosquitoes buzzing in his ears and crawling over his blood-caked face would have driven him mad if he hadn't already been close to it.

Was he helpless to save Kelly? To save himself? Would death be like slipping from wakefulness to a dream, or was life the dream? Would Franci be there to wake him? Adam watched Kelly stand like a goddess in the middle of the clearing even though a madman lurked nearby. Like Franci, caught in the swirls of the river, Kelly, trapped in the current of a nightmare, was only a few feet away. It may as well be a million miles. Impervious to the pain, Adam began to scrape faster and harder. He would not lose Kelly. The bark dug deeper into his arms, but he went beyond the pain. He had lost a lot of blood.

★

After Kelly rinsed, Kyle said, "Put your panties back on." He pulled a white dress from another shopping bag and threw it to her. "Then put this on." She stepped into it and slowly started buttoning it up. Kyle said, "Take the tape from your mouth, and say, "It's you! Just like that." Kelly removed the tape and stared at him. "You heard me," he said. Kyle laid the 45 down and pulled out his knife. "No funny stuff or I will flay the runt." Kyle had to tame Kelly. He had enjoyed watching Adam suffer, but Kelly had shown no fear. Kyle had seen only anger in her eyes. Now he craved to see terror. Without the fear there was no erection. He moved toward Kelly. "Say it now!" he shouted.

"But I'm not dressed yet," Kelly said, struggling to keep her voice steady. She continued to fumble with the buttons.

★

Phoenix stomped up the stairs of the lighthouse to the observation deck. She searched up and down the beach highway, but saw no sign of Barbara's red Camry. Reaching for a cigarette, but finding none, she huffed down the stairs to the second floor and lit up. Too mad to sit, she paced. Barbara had never been gone this long before. Phoenix poured herself another gin and tonic. She took a long drink.

She vaguely heard the TV newscaster say, "Tragedy in Tampa. The sometimes controversial Dr. Luther Huntley is dead. The man who recently claimed to have been contacted by a mysterious Mr. X, who planned to commit suicide to prove the existence of life after death, was shot..." Phoenix ran and turned up the TV. She plopped down and listened as the announcer rattled off the details. All hope vanished. Phoenix had counted on Dr. Huntley's promised help, now there would be none. She tossed back the gin then poured another.

★

Adam felt the tape binding his hands break, but he never took his eyes off Kyle, who concentrated on Kelly. Shielded by the tree from the moonlight, Adam used his hands to lift and pull away the tape that wrapped around his chest and the tree. He ducked under it and quickly started to snatch the remaining tape from his ankles. Adam worked as quietly and quickly as possible. He was feeling dizzy. Maybe he had sliced an artery.

Kyle waited until Kelly dropped her hands. "Now, bitch. You say it now or I cut the butcher's throat." Both Kelly and Kyle looked at Adam just as he ripped the last piece of tape from his ankle and was struggling to stand. Kyle rushed toward his captive, who managed to get to his feet and dive headfirst into the killer's stomach. Adam's legs were rubbery and his momentum weak, but Kyle doubled up. Unfortunately, not before crashing the butt of his knife on Adam's skull.

His heroics over, Adam collapsed to the ground, but his refusal to accept another loss made him fight to maintain consciousness. He blinked his eyes to clear his vision and struggled to get to his knees. He couldn't, but he did hear a sickening thud and see the big boots that had been before him disappear to be replaced by the smaller bare feet of Kelly.

★

Kelly did not hesitate. As soon as Kyle's attention turned to Adam, she moved in. Kyle rushed toward Adam and Kelly locked onto him like a guided missile. He was big and clumsy, and her timing was perfect. She leaped into the air, cocked her right leg and drove her heel into Kyle's temple. The kick propelled Kyle into the side of the van, and like a wrestler coming off the ropes, he bounced back toward Kelly completely off balance and off guard. His brain rattled like a BB in a baby toy.

★

Adam, his mouth still taped, rolled to his side. As he continued his struggle to stand, he saw Kelly jump straight up and kick Kyle in the face. Kyle, his forward momentum halted by the power of Kelly's kick, again flew backwards, but this time spinning like a whirlwind. Blood gushed from his nose and swirled about him. With a loud bang, Kyle slammed against the van, twisted around again, and took two wobbly steps forward. Kelly stepped to the side, twisted on her left foot, leaned away from Kyle, cocked her right leg, and with a powerful thrust drove her heel into his knee. There was a sickening crack, followed by an agonizing scream as Kyle fell writhing to the ground like a chicken with a wrung neck. Adam could smell the man. His bowels had voided.

★

After the kick, Kelly stepped back for balance and discovered the 45 automatic under her foot. She scooped it up and pointed it at Kyle. As a psychologist she knew that Kyle was sick, she understood that he needed help, but as a woman, she hated the bastard. His mouth still taped, Adam's muffled shouts and pleas to stop went unheeded. Kelly fired. She deliberately missed, but it had been necessary to pull the trigger.

★

Adam ripped the tape from his mouth just as Kelly fired. He jumped at the retort and marveled as her arm flew above her head from the recoil. Kyle, unconscious, lay sprawled in his own excrement. Kelly continued to stare at the boy, and Adam, finally on his feet, hobbled over to her. She didn't respond to his touch. He eased the pistol from her hand and tossed it. She looked at him for the first time, her expression blank. Adam nodded at Kyle, and grinned slightly. "Guess that will teach him to mess with me, huh?"

It took a moment, but Kelly began to giggle, then laugh and cry at the same time. Adam put his arms around her and whispered in her ear, "I've decided to love you too." His head began to spin, and he collapsed in her arms. He was bleeding badly. Kelly was applying a tourniquet when Bulldog wheeled up.

★

Nigel parked his work car, an old sedan that he kept hidden in a rented garage, in a crowded tenement parking lot one block away from Clarence Fardy's building. He quickly shut off the motor and lights and checked his surroundings for changes and movement. What with the trash heaped everywhere and the wooden buildings built on top of each other, this fire could be big, very big. Still, fires were probably like love; although he had never loved any female except his sister, he figured that for most people the first one is always the best.

Nigel was ten and his sister was twelve going on twenty-one. The month of March still blew cold in upstate New York where they lived on the outskirts of a small town with their parents. Their mother, having another baby, had been rushed to the hospital. Nigel's sister Sarah explained it all to him. How babies were made and where they came from. She also explained that her mother had lost several babies and that's why the hospital wouldn't let her come home.

Whatever the reason, with his mother gone, Nigel suffered with diarrhea and chills. His father had always been abusive to the kids, using harsh words, a cuff on the head, or a slap on the face, but mostly he just beat Nigel's helpless mother. The boy resented the woman and told himself that every father acted like his, but he didn't really believe it.

He coped by staying out of the way as much as possible. With his mother gone, both he and Sarah were terrified. The companion inside Nigel's head consoled the boy. "Don't worry, let me take care of your father." He was always saying that, but Nigel was always too scared to give in.

Nigel helped Sarah cook dinner, which they ate in silence. They cleaned the dishes, then went to bed in the small room they shared. The tiny old clapboard house had only two bedrooms so he and Sarah shared a room with twin beds. Sarah had always been his protector, their room his sanctuary.

Sleeping soundly until his father's rough hand shook him awake, Nigel yelped when he saw the man staring down at him. "Boy, you take your covers and go sleep in the living room. You stay there, you hear?" Half asleep and choking on his father's beer and cigarette breath, Nigel had trouble comprehending the orders so he didn't move fast enough. A cuff on the head woke him up and he darted from the room dragging his covers behind him. He ran toward the glowing timbers in the fireplace and wrapped his bed covers tightly around himself like a plate of armor. Now, fully awake, he realized what this meant.

He couldn't make out what Sarah said, but from the tone he could tell she was begging. His father's words, on the other hand, were no mystery. "Girl, your mother's not here so it's up to you to take care of your father. You're old enough to learn what a man needs. Besides, you're turning into a pretty girl and your mother don't take care of herself anymore."

Nigel rocked back and forth as he watched the heat rise off the glowing logs. He strained to hear Sarah's words, but he couldn't. He reasoned she carefully kept her voice low to prevent riling their father. Whatever she said, however, Nigel's father cut short with a loud slap. His father said, "Girl, am I going to have to beat you like I do your mother? She can't do a thing right, are you stupid too?" Sarah said something, then Nigel heard his father say, "Then get out of your clothes and take care of your father."

Nigel's stomach knotted up as he listened to the bedroom sounds, the grunts and groans of his father that the boy had heard many times in the past, but this time they were coming from his and Sarah's room, and they were punctuated by Sarah's muffled screams. Nigel's companion shouted, "If you can't stop it, let me!" Finally, the bedroom sounds abated and Nigel realized that he had turned blue from the cold. He placed another log on the embers and agitated the coals with the sharp poker.

As he resurrected the flames, Nigel worried about his sister. He knew that she would be awake and hurt and that his drunken father would be asleep. At least that was the way it was with his mother, she always got up afterward and walked the house. The voice in his head chided Nigel. "How long are you going to let him get away with this? So what if he is your father, now you have let him hurt Sarah."

Nigel jabbed the sharp poker into the fresh log and screamed, "Then you do something. All you do is talk." Gripping the ash-covered poker, Nigel crept to the bedroom door and put his ear against it. He could hear his father snoring. The boy slowly twisted the doorknob until it clicked open.

He detected a break in the snoring and froze until the rhythm resumed. Having been used to the light of the fire, Nigel could barely see. He crept up to the bed. Remaining on his knees, he held his breath and raised up. Holding the poker with both hands, Nigel saw that Sarah's huge brown eyes were staring at him from a face about to scream. Transfixed, Nigel didn't hear the snoring stop.

His father jumped to his knees and started clawing his way from the tangled bed covers. "Damn you, boy, I told you to stay out of here!"

Nigel recoiled like a cut spring and wound up sprawled on his butt, the poker landed several feet behind him. His father still drunk and tangled in the covers tried to climb over Sarah, but she grabbed his foot and he fell over. His face hit the cold wooden floor with a sickening thud.

"Run, Nigel, run!" Sarah screamed, but Nigel's fear pinned him to the floor.

In his mind, the terrified boy said, "See what you've done?" His invisible companion did not respond. Nigel's father pulled himself up to a sitting position and lunged for his son. His rough hands caught the boy's ankle and for an instant they stared at each other.

"So, boy, you want to know what was going on in here, do you? Well, by God, you're going to find out." Suddenly, Nigel felt himself jerked across the floor, flipped over and his underwear ripped off. He screamed as his father forced his penis into Nigel, ripping the boy in the process. His father cuffed Nigel again, but the pain of the rape was greater than the fear of his father so Nigel kept on screaming. His father snorted and grunted as usual, and when it was over, he sat back and leaned against the bed.

Nigel lay curled up on the floor whimpering, but he heard his father say, "What's this?" The boy opened his eyes and watched in horror as his father crawled over and grabbed the poker. "Well, I'll be. Maybe you ain't the sissy I think you are, boy. Too bad you didn't have the guts to use it." Then he laughed like he always did when he said something to hurt someone's feelings.

He stomped over and backhanded Sarah. "That's for tripping me, girl, now take you brother and get out of here. I've got to get some sleep." Sarah helped Nigel to his feet and supported him as they struggled to the living room. They heard the bedroom lock click closed.

The fire roared now as Sarah held Nigel trying to comfort him. Aware of the intense heat on his face, Nigel watched the log burn and wished that his father lay in its place. His companion said, "I can do that for you."

After a while Sarah wrapped herself up in a blanket and fell asleep. Nigel placed the tips of several narrow strips of lighter wood in the coals and eased away from Sarah. He rummaged through the dirty clothes until he found something to wear. He also picked out a dress for Sarah and threw it over a chair.

He went outside and wished he had his jacket from the bedroom. The March wind screamed through the trees and around the buildings and he could see every breath break up as he raced into it. He ran over to the woodshed and started stacking the wheelbarrow full with firewood, all he could push.

He quickly but quietly rolled the wheelbarrow under the window of the bedroom where his father slept. Nigel heard the snoring stop, and he froze. He wanted to scream, but knew he could not. He strained to hear above the howling wind, praying for the snoring to return. He stood motionless for what seemed like hours, but within seconds the snorts resumed. Then he filled the wheelbarrow with gasoline.

Lugging the greasy gas can, he crept back inside. He soaked the bedroom door. He ran over to the fire, snatched up the lighter wood from the coals, and threw one at the door. Flames instantly spread up and under the door, licking up the gasoline.

Protecting the flame on the other piece of lighter, Nigel raced outside and around the house. He flung the lighted stick in the wheelbarrow, which ignited with a loud explosion. The flames leaped to the roof. They engulfed the window area and lit up the night like daylight. The fire chased the shadow monsters away, and Nigel was no longer cold. Beautiful and magnificent, the flames mesmerized the boy. Watching the fire consume the bedroom wall beyond which his father slept, Nigel experienced his first ejaculation. He never even had an erection. Fire is the god of pleasure.

Suddenly, a frantic scream reached the boy, and he remembered Sarah. He plowed up the ground racing to get her. He pushed through the front door and saw his sister sitting where she had been sleeping. She sat there screaming, a hand to each cheek, her eyes fixed on the flaming bedroom door. Nigel followed her gaze and realized that his father was screaming too. The boy's heart stopped when he heard his victim fumbling with the door lock. Nigel froze, expecting his enraged father to burst screaming from the inferno. He never did though.

Nigel smiled at the memory. Having found his calling young, he was no longer a child. He left home early and never looked back, though sometimes he wondered about his sister. He would always love her.

After a few minutes, he grabbed the bag of pest control foggers, exited the car, and eased the door closed. Sticking to the shadows, he slowly worked his way to Clarence Fardy's apartment.

Nigel expertly picked the lock and slipped inside. His excitement began to accelerate, and he had to force himself to remain careful. The dark entrance forced Nigel to pause and allow his eyes to adjust to the dark after having passed under the night light outside the front door. He forced himself to breathe more normally, but his hard penis made it difficult.

He eased into the dark living room, and suddenly a rough, powerful hand seized his chin while the second hand grabbed the crown of his head. Fully aware of the quick jerk that broke his neck and snapped his fragile spinal cord, Nigel could feel nothing below his head. He knew only that powerful arms held him erect. When the rough hand slipped over Nigel's mouth and pinched his nose closed, Nigel's brain screamed to every muscle in his body to do something, but the message went unheeded. Soon, even the message stopped.

★

Lee flipped on the light, and said, "It's OK now. You and Clarence and your children are safe." He laid Nigel's lifeless body down.

Marvel stared in horror. "I still can't believe this."

Lee used his foot to roll a fogger out the way. The canisters had scattered when Nigel dropped the bag. "You would have died, Mrs. Fardy. When the spray in these cans reached your pilot light, there would have been an explosion. This old place would have burned like paper. You can bet our friend here," Lee pushed the corpse with a shoe, "would have had a ringside seat. He would have gotten off on your death. Fire jockeys are only interested in the ride."

"I don't know what to say. I don't even know your name."

"No need," Lee said. "It's like I told you. You could have called in the police, but if this scum had sensed something wrong he would have waited until he felt it was safe. Now, you're OK. Clarence believed that the only way he could protect you and his children was to do as Huntley ordered, but the Huntleys in this world always hedge their bets. His wife is dead and that meant that you would have to die too."

"Thank you, thank you so much. How can we pay you back?"

"Let's call it even." Marvel's expression asked for details, but Lee didn't venture any. He continued, "I'll get rid of this garbage. When Clarence gets home from the hospital let him know that there's nothing more to worry about. Tell him he's a free man. Tell him, tell him to spend a lot of time with his kids."

Lee handed Marvel a brown envelope, clicked off the light and stepped outside to determine if the way was clear. Seeing nothing, he walked back in and hefted Nigel's corpse as easy as he would lift a child. While Marvel peeked out, Lee stuffed the body in the car trunk. She allowed the faded curtain to fall back into place and hurried to the kitchen.

She flipped the light on, opened the envelope, and gasped when she saw all the money. With sweaty hands and shortness of breath, she counted fifty thousand dollars. What do you do with fifty thousand dollars? Clarence would believe that the honest thing would be to turn the money over to the police, but Marvel had always managed what little money they had. Clarence need never know. She would hide the money and use it a little bit at the time. She didn't want nobody asking questions.

With Clarence truly home now, he would get a job. She would continue to take in washing and ironing, she would continue to baby sit, and she would manage their money. Marvel would get the Fardy's off welfare and into a safer neighborhood. "God, I'm sorry," she said aloud. "To You the man may be a murderer, but to me he's a saint."

★

Once Bulldog convinced Cowboy that they should be friends, the big gorilla became very helpful. The detective found Adam and Kelly clinging to each other in the well field, and after a moment of great relief was grateful that once again he had help in raising Adam. Now, Bulldog stood waiting in the shadows, and could not have been more surprised to see LeRoy Lentz drive up.

Lee had gone to prison just after Bulldog finished the academy and became a patrolman. He had been out for a few years now and lived above The Stake Out. The two had chatted on occasion. Lee even complimented Bulldog on his successes. Said that he was probably the best detective on the force. It was thought that the ex-cop earned his living digging up information for whoever needed it, and he had even slipped Bulldog a tip or two.

Bulldog watched as Lee knocked on the Fardy door. He talked briefly to Mrs. Fardy then stepped inside. Bulldog's training told him to go in after Lee, but instinct ordered the detective to stay put. Like a statue, he waited. His antennae shot up when he saw the second man appear, but the dark house and experience suggested patience. Now Bulldog waited until Lee shut the body of the second man in the car trunk.

Bulldog stepped from behind a car. "Hello, Lee," he said.

Lee didn't even jump. He just looked around and nodded at Bulldog who continued, "Is the Fardy family safe now?"

Lee lit up a Camel. "They're safe."

"And you?"

Lee knitted his brow and shrugged. "I hear you have a daughter now?"

"A boy too."

"Love them. Spend a lot of time with them."

Bulldog nodded toward the trunk. "Anybody I know?"

"King Red might ring a bell."

"He's a bad one."

"Yeah, some people are born bad."

"Maybe so," said Bulldog. His granny always said that bad people are like a potato mound, dig deep enough and you will find something good. Bulldog continued, "Or maybe something shoves them in that direction. Not my place to judge." Each man briefly considered the other. Bulldog said, "Stay out of trouble, huh, Lee."

Lee nodded and climbed into his car. Before pulling away, he looked back and said, "If you ever need a friend."

"I'll find you," Bulldog said.

March 22, Wednesday

Adam stood close to the hospital bed and listened carefully to hear Clarence as he whispered to minimize the pain. A bandage was wrapped around his head. Adam and Kelly had brought the children who, except for the oldest, Tommy, were excitedly showing off new clothes and toys to their mother. The two youngest had already spoken to their father, but with great reservation. The flowers, so much like a funeral, the bandage, the IVs, and the smell of disinfectant were too intimidating. Tommy stood to one side, his hands stuffed in his pockets.

It was obvious to Adam that if Clarence had any sliver of doubt before, he certainly didn't now. God will part the Red Sea for any man secure enough to walk across. Or belief will. Is that what God is, just positive thinking? Or negative thinking, too, for that matter. Is it as those space movies suggested, an indifferent force to be used for good or bad? He would have to think about it.

"Have you been watching the news?" Adam said. "You'll probably be voted Father of the Year."

"For loving my children? I don't deserve that. I—"

"You do too!" Tommy said, and immediately turned red when everyone looked at him.

Adam laughed. "There you have it, Clarence, from an impeccable source."

With tears in his eyes Clarence held out a hand and Tommy rushed over to hug him. "Thank you, son. I love you too." Clarence stroked Tommy's head. He looked at Adam. "I guess you think I'm crazy?"

Adam shrugged. "You believed that no matter what happened it would be God's will, and that's where you put your trust. Me, I believe that you were very brave. You were willing to do the one thing that you thought would most likely save your family." Adam gestured toward Clarence. "You're alive. I desperately wanted to save you from Huntley, and in a way I did because of the most bizarre series of events imaginable. A coincidence? I don't know, but I guess we all got what we wanted. You never lost your faith in God, or Jesus…" Adam scratched his head. "You know, I have never figured out that trilogy concept, God, Jesus and the Holy Ghost. That's three gods to me, and then if you throw in this Mother Mary mess as some do, that makes four. Who do you pray to, Jesus because he died for your sins?"

"Mr. Eden, I don't accept eternal damnation or vicarious atonement. God is love. His children have eternity to correct their mistakes. Jesus is my savior because he showed me how to live. Through his complete love for everything, he died on the Cross and taught me that there is no death. He taught me that love is God and that fear is the devil. The Master taught me to love myself. Most importantly, He taught me that we are all brothers."

"No second thoughts, huh?" said Adam.

Clarence thought a moment. "My only regret is that Dr. Huntley died angry. I feel that I failed in that regard."

"I'm told that even Jesus failed with Judas, Clarence, so say a prayer for him and put it behind you." Adam studied the children a moment before turning again to Clarence. "You've got me curious about one thing, however. You say God is love. I say that allowing Reverend Meeks and Susan Barrett to be murdered is not love. If there truly is a god in charge then such blatant omissions amount to criminal and moral neglect."

"Mr. Eden, there are no easy answers, but I believe that God is All That Is. Symbolically man has chosen to live on the fruit of the tree of the knowledge of good and evil, thereby denying true understanding. At some level, did Reverend Meeks understand that her life's goals had been accomplished? Did the director of the clinic? Did their horrible deaths chip away at some past karma? On a level beyond our ken, did they at least partially accept that avenue of death just to help that poor, troubled boy? To help me, perhaps? I don't know. I merely trust in the Higher Will."

Adam started to speak, but suddenly Clarence stared at Adam and continued. "Maybe they also played a part just to help you find your way. We're all a part of the Whole, Mr. Eden. I've heard your friend, the detective, joke about how you have always been one to stir things up." Clarence adjusted his bed to get more in a sitting position. "Believe me, Mr. Eden, the ripples you set in motion here are merely a slight disturbance on the face of a puddle compared to the tidal wave that your efforts send rushing through creation. You are like the storm-swollen creek that cuts a new channel through the valley. Compare that power with the movement your quest to understand your friend's suicide causes throughout creation and you get the Grand Canyon. It is the same for every man who confronts emotional issues. What action we consciously perceive is as a simple exhalation of breath; what we set in motion is as a hurricane. Maybe one day we will better understand cause and effect when we once again begin to harvest the fruit of the tree of life."

Adam said, "What do you mean?"

"To eat of the fruit of the tree of the knowledge of good and evil is to see life as a puzzle, to see all things as relative and out of context. To eat of the fruit of the tree of life is to experience the beauty of life as a completed picture. One is to follow individual will, the latter is to follow the Higher Will."

Clarence looked somewhat embarrassed. "I do not think these ideas up, they just come to me unexpected like an Indian leaping onto my path from behind a tree. That is why I believe that there is an inner knowing to which each of us is connected." Clarence lightly touched his bandage. "You will probably think that the bullet addled my brain, but since I got shot, sometimes as I read the Bible and form ideas, it's almost as if someone is talking to me. I often see a face, sometimes many faces."

"Indian?" Adam repeated. You know, I don't remember where but I met an Indian who talks about the same stuff you do." Adam scratched his head. "Then again, maybe I just dreamed it."

He stared out the window. First Glory, then Kelly, now Clarence. Maybe it's something in the water. Adam decided to stick with wine. At least when he started hearing voices he would have an excuse.

St. Francis Hospital sat on the banks of the Hillsborough River, and Adam watched the black water slowly flowing toward the bay. The river remained the same; the name never changed. However, the water that Adam studied now was not the same murky water that had grabbed Franci and pulled her under to die. Or was it?

Like the river, did she remain the same yet somehow different? Could droplets of that same life-taking river water be currently sustaining the pot of yellow mums next to Clarence's bed? The water in the plant is physically separated from the river, but it is still water. While a man believes himself to be an individual, is he inescapably an inseparable part of a whole? Is a man created with a picture perfect life, and does he spoil it with a chainsaw? He had no idea, but he might think about that fruit thing.

Adam watched Clarence praise his son. Like clothes in a dryer, Adam's beliefs concerning life and death tumbled in turmoil, while Clarence's rock solid faith had been vindicated. Facing life with a nasty scar testifying to that faith, Clarence lay contentedly in bed admiring his family. Adam looked again at the benign river, and then eyed the sky. Contentment had never been Adam's cup of tea. He couldn't live without waves in his teacup.

He no longer fully disbelieved life after death, but rather than blind acceptance, questioning the unanswerable should prove to be infinitely more interesting. A real god wouldn't let his urine get hot just because a person seeks proof. Turning people into pillars of salt and sending floods isn't much of a way to endear oneself to others, especially to one's children. Ruling by fear and intimidation? Man could do that on his own. Always has. No, Clarence is right; a real god would be a god of love. He wouldn't suffer with insecurities. A real god has no need to be worshiped. He would simply rejoice at a man's progress.

Kelly nudged Adam. "It's time we left so Clarence can spend some private time with his family."

★

Two A.M. and Barbara had not returned. While slugging gin and chain smoking, Phoenix maintained vigilance from atop the lighthouse. Several empty and crumpled cigarette packages littered the floor, as did a deadly trail of snuffed out butts. There was no longer room in the several ashtrays that overflowed like trashcans at a frat party. Like a caged bear, she paced around and around the lookout walkway, eagerly studying the now infrequent headlights that moved her way.

Barbara was a whore. How could someone who has been so satisfied leave the way she does? If she wanted more, why not ask? Phoenix would not have said no. She had never said no. In fact, Phoenix had never hurt Barbara in any way, so how could the ungrateful tramp be so cruel? How could anyone so callously take advantage of another's trust? Phoenix raised her glass but it was empty. Now she would have to trudge back down the spiral staircase three floors to the kitchen, and each trip became more difficult. There was no choice however. She wanted another drink.

Phoenix reached the kitchen and began to cough. As she clung to the stair rail each violent spasm was like dragging a file across her abused throat. She was a wreck but the drink would stop the hacking. She plopped a couple of ice cubes in her glass and picked up the bottle of gin. Then she dropped it. She knew she was high, but not drunk. Why did that happen? Especially now, for Christ's sake.

Ignoring the broken glass, Phoenix snatched open all the cabinet doors and shoved the contents about, desperate for more booze. She slammed the last one shut. There wasn't even a car to find a liquor store. The cheating bitch had left Phoenix stranded. Desperate, Phoenix jerked out all the drawers although knowing there would be nothing to drink. There was a tool drawer, however. She stared at it for a while before picking up the hammer. Eventually Barbara would return. She always did. The two-timing slut had hurt Phoenix for the last time.

★

Kelly sensed Adam's preoccupation and rode quietly, waiting for him to speak. He was so funny when he got like this. Like a teapot, one could sense that if the steam didn't escape the kettle would explode. Old Faithful, he is.

Adam squealed around a sharp turn. "Kelly, you're so quiet. Are you awake?"

"After that turn? I should think so. Besides, you're thinking so hard I can hear you."

"I told Clarence that we all got what we wanted, but Huntley and the religious psycho didn't. I hope the kid gets the help he needs, though. He lost his mother when he was young, you know."

Kelly did know. This was probably the tenth time Adam had mentioned it. "Perhaps they did too," she said.

"What?"

Kelly sipped her Gatoraid. "Kyle and Unc, uh, Luther. God, I feel sorry for him too. He wasn't all bad you know." Adam shot her a look. She continued. "No, really, he wasn't. He had his moments. Anyway, maybe they got what they wanted too."

"You think the kid wanted to be locked in a padded cell?" said Adam.

"I think he was crying out for help. Now he will get it."

"What about Huntley? You think he wanted to die?"

"I believe he wanted to be with Aunt Jean."

"I take it you don't believe that there is a hell or heaven, because if there is old Huntley would be working up a pretty good sweat by now. He couldn't possibly be with your aunt."

"I believe that heaven and hell are states of mind. You are in one or the other whether in the physical body or in spirit. Depends on your beliefs, your attitude. Remember?"

"Well, all that aside, I can't see Huntley with his wife. He's not the type to truly love someone. He collected people only to feed off the attention they brought. When he lost your aunt, and you too actually, when you stopped seeing them so often, he lost possessions. The losses wounded his ego."

Kelly said, "He is, ah, *was* as you say, but I believe that he also truly loved Aunt Jean. Maybe that was part of his undoing. He would have considered needing another to be a weakness, and no matter how much he may have wanted to be otherwise, he hated weakness. A sign of his own insecurity."

"Maybe. You would know better than I, but seems to me that real love breeds spontaneity. I'm sure that Huntley never did one thing in his life that wasn't calculated," said Adam.

Kelly shook her head in agreement, and Adam continued. "And I'll tell you something else, somewhere there is a con artist who was probably paid royally for future services that now will never need to be rendered. I bet that person got more than what they wanted, but not what they deserve," said Adam. He shook his head and slapped the steering wheel. "I wish I could get my hands on that person." He thought a moment then grinned at Kelly. "So that you could beat them up."

Kelly didn't even smile. Adam didn't mean to, but he had struck a nerve. "Oh, Adam, I wanted to kill that boy so badly."

"Yes, but you didn't."

"You don't understand. As a rape counselor, I have to deal with the aftermath of brutal violence practically every day. Sometimes it takes all my strength to will myself not to hate. Vengeance is a tempting seducer, but I know that Kyle and others are no different than you and me. We all go to our closet each day and decide what to wear based on individual and collective consciousness."

"What?" said Adam. "Kelly? Kelly, what did you say?"

"Huh? Oh, ah, I was just thinking out loud I guess. I was remembering a conversation that Reverend Meeks and I often had."

"About people hanging around in their closet? I thought you mind worms recommend that people stay out of boxes."

She giggled. "I'm talking about possible paths, probable futures."

"I've heard that you have to be nuts to be a successful shrink. Now it's confirmed," said Adam.

"We're multidimensional, my little mule. Remove the blinders for a moment and listen. We all have a closet filled with different outfits and each day we open the door and choose one for the occasion. Likewise, the individual also has probable pathways or alternate lives from which he or she constantly chooses what we call the future. As a youth sailor, I could have chosen to become an Olympic competitor and eventually a sponsored world-class winner."

She patted Adam's leg. "I used to keep a diary too, as I traveled with Aunt Jean and Uncle Luther to exotic places. At night I often dreamed of becoming an adventure writer. I could have too, but eventually I recognized Luther's hugs for what they were. On that day, I changed clothes."

"But you're just talking about choices. We make choices all the time."

"It's more than that. Think of your life as an apple. You are part of a tree and on that tree are many apples. They are all you, this can better be understood if you consider your dreams; it is not so apparent in the physical world where we choose to experience existence linearly. Nevertheless, there is interaction, the experiences from each benefiting the whole. One day you concentrate your efforts following one pathway, and the next you may be prompted to change. Each is a valid part of your existence, as are many of your dreams."

"You're not talking about possession then?" said Adam.

"No. To extend the metaphor, for reasons we are unable to discern, Kyle selected an outfit that we consider wrong, like wearing Levis to the Met."

"Well, yes we consider it wrong. It *is* wrong to murder and rape. Period."

"After losing your mother and Franci, you could have become a murderer. If perhaps you could have located this Phoenix who you told me conned the mother of a suicide, you might have murdered her. You are passionate. A parent, a respected citizen can kill a drug dealer or rapist. Aunt Jean's love could have aided Luther to become a warm, loving person, instead he chose to become a monster."

Adam said, "Yes, and I repeat, what he and the kid did isn't just *considered* wrong, it *is* wrong."

Kelly put her hand on Adam's leg and left it there. "Once, when I was agonizing over my hurt after learning of my husband's affairs, I finally gave up on trying to make sense of it and thought, 'Oh, well, a better day is coming.' Immediately, a voice in my head said, 'No, child, a different day is coming, but it is one that you will like better'."

Adam glanced at Kelly, waiting for more. She said, "Don't you see, life is forever, and all experience eventually teaches us to love. In that context, there are no negatives, all experience is positive."

"Maybe," is all that Adam would concede.

"Adam, we can't really know, but I believe that Luther lives on. All paths ultimately lead to God, to love, so somewhere Luther is walking his. And the psychic; that person's prayers will be answered too, because we each write our own music."

"Yeah, Reverend Meeks mentioned that."

Kelly nodded. "Reverend Meeks used to be fond of saying that existence is a never-ending composition to which each individual contributes. One's improvisation may produce harmony as well as discordance, but every note we produce teaches us to become better musicians."

"Maybe," Adam repeated. "Maybe."

★

Phoenix opened her eyes and blinked at the late morning sun shining through the window. She fought to a sitting position and held her head with both hands. Had she heard something? She recognized the sound of a car door slamming. Barbara always slammed the door shut, because her arms were always full of peace offerings.

Hysterical one minute, livid the next, Phoenix had alternated between wanting to beg Barbara to stay and wanting to bash in her skull. She hated herself for being weak. What did Barbara contribute besides unbelievable beauty? And she didn't really contribute that, it was just an advantage she used for her own selfish end. Sometime during the early morning hours Phoenix fell asleep.

Now, what was she to do? Barbara's beauty did bring great pleasure to Phoenix. Also, she and Barbara enjoyed laughing at the gullibility of the faithful while reviewing files on clients and preparing for séances and private readings. In the hands of a skillful manipulator, an ounce of belief could be multiplied like fishes and loaves. An unwary mind was a vacuum ready to suck up any hoax laid down by another with the fortitude and imagination to try. Distraught people, their emotions out of control, were easy marks. They wanted to believe. Phoenix was convincing. They gave her their trust.

Phoenix and Barbara made a good team. Phoenix excelled as a skilled hustler, a street-smart psychologist. No gambler or pitchman had ever explained partial reinforcement to Phoenix, she simply figured it out and applied it expertly. Toss the hungry an occasional crumb and they will keep coming to the bakery.

Barbara wasn't bright enough to figure that out, but she was beautiful. Most men and a lot of women opened up to Barbara, either because they were blatantly attracted to her or more often intimidated. It didn't matter. The results were the same; precious seeds of information were freely given for Phoenix to spice up and feed back to the hungry giver.

The ebb and wane of the relation was always the same. First, Phoenix cursed Barbara and swore to kick her out, only later to beg God to help for fear that her love would not return. "Oh, God, I am such a mess," she said, and she cried a bit. She wrung her hands. "I can't handle this anymore." She reached for another cigarette, started to light it then hesitated. She had forgotten about the hammer but there it lay on the night stand.

She started to light up but dropped the lighter. Just like she had the gin bottle. Maybe this was a sign. Maybe she should quit. She had never considered it before. In fact, she despised the current backlash against smokers as an attack on her personal freedoms. Now, however, she stared at the lethal little coffin nail that had been a source of pleasure for thirty-two years and tossed it across the room. The door clicked and Barbara bounced in smiling and jabbering as if she had gone only to the corner market.

"Hi, Phoenix," she said. "You won't believe…"

Phoenix lost it. She was about to slap her wayward lover, when the old con artist suddenly stopped and stared at Barbara as if seeing her for the first time. The fatigue was washed away, and Phoenix experienced a passion different from any she had ever known. The younger woman rattled on, obviously trying to distract Phoenix and calm her down as usual, but Phoenix paid no attention. The anger was gone. An overwhelming hunger to possess Barbara, to own her actually, and a resolve to dominate the woman seized the psychic.

Barbara rattled on about her shopping spree, and like a magician she pulled out item after item, displaying them on the bed. Phoenix approached and noticed her partner become nervous; her big expressive eyes danced about, unable to focus. Barbara always controlled intimacy. She doled out the privilege to Phoenix as a matter of control; it was a game of denial or reward, or at other times the young woman simply wanted her own prurient needs satisfied. Partial reinforcement at its purest, but Barbara could not have labeled it.

She began to dig faster into her purchases, her hands moving in concert with her speedy explanations about where she bought this or that, and for how much. Never averting her eyes from Barbara's, Phoenix reached out and began to stroke her friend's arm. "Look, Phoenix, look what I bought for you." Barbara held up a cigarette lighter like a shield. Phoenix didn't look, and found it amusing when Barbara glanced up to check the psychic's response then quickly averted her eyes.

Phoenix leaned close and spoke softly in Barbara's ear. "You are never going to cheat on me again." She kissed Barbara on her neck then on her cheek. Phoenix breathed deeply to control her passion.

"Uh, Phoenix, I, uh, I need to bathe. Yes, I need a bath. I've been shopping all morning. I'm sweaty. You know how I like to smell good for you." Barbara tried to step around, but Phoenix blocked her.

Phoenix drew the backs of her fingernails down Barbara's bare arms. "There will be time for that later, my darling." Breathing hard, Phoenix leaned into Barbara, forcing their bodies to meet. The older woman gently massaged the frightened woman's shoulders and kissed her eyes.

"Phoenix, I, I'm sorry that I ran off. I—"

Pressing a finger to Barbara's lips, the psychic began rotating her hips and moved her hands to unbutton the blouse that held great treasure. She looked into Barbara's eyes and saw fear. "Don't be afraid, baby. I'm not going to hurt you. You and I are going to have a good time, and you're never going to cheat again. You are going to be a good girl, aren't you?" Phoenix unbuttoned Barbara's skin-tight jeans and slowly unzipped them. She eased the blouse back across the shoulders and down Barbara's arms, but left the sleeves buttoned around the wrists.

As usual, the narcissistic tease did not wear a bra. Phoenix cupped first one breast in her hands and kissed it then moved her attention to the other. Barbara's nipples stiffened, and Phoenix noticed that some of the fear had gone from her eyes. Phoenix pushed aside the dime store purchases and lowered her love to the bed.

Phoenix worked Barbara's jeans over rounded hips and began to rub her shapely tan legs with one hand while peeling the panties with the other. She freed Barbara's hands from the blouse then began kissing and touching the younger woman everywhere except the magic spot between her thighs. Phoenix would come close, first with a finger then with her tongue, and sometimes with her warm breath, but her movements were timed to tease. The touching, caressing, kissing, and teasing went on and on and on until Barbara said, "Phoenix, please."

The older woman moved her finger slowly around and over Barbara's clitoris as Barbara frantically elevated her hips, chasing the illusive digit. "Please," she said again.

Phoenix placed her lips close to her selfish companion's and said, "Kiss me." Barbara never had before. Phoenix slowly and rhythmically kissed the younger woman's neck and her cheeks, then Phoenix touched her lips to those of her self-indulgent lover at the same time that the bewitching finger eased into Barbara's crevice. Barbara grabbed Phoenix's head with both hands and kissed her long and passionately while thrusting her hips forward to possess the instrument of her pleasure. Breathless, Barbara sent her tongue to explore everywhere it could reach, signaling the desire burning between her legs.

That first kiss brought Phoenix to a surprise climax that seemed to excite forever. It marked the beginning of a long night of lovemaking. It became a night of frolicking on the bed and rolling on the floor while using their legs, and hands, and lips, and tongues to explore every possible avenue to give each other pleasure. When they were finally spent, Barbara lay curled up in Phoenix's arms like a contented child.

Phoenix, on the other hand, lay wide awake. She wanted a cigarette, but each time she had the thought, another thought said she didn't. She felt over-stimulated, like when she drank too much coffee and puffed too many cigarettes. She admired Barbara's nude body curled up next to her like a little girl, a valued artwork, a treasure to guard, an acquisition to display. Sex had never been so satisfying. Barbara had actually returned the passion. She even used her tongue to bring Phoenix to multiple orgasms. Unbelievable!

Phoenix rubbed her face. It felt covered with cobwebs. She was giddy as if too much blood rushed through the passages of her brain. When Phoenix looked away, her eyes seemed to float as if detached from her control, and despite her efforts they always came back to rest on the nude body of Barbara. They felt strange, flooded in a way, as if everything she saw had to be processed twice before the image registered in her mind.

It was a struggle to think. It was as if she were fighting her impulses. She was simultaneously flushed with excitement and frightened by the change. As Phoenix tried to reason what was different, she slowly stroked her chin. For the first time in her life, Phoenix had made contact with the dead.

*

Later, at home, Adam brewed a cup of tea and sat down at the computer. He wanted to write, he needed to write, but his injured wrists had prevented it. He was desperately tired, and thought he could sleep; there had been no nightmares since the evening in the well field. However, he had packed years of living into a couple of weeks, and he couldn't relax until the thoughts that kept stampeding through his head were corralled. Writing can be like that. Something inside has to get out. Thoughts start kicking on the barn door until it breaks open and they gallop to freedom.

He and Kelly had driven out to John's Pass on the Gulf beaches, and watched the sun extinguish itself in the Gulf of Mexico. They did not talk much, just held each other's hands and sat transfixed as the bright orange ball dropped into the sea. Conversation would have been intrusive. Is there a formula for that kind of contentment? Is there a recipe for such happiness? If so, is a god an ingredient? How could a god claim that man has free will, but require that individuals submit to total obedience or be punished or denied token rewards like a trained pet? To label such a god a supreme being is an oxymoron. Adam began to write.

My Relationship To The Sun

The sun is central to survival. Light makes the plants grow on which man depends directly and indirectly. Plants produce oxygen, and humans feed on the vegetation as well as the animals that survive on the plants. He extracts medicines, spins fiber for clothing, cuts trees into wood for shelter, and surrounds himself with brilliant color.

Sunlight also makes possible the rhythm of life that allows man to rest, to work, and to play. The sun is essential to sustaining life, yet it is much more than that. A dazzling rainbow, a magnificent dawn, or a breathtaking sundown inspires man to hope, to dream, to believe that there is more to life than just the individual. Old Sol is all this, yet man no longer worships it.

As the sunlight is to the physical self, the radiance of God is to spirit. Light, understanding, is God's first born. Existence flourishes within this spiritual light as a fish swims within the waters of a pristine lake. When one becomes irradiated by this light the door to Infinite Potential swings open. Now, however, man lives with limitation due to the narrow perception of the ego. When the physical ego dies the spirit self is freed. Symbolically, one is born again. Spiritual light is all that and man worships the source.

In order for plants to grow, the seed husk must compromise. If the mighty oak that lives within the tiny acorn is to be, the tough shell must first surrender and allow in the sunlight. If the spirit that lives within is to reach its potential, ego too must surrender to the light. Jesus spoke of the faith of the mustard seed. To the ego this is nonsense. Nevertheless, it is true. Faith is the vehicle that propels life. Life without faith is death.

Every plant, insect, animal, fowl, and fish lives by the grace of faith. The acorn hull understands that it is a part of something greater than itself; therefore, it willingly opens to the sunlight. The protective armor of the acorn willing submits otherwise the majestic oak can never be. The ego, however, fights for self-preservation.

Man no longer kneels in supplication before Sol, nor does he beg for forgiveness. Now, man simply accepts the golden orb and is grateful for the sunlight. He appreciates the power of the sun and is free to harness it without end, subject to the limits of his understanding. Humans marvel at the gas giant's majesty.

In comparison to the past worship of the sun, man now kneels in supplication before God begging forgiveness and seeking abundance or relief from pain and suffering. Nevertheless, God's radiance, like sunlight, is always there whether man worships the source or denies its presence. God's radiance exists always whether man uses it wisely or foolishly.

Humans have free will and may do either, but wisdom suggests that rather than supplication, man should merely love life. Embrace it with enthusiasm. Smell the roses and rise to a challenge. Marvel at the beauty of existence. Imprisoned, the tiny mustard seed opens within the darkness of sod, and a fragile shoot climbs toward its destiny. It harbors no doubt that sunlight is waiting above with a life-sustaining embrace. Should a man do less?

I should trust my impulses. I should believe in the benevolence of my spiritual self. My ego should surrender and allow in the light so that my spirit may soar. It is not necessary that I worship God, but rather I should choose to honor existence with goodwill and good deeds, and cheer creation each day just as I cheer the dawn.

Adam read what he had written. Strange stuff, but he felt a kinship to it. He could sleep now. He printed a copy to study later. Perhaps he would crack the door sealed since his girlfriend's death and take a peep into the possibilities that might lie beyond. Maybe the dead can hear. He would strive to no longer be handicapped by guilt. He would monitor his beliefs. He would work to be more open-minded and respectful of other's opinions. He grinned. Or maybe not. Suddenly, the room pulsated with energy and the hair on his arms stood to attention. Something familiar made him sniff the air, and it greeted him with the unmistakable scent of chocolate peanut butter cups. "Hello, Franci," he said. Just in case.

God, whose boundless love and joy are present everywhere:
He cannot come to visit you unless you are not there.

Angelus Silesius
1424–1477